# Covenant

A JERICHO NOVEL

**Ann McMan**

Ann Arbor
2021

Bywater Books

Copyright © 2021 Ann McMan

All rights reserved. No part of this book may be reproduced, stored in a retrieval system, or transmitted in any form or by any means, without prior permission in writing from the publisher.

Print ISBN: 978-1-61294-191-2

Bywater Books First Edition: July 2021

Printed in the United States of America on acid-free paper.
Cover design: TreeHouse Studio

Bywater Books
PO Box 3671
Ann Arbor MI 48106-3671
www.bywaterbooks.com

This is a work of fiction. Names, characters, places, and incidents are the product of the author's imagination, or, in the case of historical persons, are used fictitiously.

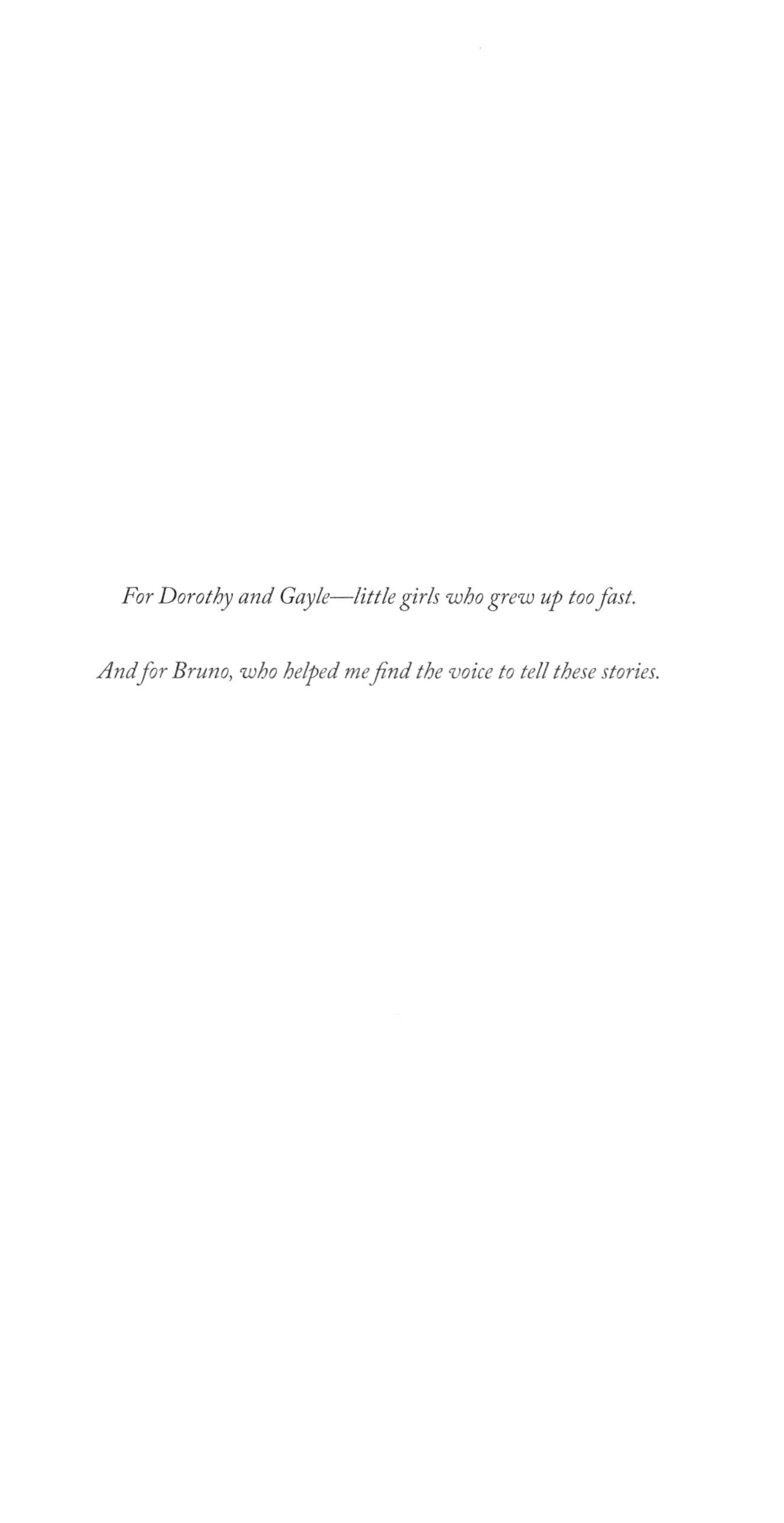

*For Dorothy and Gayle—little girls who grew up too fast.*

*And for Bruno, who helped me find the voice to tell these stories.*

# Books by Ann McMan

## Novels

*Hoosier Daddy*
*Festival Nurse*
*Backcast*
*Beowulf for Cretins: A Love Story*
*The Big Tow*

### The Jericho Series

*Jericho*
*Aftermath*
*Goldenrod*
*Covenant*

### Evan Reed Mysteries

*Dust*
*Galileo*

## Story Collections

*Sidecar*
*Three Plus One*

# Covenant
A JERICHO NOVEL

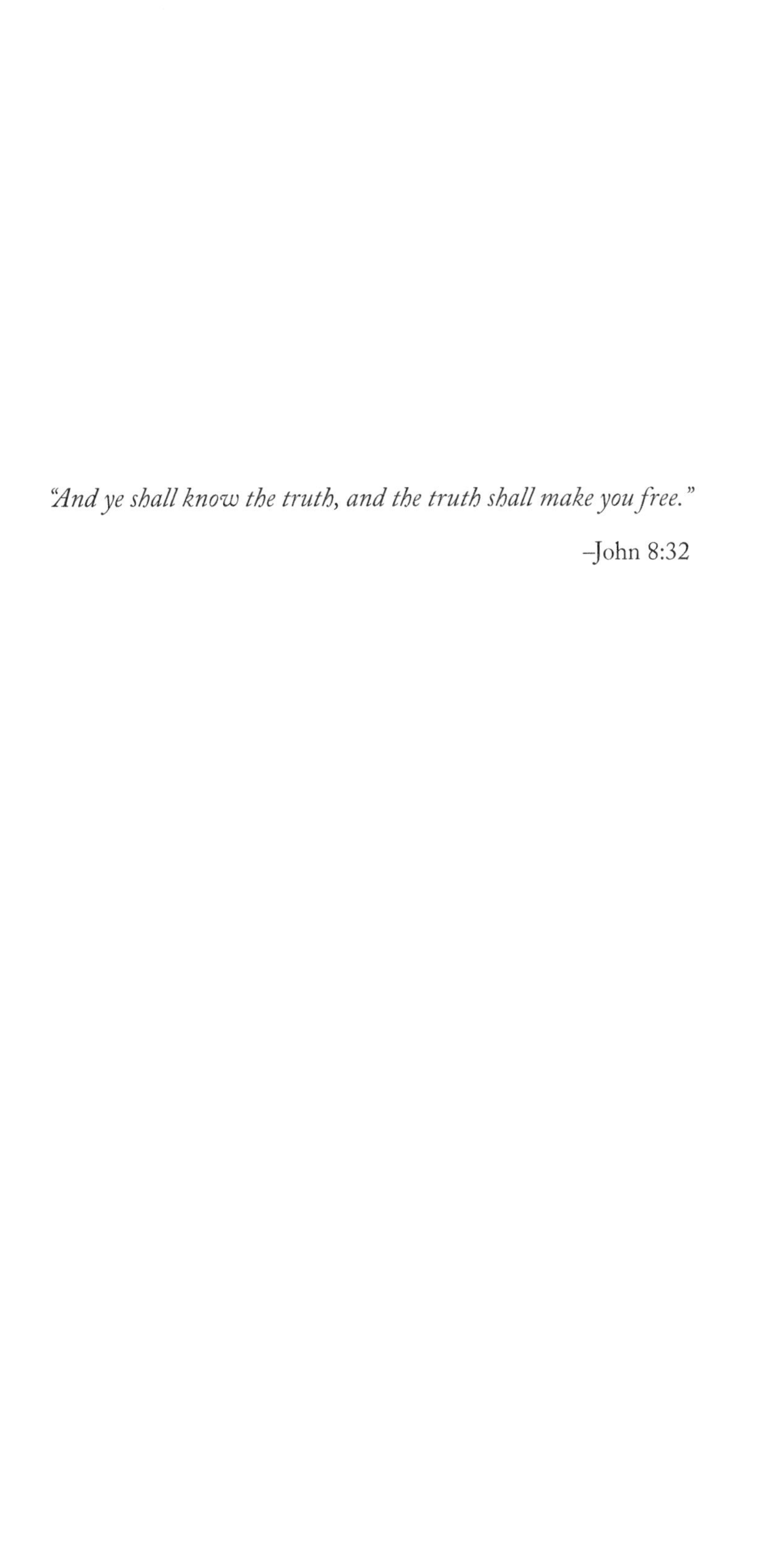

*"And ye shall know the truth, and the truth shall make you free."*

–John 8:32

# Chapter One

*Recorded Interview*
*Preliminary Inquest Investigation*
*Death of Mayor Gerald Watson*

"My name is Dorothy Gale."

*The old ones will tell you they can sense when a change is coming. They watch for signs—the way poplar leaves curl up before a thunderstorm. Or how bones that have been broken will ache and grow stiff ahead of a snow.*

"It was an accident."

*I had my own ways of knowing. The broken parts of me would buzz and bang against my insides like flies inside a hot car—warning me to escape. Telling me to run. So I paid attention to them, and I learned how to read his signs.*

"I didn't mean to hit him so hard."

*He wasn't always so mean. He used to try to do better. He used to fight his darkness. But he gave up on all of that when Mama died. After her funeral, he sat at the kitchen table drinking from a big bottle of Jack Daniel's. He sat there for hours. It was that night he told me there was an ugly animal inside him, and it wanted to hurt people. I didn't believe him at first. But then I began to see flashes of it moving behind his eyes. His animal. Waking up. Moving around. Hungry, and crazy to find a way out.*

"I was just trying to stop him."

*Sometimes, I could get away before his animal got loose. Most times I couldn't.*

"If I hadn't stopped him, he would've killed Buddy. I could see it in his eyes. His animal was out."

*At first, I tried to fight him. To make him stop. But when I did, he just got madder. Then he would hurt me worse, and do . . . other things. So when I knew I couldn't hide, I didn't struggle.*

"I didn't mean to hit him so hard."

*I only fought back on that day because I had to. I had to.*

"My name is Dorothy Gale, and I killed my father."

*Clair de Lune.*

She recognized it immediately. Nothing else sounded like that—especially the way her mother played it. Quiet. Tentative. Full of nuance. *Pianissimo,* she reminded herself. *Softly*. How many times did Celine caution her? Slow her down? Tell her to linger over the notes? Not to be in such a hurry?

They could've been talking about a thousand different things.

Probably, they had been. It was about as direct as any of their conversations got back in those days.

"Debussy meant for us to take our time here," she'd say. "He wanted us to set our own pace for the transitions from note to note."

As it happened, Maddie's preferred pace was always a bit more *presto* than Celine's.

The simple truth was that Maddie never cared much about connecting with the music in the ways her mother did—in the ways her mother desperately wanted her to. It took decades for Maddie to understand the method behind her mother's passion: music was Celine's currency. It had been the common language of the Heller family—the only vehicle Celine's parents ever used to convey their deepest emotions. Growing up, Maddie learned to gauge her mother's moods by how she played her piano.

She leaned against a support post on the front porch of Celine's bungalow and listened while her mother finished the piece.

After three days, it had finally stopped raining, although the late summer heat had not abated one bit.

The tempo of the music perfectly matched the sun's slow descent behind Buck Mountain. Maddie waited and watched as the color slowly drained from a wide meadow filled with soft yellow sedge and the pale red of early autumn azaleas.

*Celine was sad today.*

That wasn't hard to understand. Ever since the nightmarish events at the river on July 4th, the entire town had been moving slow. They were all a bit sluggish, like unmoored boats dragging their anchors. They were like refugees from an Emily Dickinson poem.

*"The Feet, mechanical, go round—A Wooden way . . ."*

She felt it herself: that same creeping malaise. It was impossible to shake off. Watson's murder had changed everything. Had changed *everyone.* Jericho had lost its innocence. Now its residents slept, if they slept at all, with one eye open.

"Knock, knock." She opened the front door and stepped inside.

"In here," Celine called back. Her voice came from the kitchen.

Maddie was confused, but made her way from the small foyer to the bungalow's big kitchen. Celine was standing at the island, pitting cherries from a large bowl. Something smelled wonderful—spicy and exotic. *Chili maybe?*

"What are you making?" She hugged her mother from behind. "It smells great."

Celine leaned back against her. "Chickpea lentil stew. These cherries are for the couscous."

"Oh, man." Maddie released her and walked over to the stove so she could peer inside the large Dutch oven. "For about two seconds there, you had my hopes up." She replaced the heavy lid. "How'd you get in here so fast?"

Celine looked at her. "What do you mean?"

"From in there." Maddie jerked a thumb toward the living room. "Did you fold space or something? I was just on the porch, listening to you play."

"Oh." Celine smiled. "That wasn't me."

"It wasn't? What was it? The stereo?"

"Nope. Go duck your head into the living room."

"Okay . . ." Maddie left the kitchen and crossed the foyer to peek into the living room.

Dorothy heard her approach and looked up from the piano. She'd been flipping pages of sheet music. "Hey, Maddie." She pushed the stool back and stood up. "Are you here for dinner? Byron's coming, too." Her tone was hopeful.

"Um. No. Was that *you* playing when I got here?"

Dorothy dropped her eyes. "I know it wasn't right. I've been trying to practice."

"Are you kidding me? It was *perfect.* I thought it was Mom."

Dorothy's eyes grew wide. "Really?"

"Yes, really." Maddie could tell the girl was trying hard not to smile. "You're a natural."

"There's nothing 'natural' about it," Celine's voice carried across from the kitchen. "It's hard work and determination."

Maddie raised her eyes to take in the ceiling before bending toward Dorothy and lowering her voice. "*This* is the bane of my existence."

Dorothy did smile now. Maddie was moved by how the simple action drained the years from her young face. Dorothy didn't smile much these days. She didn't have a lot of reason to. Maddie was confident that her coming to live with Celine would change that.

"Come on, kiddo." She held out a hand. "Let's go to the kitchen and liberate some cherries."

Dorothy crossed toward her and only hesitated a second before taking her hand.

*Progress*, Maddie thought. She tightened her hold and led Dorothy back to the kitchen.

"Want me to finish pitting those for you, Mom?" Maddie offered.

Celine eyed her with suspicion. "I don't think so."

"Why not?" Maddie was disappointed. Something occurred to her. "Hey . . . I'd do it right."

Celine selected a fat cherry from the stoneware bowl and wielded her stainless steel pitter with a flourish. "Doubtful."

"Excuse *me.*" Maddie feigned exaggerated umbrage. "I did a standard surgical rotation."

"It's not your facility with implements that concerns me," Celine replied. She expertly pitted another cherry. "It's how much product I would lose in the exercise of so much beneficence."

Maddie looked at Dorothy for support.

"I don't really know what *beneficence* means," Dorothy said. She walked to the refrigerator and pulled out a cardboard container. "But we do have these extra ones."

"Culls," Celine added.

"Seriously? You culled the cherries?" Maddie asked.

Celine lowered her head and looked at her daughter over the rims of her glasses. "Do you know me at all?"

"Good point." Maddie pulled up a stool and sat down at the kitchen island. "Come on, Dorothy. Let's dispatch the culls."

Dorothy joined her. Together they sorted through the carton of cherries deemed deficient, dividing them into two piles: mushy; or still viable with blotchy bits of skin. Maddie was amused by the way they fell into the same sorting rhythm without advance discussion.

"This one's a goner." Maddie held one up. Dark red juice ran down her fingers.

Dorothy regarded it. "I'd eat it anyway."

"My thoughts exactly." Maddie popped the offending fruit into her mouth.

"Do you want to stay and eat with us?" Celine offered. "We have plenty."

"That's very generous. But Syd and Henry are meeting me at the café for dinner. We're celebrating," she added.

"Oh?" Celine asked. "What are you celebrating?"

Maddie smiled "Henry *finally* mastered his multiplication tables. We promised him a dinner at the restaurant of his choice."

"And he chose the Riverside Café? That surprises me. I thought he shared your penchant for fast food."

"Me, too." Maddie shrugged. "I asked him three times if he wouldn't rather go to Aunt Bea's."

"It's Wednesday," Dorothy explained. Maddie and Celine both looked at her. "The special on Wednesday is chicken and biscuits."

*Of course*. Enlightenment dawned for Maddie. "You mean fairy sprinkles?"

Dorothy nodded.

"Nadine puts red pepper flakes in her biscuits," Maddie reminded Celine. "David convinced Henry that they're 'fairy sprinkles.'"

Celine laughed. "Too bad he was never able to persuade you that zucchini is a green banana in disguise."

Dorothy gave Maddie a look of solidarity. "I hate zucchini, too."

"See?" Maddie argued. "It's slimy."

"That's *okra*, not zucchini." Celine finished pitting her cherries and headed for the prep sink to rinse her hands.

"You say tomato . . ." Maddie glanced at her watch. "What time did you say Byron was getting here?"

"I didn't say. But I suspect it'll be soon." Celine looked at her. "Do you need to talk with him?"

Before Maddie could answer her, Dorothy got up from her stool and headed for the atrium door that led to the patio. "I hear his car," she said with excitement. "I'll go get him."

She left them alone in the kitchen.

Maddie was surprised by Dorothy's hasty exit. "She seems happy to see him. That's a good thing."

"I think so, too. Although it could as easily be Django. Those two have bonded."

"Really?"

Celine nodded. "Sometimes Byron leaves him here overnight. He sleeps on the end of Dorothy's bed."

"No kidding?" Maddie thought about that. "I bet she'd enjoy a few sleepovers with Before, too."

"Nice try. Henry's 900-pound heifer is *not* coming over here."

"You have no sense of adventure."

"You accuse the resident cougar of that—even as her cub arrives for dinner?"

Maddie laughed. "You never cease to amaze me, Mom."

"Why stop now?" Celine retrieved a small saucepan from a shelf. "I'm on a roll."

"In fact, I did want to run something by you—about Dorothy."

"Oh? What is it?"

Maddie glanced toward the patio doors. "I found out last week that Avi Zakariya, a classmate of mine from Penn, is doing a locum for a pal in Roanoke and is looking to move her practice when that arrangement ends. She's a top-notch child psychologist. I touched base with her earlier today, just to get caught up."

Celine nodded. "And in the course of your conversation, it occurred to you that perhaps Avi could meet with Dorothy?"

"Exactly. I wanted to see what you and Byron thought about

it before I pursued setting anything up."

"I'll talk with him about it, certainly. But at first blush, I think it's a good idea. Would Avi be willing to come here?"

"I honestly think she might. She expressed interest in possibly setting up a practice in this area, versus looking at more lucrative markets. There may be possibilities for her to use space in my clinic." Maddie was lost in thought for a moment. "Avi came to visit a couple of times when Dad was still alive. Even then, she created quite a stir in town."

"Why was that?"

"She's androgynous—or was back then. Although," Maddie recalled, "she always used female pronouns. I honestly have no idea how she identifies now, and it felt absurd to inquire—not to mention, it's totally irrelevant. I fell all over myself trying to avoid the pitfalls of making assumptions—like any of that even *mattered.* It was mortifying. I'm sure I sounded like an idiot."

"I doubt that." Celine smiled at her. "We're all playing catch up. But the good news is that every time our understandings evolve, we end up with more winners than losers."

"You should run for office."

"I don't think so." Celine pitted another cherry before magnanimously offering it to Maddie. "Besides, we already have a woke mayor."

"Are you talking about David?"

"Is there more than one mayor?"

"No," Maddie admitted. "Just the one. I confess it's still a struggle to get my head around the idea that David is now the chief executive of Jericho."

"It is rather a paradigm shift."

Maddie laughed. "That's putting it mildly. It seems like only a week ago that he was shoplifting cigarettes from Freemantle's market."

"I'd prefer not to be reminded about those exploits of yours."

"*Mine?* He was the aspiring felon. I was just his stooge."

Celine glared at her. "Spoken like every accomplice who denies culpability."

"Who's denying culpability?" Byron entered the kitchen from the patio with Dorothy following close behind. His mutt, Django danced happily around her heels.

Celine smiled at him. "We were discussing Maddie's former life of crime."

Byron laughed and crossed over to where Celine stood. He peered into her bowl before kissing the side of her head. "Sorry I'm late," he apologized. "Gladys Pitzer's car alarm kept going off and she was positive it meant someone was trying to steal her dry goods. I had to go over there to persuade her that the culprit was rusted battery terminals."

"Her dry goods?" Celine asked. "Why on earth does she keep them in the car?"

"Wait a minute." Maddie held up a hand. "Before you answer, what the hell are 'dry goods'?"

"Seriously?" Celine glared at her.

"It's stuff like flour and sugar," Dorothy interjected. "Things you use in baking."

"Hence your unfamiliarity with the term." Celine shook her head.

"Yeah, *whatever.*" Maddie looked at Byron. "So why is she keeping her 'dry goods' in the car?"

Byron shrugged. "She said the damp nights we've been having are making the mice come inside. Apparently, Sonny is running behind and hasn't been out there yet to deal with them."

Maddie was baffled by Gladys's logic. "Why doesn't she just store the stuff in airtight containers?"

"That one is above my pay grade." Byron crossed to the stove and inspected the savory concoction simmering in the big Dutch oven. "You're making chickpea stew? It's my favorite."

"I gathered that," Celine observed. "Especially after I found the cookbook opened to this page no less than five times."

"So sue me." Byron returned the lid to the big pot. "Sometimes it takes you a while to pick up the clue phone."

"You could always just ask for it," Celine replied, "and avoid the obfuscation."

"Where's the fun in that?"

Celine swatted him with a dishtowel.

Maddie was charmed by their casual intimacy. She couldn't recall any interactions like this between her parents. They'd always been polite to each other, but had behaved more like professional colleagues than life partners.

"Besides," Byron continued, "we like a bit of obfuscation now and then, don't we, Dorothy?"

Dorothy looked at Maddie for help.

"I am *so* not getting into the middle of this one." Maddie checked her watch. "I gotta scoot. Walk me to my car, Dorothy?"

"Sure." Dorothy patted the side of her leg. "Come on, Django."

"I'll call you tomorrow, Mom. See you around, Byron."

Byron gave her a small salute. "Watch for deer by the river," he cautioned. "I passed a half dozen of them on my way in here."

"Give my love to Syd and Henry," Celine called after her.

Maddie waved and held the door open for Dorothy and Django. The three of them left the house and made their way toward Maddie's Jeep.

Maddie could see a smattering of stars beginning to peek through along the western horizon. It was going to be a clear night.

"Do you still watch the stars?" she asked Dorothy.

Dorothy seemed surprised by her question. "I mostly do," she said. "How did you know about that?"

Maddie smiled at her. "Henry. He stares at the sky every night, waiting for the appearance of some mysterious horse he says you told him about."

"Oh. That's Pegasus. The constellation. I told him he would be able to see it in the fall."

"That explains it. He wants to be sure not to miss it. At first, I thought it was a ruse to get to stay up later. But I get the impression he thinks it's going to gallop across the sky like Maximus in *Tangled*."

"I'm sorry. It was in a story I told him one day, when we were reading a book together."

"Don't be sorry about that. Henry loves his bookmobile dates with you."

"I like them, too. It's really nice that Syd brings him over here so we can go together."

"That's right," Maddie recalled. "Roma Jean does a stop out here now, doesn't she?"

Dorothy nodded. "Just for the summer, until school starts."

"I bet you like that."

"Yeah. It's a lot easier than . . . than it used to be."

Maddie fought an impulse to wrap an arm around the girl and pull her closer.

"Mom likes having you here," she said.

Dorothy looked up at her with a hopeful expression. "Do you think so?"

"No. I *know* so. You're great company for her—and she loves having a captive audience."

"A captive audience for what?"

Maddie bent down to whisper. "*Piano lessons.*"

That made Dorothy laugh.

Maddie felt irrationally proud of herself for making Dorothy laugh—a rare occurrence of late.

She smiled smugly.

*I cannot wait to tell Syd . . .*

—∞— —∞— —∞—

Henry was busy flipping through a glossy magazine that Uncle David had just dropped off. It was very fat and full of shiny pages. Most showed big photos of pretty, smiling women with fussy hairdos. They were all dressed in floofy white gowns. The pictures showed them walking through arches covered with flowers, or standing outside in gardens beside long tables that were loaded with fancy fountains and towers of shiny glasses.

He could tell by their outfits that the women were all brides. Many of them stood with tall, handsome men wearing fancy black or gray suits. Some of the men even wore hats.

He looked and looked, but no matter how many pages he turned, he didn't see any pictures of brides with *other* brides—just brides with men.

*Grooms,* he reminded himself.

But he supposed that was okay because Maddie wouldn't want to wear any of these fussy dresses, either.

He couldn't imagine that.

Maddie said she wanted him to be her best man. He wasn't sure what kind of job that was, but he knew it was important. He wanted to do it right.

He just hoped it didn't mean he'd have to wear one of those hats. They looked really silly. He liked his green "Murderous Quakers" hat—the one Maddie gave him when he first came to live here. She said it had been her hat in college. Henry wore it all the time—but Syd always made him take it off inside the house.

"Are you ready to go, Henry?" It was Syd. They were meeting Maddie for dinner at the café.

He looked up at her. "Is Uncle David coming, too?"

"No can do, bucko." Uncle David looked at his watch. "I have a meeting in town and I gotta boogie." He waved goodbye. "Save me some sprinkles." He gave Syd a kiss on the cheek. "Let me know what you think about those bowl food ideas and grazing tables. Both approaches are pretty hot right now."

"I will." Syd held the door open for him. "The only thing I'm sure about is that we'll have to include some vegan options, whatever we decide."

David held up a hand. "I do not have the bandwidth to even *think* about that. Considerations of wholly tasteless, cardboard canapés demands more time than we have right now—and will require at least *two* bottles of the good hooch Maddie keeps hidden in the barn."

Syd looked confused. "Is she still doing that?"

"It's in the old refrigerator," Henry piped up. "Behind the workbench."

"The workbench?" Syd sounded confused. "That fridge hasn't worked since *I* moved out here."

"She fixed it," Henry added. "But she told me it was *entre nous*."

Syd shook her head and looked at Uncle David. "How did *you* know about this?"

"You're kidding me, right? That woman is about as opaque as cellophane."

"True," Syd agreed.

"I gotta scoot." David waved at Henry. "See you on taco night."

"Bye." Henry watched him leave. After Syd closed the door, he lifted up the heavy magazine. "How come there aren't any pictures of brides with brides?"

"What?" Syd walked over to the table.

"In here," Henry explained. "There are only pictures of brides with grooms."

"Oh." Syd smiled at him and pushed his hair back from his forehead. "I guess that's because many of these magazines are more concerned with selling things than taking care to show all kinds of families."

That confused Henry. "I don't get it."

"I don't really get it either, sweetheart. But our family is just as important as any of these, and we can't forget that."

"Do I have to wear one of those big hats?" Henry had moved on.

Syd laughed. "No, honey. Nobody is going to ask you to wear a hat."

"Will Maddie have to wear one?"

Syd took a moment to consider her answer. "Unlikely. In fact, we'll be lucky if we can get her to toss the wingtips and wear girl shoes."

"What are 'girl' shoes?"

"They're . . ." Syd reconsidered. "Let's talk about it on the way to the café. Maddie will be there waiting on us."

"Okay." Henry closed the magazine. They left the house and walked together toward the barn, where Syd's new Volvo was parked. Henry was fastening his seatbelt when something else occurred to him. "Will Uncle David let us have fairy sprinkles at the wedding?"

Syd chuckled as she started the car.

"I'm pretty sure there'll be fairy sprinkles a-plenty."

"Want me to top off your coffee?"

Coralee Minor had appeared next to Lizzy's table, brandishing a fat pot with a bright orange rim. *Decaf.* It was full, too. It looked like Coralee had brewed a fresh pot just for her, because there were next to no other patrons at Waffle House. Small wonder. It was nearly 8 p.m.

Tom was running late. *As usual.*

"Sure." Lizzy held up her mug. "Why not?"

Coralee promptly filled her cup. "Do you wanna order something to nibble on while you wait on Mr. Murphy?"

Lizzy smiled at her. "No. Thanks, Coralee. He should be along any minute now."

"Okay. Just holler at me if you change your mind." Coralee headed back toward the service area.

Lizzy returned her gaze to the article she was reading in the latest issue of *The New England Journal of Medicine*. It was depressing the hell out of her.

"The Ongoing Ebola Epidemic in the Democratic Republic of Congo, 2018–2019."

Zoonotic diseases. They kept cropping up—faster and faster now. She remembered a conversation she'd had a few weeks ago with their Upjohn rep.

"This crap is going to get a lot worse," he had said. "It's as if Mother Nature's pissed with us and the ways we keep jacking up the planet. 'You refuse to do right and clean up your acts? *Fine.* I'll find a way to get your attention.' That's what's happening with all these viruses that jump species." He shook his head. "Mark my words, sooner or later one of these will take us all out."

God help them if he ended up being right.

Lizzy sipped her hot coffee and kept reading.

> *Scientists do not know where Ebola virus comes from. However, based on the nature of similar viruses, they believe the virus is animal-borne, with bats or nonhuman primates (chimpanzees, apes, monkeys, etc.) being the most likely source.*

In frustration, she closed the journal and pushed it away. This wasn't the kind of dire prognostication she needed, front-loading another sleepless night. She already had enough incentives to lie awake.

Car headlights flashed across the front windows of the tiny restaurant. She saw a man get out and head for the door. His blond hair was unmistakable. Tom. *Finally.*

He looked around the interior and waved when he spotted

her. He smiled as he slid into the booth.

"Sorry I'm late. Have you been waiting long?"

Lizzy looked at her watch. "Nearly an hour. I got here a few minutes after seven—as we agreed."

"Don't start, okay?" He held up a palm. "I got snagged on a call and didn't get out of Blacksburg until nearly six-thirty."

"Why didn't you text me to say you were running late?"

He shrugged. "I had to make some calls during the drive." He continued before Lizzy could react. "They were important, okay? Don't be pissed."

Lizzy gave up on bothering to chastise him. It was pointless. She sank back against the booth.

"Are you going to tell me about these important calls?"

"Yeah." He nodded and twisted around to catch Coralee's eye. "As soon as we order some food. I'm starving."

After Coralee had taken their orders and brought Tom his iced tea, he stretched his arms out along the back of the booth and yawned.

"Tired?" Lizzy asked.

"Damn straight. I've been busting my hump all week. It sucks that I have to drive back after we eat."

That surprised Lizzy. Normally, Tom stayed over at her place whenever they connected on weeknights.

"You're going back to Blacksburg?" she asked. "Tonight?"

"Have to. I've got to get some paperwork in order. And I have to meet with the Dean tomorrow morning."

"What's going on, Tom? You normally lay a patch whenever you have the chance to get out of Blacksburg."

He dropped his arms and leaned over their narrow table.

"I've got *great* news, Babe."

"You do?"

"Yep. That's why I'm late tonight."

Lizzy thought about pointing out that Tom was nearly always late, but didn't want to rain on his parade. It was clear he was excited about something.

"Are you going to share it with me?" she asked.

"Oh, yeah." He nodded smugly. "I got a job. A *great* job."

"A job?" Lizzy was flummoxed. "I didn't know you were interviewing anyplace."

"Of *course*, I've been interviewing. I graduate in less than nine weeks."

"But you didn't say anything to me about this—this job prospect."

"Nope. I wasn't sure it would pan out, and I wanted to surprise you."

*Pan out?* Something had "panned out"—*already?* Before they'd even discussed any possibilities?

"Well?" Tom sounded impatient. "Aren't you gonna ask me about it?"

"Yes. Sure." She did her best to sound upbeat. "What is it?"

"Brace yourself. It's a sweet gig—a clinical pathology residency with Zoetis labs."

Lizzy was confused. "You're applying for a lab residency? I thought you wanted to practice."

"I was never more than 50/50 on the whole vet clinic track. You know that. Research is where the big bucks are. I put in my two years with Zoetis, and I can pretty much write my own ticket." He reached for her hand. "This is the brass ring, Babe. We can live anywhere we want."

"Two years?" Lizzy's head was spinning. "Where is this residency?"

"That's the best part: Denver. Great skiing. Hospitals every twenty feet. You'll have *no* trouble finding a job."

*Denver?*

"Wait a minute, Tom. You expect me to move to Denver with you?"

Tom's face fell. "Sure. I mean, why wouldn't you?"

Lizzy withdrew her hand from his. "For starters, you haven't asked me to."

"What's that supposed to mean? Of course, I want you to go with me. It's a no-brainer."

"Tom? This might surprise you, but assuming I'll jump at the chance to move across the country with you isn't the same as asking for my opinion on the matter."

"Oh, come on. Don't do this."

"Don't do what?"

"*This.*" He waved his hands at her. "Get the way you get whenever we don't talk something to death."

"Tom, we haven't talked about this *at all*—much less to death."

Coralee showed up and timidly deposited their two plates of food.

"Y'all let me know if you need anything else, okay?"

She retreated before either of them could reply.

Tom picked up his fork and angrily speared a hunk of hash brown.

"I don't see what the big damn deal is. This is a fantastic opportunity for me. I thought you'd be jumping for joy."

Lizzy gave him one of what she knew he called "those" looks.

"Okay. *Whatever.*" He chewed a forkful of food. "You never jump for joy about *anything*. I don't know why I thought this would be different."

"Well, that makes two of us."

Lizzy dropped her eyes and stared at her mushroom omelet. It was ironic: she'd nearly ordered a Denver omelet, but decided the combination of onions and green pepper would give her trouble later on. *How prescient that decision was turning out to be....*

"Tom, I don't see how it could surprise you that I might have opinions—*strong* opinions—about relocating. Especially to a place more than halfway across the country."

Tom seemed nonplussed by her comment. "Why would you want to stay here?"

Lizzy hadn't had much of an appetite when she'd arrived. Now it was completely gone. She pushed her plate away. "The fact that you even ask me that question tells me you'd never understand my answer."

Tom gave her an exaggerated eye-roll. "You act like you're some kind of missionary."

Lizzy was too tired to argue with him. It was clear that his mind was made up.

"I need some time to think about all of this," she said. "And you said you need to get back to Blacksburg tonight." She looked at her watch. "If you leave now, you can get there before ten." She collected her journal and dug a ten-dollar bill out of her purse. "This should cover my dinner."

"You're leaving?"

Lizzy noticed that he didn't offer to pay for her meal.

"Yes, Tom. I'm going home."

He blinked. "Can I at least call you later?"

*Can I stop you?* she thought. "Maybe tomorrow," she said instead. "I'm kind of tired. Goodnight."

She waved at Coralee on her way out. Coralee jerked her head toward Tom's back and made what looked to Lizzy like a rude gesture.

Even as deflated as she felt, Lizzy had to fight an impulse to laugh.

Roma Jean looked at her watch for about the fifth time in the past fifteen minutes. She'd only been sitting on Charlie's side porch for half an hour, but it felt like longer.

Of course, she didn't *have* to wait outside—Charlie had given her a key two weeks ago. But Roma Jean still felt like letting herself into the small house when Charlie wasn't at home was ... *inappropriate.* It didn't seem like the kind of thing "nice" girls did. And one thing Roma Jean got plenty of was reminders about how "nice" girls behaved. Her mother was famous for randomly tossing those helpful hints off whenever the two of them were busy doing just about any mundane task around the house—like sorting dirty clothes or emptying the dishwasher. It drove Roma Jean nuts. But even with all that, she knew it could be a lot worse. All things considered, her parents had handled things with Charlie pretty well. But "things with Charlie" was still kind of a moving target in the Freemantle family.

"Moving target" made her think about Grandma Azalea. The old woman had more or less adopted Charlie at the 4th of July picnic after Roma Jean had lied and said Charlie was related to Jefferson Davis. Now Charlie had regular dates with Azalea to visit the county shooting range. Charlie said it was so she could teach Grandma Azalea about gun safety—but Roma Jean knew it *really* was because they both shared a passion for target shooting. Charlie said she'd never seen anybody empty a chamber as fast as Azalea—and into such a tight grouping, dead center on the target.

As nice as that strange relationship was, Roma Jean still knew that where information she shared with her parents was concerned, less was more.

And her parents weren't the only ones ready to dispense unsolicited behavioral advice. Last Sunday after church, Grandma Azalea had pulled her aside and shaken a crooked finger in her face, reminding her that "the law is not made for a righteous man, but for the lawless and disobedient, for the ungodly and for sinners." After that, she reminded Roma Jean to be sure and reserve her a leg quarter and some broccoli slaw if she got to the Riverside Café first.

*Like they'd ever run out of chicken legs on a Sunday . . .*

Roma Jean thought Grandma Azalea's admonition was pretty ironic since it came from the same person who spent most of her waking hours beta testing *Grand Theft Auto, Cayo*

*Perico*, which came with about twenty-five warnings for extreme violence and graphic nudity. Not to mention her own budding, second-amendment-based friendship with Charlie.

A beat-up car passed the house . . . slowly. It sounded like it was running low on power steering fluid. Her Caprice made that same noise last month—a loud screech whenever she turned the wheel. She didn't recognize the car, but she could tell the person driving was taking a good look at Charlie's house—and at Roma Jean's car, parked big as life, in the driveway. She grimaced, thinking again about the big new dent on its hood.

On her way to Charlie's tonight, she'd been following a pick-up truck that was missing its tailgate. Right before she turned off Highway 58, something had rolled out of the truck bed and smacked down on the hood of her car. The noise it made was so loud, it scared the crap out of her. She pulled off the road to see if the object left any damage. It had. *Of course*. The dent on the hood was pretty deep, too—and when she looked back up the road, she could see a can of something still rolling around on the ground. Roma Jean had backtracked and picked it up.

*Cling peaches in heavy syrup.*

*Just her luck.* She knew her father would never let her hear the end of this, even though it wasn't her fault. She kept the can of peaches just in case. *Maybe she could make it up to him by baking some cobbler?*

No. *That would never work.* She could just hear her mother saying Daddy couldn't eat them kind of peaches because of his "sugar."

She was praying maybe Charlie could pull the dent out with a plunger. That was partly why she kept waiting here on her: she didn't want to risk having her father see the car before she could get it fixed.

Sitting outside Charlie's house this long was creating other problems, too. She knew they wouldn't be able to keep their relationship secret for much longer—especially if she kept hanging out on Charlie's porch like some kind of fanatical Jehovah's Witness.

She looked at her watch again. Charlie had said she'd be home shortly after her shift ended. Roma Jean couldn't risk being late for supper, so she hoped Charlie would get there soon. As much as she wanted to, she could never stay overnight. *That* would be a bridge too far—at least when she was home from college and unofficially living with her parents. Her classes started in a couple of weeks, and she'd have more freedom then.

The ratty car came toward the house again. She heard it before she saw it. This time, it turned into Charlie's driveway and parked beside Roma Jean's Caprice.

She felt her pulse rate tick up. It seemed really quiet after the driver shut his engine off. The only sound came from a chorus of peep frogs that must've taken up residence in the abandoned above-ground swimming pool next door. For the first time, she realized that sitting outside hadn't been the best idea. That insight made her feel even more nervous.

After a few moments, a skinny man with pale skin and a gaunt face climbed out of the car. *Who was he?* And whatever would she say to him about why she was sitting there on Charlie's porch, so late on a Wednesday night?

The man approached her. She could make out the faded outlines of a tattoo creeping up above his shirt collar, on the sagging skin of his neck.

"Excuse me, young lady." He inclined his head toward her. "Is this here where Charlene Davis lives?"

"Yes, sir," Roma Jean replied because she wasn't certain how else to answer him. "But she's not at home right now." *Oh, real smart,* she chided herself. *Go ahead and advertise that you're here all alone.* Something about his sudden appearance was making the hairs on the back of her neck stand up. And nobody in Jericho ever called Charlie "Charlene." Roma Jean had first thought about reaching for her cellphone, just in case she needed to call for help, but the man seemed pretty harmless.

"I don't mean to trouble you none," he continued, "but could you tell me when you expect her back?"

"Um. Any minute now. She's on her way home from work."

He stared at the cracked pavement on Charlie's driveway.

"I won't trouble you no more," he said. "But if you don't mind tellin' her that Manfred stopped by, I'd appreciate it."

"Manfred?" Roma Jean repeated.

"Yes, ma'am. Manfred." He nodded at her and returned to his car.

He got back into his car, started it, and slowly backed out of the driveway. Roma Jean watched him leave, listening to the whine of his power steering until his car disappeared down the road. He drove off at the same deliberate speed—like he had nowhere else to be. This time, she noticed the palmetto tree on his license plate: South Carolina.

*Okay, that was weird.*

Who was this strange-looking man who showed up at this hour of the evening looking for "Charlene"? She'd just about decided to call Charlie and ask where she was when she saw the flash of headlights and realized that Charlie's patrol car was making its way up the street.

Roma Jean walked out to meet her.

The smile on Charlie's face could've lit up the night. Roma Jean felt the same little shiver she always felt when she saw Charlie. It was like an electric shock—only a lot nicer . . . and it didn't leave burned marks.

"What a great surprise," Charlie said, while she locked her patrol car. "How long have you been here?"

"About half an hour," Roma Jean explained. "I can't stay much longer. My parents will go ballistic."

Charlie's face fell. "I'm sorry I didn't get here sooner. I had to drop off some paperwork for Byron. I was lucky he was out at Dr. Heller's, or it would've taken me an hour."

Charlie took a step toward her like she wanted to hug her, but Roma Jean knew she wouldn't—not out here in the driveway. Then Charlie seemed to notice something on Roma Jean's car.

"When did that happen?" she asked, pointing at the dent.

"Tonight." Roma Jean sighed. "On my way over here. A can of peaches rolled out of the bed on the pickup truck I was following. Of course it landed on my car."

"How close were you following?"

Roma Jean glared at Charlie. "Don't go all deputy sheriff on me, okay? It was right before the turnoff on Redd Road."

"Okay, okay." Charlie held up her hands. "Don't get spooled up. I won't say anything else."

"Good. I was thinking maybe you could pull it out for me?"

"Pull it out? How?"

"Don't you have a plunger?" she asked. "You know," she made dramatic plunging motions, "use some suction to pull the dent out?"

Charlie ran a hand over the dent. "Honey, I don't think that's gonna work here. It's too deep. And the paint is cracked, too."

Roma Jean was grateful Charlie didn't make fun of her idea. "*Great.* How am I gonna tell Uncle Cletus I ruined his car?"

"You didn't ruin it. Junior can fix this—pretty easily, I think."

"Just my luck." Roma Jean was frustrated. "Maybe if the dang peaches had been in *light* syrup, instead of heavy, we could've fixed it ourselves."

Charlie smiled at her. "Maybe."

"Will you follow me out to Junior's tomorrow morning?"

"Of course."

"Then you can drop me off at the library. I have to take the bookmobile out early." She cast her eyes toward heaven. "I better try harder to avoid flying cans of fruit."

Charlie laughed. "Do you wanna come inside for a while?" She sounded hopeful.

"I'd love to, but I can't. It's too late now. Mama will be sending out a posse if I don't show up soon."

Charlie's face fell. "I'm really sorry I was late tonight."

Roma Jean laid a hand on her arm. "It's okay. Coming by here was just an impulse."

Charlie covered her hand. "It was a good one. I hope you have a lot more of them."

"That's just it." Roma Jean gave her a shy smile. "I have them all the time these days."

Charlie squeezed her hand. "Me, too."

"Okay. I gotta go." Roma Jean opened the door to the Caprice. "Oh. I almost forgot. Some strange man stopped by here looking for you. He asked me if Charlene lived here."

It wasn't quite dark, so Roma Jean had no trouble seeing the color drain from Charlie's face.

"Did he leave his name?" Charlie's voice sounded strange—like it had traveled a long distance to be heard.

Roma Jean nodded. "Manfred."

Charlie closed her eyes. She stayed silent for so long, Roma Jean began to worry.

"Do you know him?"

"Yeah." Charlie let out a slow breath.

Roma Jean waited, but Charlie didn't seem to be in a hurry to say anything else.

"Charlie?"

Charlie finally met her eyes.

"Yeah. I know him, all right." Roma Jean hadn't ever heard that cold tone in Charlie's voice. She didn't sound like herself. "I know him," she continued. "He used to be my father."

—~— —~— —~—

This was the first time Sonny had been to services out at Bone Gap in more than a year. Heck. *Two years.* He'd been to Nelda Rae Black's on Monday to spray for stink bugs, and darn if Nelda Rae hadn't twisted his arm and got him to promise to come out to her tabernacle for preaching on Wednesday night. She said there was some "special feller" in town visiting that he might remember. But she wouldn't answer any more questions about it.

Sonny always had been a sucker for mysteries . . .

He tried to get Bert to come out with him, but Bert said he was nuts.

"I ain't goin' all the way out to Bone Gap tonight. I gotta watch *Chicago Fire.*"

Sonny tried to argue with him. "If you weren't so damn cheap, you'd TiVo them programs."

"Well, if you weren't so damn weak you'd never've let that Nelda Rae Black talk you into going, neither."

Bert had a point.

There'd been no use asking Buddy to go with him, either. Wednesday nights were his "repair" nights.

You didn't mess with none of Buddy's routines.

Bert and Buddy had been at Sonny's house for dinner earlier, just like every Wednesday night. They always had Salisbury steak because Bert said Sonny's was the best—even better'n Nadine Odell's, but nobody could ever say that out in public. They'd been doing these Wednesday dinners together ever since Buddy came back to live with Bert—after his ex-wife, Ruby, run off with that Bath Fitter guy. That's how Buddy came to start fixing things over at Sonny's. Bert's double-wide didn't have much extra room, so Sonny let Buddy use his dining room as his workshop. It didn't take folks in town long to figure out this arrangement, and people started leaving things for Buddy to fix at Sonny's house. Buddy would sit at Sonny's dining-room table for hours, too, fixing all kinds of broken stuff with that dern car tape.

When Sonny'd left the house to drive out to Bone Gap tonight, Buddy was already hard at work, taping up a couple of lamps that had ripped shades and frayed power cords. Sonny had found them in a box on the front porch with a note attached: *These lamps been in my wife's family since James H. Price give them to her granddaddy back during the Great Depression. I was gonna throw them out, but she asked if maybe Bert's boy could have a go at fixing them. Regards, James Halsey, Sr.*

That's how it always went, too. Every week, folks would drop stuff off for Buddy. It was kind of crazy, if you thought about it. But then, Buddy always did manage to fix whatever Sonny hauled in from the porch. Except that one Wednesday night, when some feller from Sparta drove up and asked if Buddy could reattach the back bumper on his Crown Victoria. He explained that he'd accidentally backed over some new-fangled kind of Japanese shrub Raymond Odell had planted at the entrance to the Riverside Café, and damn if it hadn't ripped the thing clean off when he tried to pull forward. Sonny could see the bumper stuffed into the back seat of his car. Part of it was sticking out the passenger-side window.

Sonny had gone inside and got Buddy, but Buddy had said no. He could fix it temporary, but car tape wouldn't hold it long without new clips soldered to the frame.

Good thing, too. Sonny didn't want that bumper added to the pile of busted stuff piled up around his dining room.

Buddy was real scrupulous about fixing things in the order they was presented, and Sonny estimated he had about a month's worth of Salisbury steak dinners to cook before Buddy even got close to being caught up.

Sonny scratched at his collar. He wasn't used to wearing a dress shirt and tie and it was hot inside the tiny sanctuary. Seemed to him like they could've at least set up some box fans to move the air around. It smelled like mildew, too. Probably a lot of that came from all the cast-off hymnals that had been collecting dust in these old pew racks since Methuselah was in short pants. Nobody ever used them. They all knew the songs by heart. And it wadn't like they ever sang more'n the first and last verses, anyway. He didn't even know why they kept bothering with them altar calls. It wadn't like everybody in three counties hadn't *already* been saved . . . more'n once, too.

He supposed that's why they said the Lord moved in mysterious ways.

Skipping all them middle verses must've been part of that plan.

He kept looking around the congregation to see if he could spot Nelda Rae's special visitor. So far, he didn't see nobody who stood out. Not unless you counted them Lear twins, who were sittin' up front with new hairdos. His son, Harold had told him about two fellers who come into his shop wanting them Patrick Mahomes haircuts—with a twist. One wanted his top hair dyed purple; the other wanted his lime green. Harold said he did it, but when they left the shop, they looked like Tinky Winky and Dipsy from the *Teletubbies*.

*Figures it'd be the Lear twins. Them boys always was one brick shy of a load.*

He'd just about given up on seeing anything and began to wonder if he could slip out before the service got started when he saw a tall, thin man make his way in from the tiny vestibule.

*Well I'll be damned . . . if it ain't Manfred Davis.*

Sonny was stunned. Nobody'd seen hide nor hair of him since Sheriff Martin run him out of town more'n a decade ago. Last anyone had heard about him, he was working at some air-bag plant down in Cheraw, South Carolina. There were rumors that he'd taken up with some new woman, too. A widow lady, they said. With a couple of kids.

Sonny hoped that last part wadn't true—not after what all

Manfred did to Charlie. He beat that girl so bad she ended up in the hospital. That's when Sheriff Martin told him that unless he wanted to end up livin' in a cell out at River North, he'd pack up his stuff and get out of town.

But here he was, big as life. Well. *Maybe not as big*. Manfred looked like he'd aged—he'd lost a lot of weight, and the little bit of hair he had on top was streaked with gray.

*What was he doing back in Jefferson County?*

And why did Nelda Rae seem so hell-bent on making sure he knew about it?

One thing was for sure: it wasn't gonna be good news for Charlie Davis.

Sonny's neck itch fired up again—and this time, it was runnin' down his back.

A thought occurred to him. Nelda Rae knew him and Bert were still working out at Dr. Heller's. He began to think maybe she wanted to be sure news about Manfred got back to Sheriff Martin. Everybody in the county knew about Sheriff Martin's special . . . *friendship* with Dr. Heller—and that he spent a lot of time out at her place.

It would be just like Nelda Rae to be all up in *that* business, too. That woman was a menace.

Bert was right. Sonny was a sucker to let Nelda Rae drag him into something. He cursed his weakness.

*Chicago Fire* or not, he was gonna call Bert as soon as he got outta there . . .

It was Maddie's night to get Henry settled for bed. They'd been reading a bit of Henry's latest "grown-up" book every night before lights out. Their dog, Pete seemed to enjoy these story times, too. He was already sound asleep on his blanket at the foot of Henry's bed.

Roma Jean had suggested the book they were reading, *Danny the Champion of the World*. She thought Henry would especially like this story about the special bond between a boy and his father. As usual, Maddie found her instincts to be on point. Henry was wholly engrossed by the tale of a motherless English boy and his mechanic father, living in a Gypsy caravan behind a service station, and poaching pheasants from a nearby estate for food.

Maddie knew how much Henry missed his own father, who'd left Jericho weeks ago to rejoin the Army transportation corps in Texas. James called Henry every week, and sometimes they'd do family FaceTime sessions. Maddie was happy that Henry was so engrossed in this dramatic tale about a young boy and his dad. She and Syd did all they could to be intentional about including James in conversations and to remind Henry that his father was still very much engaged in his day-to-day life. They were hopeful that when James got his first significant leave in November, he'd be able to spend the time with them at the farm. Maybe for Thanksgiving?

Henry had been quiet tonight at dinner, which was especially unusual when they splurged and ate at the café. The only real animation he'd shown was when the basket of hot biscuits with "fairy sprinkles" was delivered to their table. Maddie wondered if he'd come down with something. School had only been back in session for two weeks and already her clinic was overrun with cases of ear infections, conjunctivitis, and stomach flu. But Henry met all of her entreaties about his health with emphatic assertions that he felt fine. She wasn't sure she fully believed him, but when Syd had nudged her leg beneath the table, she knew it was time to back off.

They finished tonight's chapter—an exciting one where Danny helped free his father, who'd become caught in a trap while out hunting pheasants after dark. This led to a long series of questions about what "poaching" meant, and why it once had been considered such a dangerous and serious crime.

Henry seemed satisfied with Maddie's explanation, but he wasn't at all sure why someone could be thrown in jail just for trying to feed his family.

"It was a different time, Henry." Maddie explained. "People who owned large estates maintained flocks of birds and other animals to hunt and shoot for sport. They didn't want common folk trespassing on their lands to kill their game. Intrusions like that were considered to be serious crimes—like theft of personal property—and people who got caught committing those crimes could be sent to jail for many years, or worse."

"But they needed the food."

Maddie nodded. "That's true. It was an unjust law that punished the poor."

Maddie could tell Henry was trying hard to make sense of it all.

"I'm glad Danny knew to go look for his daddy."

"He was very brave," Maddie agreed.

"If they got caught, would Danny have been sent to jail, too?"

"I honestly don't know, Henry." Maddie thought about it. "Maybe we can try to research this some more tomorrow, and find out."

"Okay." Henry stared down at his covers for a moment before looking up at her. "Do I have to wear one of those funny hats?"

"What funny hats?" Maddie glanced at his green Quakers hat, hanging from the bedpost. "You mean like your ball cap?

"No." He shook his head. "The ones in all those magazines that Uncle David keeps bringing Syd."

*Magazines?* Enlightenment dawned. "*Oh.* You mean the bridal magazines?"

Henry nodded.

"I don't think so, Henry. Nobody is going to make you wear anything you don't feel comfortable in." She rethought her statement. "Did you ask Syd about this?"

He nodded again.

"What did she say?"

"She said I didn't have to—and that you probably wouldn't, either."

Maddie felt irrationally relieved. Syd hadn't approached her yet for any discussions about wardrobe choices for their wedding, but she knew she was on borrowed time. At the rate the bridal magazines—most containing dozens of pages bearing colorful tabs—were piling up downstairs, she'd be unlikely to dodge this bullet for very much longer.

*Why couldn't they just have a quiet ceremony at home?* Or better yet, elope and do some kind of destination wedding . . . just the two of them.

*Fat chance.* Syd was determined to insist on the whole enchilada: gowns, guests, music, food, champagne, and cake . . . probably an obscenely overwrought creation with twenty tiers, if David had anything to do with it. *And he did.* He'd been Syd's coconspirator ever since Maddie put Oma's ring on her finger. Maddie did her best to tolerate what she viewed as Syd's excessive interest in the minutiae of the event. She knew that Syd's first wedding to Jeff had been, by her own admission, an afterthought—what she called a throwaway affair at city hall with no family or friends present. She was determined not to repeat that experience. "Especially," she explained, "not with *you*—not when it all matters so much."

*But hats?* No. They weren't going to be wearing any hats . . .

Henry yawned.

Maddie stood up and adjusted his covers. The nights were so warm that Syd had swapped out Henry's usual Spiderman bedspread for a lighter weight throw. This one had happy little cartoon cows all over it. Maddie suspected that if the cows hadn't borne some resemblance to Before, Henry would've strenuously objected to the change.

Maddie placed the book on Henry's little school desk—the same one she'd used when this had been her room. She noted that the top of the desk was strewn with parts of an old alarm clock that had stopped working months ago. Henry had retrieved it from the trash and was determined to "fix it." When Maddie gently suggested the thing was beyond repair, he insisted that he could figure it out. So back into the house it came, and here it sat—in about sixty pieces.

Before turning off the bedside light, she smoothed his unruly bangs away from his forehead. No matter how hard they tried, Henry's hair would not be tamed. Hers had always been the same way. Celine used to get so exasperated, she'd threaten to shave it off with a Flowbee.

"You go to sleep now, Sport." She kissed him. "No more worries about wedding clothes. Okay?"

"Okay." His voice sounded smaller.

Maddie could tell he'd be asleep before she reached her own bedroom. She turned off the lamp and retreated to the door. Before she could close it, she heard his voice again.

"Maddie? What are 'girl shoes'?"

Syd was sitting in the nook in front of their bedroom fireplace when Maddie returned from Henry's room. Mercifully, she didn't have the gas logs turned on.

"That was a long chapter tonight. Here." She handed Maddie a short tumbler containing an amber-colored liquid. "I thought we deserved a special treat, too."

Maddie sniffed the glass. *Score.* "Is this what I think it is?"

"Uh huh. Come sit down beside me."

"You don't have to ask me twice." Maddie collapsed on the settee beside her and kicked off her shoes. "What are we celebrating?"

"Multiplication tables. Remember?"

"How could I forget? The sixes and nines about drove me insane."

"That's probably because you don't know them, either."

"Hey." Maddie feigned umbrage. "I went to medical school."

"Hey." Syd bumped her shoulder. "You also have to use a calculator to figure out a 20 percent tip."

"Do not."

"*Do, too.*"

"What-*ever.*" Maddie sipped her drink. "Ohhhhh. This isn't the cheap stuff."

"That's because we don't *have* any cheap stuff."

"We ran out?"

"In a manner of speaking. David was here, and he polished it off."

"*All* of it?" Maddie shook her head.

"Relax, cheapskate. There wasn't that much. And he only drank it under duress."

"Meaning he couldn't find the good stuff?"

"Precisely."

"And you told me hiding this one in the dirty clothes hamper wouldn't work."

"I happily stand corrected." Syd yawned.

"Tired?"

"Uh huh. It was a long day. Getting ready for the book sale is wearing me out. People keep bringing in boxes of old magazines and get irate when I explain that we can't take them."

"You don't want magazines? I'd think some of them would have historical value."

"Yeah," Syd looked at her, "not when they're fifty-year-old copies of *TV Guide.*"

"You're kidding? Somebody had fifty-year-old copies of *TV Guide*?"

"Yes. Why? Are you interested in researching any episodes of *Bonanza* you might've missed? If so, I'd be happy to drop them off at your office."

"I thought you said you wouldn't take them?"

"I lost that argument."

Maddie chuckled. "How come you never lose any arguments with me?"

"Because you, my darling, are a pushover."

Maddie wanted to disagree with her, but she knew Syd was right. Something else occurred to her.

"I meant to tell you that I talked with Mom about Avi and Dorothy."

"Oh?" Syd sounded pleased. "What did she say?"

"She thinks it's a good idea. So I called Avi on the way to the café. She's coming down tomorrow."

"That's great. How'd you finagle a meeting so quickly?"

"Avi is interested in looking for office space to expand her practice into this part of the region. She's taking a couple of weeks off to scout the area. I thought maybe she could make use of that extra office in my clinic."

"That's a great idea."

Maddie nodded. "Keep it under your hat for now. At least until I get to talk with Lizzy."

"Sure. I assume you're going to approach her tomorrow?"

"That's the plan." Maddie sipped her cognac. Her mention of hats reminded her of Henry's question.

"Apropos of hats," she began, "Henry asked me some random question about hats for the wedding."

"Oh, god." Syd sighed. "I forgot about that. He's worried that you both might have to wear something formal at the wedding."

"He's not the only one."

"Maddie . . ."

"Okay, okay." Maddie held up a hand. "Don't get riled up. I know I said I'd think about it."

"And have you thought about it?"

"Hats?"

Syd socked her on the arm. "No. *Not* hats. *Clothes*. Dress clothes. As in some kind of ensemble that includes shoes and garments not made of flannel."

"I rarely wear flannel."

"You know what I mean. Have you thought about it?"

"What's the big rush? The wedding is still months away—*nine* months, to be exact. We've got plenty of time to argue about whether or not I have to wear girl shoes."

Syd raised an eyebrow.

*Shit.* Maddie knew her unfortunate choice of words was tantamount to granting Syd license to release her inner bridal kraken.

"I didn't mean to say *argue*," she hurriedly corrected. "I meant to say *discuss*."

"Of, course you did." Syd's tone was dripping with sarcasm.

"Come on, honey." Maddie took hold of her hand. "I *want* to talk about all of this. It's just . . ."

"Just?" Syd prompted. "Just what?"

"Just . . ." Maddie was floundering. "It just seems premature—at least for me. Can't I have a bit more time to get my head around all of this before we commit to anything?" She tugged on Syd's hand. "Please?"

"Maddie? What do you think this process will be like once you make up your mind about what you will and won't consent to wear?"

"I don't know. I guess we order it someplace."

"*Someplace?* Like where? JC Penney? Men's Wearhouse?"

"Very funny." Maddie slugged back the rest of her cognac. It was going straight to her head. She began to feel overheated and slightly dizzy. What she really wanted was to change the subject. She shifted on the settee so she could face Syd. "Honey? You know I love you more than anything, and I cannot wait to be married to you. It's not that I never think about it. It's that

I think about it all the time. I don't want to wait nine more minutes, much less nine more months. Any time you hear frustration in my voice, it's only because I don't want to have to wait so long to make you mine. I just want us to get married. *Now*. Right away. Without any big fuss or hoopla. Does that make sense?"

She could see Syd's expression soften. Well. Maybe soften a *little* bit.

"Maddie, I understand that a big wedding will push you out of your comfort zone—and I'm sorry about that. I know you'd like nothing more than for us to elope and find a justice of the peace someplace. But please try to understand my perspective on all of this. I made that mistake with Jeff, and I've *always* regretted it. I promised myself that if ever I chose to be married again—and, truthfully, until I met you, I never believed I'd even consider it—I'd make sure the vows I took were respected and honored in all the ways they should be."

"I know that. I want that, too."

"Do you?"

"Of course."

Syd seemed a bit calmer. "Then try to understand this when you get frustrated with me—and with the timetable. No one stood up with me. No friends. No neighbors. No grad school classmates. *No one.* My parents were excluded. I didn't even change my clothes. I sailed through the experience with the same careless inattention I'd grant to . . . I don't know . . . renewing my driver's license or paying my taxes." She wiped an impatient hand across her eyes. "I love you. I want to make those solemn promises to you in front of everyone who matters to me . . . *to us*. That *matters* to me. Making a public demonstration of my commitment to you—especially now, especially after everything this community has just gone through—matters more to me than just about anything. I want our friends and neighbors to know that we love each other and are not ashamed to declare it."

It was hard for Maddie not to feel the same emotion Syd was expressing. And she felt like a cad for dragging her feet on something she knew in her viscera was this important to Syd—and to herself. The last thing she ever felt was shame about her life with Syd. It mattered that she own the truth of it, too. Publicly. *No matter how uncomfortable the damn shoes were.*

"Okay, baby." She raised Syd's hand to her lips and kissed it. "I want us to do this right, too."

"Do you really mean that?" Syd sounded hopeful.

"I do." Maddie gave her a wry smile. "See? I recited my lines just fine."

Syd laughed. "Don't get ahead of yourself."

Maddie tugged her closer. "I love you. You know?"

"Yeah. I think I got that memo a while back."

Maddie kissed her. When they drew apart, she nudged Syd.

"Well? Don't you have something you want to say to me, too?"

"How'd you know?" Syd smiled impishly and held up her empty glass. "It's your turn to go downstairs for refills."

"How about I just go get the damn bottle?"

"Even better." Syd relaxed against the settee and yawned again. "I wonder why arguing with you makes me horny?"

Suddenly, Maddie was feeling overheated for a new reason altogether.

*Screw the cognac.*

She hauled Syd to her feet and led her toward their big and welcoming bed.

# Chapter Two

*Recorded Interview*
*Preliminary Inquest Investigation*
*Death of Mayor Gerald Watson*

"My name is Bertrand L. Townsend, Sr. Everybody just calls me Bert. I wadn't down by the water when it happened—not on that part of the river, anyways."

*Good thing I wadn't, too. I wouldn't a helped that man, no way.*

"The first thing I heard about the ruckus was when Natalie Chriscoe came runnin' down to tell us that Buddy and Dorothy come up from the water, and she was cryin' and beggin' for help."

*I don't know nobody who's sorry he's dead.*

"She said Buddy was limpin' bad and Dorothy was helpin' him walk. She said she heard Dorothy say that her daddy'd done kicked Buddy real hard."

*That made me wanna go down there and give that man what for, but Sonny held me back because we had to finish the fireworks.*

"Natalie said Buddy kept mutterin' somethin' about Goldenrod bein' redeemed. That's what he always calls Dorothy—Goldenrod. It's a kind of nickname of his. He has 'em for lots of people he's special friends with. I didn't pay no special attention to that. I told her he mostly talks that way when he's on to something that upsets him. Sonny told me he could finish up the fireworks his self, and I could skedaddle and go check on Buddy. So I followed Natalie back to where they was."

*Before I left, Sonny told me he thought this all was a bad sign. He said somethin' "dire" had probably happened—that Watson had been beggin' for it. He told me I needed to go on and protect my boy because Buddy wadn't always good at takin' care of his self.*

"By the time me and Natalie got up from the river, Dorothy was talkin' to Sheriff Martin, and Doc Stevenson was lookin' at Buddy's leg. Buddy was rocking back and forth on a bench and mutterin' about them cannons being finished. I told him everything was okay and that Sonny was wrappin' it all up. After that, everything pretty much happened the way you know. They found Watson in the water and nobody saw what happened."

*I ain't sayin' that he got what was coming to him—but we all know he did. Ain't nobody in this town sorry that man is dead.*

"You ain't asked for my opinion, but I'll tell you that I don't think nobody did him wrong. I think that man did for his own self. End of story."

*Kohlrabi. Collards. Kale. Cauliflower.*

It was time to move the seedlings from the shed and plant them in the Quiet Lady's garden.

The frost would come late this year. The farmers all said October twelfth. But October twelfth was wrong.

The frost would come late. Buddy could see the signs. Nights were too warm. Tall weeds choked the orchard grass. White butterflies swarmed the garden.

The frost would come late this year.

*Kohlrabi. Collards. Kale. Cauliflower.*

He laid out the plants. *One. One. Two. Three. Five.*

Five was part of phi. Phi was right when the frost came late.

*Roots. Stems. Leaves.*

*One. One. Two. Three. Five.*

Five from one. The Golden Ratio.

Five and three. *The Divine Proportion.*

God told Moses to use phi to build the Ark. The Ark held God's Covenant.

Warm nights.

White Butterflies and Orange Dogs came early. They made five less than zero.

Less than zero was little phi. Little phi was not right for a garden.

Little phi broke the Covenant.

The frost would come late. It would come late because nights were too warm and the Covenant was broken.

Goldenrod was broken. Goldenrod helped Buddy plant the seedlings.

Goldenrod didn't talk. Goldenrod was broken.

Her ratio was less than zero.

Goldenrod was little phi.

Little phi was not right for Goldenrod.

Goldenrod's ratio was wrong because nights were too warm and God's Covenant was broken.

The Orange Dog came for her at night.

*One. One. Two. Three. Five.*

Goldenrod planted the kohlrabi in the holes Buddy dug for her. The earth was the Ark of God's Covenant.

*One. One. Two. Three. Five.*

Phi was The Divine Proportion. Phi-Prime was right for Goldenrod.

*Roots. Stems. Leaves.*

Goldenrod would be less than zero until the Orange Dog went away.

*Kohlrabi. Collards. Kale. Cauliflower.*

The frost would come late this year.

—∞— —∞— —∞—

Inside the small library, Miss Murphy and Roma Jean had a wager.

Miss Murphy had bet Roma Jean she couldn't guess who'd donated some of the books by just looking at their titles.

Roma Jean was pretty sure she could.

They'd been emptying out the boxes and sorting the books into stacks by type for more than two hours now. So far, Roma Jean had been able to nail donations from Gladys Pitzer (*Fifty Best Designs for Winter Casket Sprays*), Harold Nicks (*A Guide to Cutting Hair the Sassoon Way*), Raymond Odell (*Better Homes Guide to Zone Six Ornamental Shrubs*), Natalie Chriscoe (*QuickBooks for Dummies*), and Edna Freemantle (*Living with Toxic In-laws*).

That last one had been super easy because Roma Jean had bought copies of the book for pretty much everyone in her family. Mama said it was a pretty strange stocking stuffer, but Roma Jean noticed she kept her copy on the nightstand next to her bed.

"Okay, smart aleck." Syd hauled another cardboard box up from the floor. "I'll bet you a hot dog and a Diet Coke you can't get *these* right."

The first two were real posers. It didn't help that Miss Murphy told her they came from the same person. One book was a dog-eared hardback copy of something called *Deutsch Aktuell*, and the other was an oversized paperback called *The Moosewood Cookbook, Revised Edition*. Roma Jean pondered. Who did she know who read books in German and cooked weird hippie recipes from about a hundred years ago?

A lightbulb went off.

"Dr. Heller!" she cried.

Miss Murphy's face lost its smug expression. She sighed

dramatically and dropped the two books back into their box. "So what do you want on your hot dog?"

Roma Jean felt ten feet tall. It wasn't usual for her to get the best of Miss Murphy. It was a change in the way their relationship was developing.

There were other changes, too.

For one thing, Miss Murphy kept asking Roma Jean to call her Syd. As much as Roma Jean tried to remember, the informality of that just felt . . . *weird.* It was hard for her not to remember the days when she'd ring up Miss Murphy's—*Syd's*—groceries at Food City. She thought back on those days with mortification—especially when she recalled how she'd practically pass out whenever Miss Murphy came in with Dr. Stevenson. Roma Jean had been *so* crushed out on the dark-haired, blue-eyed doctor. *It was so embarrassing.* She'd always acted like a moron around them both, too. Dropping things. Tripping over stuff. Making really stupid comments.

Well. She *still* said a lot of stupid stuff. That hadn't changed much.

But she'd never understood how the two women had been able to see past her dorky behavior and take such a strong interest in her future. On her own, Miss Murphy had established a scholarship fund that pretty much paid for Roma Jean's college tuition. And now she'd given her this part-time job driving the bookmobile on weekends and during the summer months, too.

She owed them both a lot.

But so did a lot of people in this town. Too bad not everyone was as grateful.

Everything that Gerald Watson had tried to do to them was awful. The things he said about their relationship—and her own with Charlie—had hurt a lot of people. Including her parents. It was hard for her to admit that there were other people in Jericho who felt the same way he did—people who believed that women who loved other women were ungodly or some kind of affront to nature.

But those people did exist, and a lot of them lived here. She could feel their eyes on her at church. Aunt Edna noticed it, too. One time, she even saw Aunt Edna take two of them aside in the church parking lot after services and give them a talking to. She couldn't hear anything Aunt Edna said, but from the way she shook her head and pointed her index finger, she could guess. Later, at lunch, Aunt Edna told Roma Jean to ignore them. She said that Mr. Watson had freed them all up to show their ignorant butts in public, and, even though he was gone, his ilk was still out there sowing hate. It would take a while, she said, for their meanness to get siphoned off and sink back underground.

But she warned Roma Jean that it would never go away.

Roma Jean knew Aunt Edna spoke the truth because she'd had a lot of firsthand experience living with bigotry. Her decision to marry a white man more than thirty years ago and move back here with him to live had made sure of that. Roma Jean never even thought of them as an "interracial" couple. They were just Aunt Edna and Uncle Cletus. But she knew there were *other* people who didn't see them that way. It wasn't something her family ever talked about—not even Grandma Azalea, who didn't hesitate to offer up opinions whether you asked for them or not.

But then, her family never much talked about *anything* difficult. It wasn't their way.

Roma Jean's relationship with Charlie had become one of those topics that never got discussed.

Miss Murphy's relationship with Dr. Stevenson was another one.

That was mostly why Roma Jean never told Miss Murphy about some of the whispered comments she'd heard at a bookmobile stop out in the eastern part of the county. It was one of the days that Henry was riding along with her. The women clucked their tongues and talked about how Miss Murphy and Dr. Stevenson were committing a sin by raising James

Lawrence's little boy—about how immoral it was, and how right the mayor had been to say the law shouldn't allow it.

It made Roma Jean furious. And it took all of her strength to hold her tongue in front of Henry, and not set those nasty biddies straight. When she told Charlie about it that night, Charlie laughed at her.

"Roma Jean, they're *already* 'straight'—and self-righteous. It's a dangerous combination, and that's part of what drives their hatred toward things they don't understand."

"Well, I don't *care* what drives it." Roma Jean was disgusted. "It's *wrong*—and if they ever read the gospels, they'd know they need to sow less hate and be more Christ-like. Jesus *never* treated people so meanly. He taught us not to judge others."

Charlie did not disagree with her.

She was sure Miss Murphy wouldn't either, but she still wasn't going to tell her about it. She just prayed Henry hadn't overheard their whispers, too.

Her stomach growled. A hot dog was sounding pretty good.

Miss Murphy noticed. "Let's just finish this one box and we'll take a break to go and get some lunch."

Roma Jean lifted another stack of books out and set them on the sorting table. They were mostly biographies. The top one was about the World War I pilot, Baron Manfred von Richthofen—"The Red Baron."

Roma Jean stared at it for a minute before asking Miss Murphy, "Did you know Manfred Davis?"

Miss Murphy seemed surprised by her question. "Do you mean Charlie Davis's father?"

Roma Jean nodded.

"I didn't know him personally. He was gone many years before I moved here. But I probably know as much about him as you do."

"I don't really know anything," Roma Jean replied. "Why did he leave Jericho?"

Miss Murphy seemed to hesitate. "Did you ask Charlie about him?"

Roma Jean shook her head.

The truth was that Charlie hadn't explained anything else about the strange man who'd appeared last night—after her one revelation that he "used to be" her father. Her mood had quickly grown so dark, Roma Jean knew it wasn't the right time to press her for details.

"I saw him last night," Roma Jean added. "He came by Charlie's house before she got home from work. He told me he was looking for 'Charlene.' He seemed kind of creepy, but harmless. Charlie pretty much freaked out when I told her about him. She wouldn't say anything else after telling me he was her father."

"Oh." Roma Jean could tell Miss Murphy was trying to figure out what to say.

"It's okay if you don't want to talk about it, Miss Murphy. I was too nervous to ask Charlie for any details."

"No. It's okay. I don't know a lot about him, except that he was pretty brutal toward Charlie when she was growing up. I gather that Sheriff Martin was instrumental in getting him to leave town after some altercation led to Charlie ending up in the hospital."

"He *hurt* her?" Roma Jean was stunned. "Bad enough to put her in the hospital? Why?"

"I don't know many more details, Roma Jean—and I don't want to offer conjectures. I think you should ask Charlie about it."

*That was going to be a lot easier said than done . . .*

Roma Jean dejectedly continued sifting through her stack of books. One of them caught her eye: *The Everything Bridesmaid Book* by Holly Lefevre. She discreetly flipped it over to scan the back. *This book can be your go-to companion*, the description proclaimed. The blurb went on to promise the book could provide readers "quick intel" on bridal showers and bachelorette parties.

Roma Jean thought about sneaking it into the discard pile before Miss Murphy saw it.

*Too late.* When she made her move, she realized Miss Murphy was watching her.

"What's that one?" she asked.

"It's some bride thing." Roma Jean tried to wave it off.

"Ohhh, lemme see." Miss Murphy reached out for it.

Roma Jean reluctantly handed it over.

*Great.* Now they'd have to spend their entire lunch talking about peach and prosciutto versus smoked salmon canapés—or whether white lilies were too somber for a spring wedding.

Miss Murphy was flipping through the pages of the book. "I think this one is a keeper."

"I don't know." Roma Jean decided to give it a shot. "Do you think maybe you already have enough books about wedding planning? Too many could just make the choices more confusing."

One shelf in Miss Murphy's tiny office was already full of books stuffed with interlibrary loan tags—all of them about different aspects of planning weddings.

"Too many?" Miss Murphy sounded confused by her question. "Not at all. I want to be sure I make the best choices. A woman only gets to do this once." She smiled. "Okay . . . *twice*, in my case. But you know what I mean."

"Yeah, but the thing is . . ." Roma Jean stopped herself.

"The thing is . . . what?"

"Well. The thing is to . . . maybe . . . try not to go all . . . sort of . . . *Real Housewives* . . . on some of this stuff." Roma Jean was floundering. "You know?"

Miss Murphy looked flustered. "Is that what you think I'm doing?"

"Well. Kind of . . . a little bit? *Maybe?* Just now and then."

Miss Murphy sighed and tossed the book onto the discard pile. But Roma Jean knew she wouldn't leave it there. She was pretty sure that later, before she locked up the library and left for the night, that book would join the others on the shelf in her office.

*She'd bet another hot dog on it . . .*

When Lizzy arrived at the clinic on Thursday morning, she found a note from Maddie on her desk. For once, her handwriting looked relaxed and more than halfway readable.

*Good morning,* the note read. *After you get settled, come by my office. I have some news to share with you. P.S. Bring coffee.*

Lizzy smiled. She looked forward to these informal chats with her boss. They tried to arrange these coffee dates at least two mornings a week. Lately, however, the workload had escalated so much they'd been lucky to wave hello as they passed each other in the corridor. It wasn't just that school was back in session and they were dealing with the inevitable surge in cases of stomach flu and head colds. The only other independent medical clinic in the county had closed its doors less than a month ago, and they'd been steadily taking on more new patients than they could reasonably handle. Something was going to have to change. She guessed this was likely part of what Maddie wanted to discuss with her. She hoped the "good news" meant the clinic would be acquiring another set of hands.

That was truer than ever since the grant that funded her position was set to expire at the end of the calendar year. Maddie would have to figure something out, and fast. Against all hope, Lizzy prayed Maddie would engineer a way to make her position permanent, but she was afraid to pin many hopes on that outcome. It just didn't seem economically feasible. The reality was that she'd probably have to go back into hospital nursing, which she hated. And knowing this made it even harder for her to cobble together reasonable explanations for why she didn't want to move to Colorado with Tom.

It wasn't that she didn't want a life with Tom. It was more that she wanted to have that life here. She'd never before felt the sense of belonging she'd inherited when she accepted Maddie's job offer all those years ago. It was true what the old-timers said: Jericho, with all its quirks and provincialities, wormed its way under your skin and pretty much ruined you for life anyplace else. Jericho had become her home and she didn't want to leave it—even if it meant she'd have to take a job she loathed to be able to stay here.

*She just wished Tom felt the same way . . .*

Lizzy checked her appointment calendar before heading to their tiny kitchen to fix a mug of coffee.

It was a few minutes past seven. Peggy wasn't in yet. She didn't usually show up until seven-thirty—thirty minutes before they started seeing patients. She and Maddie should have time for a decent chat before the onslaught of patients began.

Maddie's office door was open, as usual, and she was seated behind her desk going over some printouts. Lizzy tapped on the doorframe.

Maddie looked up and smiled. She was wearing what Syd called her "nerd glasses." They were horn rims with bright blue frames—a detail Maddie described as her one concession to fashion.

"Come on in." She waved Lizzy toward the small sitting area opposite her desk. "Let's get comfy."

Lizzy sat down in one of the upholstered chairs and waited on Maddie to join her.

Maddie had some music playing at a low volume. It was something classical. Maybe Debussy? Lizzy regretted that her music education was so flimsy. She'd thought many times about asking Syd to give her piano lessons.

Asking Dr. Heller would've been a bridge too far. Although a likelier candidate for offering instruction, Maddie's mother was just too . . . *enigmatic*. It was ridiculous, but Lizzy always felt a bit clumsy around Dr. Heller. She reminded Lizzy of her clinical master's degree adviser at Vanderbilt, Julia Smyth Barroso. Dr. Barroso had been that same way. Reserved. Almost mysterious. The women were similar in appearance, too: both tall and patrician with impeccable posture and classic beauty. They oozed competence and confidence in equal measure.

Frankly, they scared the hell out of Lizzy.

Maddie was like her mother in a lot of ways—most ways, actually—but she had far less reserve.

"So." Maddie had joined her and promptly propped her feet up on the small coffee table between their chairs—another difference from her mother. Lizzy couldn't imagine Dr. Heller ever doing something so casual. "How're things going with you?"

Lizzy demurred in responding. "Do you want the polite answer or the long version?"

"The long version, of course." Maddie's voice dropped into its more serious octave range. "What's going on?"

"It's Tom." Lizzy chuckled. "Of course."

"Uh oh."

"Yeah. This one's a doozie, too." Maddie gave her time to continue talking. "I met him for dinner last night at Waffle House. He was an hour late . . . also not uncommon. And when he finally arrived, he explained that he'd been held up because he'd been negotiating a job offer."

"Really? Isn't that a good thing? He's nearly finished with his program, isn't he?"

Lizzy nodded. "Only nine more weeks."

"So I take it the job in question is not to your liking?"

"You might say that. It's in Colorado."

Maddie's face fell. Lizzy could've been mistaken, but she thought Maddie's knee-jerk reaction to the news expressed about as much dismay as she'd felt herself when Tom shared it with her.

"Well, I'll be damned . . ." Maddie searched Lizzy's eyes. "I guess this means you've got to do some soul searching."

"To say the least. I think I slept about forty-five minutes last night."

Maddie was drumming her fingers against the arm of her chair. Her agitation was evident.

"I'm flattered that you seem to share my reaction to this news," Lizzy observed. "But you seem to be nearly as frustrated by it as I am."

"Well, that's an understatement." Maddie let out a deep breath. "Remember I told you I had some good news I wanted to share?"

Lizzy nodded.

Maddie set her coffee cup down on the table and folded her hands. "Guess there's no time like the present. I've run all the numbers and have concluded that the clinic can now support adding your position, *adding you*, full time—as a partner in the practice. That is, if you're interested. I mean," she hastily added, "as you consider this other . . . possibility."

Lizzy was too stunned to speak. Maddie was offering her a permanent job? And a partnership in her clinic . . . her *father's* clinic?

Maddie leaned toward her. "It's okay to speak. It's not like I offered to give you my left kidney or anything."

Lizzy laughed. "It's actually pretty damn close. You have no idea how much I've dreamed about being able to stay on here after my grant runs out. I thought it was impossible."

"Not so much, as it turns out. And by the way, that was always *my* dream scenario, too. You've been an incredible asset to this community, Lizzy. I'd be crazy not to move heaven and earth to keep you."

"But *are* you moving heaven and earth? Can the practice truly afford to do this? Are you sure it won't become untenable down the road?"

"Truthfully, none of us knows what manner of dragons lurk

down the proverbial road. As we know, the only other private clinic in the county just shut its doors after thirty-five years. My thought is that by having you join me as a partner in this journey, it'll be up to both of us to be sure we can face whatever changes lie ahead. I've always been an optimist, although Syd tells me I'm actually more clueless than hopeful. But she agrees that making this commitment to you and to a shared future taking care of people in this county is a no-brainer." Maddie smiled. "And as you know, I always do what she says."

That made Lizzy laugh. Her head was still spinning.

"Would it be okay if I took some time to think it over? Just for a little bit?"

"Of course you can. In fact, I have a preliminary contract drafted for you. Take it with you and go over it. Have an attorney examine it, too. And mark it up with any questions or changes. I was just looking it over when you got here."

Lizzy struggled to find the right words to express all she was feeling. It was a tall order because she honestly had no idea how she felt. Right now, there were simply too many variables and they were all slamming into each other like cars in a demolition derby.

"Maddie," she finally managed. "It matters to me that you know how much this means to me. And not just the incredible offer—but the demonstration of trust and confidence it means you're placing in me. It's . . . humbling."

"I think I know," Maddie replied. "But don't give me too much credit. It's just like Syd said: a no-brainer."

The phone on Maddie's desk buzzed. They both jumped at the interruption.

Maddie glanced at the wall clock. "I guess Peggy's here. Excuse me."

She got up and went to her desk to answer the phone. "Good morning. When did you sneak in?" She listened for a moment. "She is? That's great. Send her right on back." She hung up and faced Lizzy.

"A med school chum of mine is here—a child psychologist. She's looking for remote office space in this area. And I thought I'd co-opt her to have a conversation with Dorothy."

"Great idea. Do you want me to scoot?"

"Not at all." Maddie waved her back into her chair. "I wanted you to meet her, anyway. If it works out, I thought she could use the extra office here."

Lizzy was impressed. It looked like Maddie had more than one idea in the works to expand their practice.

*Their practice.*

She'd always thought of it that way. Now there was every chance it could truly be theirs—if Lizzy could unravel the confusing situation with Tom. She was determined to figure it all out.

A slender, olive-skinned woman with very short hair tapped on Maddie's door. Her appearance was striking and faintly exotic. She was wearing stylishly cut clothes that still managed to look casual—and comfortable.

"Excuse me, but the nurse up front told me I might find a singularly mirthless physician lurking back here, devising new ways to commit Medicare fraud. Have either of you seen anyone matching that description?"

Lizzy stifled a laugh and got to her feet.

"Get in here, nitwit." Maddie crossed the room and gave her friend a warm hug. Maddie topped her by several inches. They both turned to face Lizzy. "Avi, meet my partner in crime and resident nurse practitioner, Lizzy Mayes. Lizzy, this is Avi Zakariya. Be careful not to look too closely into her eyes. Word on the street is that she's a total shaman."

Avi crossed to where Lizzy stood and extended a hand. "My pleasure. I heard that any gig working here came packaged with hazardous duty pay. Is that so?"

Avi had a nice handshake. Firm, but not bone crushing.

Lizzy dropped her chin and lowered her voice. "Just avoid the office karaoke jams on Friday afternoons. They're the worst."

Avi laughed. "Noted." She flopped into a chair. "Are we sitting, or what?"

"We're sitting." Maddie waved Lizzy back into her seat. "Did you get any breakfast?"

"Nope. I left Roanoke at o'dark-thirty." She looked around the office. "You got any bagels in this joint?"

Maddie looked at Lizzy hopefully.

"No bagels," she answered. "But the last time I checked, there was a partial box of prehistoric Fruity Pebbles in the kitchen."

Avi looked at Maddie with a raised eyebrow.

"So sue me because I *never* get stuff like that at home." Maddie regarded Lizzy. It was obvious she had an idea. "When's your first appointment?"

Lizzy blinked. "Nine-thirty."

"Hallelujah. Mine, too. Why don't we blow this pop stand and go get a quick bite to eat?"

Lizzy was surprised. "You mean, all three of us?"

"Sure. If this joint's going condo, I want you to be equally responsible."

"You don't have to ask me twice." Avi stood up. "Who's driving?"

Dorothy was distracted. She kept stumbling over the transition from down-tempo E minor to double tempo A minor in the Beethoven piece they were practicing. After the fourth misstep, Celine realized today's lesson was going no place. She decided to call it quits, and suggested that Dorothy go outside to help Buddy plant the vegetable garden. Dorothy jumped at the chance.

At the doorway, Dorothy stopped and turned back to face Celine.

"I'm really sorry. It isn't that I don't want to try to get it right. It's just . . ."

Celine stopped her. "It's fine, Dorothy. Some days are just not conducive to practice."

"Really?" Dorothy's tone was hopeful.

"Really," Celine lied. The truth was that in her experience, there'd never been any excuse not to practice. Her mother wouldn't hear of it. "You go on outside," she told the girl. "Ask Buddy if he wants to stay for lunch."

"Okay, Celine. I will." Dorothy disappeared into the kitchen. Celine heard the patio door open and close.

*Celine.* The word still reverberated in her mind.

Convincing Dorothy to use her name, instead of continuing to call her "Dr. Heller," had been a Herculean task. Celine felt the significance of Dorothy speaking her name any time the girl remembered to use it. It mattered that the two of them found some way to level the terrain that separated them in both age and life experience—especially now that Dorothy was staying with Celine. It might seem like a small thing to any onlooker, but Celine understood what an act of daring—and courage—it was for the girl to express any kind of intimacy with her.

That was another departure from Celine's relationship with her own mother.

Of course, she quickly reminded herself, she was *not* Dorothy's mother. But for right now, at least, she was Dorothy's caretaker, and those lines sometimes became blurred.

At least they did for her. She wasn't sure about Dorothy's perceptions. The girl said little about her status. Although she appeared to be very comfortable sharing space here in the old farmhouse that was still undergoing renovation. Most days, they moved around each other quietly. Dorothy had taken to getting up early so she could make breakfast for them before heading out to catch the bus for school. Celine had developed what she knew was an unhealthy fondness for Dorothy's sweet scratch biscuits. And as much as she knew she should ask the girl to stop baking them so frequently, she understood the symbolic significance of Dorothy's desire to gift Celine with something special. So Celine was willing to indulge her less-than-secret appetite for the hot confections, and express only modest concern for the integrity of her waistline.

They'd meet in the late afternoons, after Dorothy had finished her homework, for piano lessons. Once those were completed, they'd make supper together. More often than not, it was a platter full of late season vegetables from the garden, garnished with cheeses and bits of cut-up fruit. They'd carry it outside to the patio, where they could sit in the shade beneath a large market umbrella. By that late in the day, the August sun would be low and hot. So most evenings, it was prohibitive to remain outdoors for very long.

Celine would then retreat to her office to read or answer correspondence, and Dorothy would often retrieve her latest book and curl up on the window seat near the Steinway.

The girl was a voracious reader and her tastes were exceptional. Celine marveled at the skill Roma Jean had employed to introduce Dorothy to the world of Southern fiction titles—all written by women. Carson McCullers. Lee Smith. Dorothy Allison. Eudora Welty. Olive Ann Burns. Sheri Reynolds. Sharyn McCrumb. Right now, Dorothy was engrossed in a book of Celine's that she'd pulled from a shelf in the living room: *Heading West* by Doris Betts.

Sometimes, they would watch a cooking show on TV—usually on the nights Byron joined them for dinner. Dorothy tended to enjoy competition shows more than straightforward, recipe-driven formats that were what she called too "cheffy." She'd sit on the floor with Django, who always seemed captivated by whatever was happening inside the big, bright box. For his part, Byron liked to argue with the celebrity judges.

"They're nuts," he'd bellow. "There's no way that was the best dish. The plating was a nightmare. It looked like a five-car pileup.

Wasn't it a mess, Dorothy?"

Celine observed that Dorothy would always agree with him, whether the plating had been bad or not.

Byron would look at Celine with a smug expression. "See?" he'd say. "Dorothy agrees with me."

"I somehow think it's less that she agrees with your opinions than she respects the trappings of your office."

That was essentially the way their evenings would unfold. Byron would always leave for home at a respectable hour. Sometimes, on weekends, he'd leave Django with Dorothy for a sleepover. But he never stayed the night himself—and hadn't since Dorothy had come to live there. This change in circumstance created some logistical issues for the two of them. But whenever Dorothy spent the night with Henry at Maddie's farm, Celine would join Byron at his home near Iron Mountain.

Celine was gratified that Byron was being so tolerant of these arrangements, and doing so generally without complaint. Although his entreaties that she quit resisting his offers and agree to marry him were becoming more insistent.

*That wasn't going to happen.* She was determined. And she told him as much. Even when Byron insisted that getting married would immediately short-circuit the wagging tongues of the county biddies, Celine refused. She knew her limits, and taking a step like that exceeded them all. She cared deeply for Byron. More deeply than she'd cared for any man since Maddie's father. But marriage, even to him, was likely to remain a bridge too far for her.

For now, Byron reluctantly seemed to accept her protestations—even respect them. Celine feared the advent of the day he might cease to do so, but knew there was precious little she could do to forestall it.

In the meantime, the three of them—four including Django, who was rapidly becoming Dorothy's best friend—were slowly making their way toward something resembling a family.

She tried for the tenth time to return her attention to the magazine she'd picked up.

She scanned the listings in "Talk of the Town," the event calendar in *The New Yorker*. It was a habit she'd acquired many years ago when monitoring the New York concert scene became an obsession. That had been especially true after she'd left Virginia and moved to Los Angeles, a city she always believed to be bereft of refinement—at least when it came to classical music.

That belief was a prejudice she'd inherited from her parents, who never ventured more than a few city blocks beyond their known worlds at Juilliard and The Metropolitan Opera.

It surprised Celine how much she missed New York. She and Maddie's father had always managed to juggle their schedules to allow them to make frequent trips to the city for concerts or the ballet. Sometimes, Celine would go by herself, and reconnect with her former teacher at Juilliard, the virtuoso Joseph Bloch. It amazed her that he always made time to see her, and that, no matter how many years intervened, he still managed to recall *every one* of her foibles and proclivities. It had been *his* constancy and lack of judgment that single-handedly salvaged her love of music after she decided to leave Juilliard and enter medical school.

The same had decidedly not been true of her musician parents.

Celine redirected her attention to the list of upcoming concerts and recitals. The autumn promised to be a good season in town. Mitsuko Uchida was scheduled to appear with the Mahler Chamber Orchestra at Carnegie Hall next week. It was an all-Beethoven program. There were two performances: one on Thursday and one on Saturday night. Her mind began to race ahead.

*They could drive to Charlotte and hop a direct flight. Be back on Sunday before suppertime.*

No. It was an insane idea. She'd *never* be able to get tickets this close to the event.

But Uchida's style was so mesmerizing . . . filled with emotion and veracity. Her light touch was subtle, full of passion and sheer tenderness.

*Just like Dorothy's . . .*

She put the magazine aside and went in search of her cell phone.

A former grad student of hers was the son of a trustee on the Carnegie Hall board. Celine had helped him land a plum residency at Presbyterian.

It was time to call in a favor.

Nadine wasn't too impressed with Michael's menu.

It was Thursday, and her turn to be sous chef in the kitchen at the inn. That was their deal: Michael cooked with her two nights a week at the café, and Nadine donned an apron two nights a week in his kitchen.

"What is it you call this mishmash?" she asked for about the fifth time. She was peering into the flat pan with a look of displeasure. Steam wafting up from the stove had fogged the lenses of her wire-framed glasses.

"Paella." Michael stirred the mixture. "It's Spanish. This version is Valencian. No shellfish."

"Well, whatever version it is, you're burning that rice."

"I'm *not* burning it. I'm making *soccarat.*"

"You're making what?"

"*Soccarat.* It's the layer of caramelized rice that forms on the bottom of the pan."

"You can call it by any fancy name you want, but it smells *burned* to me."

"Trust me." Michael spooned liquid over the chicken thighs and medallions of hare. "It's the best part of the dish."

"You're dreaming if you think anyone around here is gonna volunteer to eat something with *rabbit* in it."

"It's not rabbit. It's wild hare."

Nadine huffed. "Does it bump its fluffy little cottontail ass when it hops around? I call that a *rabbit*."

"Nadine? Will you please just roast the red peppers and make the sherry vinaigrette?"

"They're both done." She walked back to her prep station and held up a hunk of Manchego cheese. "What do you want to do with this?"

"Slice it up in little wedges and put it on a plate with some of that Serrano ham and a couple pieces of baguette."

"It's a good thing you got some of that butternut squash soup left. I think I ought to make another batch of biscuits, just in case. You're likely to need 'em."

"Thanks for the vote of confidence. But if you're up for it, go on ahead. You know David will always eat any that are left over."

"Where is that boy, anyway? Normally he's back here getting on my last nerve."

"He's in town. *Again*. Third night this week he's had meetings."

Nadine walked to a utensil cabinet and started rifling through its drawers. Loudly.

Michael turned around. "What are you looking for?"

"That cheese knife."

"What cheese knife?"

"The one I *always* use. The one you keep hiding."

"I don't hide any knives from you."

"Oh, no?" She held up an old, all-purpose Betty Crocker knife that was missing part of its handle. "Then why was this buried in the bottom of a drawer?"

"Nadine, that thing is ancient and duller than a tablespoon. I think David bought it out of a bargain bin at Dollar Tree."

"It works great for cheese."

"That's *impossible*. He used it to cut florist wire."

"That's why it's great for cheese. Especially these soft damn goat's milk cheeses you gay boys seem so partial to."

"Okay. Whatever."

Nadine set about slicing the Manchego. Michael watched her work. Strangely, the world's cheapest knife seemed to be doing the job just fine. She dispatched the cheese in record time.

He should know better than to question Nadine. *Except when it came to soccarat.*

The paella was coming along great. He hadn't made it in years. Not since he'd worked at The Peninsula Grill in Charleston. The dish had been a seasonal mainstay there—although they always prepared it with clams and chorizo. He preferred this more traditional field variety. It was anybody's guess how well it would go over tonight. But he figured Thursday would be a safe night to try something new. And they had a couple of guests from Richmond staying there. He hoped they might be a bit more adventurous when it came to international fare.

If the dish bombed, as Nadine was kind enough to predict, he always had her biscuits as a backup. He could pair those with anything else on the menu and have a hit on his hands—especially if he could coerce her into making some of her chicken and Andouille sausage gumbo. He had even procured a bit of tasso ham she could toss into it. She'd grumble that there wasn't enough time to make it decent, but Michael had seen her pull the savory stew together in less than an hour—and still manage to create a stock with incredible depth of flavor.

He glanced up at the big wall clock.

They had more than two hours until the first seating.

It was now or never. *He was going in . . .*

"Hey, Nadine. Since you've been so fast taking care of all those sides, how about whipping up a batch of that gumbo you made last week?"

Nadine looked at the clock. "We don't have enough time for that."

"Sure we do. We have more than two hours."

"The broth will be weak."

"No it won't. I got some tasso ham for you to add in." He pulled out the big guns. "I ordered it special because I know how much you like it."

Nadine glared at him. "Don't suck up to me, boy. It's a waste of time."

He noted, however, that she retrieved a deep cast-iron skillet from the pot rack and slammed it down on the range.

Michael tried not to smile. "The andouille is on the top shelf of the walk-in."

"I *know* where it is. You just tend to your burnt rice."

Michael decided to change the subject. "I think Sheriff Martin and Dr. Heller are coming in for dinner tonight."

"That so?" Nadine was dicing big yellow onions for her *mirepoix*. "I'm glad they're getting out and not listening to any of the bad talk."

"Bad talk? Really?" Michael was alarmed by her observation. "What are you hearing?"

"I ain't hearing much of anything. Folks know better than to speak that mess to me. But Nicky said there were some of Nelda Rae Black's people in the café last night, and they were going on about it. And one of them was that nasty Manfred Davis. Lord knows what he's back in town for. But mark my words: it can't be anything good."

Michael slapped his spoon down on the stainless steel countertop. "Why can't people just mind their own goddamn business?"

"Don't you blaspheme in front of me, boy." Nadine shook her knife at him. "I don't like it no more'n you do. But these hateful people've always been among us, and they ain't gonna be silenced anytime soon. Not since that idiot mayor and his unholy flock of followers got a big damn megaphone. Now, half the people in this county think they have a God-given right to spew hate-speak right out loud in public."

"It makes me *sick*, Nadine. I thought I left all this behind in damn South Carolina. And I've *never* seen abject bigotry accepted and treated as gospel anyplace like it was there. My mama nearly lost her job at the mill because I had a Black classmate come over and spend the night at our house. We were *kids* . . . not even ten years old." He made a disgusted grunt. "I thought I left that all behind when I came here."

"Bigotry ain't never left behind, boy. Sometimes it hides its face, but it's always there. It don't matter where you are. It's gonna be right there—simmerin' away like that damn rabbit you're stewing. The only thing that ever makes it get gone is ridding the world of vermin like that godforsaken mayor. They're the dangerous ones—the ones who rise up to positions of power. The ones who use their elected offices or, God help us, their church pulpits to spread their lies and hatred. The ones who use their words to make people afraid of their neighbors—afraid and suspicious of people they been knowing for years. That mayor and people like him are the ones who gave people like Nelda Rae permission to let their worst selves crawl back out of the darkness—and we're all gonna pay the price for it. You ask me, whoever took that man out did this county a *service*."

Michael was rattled by her declaration.

"Do you really think somebody killed him? That his death wasn't an accident?"

"Count on it."

Nadine's words chilled him to the bone.

Mostly because he knew she was right, and that admission scared the crap out of him.

That night at supper, Maddie filled in Syd on her meetings with Lizzy and Avi.

They were having sloppy joes—one of Henry's favorites.

Maddie had been surprised that Syd was treating Henry to another special meal, coming right on the heels of their café outing—but she wasn't going to complain.

She loved sloppy joes, too.

And she didn't protest when Syd conscripted her to peel potatoes for the oven-baked fries. The happy departure from their usual weekday fare, which invariably included at least two vegetables from the list of foods she loathed, made her more than amenable to helping out with any kitchen task.

Henry sat at the kitchen table, finishing his homework while they completed preparations for the meal. He'd occasionally interrupt them to ask for help with an arithmetic problem or a question about how to use a vocabulary word in a sentence.

"Absorb. A-B-S-O-R-B," Syd explained. "It's a verb that means to take in or to suck up. Like a sponge absorbs water, or the way Uncle David absorbs Maddie's wine."

Henry giggled.

Maddie glowered at her. "I don't think that's the meaning they had in mind."

"Who cares? It works."

"Don't write that one down, Henry." Maddie plucked another potato from the bag. "It's not a correct usage for the word."

"How do you spell *usage*?" Henry asked.

"U-S . . ." Maddie began, before thinking better of it. "Never mind. Just go with that whole sponge idea."

Syd examined Maddie's pile of peeled potatoes. "I don't think we need any more of those."

"Just a couple more."

"Maddie, you already have about three pounds peeled."

"So? We *like* French fries. Don't we, Henry?"

Henry nodded enthusiastically. "Can I have ketchup *and* mustard with mine?"

Maddie gave Syd a smug smile. "He learned that from *me*."

"I know. He also learned leaving his dirty socks on the bathroom floor from you."

"My socks are rarely dirty."

"Unfortunately, we cannot say the same for Mini Me over there."

Maddie reluctantly surrendered the bag of potatoes to Syd, who promptly restored it to the pantry and quickly sliced the potatoes into fry-shaped planks with the food processor.

"Are you going to tell me how the conversation with Lizzy went?" she asked when she'd finished.

"Yeah." Maddie hauled a stool over to the kitchen counter and sat down on it. "I think she was genuinely unprepared for the offer. She seemed undone by it. Gratified but cautious."

"You mean she didn't immediately accept?" Syd looked surprised. "I was certain she'd jump at it. We both know how much she loves it here."

"I know. That's what I thought, too. But there's a fly in the ointment."

Syd was now browning the ground turkey with a bit of diced onion. It smelled heavenly. A mixture of spices and some chopped tomatoes sat beside the range in a glass bowl.

"What kind of fly?" she asked.

"The Tom-shaped kind."

Syd threw her head back and gazed at the ceiling. "You've *got* to be kidding me. What now?"

"It seems he has a job offer—in Colorado. And before you ask, Lizzy told me about this, but Peggy supplied most of the details."

"Of *course,* she did. That woman should hang out a shingle."

"Yeah." Maddie snagged a piece of cut potato and shook some salt onto it before popping it into her mouth. "I think she got the skinny from Coralee Minor. Apparently Lizzy and Tom had dinner at Waffle House, and Coralee overheard their conversation."

"Remind me to always pull my jobs out of town."

"It's a deal. Anyway, Tom got a job offer and he wants Lizzy to go with him. I gather this is the reason for her hesitation."

"Do you think she'll go with him?"

Maddie shrugged. "Who knows? I can't venture a guess until she tells me about it."

"Tom." Syd sighed with disgust. "He just can't get it right."

"What do you mean? Maybe they've talked about it. Maybe Lizzy wants to go with him. Maybe he's learned that he needs to include her in his plans."

"Yeah? And maybe Rosebud, your tuxedo-cat-shaped nemesis, has learned that pooping on your tools is a bad idea, too."

Henry giggled again. "Syd said *poop*."

"Do your homework," Maddie and Syd ordered in unison. Henry dutifully complied.

"Look," Maddie continued. "You know we can't mention this to anyone, right? Not until Lizzy and Tom have time to sort it out."

"Maddie . . ."

"I know, I know." Maddie held up a hand to halt her tirade. "*I apologize.* It's a function of my own guilt and trepidation about spreading idle gossip."

"Well, for my part, I think it's more than idle gossip. This sounds exactly like something my brother would do. If he messes up royally like he did before, there'll be no coming back from it. And I, for one, will not try to help him. He needs to learn that sometimes there are no do-overs. And if you ask me, this could be one of those times."

"Maddie?" Henry asked. "What's 39 + 8 - 12?"

"It's . . ." Maddie hesitated for a moment before appealing to Syd.

"*Seriously?*" Syd faced Henry. "Thirty-five."

"Thanks." Henry erased something on his paper and carefully wrote down the correct answer. "I'm all finished, now."

"Good. I'll check it over for you after supper. Now run upstairs and wash your hands."

"Okay, Syd." Henry pushed back his chair and started for the back stairs.

"Henry." Syd stopped him. "Pick up your homework first, and take it to your room."

Henry dutifully collected his books and papers and dashed to the stairs.

"Don't run, Sport!" Maddie called after him. But she was too late. Henry had already disappeared from view. She looked back at Syd with a sorrowful expression. "There are too many rules in this joint."

"I would only amend your statement to add that there are too many rules in this joint that go ignored."

"That is *not* my fault."

"The anthem of the unrepentant."

Maddie stole another potato.

"Quit eating those." Syd slapped at her hand, but Maddie yanked her treat out of reach. "You'll ruin your dinner."

"Fat chance. Not when we're having reality-based food."

"How is it possible for you to have an IQ in the quintuple digits, but stubbornly cling to a preteen palate?"

"Because I'm a marvel of science?"

Syd looked her over. "I won't disagree that there are many marvelous things about you, my dear. But your dietary proclivities would not be among them."

"You're just jealous because I'm taller." Maddie ate her potato. "Oh, I invited Avi to come out for dinner tomorrow night."

"Good. I hope she will." Syd brightened up. "Why not invite Lizzy, too? It'll give those two a chance to get to know each other better—especially since Avi's going to be in the clinic part of each week."

"Great idea." Maddie agreed. "Maybe Lizzy can give her a ride out here?"

"That'll work. Dorothy is coming home with Henry after school tomorrow, and will stay the night. If both Avi and Lizzy are here, that'll give them an easy and casual introduction."

"Mom had the same idea—at least with regard to Avi." Maddie smiled. "I guess this means Mom is getting a booty call tomorrow night?"

Syd's eyes widened. She made a rapid slashing gesture beneath her neck. "What's the matter with you?" she whispered.

Maddie jerked a thumb toward the upstairs. "He can't hear us. He's got the bathroom water running full blast . . . it's probably over the sink and halfway down the hall by now."

"I reiterate: Mini Me."

"Very funny. At least he seemed a little more engaged tonight."

"You noticed that, too? I was beginning to think maybe we needed Avi to finagle a way to talk with him, as well."

"Not a bad idea. Whatever has been on his mind, he's not going to share it with us."

"I know. I wonder if he'll talk with James about it?"

"Maybe. When's their next FaceTime chat?"

"Sunday. I think we should give James a heads-up and contrive a way to leave them alone to talk."

"Good idea," Maddie agreed. "I just hope he's not getting flak at school."

"At school? Flak about what?"

"Take your pick. Watson might be gone, but he cast a long shadow. Henry's churlish teacher, Hozbiest, and the legions like him won't just fade into the woodwork. The whole community knows that Henry is living with two women now. And not just *any* two women—an out lesbian couple. I want to be sure he isn't getting bullied or intimidated by anyone."

"Dear god. I hope that's not happening."

"Me, too. But I think we have to be prepared for the possibility."

"People can be such cowards." Syd slowly shook her head.

"Why do they direct their fear and ignorance at children?"

"It's a shitty system, to be sure."

"Everything Dorothy is going through . . . everything she's already *been* through—it just makes me furious. And sick at heart. I just want to rage against it."

"I know, honey. None of it is right. None of it makes sense. We all have to be better than this."

"How can we keep failing to protect them? And how do we make these horrors stop happening *to* them?"

Maddie got up and wrapped her arms around Syd from behind.

"We have to be brave enough to call it out when it happens, and to face it openly. We have to be willing to say its name out loud, and to show we're not afraid to stand up against it. That's the only way to take away its power."

Syd leaned into her. "It scares me, Maddie. It scares me for Dorothy—and for Henry. For all of the children who stand to inherit this legacy of ignorance and fear."

"I know. It scares me, too. But we have each other. And we have good people like Avi who can help us find the right vocabulary to fight back."

They heard the sound of Henry's footsteps thundering down the hallway above them.

Maddie kissed Syd's head and stepped back. "Okay. So, where do you want me?"

"Where?" Syd turned and gave her a small smile. "I want you right where you always are—hanging on to my last, best hope."

Maddie smiled back at her.

"I think I can do that."

# Chapter Three

*Recorded Interview*
*Preliminary Inquest Investigation*
*Death of Mayor Gerald Watson*

"I'm Curtis Dwayne Freemantle. That's D-W-A-Y-N-E. Me and my wife, Edna, run the market here in Jericho. I was at the river all day with my family, down by the water where we always set up to watch the fireworks. I only heard about what happened when Sheriff Martin called Charlie Davis on her radio, and told her to meet him at the water. Charlie told us there'd been some kind of ruckus involving the mayor."

*I don't know why they're asking all these questions of everybody. We all know the whole town is better off with that man gone. Nobody cares about how it happened. We're all just relieved.*

"We didn't see that argument he had with David Jenkins before the debate. We only heard about it later from Nadine Odell."

*Nadine said she'd never seen David act the way he did that day. She said he was like a scared animal who just wanted to run away and hide. She said nobody knew where he went when he disappeared—not even Michael.*

"No. Nadine said she didn't see David again until right

before the fireworks. She said his partner, Michael, ran off to try and follow him."

*I'm not saying anything about Michael not being able to find David. Nobody thinks David could ever hurt anybody. That idea is just crazy.*

"It's true that Watson came into the market the week before and had words with . . . well . . . with just about everybody who was in there. When I told him to leave, he even attacked my daughter. Me and Edna couldn't stand for that. Roma Jean is a good girl."

*If you're looking for suspects, you're pretty much gonna have to interview the whole town. That man made enemies everywhere he went.*

"He went after Roma Jean because she's . . . special friends with Charlie Davis, that deputy sheriff. He called her terrible names, too. That's just not right. Roma Jean and Charlie aren't hurting nobody."

*Dear lord. I hope they don't think I went after Watson to get even for what he said about Roma Jean. If I'd wanted to hurt him, I'd a done it that day in the market—not a week later.*

"No sir, I don't know anybody who would've tried to do harm to that man. Most folks didn't care enough about him to try and plan anything like that. He was a big ole bad penny, and everybody just wished he'd pack up and go away."

*But we all know he's never gonna go away. Not now. He's gonna keep right on messin' in everybody's life—one damn interview at a time.*

Charlie and Byron were having breakfast at Aunt Bea's. They did this every Friday.

The worst of the rain had moved out, but there still had been a light drizzle falling. Even with that, the small restaurant was close enough to their office that they could walk over. But Byron was a stickler about protocol, so they always took their patrol cars. He said they never knew when a call might come in and they had to be ready to jump up and go. That had actually happened a few times, too. Last week, two cars had slid in some pooled water on the bridge over Little Wilson creek, and run into each other. One of the vehicles, a pickup belonging to Al Hawkes, had gone into the water. Nobody was hurt, but it took a couple of hours for Junior to get there from Troutdale and haul the thing out.

Al was in the restaurant this morning—just like he was every Friday. He was still driving Junior's loaner car, too. The yellow Cutlass Ciera was parked out front, commando style. Charlie figured that was because the winch on the front of Junior's Cutlass stuck out too far, and crowded the sidewalk near the entrance.

Al always got to Aunt Bea's early, so he could lay claim to the best parking spot. In Jericho, that eighteen-foot piece of real estate was one of the most coveted in town.

Charlie and Byron ordered their combo breakfast plates and sat down in their usual spot: the big corner booth that afforded them a clear sight line across the square toward the entrance to their office.

Byron seemed to be in an especially good mood this morning. Charlie guessed that was because it was Friday, and Dr. Heller usually stayed at his house on Friday nights. Of course, Charlie only knew that because Roma Jean had told her that Dorothy tended to spend Friday nights with Henry at Dr. Stevenson's farm—and that meant sometimes they'd both ride out on the bookmobile with her on Saturdays.

While they ate breakfast, Byron had been filling her in on the progress of the inquest on Gerald Watson's death.

Nobody was officially calling it anything other than an accident. Not yet, anyway. The full autopsy report hadn't yet come in from the Western District Medical Examiner. The immediate report showed only that Watson died by drowning. Byron said the final reports sometimes took as long as eight to ten weeks—it just depended on the workload in the district ME's office. The full autopsy would tell them exactly how Watson died, and whether or not there were any signs of misadventure or foul play.

So far, investigators from Roanoke had only interviewed a couple of the dozen or so people they wanted to talk with. Charlie wasn't sure how they arrived at their final list. When she asked Byron about it, he explained that they often started with just one or two people, and the list expanded from the leads they got in other conversations.

Byron seemed particularly careful about not expressing any opinions himself. Charlie wanted to ask him if he had any ideas about what might've happened that day on the river—and who, if anyone, might have had a motive to kill the man.

Charlie worried that part of Byron's silence on the matter came from his concern for Watson's daughter, Dorothy, who was now staying out at Dr. Heller's. The one detail everyone in town knew was that Dorothy had confessed to hitting her father in the head with a piece of driftwood to stop him from attacking Buddy Townsend. It seemed to Charlie that the point of the inquest was to establish whether or not anyone else had contributed to Watson's drowning—or whether his death happened as a result of the head wound he had sustained from his daughter.

That outcome wasn't one *anybody* wanted to think about—at least, not the people who had any inkling about the extent of the abuse the girl had suffered at the hands of her father. She knew this was especially true for Byron and Dr. Heller, who had pretty much become Dorothy's de facto parents since the 4th of July.

More than anything, Charlie wanted to ask Byron if he knew her own father was back in town. Charlie hadn't heard from him and, as far as she knew, he hadn't been by her house again. But hearing Roma Jean's account of how he had stopped by her place the other night had rattled her to her core. She hated the way it made her feel. And it angered her that she'd reflexively lashed out at Roma Jean, who'd only asked questions about him to be nice.

It was her own fault that she'd never told Roma Jean any details about her childhood or the circumstances that led to her father leaving Jericho. She regretted that now. She owed it to Roma Jean to come clean about it all—even though that meant telling her about her first relationship with another girl. It didn't make sense that this bothered Charlie so much. After all, Roma Jean was smart enough to know that she wasn't Charlie's first ... girlfriend. Still. Talking about what had happened at summer camp that year with Jimmie was just ... hard. It was true that Charlie's father had beaten her so badly she ended up with broken ribs and a fractured collarbone. But she thought what Jimmie's parents had done to her was worse. They'd packed her up and shipped her out to live with some crazy evangelist in Kentucky. He was supposed to "deprogram" her and save her from the sin of homosexuality.

Charlie never heard from Jimmie again. But she knew from cousins of hers that Jimmie hadn't stayed with the Kentucky family very long. She'd managed to escape during one of their remote revival tours, and she never came back.

But Charlie never forgot her. Jimmie's youth and sweetness—and the gentle, innocent first explorations they'd shared—would always live in Charlie's memory. They'd been like two newborn colts, learning to stand on their spindly legs—and, finally, daring to run free in the blazing sun.

She looked up from her coffee to find Byron watching her intently. She didn't realize she'd been silent so long.

"What's on your mind, kiddo?" he asked.

He never called her that ... not unless he was in what she called "full-frontal dad mode."

"It's ..." she nearly said, "nothing," but stopped herself.

Byron, above all people, deserved better than that. He deserved her honesty. She took a deep breath. "It's my father. He's back in town."

Byron's expression changed from one of mild interest to one of angry concern. He'd shifted into sheriff-mode.

"Where is he?" he asked. His tone was not forgiving.

"I don't know," Charlie told him. "I haven't seen him. But he came by my house on Wednesday night, looking for me. Roma Jean was there," she added. "But she had no idea who he was. She said he asked for 'Charlene,' and that he seemed 'strange,'" she made air quotes around the word, "but harmless."

"And he hasn't reached out to you in any way since?"

Charlie shook her head.

"Why the hell would he come back here?" Byron seemed to be talking to himself more than to her.

"I have no idea. But I doubt it can be for any good reason."

Byron regarded her for a bit without saying anything. He was absently rocking his empty Styrofoam coffee cup back and forth on the table.

Charlie knew him pretty well, but right now, she had no idea what he was thinking.

Finally, he spoke.

"Do you want me to find him?"

*Did she?* It hadn't been an accident that Charlie hadn't looked for him herself. It wasn't like there were an infinite number of places in town he could be staying—if he were even still *in* town. Roma Jean had described his car as an old beater with South Carolina tags. She could've at least tracked down his vehicle.

But she hadn't. *Why not?*

Was she still afraid of him? Did she want Byron to take care of him for her—just like he had the last time?

She didn't know the answers to any of these questions.

"No," she said to Byron. "No. I'll handle it."

"Okay." He held her gaze. "But you let me know if you need backup. Do we understand each other?"

"Yes, sir. We do."

"All right, then." Byron slid out of the booth. "I'm getting more coffee. You want a refill?"

Charlie handed him her cup. "Yeah. More coffee would be great."

Henry and Dorothy carried the tin bucket full of gnarled carrots, dandelion weeds and cast-off vegetable tops out to the pasture fence. Henry collected the special treats all week and saved them to give Before on Fridays, when Dorothy came home from school with him.

It was one of their traditions. Just like being allowed to do their homework outside at the table on the front porch overlooking the pond. Syd would fix them big glasses of lemonade and make sure the overhead fans were turned on to move some air around.

August had been really hot. Hotter than most summer months she could remember. Dr. Heller and Dr. Stevenson . . . *Maddie,* she reminded herself . . . both had air conditioning in their houses. Dorothy wasn't used to that. Her father had always refused to turn on their one window unit, even on the hottest nights when sleeping was next to impossible. Her room had been the smallest one on the second floor of their small house, and it had only one window, which faced east. Not even a stray breeze could ever find its way to that window. And it didn't help that Dorothy never kept the door to her room open.

Some nights, long after she was sure her father was asleep, she'd sneak out of her room and tiptoe up the stairs to the attic. She'd practiced enough times to know where all the creaky floor boards were so she could ascend the steps quietly.

She didn't ever want to wake him up.

The high-ceilinged attic had steep peaks framed with rafters, and windows in the gables at both ends. That meant there was almost always a breeze blowing through the lofty but cramped space. Dorothy discovered that even on the hottest nights, having warm air moving over you was better than no air—and even without a breeze, the space was inviting to her for other reasons.

All that remained of her mama had been haphazardly boxed up and stashed up there after her death. Dorothy spent hours going through the boxes and carefully examining each item. A scarf that still smelled like lilac. Old house shoes that resembled the feet that had worn them. Aprons decorated with brightly colored appliques that had been sewn on with tiny, even stitches. A recipe book with yellowed pages and a broken spine. Some scattered index cards containing handwritten notes—directions for how to unclog drains using baking soda and vinegar, or how to use cut-up potatoes to take the salt out of soups and stews.

And there were her mama's books—lots and lots of them. Books about everything.

Dorothy's favorites were the ones that looked like her mama's old school books: copies *of Silas Marner* and an illustrated *Great Expectations*, two books about Greek mythology, an introduction to civics textbook, an oversized copy of *Goode's World Atlas*, a three-ring notebook containing dozens of Butterick and Simplicity patterns for dresses she was sure her mother never got to wear, and her favorite: a first-edition, hardback copy of Catherine Marshall's *Christy*.

Dorothy had stayed up late many nights, squinting to read her mama's copy of *Christy* by the stray shafts of moonlight that shone through the north window. She'd read the book so many times, she had practically memorized the tale of a young woman who left the safety of her suburban home in Asheville to teach school in a small, backcountry region of the Great Smoky Mountains. Christy had been idealistic and heroic as she faced poverty and depravity on a scale she could never have imagined. Through it all, the resiliency of Christy's faith in God and her belief in the innate goodness of all people triumphed over even the worst adversity.

Dorothy was certain this had been her mama's belief, too.

And no matter how difficult things were in her life, she chose to cling to this belief like a lifeline that promised to guide her toward a better place on the other side of her father's cruelty. Most nights, that place seemed as far away as one of the distant countries in her mama's atlas. But Dorothy knew it existed. She could locate it on one of the oversized pages and outline its borders with her finger.

It was real and it was out there.

She just had to hang on long enough to find it.

Henry was busy shoving turnip tops and clumps of dandelion through the fence to the grateful heifer. Before chewed with practiced ease. She didn't need to be in a hurry because she didn't have any competition to grapple with for best access to the bucket of treats.

"Do you wanna give her some, Dorothy?" Henry extended the pail to her.

"No. That's okay." Dorothy wasn't as confident as Henry when it came to putting her fingers so close to the heifer's large mouth. "She's used to taking food from you. I might not do it right."

"It's hard to do it wrong," he explained. "Before pretty much just takes whatever you hold out in front of her." Henry demonstrated by offering the cow a couple of fat carrots, which were quickly dispatched.

Dorothy watched Before chew. "How much do you think she weighs now?"

"Maddie says maybe eight hundred pounds. But Uncle David says a thousand. He thinks Before needs to go on a 'terranean diet. Do you know what that is?"

"Um. Do you mean a *Mediterranean* diet?"

Henry nodded. "He said she was starting to look like somebody called Lizzo—only without the talent."

Dorothy laughed. "A Mediterranean diet means you eat a lot of fish, beans and eggs."

"Before doesn't like fish."

"She doesn't?"

He shook his head. "Once I tried to give her half of my tuna fish sandwich, and she spit it out."

"Well, I think Before is beautiful just how she is—and so is Lizzo."

Henry thought about what Dorothy said. "Why do people say mean things?"

"I don't think Uncle David meant that to be mean. I think he was trying to be funny—like he always does."

"I know. I was thinking about other people."

Dorothy was quick enough to pick up on Henry's unintended revelation. "Is somebody being mean to you?"

He shrugged.

"At school?" she ventured.

"Sometimes."

She had to tread carefully. She knew what it felt like when people tried to trick her into talking about things she wanted to keep to herself.

"I've had that happen, too," she told him. "It isn't nice when they do that."

Henry looked at her with his clear, blue eyes. Sometimes, like right now, he really did look like Dr. Stevenson.

"Who was mean to you?" he asked.

She hesitated before answering. "Mostly my father."

"Is that why he died?"

Henry's words fell between them like chunks of iron. Dorothy felt the meaning of his innocent question reverberate beneath her feet like a tremor rising up from deep inside the earth. She was amazed that Henry didn't seem to feel it, too.

"No," she told him in a shaky voice that didn't sound like her own. "No, that's not why he died. People don't die because they're mean."

"I think maybe they should sometimes. Especially when they're mean to people who are just trying to do the right thing."

"Life doesn't work that way, Henry. People die for all kinds of reasons—because they're sick or old. Or maybe they make bad choices or have accidents they can't come back from. And sometimes, other people might hurt them. But they don't ever die just because they're bad. There's always some other reason."

"I'm sorry your daddy was mean to you."

She did her best to smile at him. Whatever was worrying him was enough. She didn't want to add her own troubles to his list.

"Thanks. I'm sorry, too."

Henry finished feeding Before the contents of his bucket and they walked back toward the barn. Maddie's golden retriever, Pete, jogged along behind them until he spotted a couple of deer who'd been brazen enough to come out before dark to try and sneak a drink at the pond. He took off at a fast lope, barking all the way.

"Maddie hollers at him when he chases deer down there," Henry explained. "But I think Pete gets confused because he's allowed to chase them away from the garden, so he thinks they shouldn't be allowed by the pond, either."

"That seems to make sense to me, too," Dorothy agreed.

"Does Django chase the deer at Gramma C's?"

"No. He pretty much sleeps on the patio. Sheriff Martin says visiting Dr. Heller's is like a night off for him."

"I like Django."

"I do, too. It's great when he gets to stay over."

"Buddy says Django is like the golden hound that protected the head god when he was little."

"Zeus?"

Henry nodded. "He said the golden dog saved Zeus from a really mean orange dog that wanted to hurt him."

"I don't know anything about orange dogs. But Django mostly sleeps on a chair in the sun."

They'd reached the barn. Henry stashed his bucket and called Dorothy over to Maddie's workbench.

"Do you wanna see the sewing machine Maddie is fixing for Mrs. Hall?"

"Sure." Dorothy approached the workshop area of the big barn. She noticed the big tuxedo cat, Rosebud, stretched out across the hood of Maddie's Jeep. Rosebud stretched lazily before jumping down and following her.

Henry pointed out all the small parts that had been removed from the big unit and laid out in tidy rows.

"Maddie is letting me help. My job is to keep things all together so they can go back in the right order."

"Do you like helping her?"

Henry nodded with enthusiasm. "It's great to fix broken things. Maddie says that with enough time and care, you can help most things work better again."

Dorothy wasn't sure how true that was, but she didn't want to disagree with Henry.

She picked up a tiny ring with sprockets on it. It was probably a gear of some kind.

"There are a lot of small pieces in this thing."

"Yeah. Sometimes the hardest job is figuring out a way to make things work when a part is missing. Maddie says that's when you have to be creative and not give up. She says you'll never know what might fix something until you're willing to try it."

Dorothy looked around the space. There were shelves filled with all kinds of tools and small appliances. They all had white tags attached to them.

"So she never throws anything away?"

"Nope." Henry considered his quick reply. "Well. *Sometimes.* I have an alarm clock in my room that Maddie said was a goner. But I think I can fix it if I try hard enough." He sighed. "Syd says she's giving me two more weeks, and then it's getting eighty-sixed."

Dorothy laughed.

Henry gave her a quizzical look. "What's 'eighty-sixed' mean?"

"I think it means thrown away."

"Probably. Syd doesn't like to save stuff . . . except for bride magazines. We'll *never* run out of those."

Dorothy was about to reply when they heard a car pull up outside the barn.

"That must be Lizzy." Henry was excited. "Let's go and see her."

He took off running for the driveway.

Dorothy took a last look at the dismembered sewing machine.

Maddie was right. *The hardest part* was *when there was no way to work around the missing parts.*

She knew that meant *she* was probably a goner, too—just like Henry's alarm clock.

She made her way to the driveway, with Rosebud following close on her heels.

The Osborne Motor Lodge had been the only motel in Jericho for decades—until a shiny new franchise place had opened up on the hill overlooking Food City. The only people who ever stayed at Osborne's now were hunters or fishermen, who didn't much care about things like good housekeeping or satellite TV reception. Some of the migrant men from Mexico who worked up at the tree farms on Mount Rogers stayed there, too—until they could make enough money to move into small houses spread out along the New River.

Charlie figured her best bet to find Manfred Davis, unless he'd managed to find someone willing to put him up, was to look for him at one of the two area motels. She cruised the parking lot of the new inn first, looking for the car Roma Jean had described. She wasn't surprised not to see it there. From what she remembered about her father, he'd never be willing to shell out good money just to have a view of the roof of the local shopping center.

Osborne's was her best bet. The ramshackle place was off the beaten path enough that he'd be able to avoid notice—if he were even still in town.

Something told her he probably was. She'd run into Sonny Nicks at the post office yesterday, and he told her about seeing Manfred out at Bone Gap for preaching on Wednesday night. That part made no sense to her at all. Her father had never been one for going to church on Sunday—much less, any other time.

She turned into the potholed lot at Osborne's and navigated her patrol car around mud puddles that likely concealed how deep the craters in the broken pavement were. It didn't take her long to spot the car, an old Buick LeSabre with more primer than paint, and South Carolina tags. Charlie instinctively checked the renewal sticker in the lower right corner of the tag. *May.* Manfred's car was nearly three months past due for inspection.

That figured.

She pulled past the car and made a full circuit around the motel before parking.

She got out and walked into the office to ask the desk attendant which room Manfred Davis was staying in. She noticed that the sign advertising room rates and checkout times was written in both English and Spanish.

The attendant looked at her impassively and offered no resistance to her query.

"Room 8," he told her, before immediately returning his attention to a rerun of *Star Trek* that was playing on the tiny TV set in what passed for the motel's lobby.

Charlie thanked him and headed outside. She walked to room 8 and hesitated only a moment before knocking on the door.

She heard a man on the other side clear his throat and the sound of the chain lock on the door being unfastened. Then the metal door creaked open, and her father stood before her.

Charlie was stunned by the change in him. He'd lost a ton of weight and his hair—what was left of it—had gone nearly gray. He looked gaunt and stooped over. His skin had an unhealthy pallor. Even his eyes, which once had blazed so hotly with anger, looked pale and milky.

He looked old and sick.

But Charlie knew better than to trust him.

He didn't speak, but just stood there, holding the door open with a bony hand. Charlie thought he was staring at her with something like uncertainty. She saw his eyes take in her uniform and linger over the gun holstered at her hip.

She decided to break the stalemate. "You wanted to see me?"

"Charlene," he said. That was it. It was like he was trying the name out for the first time.

"It's Charlie," she corrected him. "Nobody calls me that anymore."

He nodded. "Okay."

"You came by my house. Why did you want to see me?"

He continued to regard her with that milky, uncertain gaze. "I come back here, Char—" he stopped himself, "Charlie, because I want to make amends for the ways I done wrong by you."

Charlie cut him off. "It's too late for that. We have nothing to say to each other."

"I traveled a long way to get here. Longer'n you know. At least hear me out?"

Charlie wanted nothing more than to give him a ticket for his expired license plate, and drive the hell away from that ungodly place. But she didn't. She didn't know what made her keep standing there.

"All right. I'll listen." She stepped back from the door. "Come outside and we can go to that picnic table over there. Then you can be on your way."

"Fair enough." He retrieved a room key and met her outside.

Charlie led the way to a battered table covered with warped boards that were dotted with cigarette burns. Manfred claimed a seat but Charlie remained standing.

"Go ahead," Charlie told him. "Say your piece."

"I don't blame you for bein' finished with me. I should'a never beat you like I did. I had the devil inside me, and I know I did wrong."

Charlie made no reply. He continued.

"When Sheriff Martin run me outta town, he told me I was halfway down a path to hell, and I owed thanks to God that he didn't kill me with his own hands. I never forgot them words. My cousin in Cheraw helped me get a job in the airbag plant. He was always a good man, and he didn't put up with no kinda hijinks from me. No drinkin'. No women. Not even a pack of smokes. That's when I met Glenadine, a widow woman who works as a bookkeeper at the Buick dealership in town. She got me goin' with her to services at the Church of God. It wadn't long before I found Christ, and repented of my sins. I turned away from my evil path. And me'n Glenadine and her two young'uns have a new life together, sanctified by God's love and washed in the blood of His forgiveness. That's why I come back here to find you."

Charlie wasn't sure what to make of his story. "When did

all this happen?"

"'Bout nine years ago. I been a changed man, Char—Charlie. I come here to ask for your forgiveness."

"You say you found Christ nine years ago?"

"That's right."

"But it took you *nine* years to come apologize to me?"

Manfred didn't reply.

"You have to admit, that doesn't sound like you cared very much about apologizing for putting me in the hospital and ruining Jimmie's life."

"I didn't have nothin' to do with what them folks did to her."

That was the first familiar thing he'd said to her—shifting blame for his actions onto someone else.

"Maybe not directly. But you caused her as much pain as you did me. And for that, I can never forgive you."

"I'm here to help you find the same release from sin that I found. I want to show you that God can forgive you for your sins just like He did mine."

"Really? And what sins might those be . . . *father?*"

"I seen that doe-eyed little girl at your house. I heard from folks in town that you're still carrying on in them same perverted ways that are an abomination to God. But I'm here to tell you that you can turn away from that poison, Charlene. You can ask Christ to forgive you and cleanse your soul of them unholy passions."

Charlie had heard enough. Manfred's reference to Roma Jean made her see red.

"How *dare* you come back here under the pretense of asking forgiveness for your failure as a father, just as an excuse to falsely accuse me?" He started to argue, but Charlie held up a hand to stop him. "We have nothing more to say to each other. And if you *ever* come near me—or Roma Jean—again, I'll kill you myself. This conversation is *over*."

Charlie left him sitting there and stormed back to her patrol car. Before she drove out of the parking lot, she slowed to lower her window and call out to him.

"And get your goddamn car inspected or I'll have it towed."

When Maddie included Lizzy on their Friday night dinner invitation, she'd asked Lizzy if she'd be willing to pick Avi up at the Riverside Inn, where she was staying while she scoured the area for more suitable digs she could use on the days she planned to hold office hours at Maddie's clinic. If their arrangement became permanent, she'd look for a longer-term housing solution. In the meantime, however, although the drive to and from Roanoke was doable, it wasn't a commute Avi was eager to make on a continuing basis. Besides, she explained, her locum at the practice in Roanoke was ending in a few months, and she'd need a quasi-permanent place to live while she established a practice locally.

The inn was directly on Lizzy's route to Maddie's farm, so it had been an easy enough request to agree to. Avi had been waiting outside when Lizzy turned in at the entrance to the inn. Lizzy was struck again by the uniqueness of her appearance. Avi was wearing another stylish ensemble, every bit as subtly chic and androgynous as the outfit she'd worn the day before. Her olive-toned skin and glossy, short black hair gave her a unique air. Not European, exactly—but certainly cosmopolitan. She'd definitely be a standout in any Jericho context.

But Lizzy figured Avi would probably be a standout in any setting. There was just something intriguing about her. And that extended as much to her air as it did to her presentation.

Lizzy chided herself for being so provincial. She'd never have thought twice about someone like Avi if they'd crossed paths in Nashville. But the truth was, she'd never crossed paths with anyone who provoked her interest quite like Avi did. She was looking forward to this chance to get to know the psychologist a bit better.

*Probably because I need her expertise . . . professionally.*

Lizzy stopped the car so Avi could hop in beside her.

"I hope you weren't waiting long?" she asked.

"Nah." Avi snapped her seatbelt into place. "Whatever was cooking in there smelled too tempting. I figured I was safer waiting outside."

"I don't blame you. Michael is a fantastic chef."

"That's what I've heard. I know that breakfast this morning was amazing."

Lizzy slowly exited the inn parking lot and merged onto the main road. "Why not just stay here, then? Instead of renting someplace?"

"I can't deny that I haven't thought about it—seriously. But I think it would be too hard on my boyish figure."

Lizzy smiled. "It doesn't look to me like you have any problems staying in shape."

"Ah, but you don't know what all manner of excess lurks beneath these generously proportioned clothes."

"I'll have to warn you that healthful dining options are limited in this community."

"So I gathered. Maddie is hardly the most reliable guide to enlist for a roster of acceptable options."

"Hardly." Lizzy thought about Avi's dilemma. "Are you vegetarian? Vegan? Pescatarian?"

"Why do you ask? Do I seem some like some kind of 'arian' to you?"

Lizzy glanced over at her, suddenly worried she'd made some kind of misstep. But Avi was regarding her with a look of amusement.

"No," Lizzy explained. "I just wanted to try and suss out your tastes so I could suggest some dining options."

"Well, the answer to your question is no, no and a *big* no.

My family is Persian, and we eat *everything*—usually in massive quantities. I was raised in Minneapolis, and my parents and all three of my regrettable siblings still live there."

"How on earth did you end up in Roanoke?"

"Probably via the same kind of circuitous route that landed *you* here. After grad school, I got a residency in Richmond. That led to a job in Charlottesville. Then contacts in Charlottesville connected me with a shot at doing a two-year locum in Roanoke. And wonder of wonders, I fell head-over-heels in love with this area. I'd like nothing more than to find a way to stay here permanently—even if that means I have to subsist on a steady diet of cheese grits and ham gravy. And lord knows, there are plenty of kids who need a hand up." Avi chuckled. "I'm kidding about the cheese grits, actually . . . but I'm dead serious about the ham gravy. That information, alone, would be enough to put my maternal grandmother into an early grave."

"She hates gravy?" Lizzy asked.

"No, she's orthodox. A Jew," Avi added. "We're Jewish. At least, *they* are. I'm not too sure what I am. I've decided that I like to keep them guessing. It makes holidays in the Twin Cities a lot of fun."

"Well, your secret is safe with me. I promise not to tell anyone about your unholy passion for ham gravy."

Avi beamed at her. "I knew we'd get along just fine."

"That must be why Maddie asked me to pick you up tonight."

"Nah. The reason is way less complicated."

Avi's pronouncement piqued Lizzy's interest. "What makes you say that?"

"Because hitching a ride with you was my idea."

"Your idea? Why? I mean . . . it's not like I don't possess enviable driving skills, or anything."

"I know. But I figured if we're gonna be bunking together, so to speak, we might as well try to get to know each other a bit. Maddie told me about her offer to make you a partner in the clinic. I figure you'd be nuts not to jump at it, so it seemed I should get a head start sucking up to you right off the bat."

Lizzy was initially surprised that Maddie, who normally was the most taciturn person on the planet, would share her plans for the clinic with Avi. But since Avi was going to be working with them in some continuing capacity, she supposed it made sense.

She must've stayed quiet for too long. Avi laid a tentative hand on her arm.

"Forgive me if I spoke out of turn. I have a tendency to let my mouth roar fifty paces ahead of decorum."

"No," Lizzy assured her. "It's completely fine. Of course she'd tell you about her plans."

"Her plans?" Avi asked. "Dare I ask about *your* plans—or is that too personal?"

"It's not too personal. My plans are . . . in flux right now."

"That's the thing about flux. It can be good, and still totally muck up the works."

"Kind of like ham gravy?" Lizzy asked wryly.

"Exactly like ham gravy. Who knew a byproduct of cured meat and fat could lead to so much consternation?"

"Consternation is certainly one word for it."

"And what's another word for it?" Avi asked.

Avi was smooth, all right. Lizzy figured she must be one hell of a shrink. "Want the vernacular?" she asked.

"Of course."

They'd reached the turnoff for the lane that led to Maddie's farm. Lizzy slowed the car and turned on the blinker before shooting a nervous glance at Avi.

"Clusterfuck?"

Avi laughed the rest of the way to the house.

—~— —~— —~—

Dinner was a fairly raucous affair, mostly because Henry seemed to emerge from his funk and chattered nonstop throughout most of the meal. Syd was amazed by his transformation and wondered if it came about because Dorothy was spending the night, or because Avi seemed to have such an immediate rapport with both of the children. Whatever led to the change, she was grateful for it and hoped it would endure past the evening.

Henry claimed a seat beside Lizzy and did his best to be sure she was never without mini-biscuits, which Syd, grudgingly, had consented to make. They weren't even halfway through the meal before Lizzy had amassed a small army of them. They rimmed her plate like soldiers laying siege to the pot roast.

In truth, it wasn't really pot roast, as Henry comprehended the dish. It was *boeuf Bourguignon*, and she'd started it last night. Her mother had sent her a first edition copy of *Mastering The Art of French Cooking* she'd found at a used bookstore, and Syd was dying to try out some of the recipes. Maddie questioned if the dish was appropriate to serve on a hot summer night, but Syd insisted.

"I want to cook something homey and welcoming. Most of the vegetables in the garden are well past prime time, and throwing something on the grill just doesn't seem right for the occasion."

"I don't see why not. It isn't like we're going to be signing treaties or anything."

"When have you ever turned down an opportunity to eat beef? Besides, if you question the appropriateness of a Julia Child dish, you wouldn't understand the reasoning behind it."

Maddie grumbled her response. "Why do you always retreat to that as a defense whenever you don't have a reasonable explanation for something you've already decided to do?"

"Because it annoys you?"

"Very funny."

But the dish had turned out wonderfully, and no one—including Maddie—complained about it being too hearty. Syd noted with smug pleasure that, for all her pious protestations, Maddie crowed over the bits of crispy bacon she'd garnished the dish with, and kept trying to sneak pieces of it out of Henry's bowl whenever he was occupied passing more biscuits to Lizzy.

*Running interference at this joint was a full-time job . . .*

Avi was charming and affable. Syd liked her immediately. It was mesmerizing to watch how skillfully she navigated conversation with Dorothy. One thing was for certain: Dorothy was no pushover. It was obvious that the girl had perfected the art of saying little whenever it came to anything personal. She wasn't ever rude—but she was very adept at deflecting questions or revealing too much.

But even Dorothy seemed to warm to Avi's easy manners and playful discourse.

They'd decided to eat in the kitchen, thinking the more casual setting would defuse any ceremony that might truncate conversation between Avi and Dorothy. It seemed like a winning strategy. Even Lizzy seemed relatively at ease, which was a welcome response, given the seriousness of what all had landed on her plate . . . besides all those biscuits.

"Henry?" Syd cautioned him. "I think Lizzy has enough of those right now."

Henry's face fell. "But I don't want her to run out."

"I don't think she's in danger of running out any time soon, Sport," Maddie added. "Are you, Lizzy?"

Lizzy promptly picked up one of the biscuits and took a healthy bite out of it. After swallowing, she put an arm around Henry and bent down to whisper. "How about we make a deal? I promise to tell you as soon as I think I need more reinforcements. Will that work?"

Henry actually blushed. "Okay."

Avi reached over and claimed one of Lizzy's biscuits. "Since you've just negotiated a steady supply stream, you probably won't miss one of these."

"I should make those things more often," Syd muttered.

"You'll get no arguments from me." Maddie refilled all their wineglasses.

"Go easy on mine," Lizzy warned her. "I'm driving."

"Don't worry." Maddie topped her off, anyway. "It's just a pinot and not very big. And Syd has *major* plans for some serious carb-loading with dessert."

Lizzy looked across the table at Syd with an implied question.

"I made an apple cake. And we have some clotted cream."

Avi's eyes grew large. "No way."

"Way. They should go together very well."

Avi was ecstatic. "I haven't had real clotted cream since . . . well. Since forever."

"Then you're in luck," Syd explained. "And in the interest of full disclosure, I had nothing to do with the clotted cream. Dorothy made it."

"Dorothy?" Avi looked at her with happy surprise. "Do tell."

Dorothy shrugged. "It's not hard. My mama used to make it. I found one of her recipes . . . someplace."

Maddie was curious. "Have you ever made it for Mom?"

"Lots of times," Dorothy explained. "She always says I shouldn't, but then she eats most of it at one meal."

"That sounds about right. Mom has always had a real sweet tooth."

"I see you come by that honestly," Syd added.

Maddie feigned umbrage. "I'll have you know I come by *most* things honestly."

"Your taste in wine, for one." Avi held up her glass. "This is one of the best pinots I've ever had. What is it?"

"Ah." Maddie turned in her seat to claim a bottle off the

kitchen island. "This is a little gem I discovered years ago when I was in Portland for an AMA conference." She handed Avi the bottle. "It's a Willamette Valley pinot—estate bottled and very consistent. Syd and I call it an everyday drinker."

Avi examined the label. "If you call Sokol Blosser an 'everyday drinker,' I definitely need to raise my rates."

"Well, to clarify," Maddie amended, "*everyday drinker* here means the wine is perfect any day we drink it—not that we drink it every day."

Avi shook her dark head. "I see your level of obfuscation has not abated over the years."

Lizzy chuckled but Dorothy eyed Avi with confusion.

"It means intentional lack of clarity," Avi explained. "Something the august Dr. Stevenson has always excelled at."

"I guess that's not something you came by honestly, then." Dorothy addressed Maddie. "Dr. Heller isn't like that at all."

They were all silent for a moment, until Maddie threw back her head and laughed. "*Touché*, Dorothy. I think you've nailed us both."

Dorothy actually smiled—an indication that she understood the irony of her observation.

"Why is that just an August thing, Avi?" Henry asked. "Maddie is like that all year long. Buddy says she speaks in code."

Syd nudged Maddie. "Busted."

"In this context, Henry," Avi addressed him, "*august* means respected or impressive—not a reference to the month."

"Words are hard when they mean different things." Henry seemed unsatisfied. "Why don't they make them so they all just mean *one* thing?"

"I've wondered about that myself." Lizzy sounded like she meant it.

"This is why you study vocabulary words, honey." Syd jumped at the chance to make this a teaching moment for him. "The more you learn, the more you'll understand how words used in different combinations—called *context*—can help you understand their meaning."

Henry wasn't persuaded. "It's a lot to absorb."

"Exactly!" Syd was ecstatic. "*Absorb.* That's one of your new vocabulary words, and you just used it perfectly in a sentence."

Unlike Dorothy, Henry seemed to miss the irony of his comment. He'd clearly moved on from the usage lesson. "Can I have some more bacon?"

"*May* I have some more bacon," Syd corrected. "And, no. I think you've had enough bacon, sweetie."

"No, I haven't. Maddie ate most of mine."

"It appears he's right," Maddie said sorrowfully. "I failed miserably in my valiant efforts to obfuscate the disappearance of Henry's bacon."

Syd drummed her fingers on the table.

"I'll get it." Lizzy picked up Henry's bowl and headed for the stove.

"More carrots, too!" Henry called out.

Avi leaned close to Dorothy. "Is it always like this around here?"

"Pretty much. But bacon isn't usually involved."

"You know what, Dorothy?" Avi smiled at her. "I think this is the start of a beautiful friendship."

Syd was thrilled when Dorothy shyly smiled back.

The easy banter and staccato ping-ponging between subjects persisted throughout the meal. When they'd all finished eating, Dorothy and Henry disappeared upstairs so Henry could show Dorothy the alarm clock he was attempting to repair.

Syd suggested they all take their wineglasses outside to the porch and pray for a stray breeze.

Maddie and Avi walked to the end of the big, wraparound porch so Avi could get a better view of the pond.

Once Lizzy and Syd were settled into their Adirondack chairs, Lizzy told Syd about the situation with Tom.

"I guess by now your brother has told you about his job offer?"

"Tom hasn't said anything to me. In fact, I haven't talked with him in nearly two weeks."

"That's odd. He was over the moon about it."

"Maybe he realized I wouldn't be very receptive to the news?"

"You're not?" Lizzy asked.

"Nope. Not if it means taking you away from Jericho."

Lizzy smiled. "It's nice to hear you say that."

"I hope so. I mean it."

Lizzy took her time. "I don't know what to do, Syd."

"What do you want to do? That's often a good starting place."

"Normally, I'd agree with you. But Tom seems unwavering in his determination to accept this job—even though he knows how much I'd like to stay here."

"Sadly, that sounds like him."

"You sound nearly as frustrated with him as I am."

"It's not frustration," Syd clarified. "I'm beyond frustration. I'm pissed at him for his stupidity and selfishness."

Lizzy blinked at her. "We are discussing *your* brother, right? Shouldn't you be a bit more disposed to take his side?"

"Not when he acts like an unrepentant ass."

Lizzy laughed. "That part is certainly true." She took a moment to consider Syd's observation. "I guess I thought he'd learned something from everything we just went through with the pregnancy and miscarriage. I really believed he was more . . . committed to me. *To us*. Now, with this? Going ahead and accepting a job—*in Colorado*—without even discussing it with me? I have no idea where that puts us."

Syd knew she needed to proceed with caution. It meant the world to her that Lizzy was willing to open up to her about the situation with Tom—especially after Syd had profoundly violated Lizzy's confidence about her unwanted pregnancy. Syd continued to feel abject mortification about how badly she had bungled *that* episode. But she'd learned her lesson—the hard way. And Lizzy had seemed to fully accept her apology. Syd would never violate her confidence—or anyone else's—again.

*Never.*

She could see Maddie and Avi making their way back to where she and Lizzy were seated.

"Why don't we make a date to meet so we can talk this over with more privacy?"

"I'm always up for getting together with you. You know that. But we don't have to stop talking about this just because Avi is here." She grimaced. "I already pretty much gave her the ten thousand-foot view on the ride over here. She probably thinks I'm a total head case."

*Okay, that was a surprise.* Syd had noticed what appeared to be an easy camaraderie between the two of them at dinner, but she'd assumed it was just a byproduct of the pandemonium that typically characterized their family dinners.

"I doubt Avi thinks that. She seems pretty . . . prescient."

"Now there's a two-dollar vocabulary word for Henry."

"Remind me to add it to his list."

Maddie and Avi reclaimed their seats. Well. Avi reclaimed hers. Maddie had to dislodge Rosebud, who'd claimed the spot as her own. Maddie transferred the cat to the porch floor and shooed her away.

"That tuxedo cat is a pain in my ass," Maddie explained to Avi. After she sat down, she faced Lizzy. "So. What'd we miss?"

"Oh, I've been regaling Syd with tales of relationship angst."

"Really?" Maddie grinned at her. "How is Tom?"

Syd swatted her on the arm. "Behave."

"Is someone going to fill me in?" Avi asked, good-naturedly. "Or should I amuse myself admiring the perfection of your roof soffit?"

"It's that whole 'flux' situation I referenced on the drive over here," Lizzy explained. "My . . . *boyfriend*, for lack of a better term . . . is finishing his veterinary degree in a few weeks, and he's seen fit to accept a fellowship at a research lab in Colorado."

"Ohhhhhh." Avi gave a low whistle. "And I guess, being a sage and thoughtful man, he wants you to accompany him?"

"That would be the gist of it, yes."

"And given your consternation about the situation, I infer that you have divided opinions on the matter?"

"To say the least. Tom doesn't have the best track record when it comes to . . . inclusivity while making plans."

Syd was amazed by how easily Lizzy seemed to be sharing details with Avi. She cast a surreptitious look at Maddie, to see if she shared her reaction.

Maddie gave her a nuanced shrug before addressing Lizzy.

"Then I had to go ahead and make matters worse by dangling the partnership in front of you. I apologize for my rotten timing."

"Don't be silly," Lizzy told her. "It wasn't *rotten* timing. How could an offer like that possibly come at a bad time? I'm thrilled by it."

"Well, I'm still sorry it mucked up the process for you." Maddie sipped her wine. "Maybe Tom will have a change of heart when you tell him about it. I mean, if you haven't already told him about it."

"I have not, as it happens."

"Why not?" It was Avi who asked the question. "I mean," she continued, "one could assume that this would be relevant to his own decision-making process. Isn't *all* information better than *some* information?"

"It might be," Lizzy replied, "if ever he'd bothered to ask what I thought."

"So he's a total cad?"

Lizzy shot a nervous look at Syd.

"Okay." Avi looked back and forth between them. "What

else am I missing?"

"Tom is my brother," Syd explained. "But as it happens, I wholly agree with your assessment."

"Oh, god. I'm sorry, Lizzy. *Not,*" Avi added quickly, "that Tom is Syd's brother—but that I was so stupidly glib and said something thoughtless. See?" she said softly. "All information *is* better than some."

"Don't worry about it—*any* of you. Okay?" Lizzy looked at each of them in turn. "It's my own fault I'm in this mess, and I'll figure it out. And, Maddie? I promise not to take too long doing it."

"You take as much time as you need," Maddie assured her. "The clinic isn't going anyplace."

"Sometimes I worry that I'm not, either."

"This could be your chance to change all of that," Avi suggested in a gentle tone.

Lizzy regarded her with an expression Syd couldn't decipher.

"Maybe you're right," Lizzy said. She shifted her gaze to Syd. "Didn't you say something about apple cake and clotted cream?"

After their guests had departed and they'd finished cleaning up the kitchen—and getting the kids settled for the night—Maddie wanted to debrief. She poured them each a cognac and they returned to the porch so they could watch the moon come up behind Buck Mountain. It was a clear night. After so many days of rain, the stars seemed especially brilliant. It was like nature had pressure-washed the sky.

Pete was hard at work, making his final loop around the perimeter of the pond. He'd be loping back toward the house at any minute, insisting to be allowed inside so he could head upstairs to Henry's room.

"So what was up with all of that?" she asked Syd.

"All of what?"

"That whole business between Avi and Lizzy."

"You noticed that, too?" Syd seemed surprised by her observation. "I thought it was just me."

"Not this time. I was blown away."

"I don't think it was *that* dramatic."

"You don't?"

"No." Syd shook her head. "I thought there was some kind of spark there, but I don't think we should read anything into it."

"Spark?" Maddie was perplexed. "What spark?"

"Isn't that what you were talking about? The chemistry between Avi and Lizzy?"

"Chemistry?" Maddie felt like a deer in headlights. "There was chemistry going on?"

"Hello?" Syd snapped her fingers in front of Maddie's face. "Were you at the same dinner party?"

"Apparently not for that part of the program. I was referring to Lizzy talking so openly with all of us about Tom. She's not generally that forthcoming about personal issues."

"Oh, that." Syd waved it off. "That was nothing. I think it was part of her way to process the situation."

Rosebud padded past Syd and stopped in front of Maddie's chair. Before she could pounce, Maddie sternly warned her off.

"Don't even *think* about it, cat."

"You really should lighten up on her."

"Why should I? She's a total—"

Syd cut her off. "Pain in the ass. I know. She's a *cat,* Maddie. And for some reason, she's determined that you're her person."

"I am so *not* her person. I'm not her . . . *anything*—unless it's the unfortunate wearer of pants in need of shredding."

"She has never shredded your pants. She's just looking for a place to belong."

"Well, that place *isn't* my lap."

"Having spent a fair amount of time on your lap, I have to disagree with your assessment of its merits." Syd batted her eyes.

"Nice try. And that's only because *you* don't tend to turn my clothing into Swiss cheese." Maddie smiled. "Except for maybe that one time, back during our courting days."

"You're delusional. I never did any such thing."

"Hey. Don't ruin my fantasies. They keep hope alive."

Syd gave her a withering look. "C'mere, Rosebud." She patted the side of her leg. "*I'll* hold you."

Rosebud promptly jumped up onto Syd's lap, and curled up with her back to Maddie.

Maddie refused to be offended. "You'll live to regret that."

"I doubt it."

"So, are you going to explain what you meant about Avi and Lizzy?"

Syd nursed her cognac. "Like I said: I don't want to make too much out of it. But I think there definitely was some kind of something going on between them."

"Well that's about as clear as mud."

"Use your imagination."

Maddie thought back over the evening. It was true that Avi had been teasing, nearly playful with Lizzy—but no more than she had been with any of the rest of them. Maybe those two had seemed to be on slightly more intimate terms than might be expected after such a short acquaintance. But Avi was a shrink, and that was kind of what shrinks did. It actually was their stock in trade.

But then again, Syd's instincts were usually pretty keen about such things. After all, she'd nailed the attraction between Roma Jean and Charlie months before anyone else even had a glimmer that something was brewing there.

And it had been the same way with Maddie's mother and Byron Martin.

*But Avi and Lizzy?*

Maddie didn't see it. *Not at all.* Lizzy was straight—not to mention in love with Syd's brother. And that continued to be true, even though Tom seemed to be doing his level best to lob a hand grenade into the middle of everything.

*Idiot.*

She wondered if she should try to talk some sense into him?

On the other hand, if she *did* interfere and Tom got a clue and wised up, that might mean Lizzy would leave Jericho—and she'd be out the best nurse she'd ever practiced with.

And she'd lose a great friend, too.

It was a conundrum, and she hated conundrums. She wanted things to be straightforward and sensible.

"You cannot fix this. For either of them."

Maddie looked up to find Syd watching her.

Syd always *had* been able to read her mind.

"I know," Maddie said morosely. "It sucks."

"Sometimes it does. But it's up to them to play the cards they've been dealt, and we can't do anything but stand by and be prepared to pick up the pieces."

"True."

"Buck up, baby cakes." Syd patted her knee. "Whatever will be, will be."

Maddie narrowed her eyes. "Are you listening to David's Doris Day records again?"

"It's possible." Syd finished her drink. "Here comes Pete. Ready to head inside?"

"I suppose."

"Don't be so somber. I'll let you wear that ratty old Quakers t-shirt."

Maddie brightened up. "We still have that? I thought you threw it away."

"Nuh uh." Syd shook her head. "I've been saving it for a special occasion. Play your cards right, and I might be persuaded to sit on your lap and *shred* it."

Maddie bolted to her feet.

"Get up, Rosebud . . . *it's bedtime.*"

Michael's paella had been an unqualified success.

Maybe not *exactly* unqualified . . . but they'd sold five servings of it and, for him, that made it enough of a success that he could gloat about it to Nadine.

She hadn't been impressed. She insisted that he'd probably have sold out of it if he hadn't burned the rice . . .

The last diners had finished up shortly after nine, so he was relaxing in their bedroom, watching a rerun of *Hell's Kitchen* when David got home. Michael asked him if he'd had anything to eat and David said he'd stopped at Waffle House for a bite between meetings.

"Too bad," Michael told him. "The paella turned out great."

"Just my luck. Maybe I can have some for lunch tomorrow."

"I think there's just enough left. Avi wanted me to save her a serving, too."

"Avi? Who's Avi?"

Michael pointed above them. "The friend of Maddie's who's staying here. The psychologist from Roanoke."

"Oh . . . is *she* the totally hot-looking boi with the badass haircut?"

"Boi?"

"Duh. What would you call her?"

"I don't know. Metro, maybe?" He thought about it. "Can women be metro?"

'That would be a *no*. Women *cannot* be metro. Ergo, Avi is a *boi*."

"Why can't women be metro?"

"Because, Heathcliff, women are feminine by definition. Therefore, the 'metro' designation would be redundant."

Michael gave up. "There are too many rules about this stuff."

David was changing out of his suit. It was hard for Michael to get used to seeing David run around in dress clothes. It was a change. One of many for them since he'd assumed the mantle of mayor.

"Why are you watching that again?" David had noticed the TV program. "We've already seen that episode. Twice."

"I know. But this one is 'Fish Out of Water,' where they cook halibut for David LeFevre."

"So?"

Michael was aghast. "He's a highly regarded, Michelin Star chef."

"And *I'm* the highly regarded mayor of Jericho. But nobody wants to watch my reruns, either."

"You haven't been mayor long enough to *have* reruns."

David ignored him. "Maybe I am a little hungry . . ."

"Do you want me to fix you something?"

"No. I'll just go grab a snack. Be right back." He left their room and headed for the kitchen.

Michael had become engrossed in the episode again when David returned. He was munching on something. Loudly.

"What are you eating?"

David held up a red canister. "Pringles."

"Where'd you find those?"

"In the condiment pantry, behind two dozen boxes of corn starch."

Michael was mystified. "Where'd those even come from?"

David plopped down on the sofa beside him. "Nadine. She uses them in her meatloaf and thinks I won't find them back there."

"Did you, like, hunt truffles in a previous life?"

"Maybe. I managed to find *you*, didn't I?" David kissed his cheek. "You need a shave . . . as usual."

"It's been a long day—as you know."

David yawned. "True dat. But you could shave every twenty minutes and still be fuzzy."

"Make sure you check your messages before bed. The medical examiner's office called. Again. They said they've been leaving messages for you all over the place."

"Can I help it if I'm busy?" David snapped.

"Hey . . . dial it back, okay? I'm just the messenger."

"I don't see why they need to talk to me, anyway. I don't know anything about what happened to Watson."

"Then that's probably all you need to tell them."

David got up abruptly and crossed the room to their desk. "I wish these people would just leave me the hell alone."

"Why are you suddenly so testy? They're talking to everyone who was at the river that day."

"Not *everyone*," David snarled. "Have they asked you to come in and sit for an interview?"

"Not yet, but I'm sure they will."

"I doubt it." He slammed the can of Pringles down on the desk. "They think I had something to do with it. That's what this is about."

"You're overreacting."

"Am I? Why do you think they're so hell-bent on questioning me?"

"Probably because you had a public disagreement with him right before he . . . disappeared with Dorothy."

"Give me a break, Forest Gump. It wasn't a *disagreement.* I was practically in a *brawl* with him—and everyone saw it. They think I'm a suspect in his murder, and you know it as well as I do."

Michael didn't know what to say to him—mostly because he thought there was a good chance he was right. David and Watson *had* nearly come to blows. And after Watson had shoved him into the food table, David had run off—and Michael had no idea where he'd gone.

“Can’t you just tell them where you went?” He tried to plead his case in the gentlest tone he could manage. “Can’t you just tell *me* where you went? That would be the best way to clear this up.”

“Oh—that’s just *great.*” David swatted the can of chips and sent it flying. “*You* don’t trust me, either.”

Michael got to his feet and extended his hands in supplication. “Sweetie. You need to calm down. Of course, I trust you. But you aren’t helping yourself by being unwilling to talk about any of this.”

“Really?” David stormed across the room to the door. “You know what, Michael? *You* aren’t helping me much, either.”

He exited the room and slammed the door behind him.

Michael stared after him, dazed. For the first time, he began to fear the possibility that maybe David *did* have something to hide.

And that realization scared the hell out of him.

# Chapter Four

*Recorded Interview*
*Preliminary Inquest Investigation*
*Death of Mayor Gerald Watson*

"It's Rita. Rita Chriscoe. I work with my sister Natalie, who's the bookkeeper at Cougar's Quality Logistics. We handle moving and relocation. Sometimes we haul mobile homes. I been working there as a driver for nearly two years now. Before that, I worked out at Bixby's Bowladrome—back before the tornado tore it up."

*You can ask me all the questions you want about that waste of skin. I don't give two flips about what happened to that man. He got what he deserved. It's just too bad it came ten years too late.*

"I was at Freemantle's having lunch that day Watson come in there, madder'n a hatter. He was pretty much goin' off on everybody. Curtis had asked him to leave because he was kickin' up such a ruckus."

*I knew that rat bastard didn't see me sittn' there, watchin' everything—listening to him spread his poison. But there was no way I was gonna let him take out after that Freemantle girl like he was God almighty's avenging angel. Not after what he did to me and Eva. Not after what I* knew *he was doing to Eva's little girl. Eva knew she never should 'a married that man . . .*

"Yes sir, you heard right. He tripped over my foot on his way out. I ain't sayin' it was an accident, neither. Somebody needed to take the wind outta his sails before people in there got hurt. That man was spittin' mad. He fell ass-over-teakettle into a store display. Before you get all riled up, it didn't hurt nothin' on him but his pride. You can ask Sheriff Martin about it. He was there, too, with that Davis girl."

*I won't never forget the look on Watson's face when he saw me laughin' at him. I knew he was itchin' for a fight. And I was ready to give it to him . . . that slimy, half-assed excuse for a man. He hated me as much as I hated him—and neither of us was tryin' to hide it. He killed Eva. I knew it—and he* knew *I knew it.*

"Yes, I was by the food tables when he got into that fight with David Jenkins on the 4th. James Lawrence was with me. After it got busted up, both of them hightailed it out of there. Then I was on my way to meet up with Natalie and Jocelyn to watch the fireworks. We all heard the sirens later, at the same time everybody else did. That's when we found out about what happened down by the water."

*Am I sorry he's dead? Hell no, I ain't sorry. If you ask me, that man deserved to be killed every day of his miserable life.*

"No, sir. I ain't sorry that man is gone. I don't know of a single person in this town who is, neither. If you ask me, whatever happened to that man was a blessin'. Pure and simple. What you keep doin' here with all these questions—stirrin' things up this way? It's nothin' but a waste of time. And it's turnin' neighbor against neighbor—just keepin' that man's unholy rage alive is stirrin' up the pot."

*You might as well give it up, mister. I got nothin' else to say about any of this—so quit askin' me questions that ain't gonna get you no place.*

"I think you all'd be a lot better off just lettin' sleepin' dogs lie."

—~— —~— —~—

Henry and Dorothy were at the library with Roma Jean, helping her stock the bookmobile for her Saturday route.

Well, that wasn't entirely true. *Dorothy* was helping her. Henry spent most of his time detouring to look at brand new, face-out books displayed on low shelves in the children's section. So far, he'd pulled down about six and told Roma Jean he wanted to check them out.

"Have you finished that Roald Dahl book yet?" Roma Jean asked him.

When Henry seemed unsure about how to answer her question, Dorothy clarified.

"She means the book about Danny and the pheasants."

"Oh." Henry became animated. "Not yet. Maddie says we have *eight* more chapters to go. It's *really* good. Are there other books about Danny and his daddy?"

"I don't think so," Roma Jean said. "But when you finish the one you're reading, we can find you some other books that might be as good. In the meantime," Roma Jean held out her hands to take the stack of books back from Henry, "we should leave these here so other kids can read them, too. Don't you think that's the right thing to do?"

"Okay." Henry reluctantly handed the books to her. "I guess so."

"Tell you what. As a treat, I'll let you stamp all the checkout cards today."

"Really?" Henry forgot his disappointment. "Syd says I'm really good at that. She let me do it last week. I didn't smear the ink or anything."

Roma Jean smiled at Dorothy.

"It's a gift," Dorothy agreed. "He always stays between the lines."

"Well, I wish I could." Roma Jean sighed. "My life would be

a whole lot easier."

After they'd finished stocking the truck, Roma Jean secured the kids in their seats and they headed out for their day in the remotest parts of the county. Carsonville, Providence, Stevens Creek and Bone Gap: stops in all those communities were on tap for today. They'd take a break and eat their packed lunches at a picnic table in the park beside the New River Trail in Fries. Henry liked it there because the river was especially wide, and he could stand on the bank and throw rocks at imaginary targets on the old dam. And Roma Jean would always treat them to ice cream cones at the shop set up inside a retrofitted caboose.

Roma Jean loved the days the kids could ride along with her. It made the time pass a lot quicker—usually because Henry tended to talk nonstop. And Dorothy and Roma Jean would talk about books. Lately, however, Dorothy had pretty much outpaced Roma Jean's knowledge of Southern fiction. Now, more often than not, it was Dorothy who suggested books and authors to Roma Jean. At first, Roma Jean thought that was because Dorothy was living with Dr. Heller, who everybody knew was some kind of brainiac, just like Dr. Stevenson. But Miss Murphy said that wasn't really it. She explained that Dorothy had a good mind and a voracious appetite for knowledge. And now that it was possible for Dorothy to read anything she wanted and not have to hide it from her father, she was in flight like a bird freed from its cage.

Miss Murphy always used poetic language whenever she talked about books . . .

Dorothy told Roma Jean she was reading a book she'd found at Dr. Heller's—an older novel called *Heading West*. It was about a librarian who gets kidnapped at a picnic and soon realizes that life on the run with her kidnapper is better than the life of captivity she'd been living with her family. She said there were some very funny scenes, too, where a woman thinks her refrigerator is giving her advice about changing her life.

Roma Jean thought the book sounded good, but suggested that getting life coaching from your kitchen appliances probably wouldn't end up very well.

They'd reached their first stop in Carsonville, which wasn't much more than a crossroads on Pine Mountain Road. Sometimes, Roma Jean would park in a cleared spot beside the crumbled foundation of an old garage for the entire hour without seeing anybody. But that was part of the job. You had to wait there the whole allotted time so people had a chance to show up.

Miss Murphy was adamant about that.

Today, there were two people waiting beside their car when Roma Jean parked the bookmobile. Roma Jean recognized them right away.

Henry was excited and ran to the front of the truck to retrieve the date due stamp. He wanted to be ready and in position to perform his job.

Old Mrs. Raskin and her daughter, Beulah—who looked to Roma Jean like she was ninety, herself— sometimes showed up during her stops there. It looked like today was going to be one of their days. Beulah managed to climb up into the mobile library and pretty much proceeded to shout out book titles to her mother, who stood near the door leaning on her walker because she couldn't navigate the metal steps to get inside.

"How about one of them books by that Nora Roberts, Mama?"

Mrs. Raskin said no. She'd read enough of those to know they were all the same.

"Don't they have none of them *Twilight* books?" Mrs. Raskin hollered.

"You mean them books about Mormons?" Beulah asked.

"They ain't about Mormons. They're about *vampires*."

Henry looked expectantly at Roma Jean.

"Don't even think about it until you finish Danny," she told him.

Beulah finally appealed to Roma Jean for help.

"Do you have any of them vampire books she's talkin' about?"

"No, ma'am. But I do have two of the Anne Rice books about vampires in New Orleans."

"Mama," Beulah called out. "Do you want to read about vampires in New Orleans?"

"Is there a movie that goes with 'em, too?" Mrs. Raskin asked.

Beulah looked at Roma Jean and waited for her answer.

"Yes, ma'am," Roma Jean called out to Mrs. Raskin. "Tom Cruise is in it."

Beulah didn't wait on her mama to reply. "We'll take 'em," she told Roma Jean.

Roma Jean retrieved the two paperbacks and Henry promptly stamped their cards. Beulah descended the steps and she and her mama climbed into their mud-covered Chevy and rattled off.

"That's more activity than I've had out here in a month," Roma Jean opined.

Dorothy was looking at a third Anne Rice paperback still on the rack.

"Why didn't you give them this one, too?"

When Roma Jean saw what Dorothy was holding, she felt mortified.

"Because *that* one isn't about vampires," she explained. "And it's kind of . . ." she glanced at Henry, who was busy re-inking the stamp pad, "*NC17*, if you catch my drift. It's one of those adult . . . *fantasy* books about Sleeping Beauty she wrote back before she found Jesus."

"It is?" Dorothy handed the book to Roma Jean like it was made out of hot coals. "Why do you have it here, then?"

"It isn't supposed to be *out* here. I was at the prison last week and this one got turned in. It was an *interlibrary loan*." Roma Jean said the words like they would make sense without further explanation. When it was clear that Dorothy had no idea why that detail was significant, she lowered her voice to a whisper.

"It's *erotica*. Men out there order those books all the time. I forgot to take this one back inside."

Dorothy seemed to think about the implications of what Roma Jean had just revealed. "I don't really want to know why they ask for these books, do I?" she asked.

"Trust me. You don't."

"Are we gonna have more customers, Roma Jean?" Henry had rejoined them.

"I don't know, Henry. Probably not out here. Business has gotten a lot slower since school started."

"It's Saturday." Henry looked perplexed. "There's no school on Saturday."

"That's true. But families do a lot of other things on the weekends now."

They waited their remaining time, then closed up the truck and headed out for their next stop in Providence. Business was a little livelier there. Henry stayed very busy, carefully stamping cards while people checked out books and DVDs.

"Too bad you didn't have that Tom Cruise movie for Mrs. Raskin," Dorothy observed.

"We used to have it. People kept checking it out and keeping it way past its due date. Finally, the case for it got turned in at the night deposit box, but the wrong DVD was inside it. When Mrs. Murphy called the person who'd checked it out, he said he didn't know what happened to the right movie, but he figured sending something back was better than nothing."

"What was the movie he did send back?" Dorothy asked.

"I think it was a video of some NASCAR race in Florida."

"That's too bad."

"Not really. Miss Murphy said that race video ended up being just as popular as the Tom Cruise vampire movie."

Dorothy laughed. Roma Jean liked the way laughing changed the girl's features. It took years off her young face. It was the only time Dorothy actually looked . . . well . . . like she was fourteen. Normally, Dorothy was pretty serious. At first, Roma Jean thought that was because Dorothy didn't pay much attention to what was going on around her. But she knew the girl well enough now to know that wasn't the case at all. If anything, the opposite was true. Dorothy was clued in to *everything*—whether it directly involved her or not. Sometimes it was kind of freaky, and Roma Jean felt like Dorothy was actually the older person in their friendship. And Roma Jean did think of Dorothy as a friend. As an equal, even.

She wished sometimes she could ask for Dorothy's opinion about everything with Charlie, but common sense told her that wasn't a good idea. No matter how grown up she seemed, Dorothy was still a child. And there were some things that needed to stay off limits between them.

Still . . . she looked forward to Dorothy's quiet observations about people and general goings-on in the community. They were always offered in an understated, kind of absent way. But even Roma Jean was smart enough to understand how perceptive and on target Dorothy's assessments usually were.

Maybe Miss Murphy had been right about that whole bird thing. If Dorothy was soaring above them all, she probably could see things a lot more clearly than they could, stuck here on the ground.

After the Providence stop, they went on to Stevens Creek. There was a smattering of homes near The Church of God of Prophesy, so Roma Jean always parked in the church lot to make it easier for people to see when she was there. Sadly, Henry's stamper didn't get much of a workout in Stevens Creek, either. It was just a slow day across the board. But it was always like that out here in this remote part of the county. So Miss Murphy didn't worry too much about low service use in these areas. She told Roma Jean that educating people about the mobile library would be a process, and it might take years for people to catch on to the benefits the bookmobile delivered right to their doorsteps every week.

After they'd eaten their lunches in Fries—and Roma Jean had bought them each ice cream—they headed for their final stop of the day in Bone Gap.

Roma Jean liked the Bone Gap stop the least of just about any place she went—except for the prison. Although she had to admit that the prisoners were often a lot more courteous than some of the patrons in Bone Gap—especially the ones who tended to hang out with Mrs. Black. It had been Mrs. Black and some of her followers who Roma Jean had heard whispering bad things about Miss Murphy and Dr. Stevenson. She worried again about the wisdom of bringing Henry along with her out here, especially if Mrs. Black showed up. She didn't want the stern, judgmental woman to do or say anything to scare him.

But Henry had been so excited about their adventure today that she didn't have the heart to put him off—and she couldn't change the route without giving the patrons more advance notice.

Dorothy seemed to pick up on her nervousness.

"Are you worried about something, Roma Jean?" she asked.

"Not really." Roma Jean tried to shrug it off. "Why do you ask?"

"Because you keep looking up and down the road like you're expecting someone."

"I guess I'm just tired and want this last stop to be over with."

"I see somebody coming!" Henry exclaimed from his seat up front in the cab. "It's a car with lots of people in it."

Roma Jean took a deep breath. Henry's "lots of people" ended up being Nelda Rae Black—*of course*—another smallish woman she didn't recognize, and a man she did. Her heart sank.

It was Charlie's father.

*What was he doing out here in Bone Gap?*

Whatever it was, the fact that he was here with Mrs. Black

couldn't be good news.

All three of them approached the truck.

"Come back here and sit by me, Dorothy," Roma Jean summoned the girl. "Stay up there in the cab, Henry, so there's more room back here for the patrons. I'll hand you any books you need to stamp and you can do them up there. Okay?"

Fortunately, he agreed without argument. With luck, Mrs. Black wouldn't see him.

The unfamiliar woman made eye contact with Roma Jean, but didn't say anything. She was busy stuffing some little brochures she'd brought along into one of the bookracks near the door. Mrs. Black began looking through back issues of *Southern Living* magazine. Charlie's father—*Manfred,* she recalled—stood staring at her and plucking at some stray chin hairs.

"You're the gal I met at Charlene's, ain't you?" he asked.

That got Mrs. Black's attention. "What'd you say, Manfred?"

"This here is the gal I told you about—the one gallivantin' with Charlene."

Roma Jean felt Dorothy stiffen beside her.

"Did you need help finding a book, Mr. Davis?" Roma Jean had no idea where her bravado was coming from. Inside, she was shaking like a leaf.

"He don't need no help from the likes of you, young lady," Mrs. Black interjected. "It's more like you need guidance from *him.*"

"Not from him," the other woman corrected. "From the Lord almighty."

"That's right, Glenadine." Manfred took a step closer to Roma Jean. She didn't like the look in his eyes. He wasn't like he'd been the other night, when she'd thought him tentative and harmless. Today there was no hint of politeness or hesitation in his demeanor. No trace of kindness, either.

He looked downright menacing.

Roma Jean made herself stand up. As scared as she was, she

knew she had to take command of the situation. There was no way she'd let these people intimidate or threaten Dorothy and Henry. *They were her responsibility.* Right now, these people were probably on the verge of saying things the children didn't need to hear. She had the right to ask them to leave before things got ugly.

That had been one of the first things Miss Murphy drilled into her head after they got the bookmobile and took it out together so Roma Jean could learn the ropes.

"If you are ever in a situation where you do not feel safe, *leave*," Miss Murphy had told her. "Do not hesitate. And make sure you have your phone with you at all times so you can push the 911 button if you need help. *No exceptions.*"

Roma Jean pulled her cell phone from the pocket of the work smock she always wore on the truck, and made sure Manfred could see it.

"If there's nothing else you folks need," she said in the strongest tone she could muster, "I'll kindly ask you to leave now. We don't want to have any problems."

"I reckon we don't, missy." Manfred stared at Dorothy, then back at Roma Jean. "You ought not to be carrying on with my daughter—or anybody else's kin, neither. It's an abomination to God."

"Come along, Manfred." It was the woman, Glenadine. "Shake the dust from your feet and leave this unholy place. We can do no good here. These people are beyond redemption."

"No one is beyond redemption, woman." Charlie's father cast his milky eyes heavenward. "The Lord God almighty can wash away the sins of even the worst sinner among us." He pointed a crooked finger at Roma Jean. "Today if you will hear His voice, harden not your heart."

Roma Jean was undaunted. She took a careful step toward him. She wanted to put more distance between him and the children.

"Mr. Davis, you need to leave now. I don't want to call Sheriff

Martin for help, but I will if you don't go. Right now."

Her mention of Byron seemed to get his attention. She saw a muscle in his face twitch.

He took the woman named Glenadine by the arm, and waved Mrs. Black ahead of them toward the door. Once they were outside, he turned and addressed her again.

"The Lord hath said those that commit sins of the flesh shall not inherit the kingdom of God. Turn from this evil path before you experience the full force of His wrath."

"Come along now, Manfred." It was Mrs. Black. "We got more of these tracts to distribute."

Once they'd gone, Roma Jean rushed over to close and lock the door to the bookmobile. Then she dropped to her knees because her legs had become too shaky to hold her up any longer.

Henry had joined Dorothy, and they both rushed to her side.

"It's okay. It's okay," Dorothy insisted in a quiet voice. "You did great. *You stood up to him*. You made him leave."

Roma Jean put her arms around the children and hugged them close.

"Who was that mean man, Roma Jean?" Henry asked.

"Just someone who used to live here a long time ago."

"He was really scary."

"I know. But you were a very good boy to stay so quiet."

"I was afraid, but I knew you would protect us."

Roma Jean started to cry.

"He's right," Dorothy told her. "You *did* protect us. *You did.* You stood up to him and made him leave."

Roma Jean sniffed and tried to clear her head. She didn't need to make this situation any worse for them than it already was. They all needed to do something . . . *normal*—something that could defuse all the emotion and get their equilibrium back on track.

She thought about the one thing that always worked for her in the past.

“I have an idea,” she said. “How about we call it a day and go back to the caboose?”

“We can get more ice cream?” Henry was incredulous.

“Why not?” Roma Jean got to her feet. “Sometimes a double-dip is just the right thing.”

She got no argument from Henry, but she noticed that Dorothy kept a watchful eye on her for the rest of the afternoon.

Rita arranged her trip to Waco to deliver a load of mirrors so she could spend the night in Killeen, near Fort Hood. James had been in Texas for more than a month now, and she was looking forward to seeing him.

It had been a real loss for Rita when James reenlisted in the army. She'd always enjoyed the long hauls they'd done together. James had been quiet when it mattered, and talkative enough when it didn't. Mostly, he didn't ask anything of her, and she didn't pester him to for details about gettin' his leg blown off—like everybody else in town tried to do.

They respected each other's boundaries.

James had been surprised when Rita texted him and said she'd be in town for an overnight. But he agreed to get together for supper right away. They were going to meet at a Texas Roadhouse right off the expressway. Rita was fine with that. Steakhouses were places that always had a lot of activity, but you felt okay about holding a table for a long time—if you were having a good conversation. And if all you really cared about was eating your steak and gettin' on with the rest of your night, they were good for that, too.

Plus they always had a big bucket of peanuts on the table, and shelling them gave you something to do if you or the other person weren't in a mood to talk.

She didn't know what to expect from James. She knew how

hard his decision to reenlist had been—especially because it meant leaving his boy. But he'd only been living half a life in Jericho, workin' out at Junior's and livin' in that ratty apartment over the garage. And even though a lot of folks in town criticized him for leavin' Henry with Doc Stevenson and her girlfriend, Rita understood why he had made that choice. They were good women who led decent lives, and they would be able to give James's boy a kind of life he'd never have livin' out at Junior's in Troutdale.

James had a lot of courage—and not just because he had to figure out how to live life all over again after losing his leg in Afghanistan.

Hell. Rita had lost part of herself, too. But she didn't have the gumption James Lawrence had—that stubborn drive to quit lickin' his wounds, get up, and learn how to walk again.

She just gave up. She didn't pull herself outta her sorrow and try to start over. The best parts of her had died right along with Eva. She'd been wanderin' around like some kind of zombie for ten years now. It was no wonder her life was such a wasteland of anger and disappointed hopes. Doing these long haul trips for Cougar's gave her lots of time to think about all of that. To regret all the years she'd wasted feeling sorry for herself.

The truth was, she wanted to change. She just didn't know how.

James was already at the steakhouse when she got there. There were lots of soldiers milling around in the parking lot or sitting on the benches outside the entrance, smoking. But she recognized James right away. He always had been a good-lookin' man, and his camouflage uniform made him seem bigger. Taller, maybe. And more put together. It was like the part of him that had been missing had been put back in place.

He waved when he saw her approaching and walked out to meet her. They had an awkward moment when they stood face to face. She could tell James didn't know whether or not to hug her. Normally, that idea would never occur to Rita—but she just decided to go ahead with it. She stepped forward and wrapped her arms around him. James hugged her back, and they stepped apart without saying anything about it.

"You look good," Rita observed.

"You think so?"

"Yeah. Tanned. Healthier, maybe."

He held the big wooden door open for her. "Probably the heat down here. Or maybe it's because I'm outside most of the time."

"That'll do it for sure. Sittin' in the cab of a truck ten hours a day don't do much for the complexion."

"You look just fine, Rita."

"Nah." Rita scoffed. "You always did have bad eyesight, boy."

They got seated right away. James had suggested they meet up early for this reason. "If we wait until dinnertime, we won't have a shot at getting a table without waiting more than an hour. Too many guys come in and hog all the tables, just eating wings and drinking cheap pitchers of beer."

"Can't do that in my line of work. It just gives me gas."

"I remember."

Rita threw a peanut shell at him.

"So, how you been, Rita? Things going okay at Cougar's?"

"It's about like it was. Maybe a few more cross-country hauls in the mix, now."

"What brought you out here?"

"Mirrors. I got a load of 'em to drop off in Waco at some place that makes retail stuff for houses and general construction. On the way back, I'm picking up a load of some kind of organic felt they use for insulation in mobile homes."

"That sounds like a long trip."

"Six days in all. I don't mind. Gettin' out of town is a good distraction right now."

"How come?"

Rita eyed him. "Ain't you a chatterbox today?"

He smiled at her. His tanned skin made his teeth look extra white. He really was a good-looking man—especially when he smiled. Rita was sure he was gettin' all the attention from the ladies he wanted.

Although, looking around this Roadhouse, she figured the "ladies" around here might be on the pricey side.

That's how it always was around these military bases. The beer was cheap and the women, with some exceptions, weren't.

"I guess I just miss the local gossip. Henry doesn't usually have many details about what's happening in the community."

"You talk with him pretty regular, don't you?"

He nodded. "Every week. Maddie and Syd have been setting up the computer so we can have FaceTime chats. Sometimes, they sit in a bit, too—but just for a little while. They want to be sure Henry and me have a lot of one-on-one time."

"They're good women." Rita didn't elaborate.

Their server came and they gave her their orders. Rita was determined to treat James, so when he asked for a sirloin, she told the server to nix that and bring them both Ft. Worth ribeyes. When James started to protest, Rita cut him off.

"No arguments," she told him. "And bring the check to me," she instructed their server.

After the server—Cassie was her name—collected their menus and wandered off, Rita watched her make her way back toward the kitchen. James noticed.

"She's got a nice back yard, doesn't she?"

Rita thought about tellin' him to mind his own damn business, but why bother? They were halfway across the damn country and nobody gave two rips about her out here.

"Guess I ain't dead quite yet," she said.

"Far from it. And you don't need to be buying my dinner, either, Rita. You should be saving your money."

"Forget about it. This is a good-payin' gig and I'm feelin'

generous. So make your peace with it and shut the hell up."

"I forgot how bossy you are."

"Well, now you remember." Rita retrieved another handful of peanuts from the bucket.

"Why don't you get outta there, Rita? Start over someplace new where maybe you can meet somebody?"

"Didn't I just tell you to shut up about all that?"

James nodded. "But neither of us is getting any younger."

Rita raised an eyebrow. "You takin' your own advice, soldier?"

"Maybe." He shrugged. "But I didn't reenlist to find companionship."

"Companionship ain't what I'm lookin' for, neither."

"What are you looking for, then?"

Rita had to fight not to blurt out an answer to his simple question. What *was* she lookin' for? Absolution? Forgiveness? Freedom from a wasted life full of nothing but regret?

"Something different, maybe," she said instead.

She felt her words hang in the air over their table.

James took a minute to reply. "So, how'd your interview go?"

"What interview?" she shot back at him.

"The inquest. Maddie told me they were interviewing everybody who was there that day. I just assumed you'd had yours, too."

Rita snapped the peanut she was holding so hard the shell splintered and skidded across the table.

"Yeah. I had it. It was a waste of time—just like all them conversations. Nobody's gonna do nothin' about that man. He's as dangerous dead as he was alive."

"You don't think they'll ever figure out what happened?"

"It don't matter if they do. Nothin's gonna come out of it. Nothin' good's ever gonna come outta anything related to that waste of skin."

"I suppose you're right." James took a drink of his beer. "But maybe they can at least learn something that will help his daughter out."

"What's wrong with her?"

James shrugged. "Maddie and Syd both said she's really struggling with what happened—that she thinks she was the one who killed him."

Rita hadn't heard that. "I thought she was happier now, living out with Dr. Heller. Lord knows, she's a whole lot better off."

"Yeah. I'm sure that's true."

Rita wanted to leave it alone. She didn't want to waste any more time thinking about Gerald Watson. But she hated that Eva's daughter might still be suffering.

*It figured that man would find some way to torment the girl from the grave.*

"What makes her think she killed him? Everybody says he drowned by accident."

"I don't know," James replied. "I guess until they get the autopsy report showing anything different, she's gonna keep on thinking she killed him by hitting him on the head with that driftwood."

"Well, even if she did, it wadn't a crime. That man needed to get gone, and it don't much matter how it finally happened."

"Yeah." James nodded. "I think most folks would agree with you about that. Too bad for that little girl, though." He finished his beer. "You want another one of these? And my treat for the drinks."

Rita nodded.

*Why the hell not?* It had been a while since she'd let go and gotten good and drunk.

She drained her glass. No time like the present.

—~— —~— —~—

Bert and Sonny were replacing the last of the boards on the garden side of Dr. Heller's house. They were using HardiePlank, because Dr. Heller thought it looked almost as good as the original wood did. Or maybe as good as it *once* did, back in the '20s when the bungalow-style house had been built. Most of the wood that was left on this side of the house was rotted clean through. They'd replaced all the insulation and tacked up sheets of heavy plastic to keep it covered until the shipment of HardiePlank finally came in from Commonwealth Supply in Roanoke.

Dr. Heller didn't want to go with any of the knockoff brands they sold at Lowe's in Galax, even though they could 'a had this part of the job finished weeks ago.

After they got all the new boards hammered into place, they'd have to paint 'em, too.

They wouldn't a had to do that with vinyl . . .

Sonny kept tryin' to get Dr. Heller to change her mind—especially after the distributor told them the HardiePlank was back-ordered and wouldn't be available for four to six weeks.

"That's all right," she said. "I'd rather wait and do this right."

So that meant him and Sonny had to pick up some rolls of 6 mil. plastic sheeting to staple up over the Tyvek layer. If it had been the other side of the house, they probably could 'a got away without doing it—but this was the storm side. And it had been rainin' like cats and dogs off and on for the last month. Today was one of the first sunny days they'd had in more'n a week, so they were determined to get this HardiePlank all into place as quick as they could.

It was lookin' real nice, too—just like everything Dr. Heller insisted on.

Bert couldn't get over how good the simple house was lookin'. It was too bad most folks in town would never get to see all the work they done out here. Sonny's boy, Harold, said the place was good enough to be featured in one of them home design magazines.

Bert stepped back to take in the new siding. He supposed Harold was right.

Him and Sonny were real proud of the job they were doin' for Dr. Heller. She trusted them, too. Which most folks in town didn't ever do. Even when they had a simple job, like replacing the floorboards on somebody's sagging old porch, the people—*usually the women*—would all but stand over them while they screwed down each length of board.

Everybody was afraid of being cheated. Well. Except for them folks at the cemetery where him and Sonny went every couple weeks to mow and weed. Dead people didn't tend to kick up a fuss about much. He liked jobs like that one.

But Bert supposed he understood why some folks were suspicious. When you didn't have nothin', you were extra greedy about protectin' it. But Sonny tended to get all fractious when folks didn't trust them, or thought they might skimp and do a shoddy job so they could pocket more money. He tried to explain to Sonny that that's just how folks were and it wadn't really personal. But Sonny didn't agree with him. He thought people should have better sense and more charity.

Bert thought Sonny was spending too much time goin' to those services out at Bone Gap . . .

Buddy was in the garden again today, planting more late-season vegetables. Bert didn't know what Dr. Heller thought she was gonna do with all that produce Buddy was puttin' in.

Buddy didn't tend to do things on a small scale.

Right now, he was diggin' mounds for the beet plants. They didn't really have to be planted that way, but Buddy allowed as how they made the garden look better and made a good contrast to alternate with the plants in rows. He said it put things in balance.

Balance was always important to Buddy.

Dr. Heller seemed to like it, too. She was in the garden right now, talkin' to Buddy about . . . well. Just about everything.

Even things that didn't have nothin' to do with plants.

Bert always liked that about her. She was a nice lady and she was always real respectful toward Buddy. Sometimes, she even sat with him at her piano and they'd take turns playing pieces of music. Or she'd play something, and Buddy would play it back, exactly right.

Today, she was talking about music and her plan to take a trip to listen to some in New York.

Buddy didn't say much, but he never did say much around Dr. Heller. Bert knew that was because he looked up to her and admired her knowledge about music.

Buddy tended to be quiet around people he liked a lot.

"Mitsuko Uchida is one of the best interpreters of Beethoven right now," Dr. Heller was saying. "Taking Dorothy to New York to hear her could be a seminal experience in her music education."

"Minor to major. Transitions don't happen right. Goldenrod's ratio is broken."

Buddy wasn't making much sense, but then, Bert often didn't understand what Buddy meant when he talked about music.

"Do you mean the sonata we're been studying? I think Dorothy's tonal harmonies are working very well."

"Her ratios are broken. The transitions don't work."

"That's why I think going to this recital could be a good thing for her." Dr. Heller was kneeling down, running her fingers along the tiny leaves of the new plants. They were all bright green and stood up proud beneath her touch. Their young leaves sprang right back up to face the sun. "Dorothy needs to experience performances that are *better* than mine. I can only go so far with what I can teach her."

"Transitions from major to minor are pathways. The pathways need to be right. Goldenrod needs to find a new pathway."

"I know, Buddy. I want to help her with that journey."

Buddy looked at Dr. Heller with his clear eyes. It was unusual for him to make direct eye contact with anyone. But Bert knew he trusted Dr. Heller.

"Her ratio is broken. The orange dog comes at night."

"What do you mean?" Dr. Heller sounded confused. "Do you mean something is scaring her? Is the music too much for her right now?"

"The orange dog comes at night," Buddy repeated. "Goldenrod's ratios are broken."

Bert could tell Dr. Heller was just getting more confused.

"With all due respect, Doc," he addressed her. "Buddy is talkin' about them garden pests. That's what orange dogs are. They eat the leaves on the little plants, just like them aphids and stink bugs. Sonny said they're really bad this year on account of how hot it still is. But Sonny can spray for 'em, so don't worry too much about orange dogs."

"The orange dog comes at night." Buddy repeated. "Goldenrod is little phi."

Dr. Heller was looking at Buddy intently. Bert could tell she was trying to decipher what Buddy's rambling meant. He thought about interrupting again to tell her she'd never be able to make it out, and it was best just to go on with her day—but he stayed quiet. He knew Dr. Heller wouldn't listen to him.

She was like her daughter in that way.

So he just went back to hammering up the HardiePlank boards.

Buddy was stuck in a loop, and he'd keep right on repeating the same thing for as long as she stayed there and listened.

*He was right . . .*

"The orange dog comes at night," Buddy said.

—∿— —∿— —∿—

Maddie had tried several times to get David on the phone—all to no avail. She'd left messages on his voicemail, and with his secretary at town hall. But if David got her messages, he chose to ignore them or put them aside. Either way, he didn't return her calls.

Even if Michael hadn't stopped by the farm on Sunday morning to tell her how worried he was, she'd have had her own reasons for concern about David's uncharacteristic behavior. She could count on one hand the number of times she'd seen him since the 4th of July, and all of those encounters had occurred when they all met up for taco night at the farm. And those meals were always rollicking affairs with at least two or three additional drop-in guests.

*Perfect settings to keep attempts at serious conversation at bay.*

Syd still had semi-regular contact with him—but that was only because they shared a mutual obsession with wedding planning. When Michael asked her how David had seemed to her, she'd said "normal."

But "normal" for David had always been a moving target. And even though she understood that his new job as mayor was taking up a ton of his time, she doubted that the demands it imposed on him were sufficient to explain the entirety of his strange behavior.

Michael said he'd never seen David as angry as he'd been the other night. He said the rage David had flown into after Michael pressed him about his reluctance to sit for his inquest interview had scared him.

"He behaved irrationally," Michael told her. "Like someone I didn't know. He didn't even finish his can of Pringles."

"Pringles?" Maddie asked.

"It's a long story."

"You're right." Maddie held up a hand. "I don't need to know."

Michael asked if Maddie would reach out to him . . . try to get him to explain why he became so hostile whenever the subject of the inquest came up.

"Is he at the inn this morning?" she asked.

Michael said no, and explained that David had gone into town for a planning board meeting. Apparently, Sunday was the only day everyone could get together.

Maddie told him she'd take a ride into town and try to catch up with him, but she was as mystified as he was about the reason for David's evasive behavior.

"Why do you think he's reacting to everything the way he is?" Maddie asked him.

Maddie could tell by Michael's reaction to her question that he had a theory, but he seemed unwilling to express it.

"Michael?"

He looked up at her. "I think it's possible he knows more about Watson's death than he's telling me."

"What do you mean?" His statement alarmed Maddie.

"I mean . . . I wasn't with him after he ran off."

"But, I thought you followed him."

"I did. But I never found him. Maddie, I have no idea where he went. He didn't show up until more than an hour later, and he wouldn't tell me anything about where he'd disappeared to."

Maddie was struggling to take in what Michael was telling her. "Was his car missing?"

"I have no idea. I never thought to look for it. When I finally did find him, he was back at our booth, packing up the food that hadn't been ruined after Watson pushed him into the table. By that time, everybody else was down by the river, getting ready for the fireworks. I tried to get him to talk about what happened, but he refused. He barely spoke two words to me the rest of the night."

"Dear god . . ."

"I'm *scared*, Maddie. I don't know what to do. If they ask me to come in and answer questions, what will I tell them? If I say I don't know where David was, what will happen to him?"

"Hey, hey . . . let's try not to get ahead of ourselves. We both *know* David. He couldn't hurt a fly. It's not possible that he had anything to do with Watson's death."

"Then why won't he tell me where he was? And why does he keep ignoring their requests for him to come in and answer questions about what he knows?"

Maddie slowly shook her head. "I honestly don't know."

"I *want* to believe him, Maddie. I want that more than anything. But he has to trust me enough to tell me the truth about where he was—and he refuses to do it."

"He must be afraid of something, Michael."

"I know," Michael agreed. "*But what?* And whatever it is, is it worth what he's risking by hiding it from everyone?"

"No. It certainly isn't."

"That's why I need you to try to reach him. You're his best friend . . . the only real family he has here. He trusts you. Maybe he'll tell you what he can't tell me?"

Maddie wasn't sure about that, but she promised Michael she'd try.

After they'd finished breakfast, Maddie tried to reach David again. No dice. And his voicemail box was full, and couldn't record a message. She resolved to drive into town and engineer an encounter.

When she reached the square, she saw David's car in the lot beside the courthouse. She parked and went inside.

Since it was Sunday, David's secretary wasn't at her desk, and the door to David's office was ajar. She could hear him talking on the phone with someone, so she waited until he'd hung up. When he did, she tapped on his door and pushed it open.

"Knock, knock? Can you spare a minute for an old pal in

need of a friendly face?"

He didn't seem to mind her intrusion. At least that was good news.

"What are you doing in this part of town? Drumming up business?"

She stepped inside. "You never know. Things are slow at the clinic."

"Well, I did hear a rumor that the resident bean counter in the tax assessor's office is about to open up a vein over complaints about the rate increases. Maybe you're just in time to clean up . . . so to speak."

"One can only hope. Got any coffee in this joint?"

"Yeah," David waved her into a chair, "if you're into drinking Pennzoil."

"Then I'll pass."

"Wise decision." David sat down behind his desk. "So why are you out and about on a Sunday morning—for real?"

"In fact, I came to see you."

"Me? That *cannot* be good. And before you say anything else, I had *nothing* to do with Syd's idea to launch a hundred doves after you take your vows."

"Doves?" The reason for Maddie's visit took a momentary back seat. "Please tell me you're joking."

"Yeah. Not so much, Cinderella. Your bride-to-be has outpaced me handily in the race to plan the most Vegas-worthy wedding on the planet."

"I reiterate: tell me you're joking."

"Hardly. She makes me look like such an untutored novice that I fear my gay card will be revoked."

Maddie ran a hand over her face.

"Buck up, Bonzo." David continued. "Has Professor Boyd ever let you down?"

"I'm not sure how confident I should feel if my best hope for a modest and reasonable wedding rests in *your* hands."

"Hey, *I'm* not the one who wants you to wear that insane Alexander McQueen creation that costs, like, five times my salary."

"That *wha*t creation?"

David had moved on.

"Although, for you, those shoes would be a non-starter. Especially with your bunions."

"I don't have bunions . . ."

"But, maybe she's right? Where would we be without our fantasies? It would take all the joy out of planning your nuptials."

"David?"

"Never mind . . . it's all above your pay grade, anyway. But as long as you're here," David opened a desk drawer and withdrew an envelope, "give these applications to Syd." He passed the envelope across the desk to her.

Maddie took it from him. "Applications for what?"

"Duh. *Marriage licenses*, nimrod. Fill those out and I'll pick them up from Syd."

"Do we really need to do these right now?"

"No time like the present—unless you're getting cold feet."

"No. That's not happening."

"I'm glad to hear it. That deposit on those damn doves is nonrefundable. So . . . what'd you want to see me about?"

Maddie's head was spinning. At least this aspect of what passed for David's . . . *normal* . . . was still firing on all cylinders.

"To tell the truth, I'm here because I've missed seeing you." It wasn't exactly a lie: she really *did* miss seeing him. And she knew she had to proceed gently. She didn't want to scare him off.

Clearly, David thought she was nuts.

"What are you talking about? You just saw me on Tuesday night."

"I mean seeing you *alone*. Just the two of us. Like we used to do."

"Oh." He looked a bit flustered. "I'm sorry about that. This job is a lot more onerous than I thought it would be. Who knew a small town like this had so many moving parts?"

"Not me."

"Trust me. I've been trying to organize the committee planning for the annual 'Dining With Friends' hospice benefit. These people are knuckle-draggers. None of them thinks my idea for a 'Last Supper' theme is appropriate. *Seriously?* All I can say is there's going to be a lot of competition for who gets the Judas place cards."

Maddie wasn't certain she'd heard him correctly. "Did you say *Last Supper?*"

David nodded. "Isn't it brilliant?"

Maddie shook her head. "And here I always thought Watson intentionally inflated the demands on his time as a means to advance his notion of self-importance."

She noticed the way David flinched when she mentioned Watson. But he didn't take her bait.

"It's no cake walk, that's for sure. And I find myself having to work a lot of overtime."

"I guess that's why you haven't been able to schedule your inquest interview yet?"

David colored. "What makes you say that?"

"Michael."

David abruptly got to his feet. "So he's crying to you now?"

"Cool your jets, Kemosabe. He's not *crying* to anyone. I asked him about it."

"Oh, really? Why didn't you ask *me* about it?"

"Maybe because you won't return my calls."

Her answer found its mark. David dropped dejectedly back into his chair. "Sorry . . ."

"What's going on with you, man?" Maddie's tone was gentle. "Something's not right. What is it?"

David lowered his head into his hands and stared back at her with a bleak expression. Maddie thought he was trying not to cry.

"You know we both love you," she continued. "You know we both believe in you. Why are you shutting us out?"

"I'm not . . . I just can't . . ."

The phone on his desk buzzed. David jolted upright and grabbed the receiver.

"What?" he barked. "I'm sorry, Mrs. Halsey. It's not you. I'm just in the middle of something. No, no. I haven't forgotten. I'm just on my way. Tell them I'll be right there."

He hung up. "I have a meeting. I have to go now, or I'll be late."

"David . . ."

"Just—just give me some space, okay? I need time to figure some things out." He stood up and tried to smile, but didn't really succeed. "I just . . . need some time. That's all."

He grabbed a notepad and hurried past her out of the office.

Maddie watched him go in dumb silence.

*That went well . . .*

Byron knew better than to think too much about what he was about to do. If he did, he knew he'd talk himself out of it.

But as much as he wanted to let Charlie handle her personal situation with Manfred Davis, he couldn't overlook what had happened on the bookmobile yesterday out in Bone Gap.

Syd had been concerned enough by the story Roma Jean related to her that she'd called Byron and asked him to stop by the library.

"I don't want to make more out of it than I should," she was quick to say. "But Roma Jean felt very threatened by his behavior—and that of the two women who were with him. And you also need to know that Roma Jean had Henry and Dorothy on the truck with her when this encounter happened."

That certainly got Byron's hackles up. Manfred's making vague allegations about two consenting adults was one thing—however offensive and inappropriate that behavior was. But intimidating two children who were in no position to stand up to him, or even to understand his threats and innuendos? That was not an action he could refuse to acknowledge.

He asked Syd if she knew who the women with Manfred Davis were. She said Roma Jean recognized Nelda Rae Black as one, but the other was unfamiliar to her.

"I think she said Mr. Davis called her Glenadine."

*Glenadine.*

Last night over dinner at Celine's, Byron had tried to tease information about the encounter out of Dorothy. She'd been conservative about the details she shared. He guessed that was probably in an effort to protect Roma Jean. It was true that Byron had had doubts in the past about the kids riding along with Roma Jean on her bookmobile routes. But there'd never been a real cause for concern until yesterday.

Dorothy said enough to confirm the gist of what Syd had shared. Manfred Davis and the two women *had* behaved in vaguely threatening ways toward Roma Jean, and Dorothy admitted they were all pretty scared until Roma Jean made them leave. She also told him that Henry, thankfully, had stayed out of sight in the cab area of the truck. Byron could tell by Celine's reaction to news of the encounter that she intended to discuss the incident further with Maddie and Syd.

When Byron went into his office on Sunday afternoon, he ran a report on Manfred Davis in Cheraw, South Carolina. It seemed that Davis had been living with a woman named Glenadine Langtree—at least, his vehicle was registered at her address. He supposed she was the woman who'd joined Manfred and Mrs. Black on their little mission trip yesterday.

Charlie had said her father was staying out at the Osborne Motel, so he drove there first. There was no sign of Davis or his

Buick. That probably meant he was still out at Bone Gap for church services.

Nelda Rae Black had been a full participant in the violence Manfred and the extended Black family had perpetuated on the young teens, Charlie and Jimmie, all those years ago. It was Nelda Rae who'd suggested shipping the girl, Jimmie, off to live with a half-crazed snake handler in Kentucky, in a pathetic bid to pray the gay out of her. More than once, Byron had had to fight an impulse to go and free the girl himself. When news reached Jericho that Jimmie had managed to run off, Byron said a silent prayer for the girl's safety and wrestled long and hard with his own feelings of guilt for not doing more to protect her.

Charlie had been moved into foster care for her own safety—eventually coming to live with Byron while she finished high school. And Manfred? Well, Byron had made sure Manfred would never be able to hurt the girl again.

It now appeared that "finding Christ" had somehow emboldened the man to try and reassert himself into Charlie's life. There wasn't much, legally, Byron could do to make the man stand down. But, damn if he wasn't determined to make it clear that continuing to threaten and intimidate a town librarian and two children would land him in hot water so deep, not even the Lord would be able to lift him out.

The drive to Bone Gap seemed longer today. He didn't reach the holy-roller church frequented by the Black clan until well after twelve-thirty. Most of the worshippers had already left. There were only two cars in the parking lot, and one of them was a 1996 Buick LeSabre with South Carolina tags.

*Out of date* South Carolina tags, he noted.

He parked his cruiser and went inside.

A man he assumed to be Manfred Davis was kneeling near the altar of the church, in prayer with a skinny woman he didn't recognize. Byron took a seat at the rear of the sanctuary and waited on them to finish.

It took a while. He could hear them both muttering and gurgling, making strange sounds that weren't quite words.

They were speaking in tongues . . . *of course. The secret language of zealots.*

Byron didn't have much use for religion, and charismatics topped his list of crazies. Especially the Nelda Rae Black brand of crazy, which gave the righteous permission to explode into the middle of every controversy with hefty doses of judgment and zero charity. In his experience, "true believers" like Manfred and his ilk blew in like late summer storms—maelstroms full of crashing thunder, violent wind and lashing rain. But they tended to blow themselves out, and move on just as quickly as they appeared.

He just hoped they'd wrap up their frenzy of devotion soon. It smelled powerfully of mildew in here. He didn't want his allergies to flare up.

After what felt like an eternity, the two people got to their feet and collected their belongings from the front pew. It didn't take them long to notice him seated at the back of the church. He could see the man's expression change as his recent surge of beatification drained from his face.

It was Manfred Davis, all right—looking for all the world like a refugee from some Flannery O'Connor story.

Byron got to his feet and strode forward to greet him.

"Manfred," he said. "It's been a long time."

Davis turned to his companion. "You go along, Glenadine. I'll be out directly." When the woman hesitated, Davis gave her a gentle shove. "You go along. I won't be talkin' to this feller for long."

Byron noted that Davis called him "feller," and not sheriff—his first hint that Manfred thought their power dynamic had shifted.

The woman named Glenadine pushed past Byron and disappeared up the aisle. She reminded Byron of a thinner clone of Frances Bavier, from *The Andy Griffith Show*. He'd never actually seen a woman *scurry* before.

Clearly, one of them was impressed by his uniform.

Once his companion was safely outside, Manfred addressed him.

"I got no business with you."

"I have to disagree with you, there, Manfred. I think we do have some things to discuss."

"I got the right to come and see my girl. I ain't done nothin' here but the Lord's business."

"Is that what you call your newest crusade, threatening and intimidating women and children? The Lord's business?"

He could detect some beads of sweat forming near Manfred's receding hairline.

"I ain't done nothin' wrong. I ain't broke no laws. You got no call to be out here pester'n me."

"Again, I have to disagree with you, Manfred." Byron folded his arms. "That's not what I hear from the people who were out here on the town bookmobile yesterday. They certainly felt like you were infringing on their rights—on public property."

"The onliest thing I did was to bear witness to God's holy Word."

"Let me be clear with you about something, Manfred. You want to share God's word; you go ahead and knock your self-righteous ass out. But you do it in *here*, where people come voluntarily to listen to whatever kind of toxic mess you're spreading. Do we understand each other? Because if I find out you've gone anywhere near Miss Freemantle, or either of those two children, with the intention of spewing your hatred and vitriol again?" Byron took a step closer to the smaller man. "I'll make sure there isn't enough of your sanctified ass left to bury."

Manfred's face had turned a bright shade of purple.

"You got no call to threaten me like this."

"Oh, you thought that was a threat?" Byron chuckled. "I

must not have done it right. It wasn't a threat, Manfred. It was a *promise*."

Byron turned on his heel and took his time exiting the church.

Glenadine was standing beside the Buick, glaring at him as he headed toward his cruiser.

He stopped to address her.

"Tell your friend he's got twenty-four hours to get this heap inspected, or I'll have it picked up and sold at public auction."

She didn't reply.

Byron got into his cruiser and pulled out of the small lot that was more dirt than gravel.

With luck, he'd make it to Celine's in time for lunch.

The notes wouldn't come out right. She played them over and over, just like she'd been taught, but each time they sounded worse and more discordant. She hit the keys with greater determination, but the more she tried, the worse the sound became. The metronome kept clicking faster and faster.

There were scents of bergamot and orange. Rose and jasmine.

*Vol de Nuit.* The Night Flight. Her mother's perfume.

Jacques Guerlain created the scent in Paris before the Nazis came. Her mother'd worn it since the '40s in London. Her mother's life was neatly divided into two periods: Before and After the Nazis.

Now Celine's life was divided into two periods: Before the Music, and After her Failure.

The notes were all wrong. She couldn't get the transitions right.

Her mother was behind her, tapping her shoulder in time with the metronome. Each tap was like a hammer's blow. Each blow drove home how poor her performance was. How great her betrayal had become.

Orris root and oak moss. Oranges and sandalwood. The metronome clicked faster. The notes would not come. The piano keys turned to liquid that flowed over her hands as her fingers fumbled to find the right notes.

A creature surged and undulated in the swirling deep beneath the keys. The contours of its menacing shape eluded her. The river of dissonance it inhabited turned blood red.

Amber and vanilla. The cloying scent filled her nose and clouded her eyes. The hammer blows came faster and faster.

A snarling dog burst free from the tide of blood that covered her hands. It growled and snapped at her.

It glowed orange in the fading light.

*Modulation. Modulation.*

Her mother's voice. Stern. Full of recrimination and sharp with its familiar tone of disappointment.

The orange dog bared its fangs.

The transitions were wrong. Her failure was now complete.

The dog lunged. She knew it would drag her with it beneath the river of blood.

*Orange and bergamot.* Her failure had been foretold before the Nazis came to take the music away.

She was sinking into a blood red river of lost hope. She screamed, but no one could save her. Her transitions were wrong.

She flailed against the flood.

Other hands took hold of her shoulders, gently shaking her. Lifting her up.

"Dr. Heller? Dr. Heller? Wake up . . ."

Her eyes opened. The room was dark, but she recognized the outline of Dorothy's face, hovering above hers at close range.

"You had a bad dream," Dorothy said. "I heard you screaming."

Celine struggled to sit up and tried to steady her breathing.

"I was screaming?" she asked in a shaky voice, unlike her own.

"Yes, ma'am." Dorothy timidly withdrew her hands. "I wanted to be sure you were okay."

Celine reached out to touch the girl's hand. "Thank you for coming to wake me. I'm sorry for scaring you."

"It's okay. I know what bad dreams are like."

*I'll just bet you do, young lady* . . . Celine leaned back against the headboard.

Dorothy had been kneeling on the edge of her bed, but she moved to stand up.

"Don't go." Celine was surprised by the urgency of her request.

"Okay." Dorothy seemed to take it in stride. "Do you want some hot tea or anything?"

"No. No, I think I'm okay now."

It was quiet in the room. The only sound came from the steady clicks of the second hand on Celine's small bedside clock. The porcelain relic had belonged to her Oma, and it had been one of the few possessions her mother carried with her when her parents secured her passage out of Austria on a *Kindertransport*, bound for London. *Before the Nazis came* . . .

"Stay with me a little while?" Celine asked shyly.

She could make out Dorothy's gentle nod.

Celine shifted to make room for the girl, and patted the mattress beside her.

Without a word, Dorothy joined her beneath the covers.

# Chapter Five

*Recorded Interview*
*Preliminary Inquest Investigation*
*Death of Mayor Gerald Watson*

"Bertrand Lear Townsend, Jr. Twenty-two letters. Born on seven fifteen."

*Seven plus fifteen equals twenty-two.*

"Year 1984."

*One plus nine plus eight plus four equals twenty-two.*

"Twenty-two is the smallest number expressed by combining two primes. Two elevens make twenty-two. Twenty-two isn't phi, but twenty-two is right."

*Little phi is what happens when the numbers go less than zero. Less than zero isn't right.*

"Jericho is less than zero. Jericho is little phi. Little phi isn't right. Jericho's golden ratio is broken."

*The bad man was an orange dog. He was supposed to protect Goldenrod but he didn't. He broke the ratio.*

"The orange dog hurt Goldenrod. The orange dog comes at night."

*The bad man won't be gone until the golden ratio is restored.*

"Goldenrod can't transition from major to minor. Her ratio

is broken. The music doesn't work. The orange dog comes for her at night."

*The orange dogs broke God's covenant. They were supposed to protect their children but they didn't.*

"The sins of the fathers are visited upon the children. The stones of their covenants are broken. The ratios aren't right."

*The tablets aren't whole. God's covenant is broken. No one protected the children from the orange dogs.*

"The stones are broken. The temple veil is torn in two."

*The orange dogs are dead but they aren't gone. The orange dogs come for them at night.*

"The Golden Ratio is God's covenant with man. The orange dogs broke the ratio."

*The orange dogs won't be gone until the golden ratio is restored.*

"The orange dogs broke God's covenant."

*The orange dogs come at night—for all of them.*

Maddie stopped by the library on Monday night to give Syd a lift home. They'd dropped Syd's Volvo off at Junior's that morning because it was due an oil change and a state inspection. Junior was backed up, and apologized for needing to keep the car overnight. Al Hawkes was still using his loaner car, too, so he couldn't offer Syd the use of it. Syd told him not to worry at all and to keep the car as long as he needed.

He thanked her profusely and said he guessed he should head back into the garage to finish pulling the dent out of the hood on Cletus Freemantle's old Caprice.

"What happened to it?" Syd asked.

"Seems like that Roma Jean figured out some way to T-bone a can of peaches." Junior scratched his scalp beneath his SKOAL hat. "That Freemantle gal pretty much keeps me in business."

Syd considered asking for more details, but realized she

really didn't need any.

For her part, Syd enjoyed the chance to ride to and from work with Maddie. They didn't get very many opportunities to talk freely, unless it was late at night or just before bed. Henry was always within earshot—and that's the way they liked it. One or the other of them would invariably be engaged with him, working on his homework assignments or accompanying him on his regular circuit to feed all the animals he'd amassed since coming to live at the farm. But tonight, Henry was having dinner with Dorothy and his beloved Gramma C. So Syd was treating Maddie to a date night dinner at Waffle House.

That prospect probably accounted for Maddie's good mood when she entered the library promptly at five o'clock.

"You're nice and early," Syd called out after she heard Maddie enter the library through the back entrance.

Maddie joined her behind the circulation desk. "How'd you know it was me?"

"I heard you humming."

"I was humming?"

Syd nodded. "*Clair de Lune*. Not a bad rendition, either."

"Guess I had Mom on my mind." Maddie looked around the small space. "Everybody gone?"

"Pretty much. Mondays are usually slow." Syd was tidying up and filing a stack of little checkout cards.

"Then I'd better make hay while the sun shines." Maddie kissed her. Then did it a second time for good measure.

"You're in a good mood."

"Why wouldn't I be? I've got a dinner date with a sexy librarian."

"Awwww. You say the sweetest things when you know there's a hash brown bowl in your future."

Maddie pinched her on the butt. "One hot dish deserves another."

"You know, the quicker you quit messing with me, the

quicker we can get out of here."

"Okay, okay. Want me to go lock up the street door?"

Syd handed her the keys. "Yes, please."

Maddie dutifully locked the door and switched the sign around to read "CLOSED." Syd noticed her stop on her way back to examine something on a table.

"Where'd these come from?" She held one of the items up.

"Where'd *what* come from?"

"These." Maddie examined the pamphlet. "It's . . . a religious tract. Several of them, in fact—on a table here in the children's section." She rejoined Syd at the front desk and handed one of the printed brochures to her.

Syd grimaced as she looked it over. The cover of the tract featured a graphic, luridly colored cartoon illustration of tormented souls writhing in what she guessed was a depiction of hell. *Where Will You Spend Eternity?* the title inquired.

"Oh, *great*. And there was a second grade class in here today for story time. I wonder how many of the kids saw this thing?"

"Hopefully not many. Where's it from?"

Syd turned it over. A name was stamped in faded blue ink in an open space at the bottom of the page.

*Full Gospel Tabernacle, Bone Gap, Va. "Except a man be born of water and of the Spirit, he cannot enter into the kingdom of God." John 3:5*

She showed it to Maddie. "Color me surprised—not."

"What is *up* with those people?"

"I think we can guess. Especially after what Roma Jean shared about her encounter with Charlie's father on Saturday. I guess they wanted to leave a handy little reminder for her here, too."

Maddie was still looking the tract over. "Probably not just for her, Syd."

"You're right. We're on the same highway to hell along with the rest of the town apostates."

Maddie crushed the folded paper. "Do you think it's time for me to pay a call on our friend, Mrs. Black?"

"No, I do not. We need to let Byron handle this. He said he would. Let's give him the chance to do it."

Maddie sighed. "Against my better judgment, I defer to your suggestion."

"Good. Now throw those things away and let's get out of here. I'm starving."

"Okay." Maddie crossed the room to toss the tracts into the recycle bin beside the copier. Syd's heart sank when she saw her detour and pause to examine the control screen on the front of the machine. "Why is this thing blinking red?"

*Oh, god . . . now we'll be in here all night . . .*

"It's nothing. I'll fix it in the morning."

"Syd . . ."

"It's probably the fuser. It's been on its last legs for more than a week now."

"Do you have another one?"

"Someplace."

Maddie was opening the front panel of the machine. "Do you want to get it for me?"

"Maddie . . . could we please not do this right now?"

"Honey, it'll only take ten minutes."

"That's what you said the *last* time," she whined, "and we were stuck in here for more than two hours." She consulted her watch. "We have to pick Henry up at seven-thirty."

"We have plenty of time—and that *wasn't* the fuser last time. Fusers are easy."

Syd knew it was a losing battle. She retreated to her office and located the box containing a replacement fuser. By the time she'd returned, Maddie had already removed the offending part. Syd handed the new cartridge to her.

"Someday you'll have to explain this obsession you have to fix broken stuff."

"You mean like people?" Maddie was removing the safety wrapper from the replacement fuser. "It's not an obsession; it's part of being an MD."

"No. The *people* part of the equation I get. It's the *inanimate* stuff I don't understand."

"I like to feel useful."

"Honey, believe me when I tell you that you have *all kinds* of enviable skills that make you *beyond* useful to me. Fixing photocopiers is not among them."

Maddie snapped the fuser into place and proceeded to close up the rest of the access panels on the unit.

"*Voila*. Good as new." She turned the machine back on and waited while it cycled through its startup screens. Blissfully, a bright green READY message finally displayed. She beamed at Syd. "My work here is through."

"Thank you." Syd took the discarded part from her. "In exchange for the grace I just exhibited by enduring this repair interlude, I should be entitled to some kind of special perk. Don't you think?"

"That depends." Maddie gave her a lewd smile. "What'd you have in mind?"

"Oh, not *that*. I usually get that without having to sacrifice anything. I was thinking of something . . . more immediate."

"Immediate?" Maddie sounded suspicious.

"Uh huh. I think you should let *me* order dinner for you."

Maddie's face fell. "Oh, come *on*, Syd . . ."

"Buck up, buttercup." It was Syd's turn to pinch Maddie on the butt. "It'll be an adventure."

Maddie's grousing about her impending culinary disappointment continued until they were seated at Waffle House.

Coralee Minor brought their cups of decaf and asked if they

each wanted their usual.

"Not tonight, Coralee." Syd managed to cut Maddie off. "We're going to mix it up."

"You are?" Coralee shot an inquiring look at Maddie, who was all but pouting on her side of the table. "Okay. I'll leave these menus with you, then. Gimme a holler when you know what you want."

After Coralee retreated, Syd hissed at Maddie. "Stop acting like a five-year-old and tell me about Celine taking Dorothy to New York."

Maddie looked longingly at the color photos of hash browns and steaming bowls of Bert's Chili on her menu before sighing and pushing it away.

"That's pretty much it. She said there's a great concert scheduled at Carnegie Hall next weekend—some pianist who I gather is a true proficient, as Mom comprehends the term. She wants to expose Dorothy to this higher caliber of performance."

"Really? Do you remember the name of the pianist?"

"Um…" Maddie thought about it. "It's something Japanese … Mitsuko somebody?"

"Mitsuko Uchida?"

"That's it. Mom said she was best known for Mozart, but was branching out into Beethoven."

"Well, your mom is right: she's an incredible talent. It's a fantastic opportunity for Dorothy."

"I agree. As long as it's something Dorothy is interested in doing."

"Don't you think she would be?"

"I honestly have no idea. And I'm not persuaded Mom does, either."

This was surprising new territory. Maddie had never hinted at anything like this previously. Syd wondered how long she'd been ruminating about this.

"What are you getting at, Maddie?"

"It's nothing, really. Just something I've thought about since Dorothy started staying out there with Mom."

Coralee wandered by with the coffee pot. "Anybody ready for a refill?"

Maddie pushed her mug toward her. "I'll take some."

Syd followed suit. "I might as well, too, since you're here."

After Coralee had topped them off, she asked if they'd had time to look over the menu.

Maddie's exaggerated pout was enough to melt Syd's veneer of determination.

"Oh, for crying out loud." She snapped up their menus and handed them to Coralee. "Just bring us our damn usuals."

Coralee and Maddie shared conspiratorial smiles.

"I'll have those right up," Coralee promised, before hightailing it back to the grill area.

"You really are impossible."

"I know." Maddie gave her one of her most dazzling smiles. "But you love me, right?"

In truth, it was hard for Syd to do little else when Maddie looked at her that way.

"You're just lucky you're so damn gorgeous. So, quit flirting and tell me what you meant about your mom and Dorothy."

"Okay. For starters, you know how happy it makes me that Mom has taken Dorothy in the way she has, right?"

Syd nodded. "Of course."

"So it has nothing to do with that. I honestly think the two of them are insanely well matched. It's almost like they complete each other in some surreal way. And Dorothy's talent for the piano is . . . well, it's pretty extraordinary. We all admit that. I can see why Mom is so over the moon about teaching her—*and* jumping at the opportunity to finally have a chance to share her own great gift with such a willing recipient. Lord knows I was never all that receptive, no matter how hard she tried to get me to focus. Sadly, the same goes for Henry."

Syd laughed. "You're right about that. To Henry, even sitting down to practice scales is tantamount to Chinese water torture."

Maddie smiled. "He comes by that honestly."

"Now you sound like Celine."

"I know I do. I didn't fall too far from the tree, either. Even though I fear I disappointed Mom in the same ways she thinks she disappointed her parents."

"I don't think Celine shares that view, at all. She's proud of you and the life you've made for yourself."

"I suppose." Maddie considered Syd's suggestion. "I guess I have my own damage when it comes to wanting to rewrite the past."

"You and Celine have made incredible strides repairing your relationship. I don't think she believes you have any rewriting to do where she is concerned."

Maddie had picked up her teaspoon and had been obsessively turning it end over end. "I hope not."

Syd reached out to still her hand. "Maddie?"

Maddie looked up at her.

"You don't need to rewrite your past. I promise."

Maddie laid the spoon down. "I just don't want Mom to make the mistake of thinking Dorothy can rewrite *hers*."

"If you think there's a chance she might, then maybe you should consider asking her about it."

"Yeah." Maddie sat back and folded her arms. "I hate this kind of stuff."

"I know. It sucks you're so damn good at it."

She could tell Maddie was gearing up to argue the point. But before she could get very far, Coralee arrived with her hash brown bowl, and Maddie suddenly had a more urgent—and welcome—task to undertake.

—w— —w— —w—

Dinner at Gramma C's was always one of Henry's favorite things to do.

*As long as Gramma C. didn't make him sit down for a piano lesson . . .*

Buddy was at Gramma C's when Henry and Dorothy got off the school bus. Henry was excited to see him because they hadn't had very many chances to hang out together since school started. After he and Dorothy did their homework at Gramma C's kitchen table, she told them they could go outside and keep Buddy company while he worked in her garden. Henry was excited to go because he loved helping Buddy. But Dorothy wanted to stay inside and practice the piano.

Gramma C. gave him a big glass of iced tea to take to Buddy, since it was so hot in the sun. Henry carried it very slowly so he didn't spill any on the walk from the house.

Gramma C. really liked Buddy, and that made Henry happy. Not a lot of people were patient enough to try to understand the special way Buddy talked about things—and sometimes, they were mean to him. He knew Dorothy's daddy had been that way. But Dorothy had always had a special friendship with Buddy. She told Henry once that Buddy always tried to look after her—just like Maddie and Syd always looked after him.

*Even though* his *daddy had never been mean to him, or to anybody else.*

Henry knew Dorothy was sad that her daddy was gone, but he was glad that Dorothy didn't have to be afraid of him anymore. But it worried him that Dorothy said she was responsible for what had happened to him on the 4th of July. Henry didn't really understand what everyone was so upset about. He knew that Mr. Watson had drowned in the river, and that not everyone was as sorry as Dorothy was that he was gone.

Henry imagined how sad he'd be if his daddy had drowned. But he didn't know why Dorothy felt like it had been her fault, and he was afraid to ask her about it. She got kind of strange whenever he brought it up, and he didn't want to upset her or make her feel worse.

*People were hard to figure out sometimes.*

Buddy said once that Dorothy had the thumbprint of God on her head, and that her daddy had messed up her numbers.

Numbers mattered more to Buddy than anything. But Henry didn't understand what Buddy meant when he kept talking about things like "little phi" and "golden ratios." That sounded a lot like math problems that were way beyond what he was learning in school. He barely understood multiplication tables. And he mostly only got *those* right because he memorized the answers—not because the ways they worked out made sense to him. He didn't see patterns the way Buddy did. Buddy saw patterns in everything.

Even the garden rows he was planting.

Buddy showed him how to count them: one, one, two, three, five, seven, eleven.

Buddy said the rows made a sequence that was part of something called a "golden ratio." He said the golden ratio was what Dorothy was missing—only Buddy called Dorothy "Goldenrod." That's when he told Henry about the golden dog that was supposed to protect the children—and how the orange dog tried to hurt them instead.

Henry wondered if orange dogs were like stink bugs. Syd said the stink bugs were especially bad this year, and they were eating the vegetables in their garden at home. He remembered her talking with Maddie about spraying for stink bugs and orange dogs, and some other kind of caterpillar.

*But he didn't think anybody would ever use stink bugs to look after children . . . not even old gods like Zeus.*

Henry carried sprinkler cans full of water for Buddy to use

on the new plants. Buddy said Gramma C. would have kale and collard greens before Thanksgiving this year, because the first frost would come late. Henry didn't really like kale, but he knew Syd did. She liked to put it into smoothies she made for Maddie. One time, he saw Maddie dump one out behind the barn, but when she noticed him watching her, she told him it was *entre nous*.

He didn't much care for collards, either. Uncle David told him they were better with lots of vinegar, but Henry thought that idea was even more gross than eating them plain. He liked peas a whole lot better.

"When will these peas be ripe, Buddy?" He gently touched the tiny plants.

"Peas take seventy to eighty days, Bluebird. Peas will come before the Beaver Moon."

"What's a beaver moon?"

"The earth has imperfect alignment. The earth blocks the sun and the moon is a shadow."

Henry thought that didn't sound too good. "Is that a bad thing?"

"A Beaver Moon means imperfect alignment. It hides the light and makes shadows in the middle of the day."

"But we'll still get peas first, right?"

"Peas take seventy to eighty days, Bluebird."

Henry counted. That meant Gramma C. would have peas before Christmas.

He'd ask her about beaver moons later . . .

He wondered if Buddy would grow flowers for Maddie and Syd's wedding. Uncle David said they'd need a lot—way more than the florist in town could supply. He had showed Syd some plans for big white archways that were covered in fussy white flowers.

"I think we should have a series of these trellises," he explained. "One for each year you've been together. You can progress though them while the chamber ensemble plays whatever tiresome extended voluntary thing you decide on. It'll be sensational. The twelve bridesmaids will precede you in rows of two. I'm estimating we'll need sixty to a hundred dozen lilies."

"That's a lot of lilies," Syd said.

"That's why it's good we're planning ahead."

Uncle David rolled up the plans and handed them to Syd. "Keep these someplace safe from prying eyes. I don't want her head to explode if she sees this."

After Uncle David had left, Syd asked Henry to keep the flower thing *entre nous*.

It was getting harder for him to keep all the *entre nous* stuff straight. There was a whole lot of it going on these days.

Gramma C. called out to Henry from the patio, saying it was time for supper. She told Buddy to come along inside, too.

Buddy dropped his spade and wiped his hands on his trousers.

Henry took hold of his hand, and led him toward the house. It made him happy that Buddy held on to him like it was the most normal thing in the world.

Their conversation was going no place in a hurry.

But that wasn't unusual. Not when it involved Tom, and something he wanted passionately.

Lizzy was growing tired of beating her head against a wall. They'd planned to meet up for dinner tonight to hash some things out, but Tom had called to tell her he'd been held up . . . again. He hadn't been back to Jericho since he'd dropped the bomb about the job in Colorado on her last Wednesday night.

She didn't really think that was an accident. She knew Tom well enough to understand that the more he put her off, the further he could advance his plans, making it that much harder for her to raise objections that would get in the way of what he wanted.

When she tried to tell him that, he bowed-up, which also was a vintage defensive response of his.

"Why do you always have to accuse me of doing something underhanded? I'm not looking for reasons to avoid talking about any of this with you."

"Oh really? Then why have you been unable to follow through on any of our plans to do precisely that?"

"It hasn't been *that* long. You're over-dramatizing everything."

"Tom, I'm not doing that—and you know it as well as I do. If you really cared about my opinion, you'd make time to listen to it."

"I already *know* what your opinion is."

Lizzy couldn't mistake the contempt and frustration in his voice. She tried to moderate her own tone.

"I was surprised to learn that you haven't talked with your sister about any of this yet. When were you planning to tell her?"

"Why would I involve her? She'll just take your side."

Lizzy closed her eyes. "Nobody's taking sides, Tom."

"Oh, yeah? That'll be a first. They just want you to stay there so you keep working at that clinic for free."

"What are you talking about? I don't work for *free*. The grant pays me."

"That's the grant that's running out in . . . what? Four months? What happens to your job then?"

"If you'd cared enough to discuss any of this with me, I'd have told you that Maddie offered me a permanent position. A partnership in her clinic."

There was silence on the line. Lizzy knew Tom hadn't expected that outcome any more than she had.

"Did you hear what I said?" she asked.

"Yeah. I heard you. I suppose you want to take it?"

"I at least owe it to her to consider the offer seriously."

"More than you'll consider my offer seriously?"

"Seriously, Tom? I think I can walk and chew gum at the same time."

"What the hell is that supposed to mean?"

"It means I'm more than capable of thinking about the benefits of each possibility, simultaneously."

"Benefits?" he scoffed. "Why do you make it sound like moving to Colorado with me is nothing more than a business proposition?"

"Maybe because you've never presented the prospect to me in any way that casts this as more than a convenient arrangement for you. You've certainly never bothered to suggest it would signify anything more important in our relationship than ready access to great skiing."

"You're talking about marriage again, aren't you? I told you I wanted to defer that for some time down the road, after I'm established in a career, and have a handle on paying down my grad school loans."

"You. You. *You.*" Lizzy's frustration with his mental myopia was boiling over. "Everything is always about *you*. What *you* want. What's in *your* best interest. Where you see *yourself* in five years or in ten years. It's never about anything associated with *me*, or with what I want—with what I *need*. With how I see my own career prospects advancing and taking shape. As hard as it is to admit, I think we've reached a crossroads, Tom. Maybe even an impasse. You want what you want, and I'm not sure what you've decided is right for me."

"So that's it? That's where we are? You won't even think about going with me?"

Lizzy gazed at the wall across from her desk, but she didn't focus on anything. Not her framed diplomas. Not the bulletin board covered with notes and thank-you cards from her patients. Not the oil painting of a spring meadow on Mt. Rogers that Maddie and Syd had given her for her birthday last year. Not the chair that held the laundry bag containing her dirty scrubs. Not on any of it. Right then, her focus was entirely on the finality of the step she knew she was about to take.

"No, Tom," she told him. "No, I don't want to move to Colorado. I want to stay here, where my heart is, doing the work I love."

Tom took his time to respond to her honest declaration.

"My mistake. All this time, I thought your heart was with me."

"Like I said," she repeated sadly. "I know how to walk and chew gum at the same time."

"Go ahead. Be glib about this. What you're telling me is that we're breaking up."

Lizzy was aware of the churning in her stomach. But she knew his assessment, for once, was accurate.

"Yes," she told him. "I guess that's what I'm saying."

She didn't know whether she most wanted him to fight to keep her—or to accept her simple statement and agree they should go their separate ways.

She didn't have long to wait for him to decide.

He hung up on her.

Lizzy wanted to hurl the phone across the room, but she didn't. What would the point of that be? Tom was doing nothing but behaving in an entirely consistent fashion. She'd been so blinded by her fear and loneliness after her miscarriage, she'd thrown herself back into the same spiral that had always defined her relationship with him. Yes. Their sexual relationship had always been gratifying. Yes. He was good-looking and genial and a lot of fun at parties. Yes. She adored his family. Yes. She willed herself to believe his reason for going to veterinary school was because he had a passion for the welfare of animals, rather than the more cynical view of the profession serving as an express train to financial success.

She'd deluded herself consistently about Tom because she cared more about being with someone, no matter the compromises she had to make to do it, than about living as her authentic self.

It was a ridiculous and embarrassing admission to have to make. After all . . . she was thirty-two years old, not eighty-five. Why had she been so persuaded that Tom represented her last off-ramp on the highway to spinsterhood and a miserable life shared only with a couple dozen cats?

She didn't even *like* cats. Maddie had already tried, repeatedly, to get her to take the tuxedo cat, Rosebud, off her hands.

Lizzy stayed seated in her chair and tried to take an inventory of how she felt.

Her stomach had mostly stopped its churning. The headache she was certain had been coming on had subsided. Her respiration had returned to normal. She held out her hands and examined them. They were steady.

She actually felt . . . okay.

She knew better than to think she wouldn't wrestle with her share of *bête noire*. Sleepless nights were guaranteed. She'd have to fight her worst impulses to rethink her decision. But for now, she felt calmer about it all. Even relieved.

*And hungry . . .*

It was nearly six. Maybe she'd stop by Aunt Bea's and grab something quick for dinner so she wouldn't have to cook when she got home?

She picked up her bag of laundry and switched off the lights in her office. That's when she noticed a light shining from the office Maddie had been fixing up for Avi. She hadn't heard anyone come in since Maddie and Peggy had left for the day, so she just assumed one of them had forgotten to turn off the lights in there.

She made a detour to duck into the office, and was surprised to see Avi, unpacking books from a couple of boxes. Avi looked up when Lizzy appeared in the doorway.

"Hey, there. I heard you on the phone when I came in, so I didn't want to interrupt you." She held up the books in her hands. "I just wanted to offload these before I headed back to Roanoke to get another load."

"No worries." Lizzy held up a hand. "I hope I didn't disturb you."

In fact, Lizzy was praying that Avi hadn't overheard any of her conversation.

"Nope. I was more concerned about scaring the crap out of you once you realized somebody else was in the building. I mean . . ." Avi lowered her eyes to Lizzy's laundry bag. "You could be packing. I've heard rumors about this community's fondness for the second amendment."

Lizzy smiled. "The way my day is going, it might be something worth considering."

"I didn't want to ask."

"I suppose that means you overheard some of my phone conversation?"

"To be honest?" Avi looked uncomfortable. "Not very much. Just enough to know it was private. I promise I didn't eavesdrop."

"Don't worry. It won't be private for long."

Avi gestured toward a chair. "Why don't you sit down for a minute?"

"I don't want to hold you up," Lizzy replied. "You said you were heading back to Roanoke."

"I am." Avi claimed a seat on the small sofa. "But not until the morning."

Lizzy noted with irony that the only sofa in the clinic had been moved into Avi's office from the waiting room. *Tools of the trade, I guess.*

"Okay, then." Lizzy dropped into a chair. "But only for a minute. I don't want to keep you from unpacking."

"Right. Because unloading a couple boxes of hopelessly out-of-date psych textbooks will easily eat up my entire evening."

"I guess claiming a seat on the sofa is your way to demonstrate that I'm not a client . . . yet?"

"Oh, it's far less complicated than that. It was actually an act of selfishness: the sofa is way more comfortable than that chair. Besides, most of my 'clients' prefer to sit on the floor."

"Ah. That explains the box of toys."

"Yeah. Although, sometimes I play with them myself."

"Which are your favorites?" Lizzy had no idea why she was rambling on the way she was. She was keenly aware that she was sitting in a shrink's office, and it was making her more than a little uncomfortable.

Avi appeared to notice. "Do you really care about the toys?"

Lizzy shook her head.

"Relax, Nurse Mayes. I'm not here to analyze you."

"You're not?"

"Not unless you want me to."

"Can I take a rain check on that?"

"Of course. But how about I give you an unvarnished opinion for free?"

It was an intriguing idea. "Okay. Go ahead."

Avi crossed her legs. Lizzy noticed her bare legs. But then, she tended to notice most things about Avi's eclectic appearance. *Was it eclectic?* Or did it simply stand out in a provincial place like Jericho?

"I'll need a few more details first. That is," Avi added, "if you're comfortable sharing them."

"And if I'm not?"

"Then I'll hold my tongue. And I'll have you know that perfecting an ability to do *that* consumes about 80 percent of the curriculum in psychology."

"I fear you won't get to regale me with your hard-earned proficiency this time. It's all pretty simple: I just ended my relationship with Tom."

"Oh." The way Avi said the word suggested she hadn't been prepared for Lizzy's directness. She seemed to choose her next words carefully. "And . . . am I sorry about this?"

It was a curious way to ask how Lizzy felt about her actions. At least, she thought that's what Avi was asking . . .

"I don't know about *you*," she replied. "But I don't think *I* am. Well . . . maybe 'happy' is just too much of a stretch right now. But I do think I feel relieved."

"Relieved that you made the *right* decision, or relieved that you made *a* decision?"

Lizzy gave her a nervous smile. "Yes?"

Avi laughed. "You're gonna be fine."

"Is that the unvarnished opinion?"

"Yep."

"Wow. That was sure painless. I thought clarity was a more protracted process."

"Normally, it is. But it's late and, as we've established, you're not my patient."

"No. Although maybe I should consider it."

"Too late."

"Why?"

"Well," Avi fixed her with a steady gaze, "we're already friends, and that immediately negates any kind of therapeutic relationship. And even if it weren't unethical, it wouldn't be something I'd be advised to undertake with you."

Lizzy found Avi's reasoning a bit circular. *But maybe that was just a shrink thing?*

"Why not?" she asked.

Avi gave her a curious look. "Aren't *we* just a busy little hive of curiosity this evening."

"*You* introduced the exception. I'm just following up."

"Fair enough. Okay. Let's just say there'd be impediments to my ability to be impartial. And that obstacle would benefit neither of us."

Lizzy felt a nervous surge of . . . *something*. She couldn't identify the source of her reaction, but it was unsettling, nevertheless.

'I guess I'm not sure what that means."

"It's okay. I'm not sure I know, either."

Lizzy decided to change the subject. She'd dallied here long enough.

"So, I need to get going." She got to her feet and hefted her laundry bag. "The washing machine awaits."

Avi stood up, too. "Ah, yes. The old dirty laundry sequitur."

Lizzy smiled. "Don't you mean *non*-sequitur?"

"I was giving you the benefit of the doubt."

"Thanks. I appreciate it." Lizzy headed for the door.

"Um—" Avi stopped her. "Have you had any dinner yet?"

"No. I was gonna stop and grab something on the way home." She slung her laundry bag over her shoulder. "Folding clothes always gives me the munchies."

"Yeah. Me, too. Too bad I can never manage to fold my pants without getting a double crease."

"I think your pants look just *fine*."

Avi didn't reply right away but she smiled. Lizzy felt like an idiot.

"Would you like to join me?" she asked, quickly—mostly to cover her embarrassment.

"In fact, I'd love to." Avi retrieved her keys and messenger bag. "What do you feel like?"

"I was just going to pick something up at Aunt Bea's. But I can be flexible. Do you prefer grab-n-go, or sit down?"

"I *always* prefer sit down. Especially when I'm dining with a fellow compatriot in the relationship wars."

"You, too?" Lizzy asked. "It must be going around. And am I sorry?"

"*Touché*." Avi noticed her irony. "No. It would appear you're not the only wayfaring traveler declining to take a ride on the midnight train to Georgia."

"Woo, woooo," Lizzy sang. "Come on, Gladys. I'm driving."

Avi snapped off the lights and followed her to the parking lot.

—\~\~— —\~\~— —\~\~—

After dinner, Buddy thanked "Quiet Lady," as he always called her, and left on his little scooter just before Maddie and Syd arrived to get Henry. Henry complained about having to leave so early, but Syd reminded him that he had a math test in the morning, and they needed to work on fractions.

Henry was even less happy about having to go home and practice math problems until Syd suggested they could use a slice of leftover apple cake as a means to make sense of dividing things into equal parts.

His energy for the exercise picked up right away.

After they'd departed, Celine and Dorothy set about washing dishes and restoring order in the kitchen. It amused Celine that Dorothy seemed to be as committed to tidiness as she was. She'd noted with pleasure the way Dorothy meticulously made her bed every morning, and always took care to clear away the mixing bowl and baking sheet on mornings she made sweet biscuits before school.

Dorothy was quieter than usual this evening. Celine worried that maybe she felt awkward or uncomfortable after rousing her from her bad dream the night before.

*Bad dream?* That was too benign a term for the nightmare she'd had. It wasn't that Celine had never had bad dreams about her mother before: she'd had scores of them since her mother's passing, decades ago. And those dreams invariably involved common motifs: searing feelings of failure and disappointment being chief among them.

The aftermath of Dorothy's having gently shaken her awake last night had led to an uncharacteristic bout of intimacy that seemed, at least to Celine, to temporarily shift the power dynamic between them. As they'd sat together beneath the covers in Celine's dark bedroom, they talked about ordinary things: the progress Buddy was making planting the autumn garden, the prospects for more rain later in the week, and even details about the new book Dorothy had been reading. Eventually, they both fell quiet, and Dorothy drifted off to sleep. But Celine stayed awake, keeping a silent vigil while the girl slept. She wondered how long it had been since anyone had watched over Dorothy in a safe and caretaking way.

*She supposed it had been a very long while.*

When she awoke in the morning, Dorothy had already left her room. Celine could hear her in the kitchen, making their breakfast. The oven timer dinged and the teakettle began to whistle.

Normalcy had been restored.

Dorothy had said very little during dinner tonight. But that could've been because Henry had chattered nonstop throughout most of the meal, asking Buddy endless questions about vegetable plants and garden pests, before shifting gears and asking Celine to explain what a beaver moon was.

Celine finally decided it was better to talk about their unusual interaction last night, rather than ignore it. She didn't want to adopt a posture that would reinforce any notion the girl might have that Celine would rather forget about last night.

She'd done that same thing too often with her own daughter, with the unhappy result that Maddie grew up thinking her mother was determinedly cold and distant—or worse: emotionally unavailable to her. It had taken the two of them years to recover from Celine's mistakes and repair their relationship.

She was determined not to repeat the same mistakes now.

"I want to thank you, Dorothy, for taking such good care of me last night. I hope I didn't scare you too badly."

Dorothy was carefully folding her dishtowel into thirds—another proclivity they shared.

"I was a little scared when I first heard you," she admitted. "But I figured out right away that it was a bad dream."

"I suppose you've had your share of those, too?" Celine asked.

Dorothy nodded. "I still do a lot of nights. But I don't make very much noise. I had to learn not to do that."

Celine wanted to wrap the girl in her arms and rage at the heavens to please take her demons away.

"I'm sorry you ever had to worry about that. We can't control our dreams."

"No," Dorothy agreed. "We can't control very much that happens when we're awake, either."

"Sometimes it feels like that. But if we're open to it, we can try things that might lead us toward a different path—to a place where we can have more control."

"Is that what you did?"

Dorothy's question found its target with laser-like precision. Celine nearly staggered backward from its impact.

"Yes. I suppose it is. I had a serious injury several years ago—one I sustained in a laboratory accident. I nearly didn't survive. It gave me a lot of time to think about the choices I'd made in my life. And even more time to think about the choices I'd *never* made—the ones I avoided and allowed time to make for me."

"Do you want some tea?"

Dorothy's question seemed to come out of nowhere. But Celine nodded, and claimed a seat on one of the metal stools beside the kitchen island. She watched the girl's methodical actions as Dorothy selected two cups from a cabinet, filled the kettle, and put the water on to boil. This was a ritual of theirs. Something they did most nights before retiring to their separate spaces in the house.

Once again, Dorothy had done what she did: found a way to defuse the emotion that had been building up between them.

*She's doing this to give us both some breathing space. She wants to make this easier for me, even though my job is to make things easier for her.*

"Lemon Zinger or peppermint?" Dorothy asked.

"Peppermint, I think."

Dorothy extracted two teabags from a tin on the counter before joining Celine at the island.

"I wonder how you would feel about talking with someone about these possibilities, Dorothy?"

Dorothy looked at her with an expression that was only slightly wary.

"Talking with who?"

"You remember meeting Maddie's friend, Avi, don't you? At dinner on Friday night?"

Dorothy nodded, but made no other comment.

"Avi helps people sort through their confusion. She can be a very good person to talk with about . . ." she nearly said *orange dogs*, but stopped herself in time. "Things."

"She's a doctor, isn't she? Like you and Dr. Stevenson?"

"Yes. She is. But she's a different kind of doctor. Avi is a doctor who helps heal wounds that aren't visible on the outside." This time, she decided it *was* okay to channel Buddy. "The kind that sometimes come for us at night."

Dorothy seemed to consider what Celine had said. She met her eyes.

"Okay. I will if you want me to." Her tone gave nothing away.

"It matters more that *you* want to do it, Dorothy. I would never push you into anything."

"Not even . . ." Dorothy stopped herself. "She seemed pretty nice. And funny, too. I guess I could talk with her."

Celine gave her a small smile. "I promise if you decide it's not right for you, you don't have to do it again."

The teakettle began to whistle. Dorothy started to get up but Celine stopped her.

"My turn. I'll fix these and meet you in the living room. Maybe we can watch some *Cutthroat Kitchen*?"

Celine knew the show was one of Dorothy's favorites. The

format featured guest chefs who were hit with epic sabotages by their competitors in a mad race to create the best dish.

*Celine found its parallels to life impossible to miss . . .*

Dorothy brightened right up.

"I'll go turn on the TV."

Roma Jean and Charlie were sitting on the couch. Normally, Roma Jean was smart enough to know that if they did that, it would inevitably end up in the same place—Charlie's bedroom. But tonight was different. Tonight Charlie had invited her over so she could explain why she'd been so upset about her father showing up the way he'd done the other night.

Charlie was taking her time getting it out. Roma Jean didn't want to rush her. She'd always known there was some kind of story behind why Charlie had ended up living with Sheriff Martin through high school. But nobody ever talked about it in any way that wasn't vague and full of innuendo.

*Innuendo* seemed to be the dominant way people in this town talked about anything that hinted at bad or inappropriate happenings. Syd's revelation that Charlie's father had hurt her bad enough to land her in the hospital had really upset Roma Jean. It made no sense to her that people could be as mean as they'd been to Charlie—and to Dorothy. In Dorothy's case, at least, her father had gone away—*permanently.* Even though the circumstances were maybe not the best. Roma Jean knew a lot people, including her parents, thought Mr. Watson had been murdered. There were even some people who hinted that they thought Dorothy had killed him in self-defense. She hated that idea for Dorothy, but she found it hard to blame the young girl for it if it had happened that way. That man had abandoned his responsibility to take care of his daughter and he'd treated her shamefully. And not just her, either. Mr. Watson had pretty much behaved badly toward everyone—including her and Charlie. It was no wonder so many people hated him.

Yes, it was good he was gone from Dorothy's life.

But Charlie couldn't say the same thing. Her father had decided to come back. And it was obvious from her reaction that Charlie wasn't very happy about it.

"I first met Jimmie at Christian service summer camp," Charlie was explaining. "Out at Oil Belt. We were in the same age group so we shared a cabin with two other girls."

Roma Jean knew Jimmie was Nelda Rae Black's niece. She guessed that's why Mrs. Black had been with Mr. Davis on Saturday. But Roma Jean had never heard very much about the girl—except that she'd left Jericho as a teenager and never come back.

But the way Charlie was talking about her now suggested that this Jimmie had been someone very important in Charlie's life. Roma Jean tried hard not to reveal how jealous she was beginning to feel. She knew it was crazy. She didn't even know Charlie all those years ago.

"So Jimmie and I found out that we . . . liked each other. A lot." Charlie looked at Roma Jean intently. "More than girls were supposed to like each other. I'd never experienced anything like that before, and I didn't really understand what it meant. It all seemed so natural and innocent. But Jimmie had a better idea about it all, and she made the first overture toward me."

"What kind of overture?" Roma Jean asked. She tried to keep her voice neutral.

"We were at the swimming hole during free time one afternoon, and we'd been splashing each other and pushing each other off this big rock into the water. The other girls had already gotten tired of that game and had gone back to their cabins. But we stayed on. Then Jimmie jumped into the water and pretty much landed on top of me. We went under together and before I knew what was happening, she'd put her arms around my neck and started kissing me. I'd never experienced anything like that before."

"Was it like us at Grayson Highlands?"

Charlie must've heard the disappointment in her voice, even though Roma Jean did her best to hide it.

"No." Charlie took hold of her hand and squeezed it. "It wasn't like that at all. Nothing in my life has ever been like that." Charlie kissed her. "Believe me."

Roma Jean felt silly. "I believe you. I didn't mean to go all *Fatal Attraction* on you. I'm really sorry."

"You don't ever have to apologize, Roma Jean." Charlie stroked the side of her face. "I've never loved anyone the way I love you. That's the truth."

"I believe you. I feel the same way."

They kissed again—for longer this time. Roma Jean could tell that Charlie was starting to get distracted, so she broke away and laid a hand against her chest to hold her back. "You need to finish your story."

"I can finish it later." Charlie tried to move in again.

"No, Charlie. I want to hear about this—and about your father."

"Okay." Charlie sat back, but it seemed to be an effort.

Roma Jean hoped Charlie knew it wasn't easy for her to stop, either. They didn't get very many chances to be together this way, and it was hard to waste one.

"Was Jimmie the girl your father found out about?"

"Yes." Charlie nodded sadly. "The camp counselors caught us together one afternoon, and they pretty much freaked out. We both got expelled on the spot. Jimmie's parents came and got her. I wasn't allowed to see her, but I remember hearing her father screaming at her while they drug her to their car. He called her terrible names, too. Words I'd never even heard before. She was crying when they finally got her into the backseat. They left and I never saw her again."

"And her parents sent her off to live in Kentucky?"

Roma Jean was glad Charlie didn't ask how she knew about that.

"Yes. I guess to some kind of evangelist who was supposed to save her from being queer."

"That's crazy," Roma Jean declared. "You can't *save* someone from being how they were born. That's like saying you can save someone from having blue eyes or being terminally stupid—like those Lear twins."

Charlie smiled. "I wish I'd known you then, Roma Jean. My life might've turned out differently."

"I don't think your father would've reacted to me any differently than he did to Jimmie."

*In fact, I know he wouldn't have . . .*

Charlie agreed with her. "You're right, of course. When he found out what I'd done, he gave me the worst beating I'd ever had. And believe me, he'd beaten me a lot of times before that. He said that I was no better than an animal and that I'd humiliated him in front of the entire town—and that he refused to live with the shame I'd brought on him."

"Is that how you ended up in the hospital?" When Charlie looked at her quizzically, she added, "Miss Murphy told me about it."

"Oh," Charlie said. "Yes. I was in the hospital for more than a week. When I got out, my father was gone. He'd left town. I went to live with a foster family in Bridle Creek for a while, but eventually ended up just staying at Byron's house. He took care of me until I finished school and entered the training program to become a sheriff's deputy."

"Sheriff Martin is a good man."

"You'll get no argument from me about that."

"Why is your father back now?"

"I went to find him the other day," Charlie explained. "He's staying out at the Osborne Motel."

"That place? It's *gross*. Daddy says it's a rat trap—literally."

"I think that makes it a perfect spot for him."

"Did you talk with him?"

"Yeah. I told him to leave me the hell alone—and that I had no desire to ever see him again. But he launched into some crazy story about finding Jesus and being born again. He told me he'd come back to save me from my wicked ways."

Roma Jean's eyes blazed. "What wicked ways?"

Charlie gave her hand a squeeze. "The you and me kind of wicked ways."

Roma Jean rolled her eyes. "We might be a lot of things to a lot of people, but *nobody* except those Bible-beaters out at Bone Gap thinks we're *wicked*. Not even Gramma Azalea does—and she's two bubbles off plumb."

Charlie laughed.

"I'm not kidding. She's gotten really famous on Twitter for being a first-class nut job. Did you know those Rock Star people actually hooked her up with Kendrick Lamar?"

"The rapper?"

"Yeah. They said Nike wants to hire them both to do ads for those Cortez sneakers they both wear. Gramma Azalea is nearly as famous as he is on Twitter because of her whole *Grand Theft Auto* thing. She's got, like, a Blue Check account. They tweet at each other all the time."

"Azalea and *Kendrick Lamar?*" Charlie sounded incredulous, but it was true.

"Yeah." Roma Jean prattled on. "It's *so* embarrassing. Kendrick Lamar always calls her 'Crazy AF.' *She* thinks he means 'Crazy Azalea Freemantle.' I tried to tell her that wasn't what 'AF' meant, but Mama actually slapped me when I said it means 'As Fuck.' Nobody is allowed to curse in front of her." Roma Jean digressed to clarify. "It's an offense right up there with blasphemy against the holy spirit—or maybe washing Daddy's red work socks with a load of whites. Trust me . . . I'll never make *that* mistake again, either."

Charlie was running a hand across her face.

"I did it again, didn't I?" Roma Jean asked her. "I rambled off topic."

"Honey?" Charlie put an arm around her shoulders and pulled her close. "Just promise me you'll never change."

Roma Jean snuggled in closer. "I promise."

This time, when Charlie kissed her, Roma Jean didn't push her away. It had been a while since they'd been together in this special way, and Roma Jean was suddenly as invested in changing that as Charlie had been earlier.

They hadn't progressed very far when a loud crash and the sound of squealing car tires made them lurch apart.

"What was that?" Roma Jean was taking deep breaths.

Charlie was already on her feet.

"I don't know." She crossed to a cabinet and withdrew her service revolver and long-handled flashlight. "Stay put while I check it out," she ordered.

Roma Jean did as Charlie had directed, even though it was killing her not to look outside. She was scared, too. She didn't want anything bad to happen to Charlie.

She could hear dogs barking from behind the house next door.

After a couple of minutes, Charlie came back inside the house. She was still carrying her gun and flashlight. Her demeanor had changed. Roma Jean could tell Charlie was angry and barely containing it.

"What was it?" Roma Jean asked. "Did you see anything?"

"Yeah." Charlie returned her gun and flashlight to the cabinet. "Somebody drove by and threw a brick."

Roma Jean got a sinking feeling. "It hit my car, didn't it?" She'd only just gotten the thing back from Troutdale today.

Charlie nodded sadly. "I'm really sorry." She hesitated. "It broke the back window."

"Oh, *man*." Roma Jean sank back down onto the sofa. "I might as well *leave* the damn thing out at Junior's."

"I'm so sorry, Sweetie. I guess we both know who did this."

Roma Jean was horrified. "Do you really think so?"

"I don't think so, Roma Jean." Charlie walked across the room to pick up her phone. "I'm sure of it."

# Chapter Six

*Recorded Interview*
*Preliminary Inquest Investigation*
*Death of Mayor Gerald Watson*

"My name is Natalie Diane Chriscoe. I work at Cougar's Quality Logistics. Rita is my sister-in-law. She works at Cougar's too. And she lives in our garage apartment."

*Dear god, I hope he don't ask me any questions about Rita and Eva. That would make her look like Public Enemy Number One.*

"Yes sir. Rita and me were having lunch at Freemantle's Market the day Watson come in there and went after the Sheriff."

*He pretty much went after everybody else in that place, too. I wish Rita hadn't provoked him the way she did. It sure ain't helping her case right now. She never did have the sense to hold her peace.*

"The mayor was hoppin' mad because he said somebody tipped off them Mexicans who work up at the tree farm up on Whitetop. He blamed Sheriff Martin for it, and come in there with guns blazin' to accuse him. I guess his band of ICE raiders had just gone up there to round up illegals and didn't manage to find any. That's when he went off on the Sheriff and started accusing him and his deputy of all kinds of things."

*I'm not gonna tell them what the mayor said about the sheriff and Dr. Heller. It don't bear repeating that Sheriff Martin looked like he wanted to knock Watson's block off.*

"Yes sir. He kicked up quite a ruckus. He knocked over some snack displays and pretty much started calling out everybody who was eatin' lunch in there that day—even the librarian and her brother."

*I wonder if they already know about the words Watson and Rita had? I don't wanna lie, but I'll be damned if I'll say anything that points a finger at her. I don't even know the truth about what all happened between her and Watson's wife, Eva, all those years ago.*

"Well, I didn't really see it. But they all said Watson tripped over Rita's foot on the way to the door. Curtis Freemantle had told him to clear out. To tell the truth, Watson didn't seem to me to be any madder at Rita than he was at anybody else in there. That man pretty much hated everyone, and most people felt the same way about him."

*How much longer is this gonna take?*

"Yes, sir. He threw a bag of them Cheetos at her and stormed outta there. It was a sight to see, really. Everybody in that place pretty much stood up to him, too. Nobody was gonna take his guff. Me'n Rita finished our lunch and went back to Cougar's. We didn't talk no more about it, neither."

*They're asking me too many questions about Rita . . .*

"Yes sir. We were both at the river on the 4th. We were standin' near the food tables with James Lawrence, in line to get dessert. That's when Watson showed up and went after that Jenkins boy. He spewed all kind of mess at him, too. Then he pushed him into one of the tables and drug his daughter off. That's all we saw. We didn't know anything else that happened until later, when the whole town found out he was dead."

*Rita and James Lawrence both wandered off, and that was the last time I saw her until later that night, when it was time to head home. I hope he don't ask me if I know where she went . . .*

"If you're lookin' for people who had reason to do harm to that man, you're pretty much gonna have to look at everybody in the whole dern town. You won't find one person that had more reason than anybody else. Nobody liked him. But I don't think anybody hated him enough to bother killing him, neither. He wasn't worth it. Most people just looked the other way. You can mark my words: that man was a bad penny from first to last—and I think God knew it was time for all the torment he caused around here to end. Even now, his unholy memory is keepin' everything stirred up."

*They just need to let this rest. No good's gonna come out of* any *of this—especially for that little girl.*

Bert and Sonny were at the cemetery, trimming and weeding around all the headstones. The city paid them to head out here once a month to mow and tidy up, but it had been raining so much lately, they were more than two weeks behind.

"I can't get over how much these dern baby's breath plants have spread since we were out here at the end of June. I wish people would quit using that mess in arrangements." Sonny was restringing his line trimmer after it got caught on a burdock root near the base of the Pollard family monument.

"Well, it's all that rain," Bert told him. "Then this heat and humidity kicks up and it's like a dern greenhouse effect."

"Well, we can't be waitin' this long again to get back out here, rain or no." Sonny finished reattaching the spool containing lime green wire to his trimmer. "It's gonna take us the rest of the afternoon to get this mess sorted out."

"Did you finish cuttin' that grass over yonder?"

"Where?" Sonny asked him. "Over by them sycamore trees? No. It's too high. This push mower ain't gonna handle it. We'll have to use the zero turn."

Bert cursed beneath his breath. They didn't really get paid enough to spend a whole half-day out here—respect for the dead, or not. He wanted to get back out to Dr. Heller's today to finish puttin' up the HardiePlank on the front porch. He looked at the angle of the sun.

*Didn't look like that was gonna happen today.*

"I'll go get it off the trailer." Bert laid down his rake and headed for their truck so he could unload the zero turn mower.

As usual, they'd left their rig parked along the single lane road that wound through the property, instead of driving it across the grass so it could be closer to where they were clearing. Sonny was a stickler about not disrespecting the dead by runnin' a motor vehicle over their gravesites. Bert asked him one time why was it okay with him to ride the zero turn over them? Wadn't that disrespectful, too? But Sonny said no—that doin' what it took to keep things tidy was okay in the eyes of the Lord.

*Sometimes, Sonny sounded a lot like Buddy . . .*

Bert took a shortcut through the rows of graves to reach their truck, and that's when he noticed something off-kilter. There were small hunks of granite strewn around near a cluster of headstones. When he drew closer, he could see that one of the markers had been all busted up into jagged pieces.

"Hey, Sonny!" he called out. "Come over here and look at this. Somethin's happened to a couple of these headstones."

He knelt before the desecrated monument to try and make out whose grave it was. The thing was really smashed up. He was able to fit some pieces of it back together so he could make out the name: *Jenkins.*

*Well, I'll be damned . . . it's old Mr. Jenkins' grave.*

He looked around to see if any other graves had been disturbed. It didn't look like it.

Sonny joined him and knelt to look at the damage. "What the heck happened to it? It looks like somebody run into it with something."

"I don't see no tracks or ruts. I think somebody done this on purpose."

"Why would somebody come all the way out here just to bust up this one grave?"

Bert shrugged. "Maybe it was harder'n they thought so they give up after this one."

Sonny shook his head. "Kids these days. Don't they have nothin' better to do?"

"It would'a taken some pretty determined kids, Sonny. You'd need some kind of pipe or crowbar to bust up granite this way."

Sonny sighed with disgust. "It ain't respectful to do such a thing."

"No," Bert agreed. "I reckon we should call the sheriff."

"Yeah. Lemme go get my cell phone outta the truck." He stood up. "If this don't beat all. Sometimes I wonder what happened to people in this town. It ain't the same no more."

Bert agreed. *Everything had seemed to change after what happened at the river on the 4th of July.*

But he knew they couldn't blame the mayor for all of that. People made choices about what they did. And a lot of them followed right along with that man, without ever having to be persuaded.

He supposed a lot of the ugliness they were seeing now had always been there, too—hidin' from sight. Now it had got brave enough to move out into the open.

*And it seemed to be flourishin', too—just like these dang weeds.*

He looked around the quiet cemetery and its row after row of stones. Some of them had been there since the 1700s. There were slaves buried here, too—in tight little clusters behind old iron fences. Him and Sonny always took special care to keep those sections lookin' just as nice as the rest of the place. Even if those folks had any kin left around there, nobody would've been able to identify who was buried in them graves. Most of the markers were just random-sized hunks of rock. But him and Sonny believed those folk deserved to have their memories honored just the same as everybody else. They weren't the only ones who felt that way, either. On holidays, Gladys Pitzer always made sure to put little bunches of flowers by those markers, too. Bert could still see tattered red, white and blue ribbons fluttering next to all the little stones that tilted every which way in the slave section. He guessed they were left over from Independence Day.

*Slaves buried in the town cemetery.*

Yep. That ugliness had *always* been there . . .

People in town all seemed to think that this new time of fear and suspicion that had dropped down on them like a shroud was gonna last forever. People always thought bad things lasted forever. But Bert knew they didn't. Bad things came and went just like everything else in life.

He looked around at the expanse of rolling land that once had been a pasture, but now was full of generations of people who'd also come and gone.

*Yep. The only thing in life that lasts forever is what all these dead folks is busy doin' right now . . .*

He heard the zero turn start up. Sonny rode it over near to where he stood and parked it.

"Sheriff Martin said he'd be right out." Sonny looked down at the mess. "Should we start pickin' any of this up?"

"No. We need to leave it just like it is, so he can look it all over first."

Sonny tagged him with a gentle fist bump. "You're talkin' like this is some kind of *CSI* crime scene."

"It just might be, Sonny. It just might be."

The recording of Beethoven sonatas Celine had ordered using her Amazon Prime account arrived in two days, as promised. She never ceased to be amazed at how quickly she could receive just about anything from the massive online retailer . . . and always within two days.

*Maybe she should ask Bert to order the remaining HardiePlank they needed using her Prime account?*

Celine put the recording into her CD player and sat down to listen to it. It was a marvel of delicacy and poise—just as the reviews in *Gramophone* had said. "This is the work of an artist with colossal integrity, for whom ideation and execution are one and the same," one reviewer noted. Others had been critical of Uchida's articulation and considered it too "staged." But Celine didn't feel that at all. She heard all the proper inflections and fits of controlled abandon the sonatas commanded. To her, the performance was magical.

Dorothy had been reading in her room, but she'd heard the music and wandered into the studio to listen along with Celine.

When the final notes of *Sonata No. 30 in E Major* finished, Dorothy looked at Celine with wonder.

"What was that?"

"Beethoven. It's a new recording of three piano sonatas by Mitsuko Uchida."

"It was . . . powerful. She must be very famous."

"She is—but not for Beethoven. This is a new endeavor for her. She's mostly recognized as a leading interpreter of Mozart."

Celine handed the jewel case to Dorothy so she could examine it.

"Did you know her?" Dorothy asked.

Celine smiled. "No. But I have heard her perform many times. Most recently in Los Angeles, about three years ago."

"Wow. That must've been incredible."

"Have you ever attended a live performance, Dorothy?"

"Of music like this? No. Not ever. Once I got to hear the Richmond symphony in a Christmas program. But that was on a school trip. They were playing in Roanoke."

Celine smiled. "That counts."

"Maybe. But they played a lot of carols—just with more instruments and a lot more bells and things. There wasn't a piano."

"No. I suppose there wouldn't have been."

"I'd love to do that someday—go to a real concert."

"Funny you should mention that." Celine retrieved her copy of *The New Yorker* and showed Dorothy the page she'd earmarked. "Guess who's playing at Carnegie Hall next week?"

Dorothy was confused. "In New York?"

"Uh huh. On Saturday night."

Dorothy scanned the page. Her eyes grew wide when she saw the listing. "It's her?"

"It is. And she's playing a full Beethoven program—with the Mahler Chamber Orchestra. It should be quite an experience."

"Are you going?" Dorothy asked with wonder. "I know it will be wonderful. Is Sheriff Martin going, too?"

"Yes, I am planning to go. And no, Byron is not going with me. I hope *you* are."

"Me?" Dorothy seemed uncertain she'd heard Celine correctly. "How can I go?"

"Easy. We take a plane from Charlotte, attend the concert, stay overnight in the city, and return home on Sunday afternoon."

"You want to take *me* with you? On an airplane?"

Celine nodded. "It's the only way we can go and be back in time for you not to miss a day of school."

Dorothy lowered the jewel case to her lap. Celine could see her struggling to make sense of the opportunity.

"Dorothy? Would you like to do this with me? Please know that it's entirely fine for you to say no if anything about the prospect makes you feel strange or uncomfortable. I would not be disappointed or frustrated with you in the slightest."

"Would you still go if I didn't?" Dorothy asked.

That question brought Celine up short. She knew it

mattered for her to be honest with the girl. Dorothy deserved that from her.

"No. I probably wouldn't. But that doesn't mean you should make your decision based upon whether I attend or not. I mean that sincerely."

"Why do you want to take me?"

*Why did she? This was turning into an episode of Truth or Dare . . .*

"I think because it's been so many years since I've had someone in my life who connects with music in the same ways I do. I didn't know how much I missed that until I met you. And you have so much natural talent. You feel the music, deep inside, where it lives and breathes a life of its own. And that's not something that can be taught. I suppose I'm being selfish, wanting to share this with you. But when I saw the listing for this concert, it seemed to me that this presented an opportunity for something special we could do together—just the two of us. But I realize it's a lot to spring on you—especially so close to the event. I gave in to an impulse." She smiled. "Not something I normally do, as I'm sure you noticed."

Dorothy gave her a shy smile. "Maybe I have."

"So, maybe you can understand why I became so excited at the prospect of doing it."

Dorothy was quiet for a moment. She looked over at the large piano that dominated the room, then back at Celine.

"Can we see where they make the Steinways?"

Her question was like the sun coming out after a storm.

"I'll see what I can do."

Byron tapped again on the side door to Gladys Pitzer's small mill house in Fries. He was pretty sure she was at home. Her station wagon was pulled up beneath the carport beside the brick steps. She was probably inside watching her stories. He should've waited to come out here until three o'clock.

He heard a scuffling noise inside and the sound of a key turning in the lock. A moment later, Gladys stood gaping at him from behind her rusted aluminum screen door.

He guessed that was probably locked, too, although there was next to no crime out here in the mostly abandoned mill town.

'Hey, Gladys. I wondered if I could speak to you for a few minutes about the cemetery."

Gladys unlocked the screen door and stepped back so Byron could enter her small kitchen. Something smelled good—like brownies. It was making his stomach growl. He'd skipped breakfast that morning.

Gladys must be baking.

He was right that she'd been watching TV, too. He could hear a soap opera playing in the living room. He could tell it was a soap opera by the dramatic music that seemed to punctuate every line of dialogue.

"I ain't been out there since Independence Day," she told him. "I don't go out except for holidays."

"Yes, ma'am, I know that. And you do a great service to the town in the way you always decorate the graves for everyone."

"My husband and my son, Beau, are out there. I do it for them, so it's no matter to do it for other folks' kin, too. It's sad that most people forget about their loved ones once they're in the ground. The town used to hire me to do up the graves when I ran the florist shop in town. But they don't pay for that no more." She gestured toward her kitchen table, where there were Walmart bags full of fake, brightly colored autumn leaves, plastic acorns, and tiny American flags. "I'm gettin' these all put together for Veterans Day. It used to not take me so long, but my arthritis has got so bad, it makes everything take a lot longer. So I have to start early on the next decorations."

Gladys didn't know it, but Byron sometimes sent her

anonymous cash contributions to help defray the cost of the materials she bought for these projects. He knew the widow lived on nothing but Social Security and the little bit of pension she still got from the cotton mill, where her husband had worked his entire life.

"Well, I was out there this morning," he explained, "and I could see that you had been there to decorate for the 4th of July. There were still some ribbons here and there."

Gladys clucked her tongue. "Them groundskeepers was supposed to pick up all the flowers and such. I don't like to leave things sittin' out there until they get all faded and ruined by the weather. But it's been raining too much for me to get back out there and collect the stuff myself."

"Well, Bert and Sonny were out there this morning. And they found something disturbing. It appears that somebody vandalized two of the graves. Do you remember if you saw anything like that when you were there to place the flowers for the 4th?"

"*Two* of the graves?" she asked. "I didn't see nothin' like that."

"Do you remember when you went out there to place the flowers?"

She nodded. "It was on the 3rd. I like to be sure it's done the day before, in case people head out there to pay their respects before the town picnic. That don't happen as much as it used to, but people do still go sometimes."

"And did you see anyone else out there on the 3rd?"

"No. Not on the 3rd. It was just me and a dern gopher. I wish'd I'd a had my .220 with me . . . I could'a done for him."

Byron chose to ignore that last comment. But something about her specificity regarding the date stood out to him.

"You said you didn't see anyone on the 3rd. Were you out there on any other days?"

Gladys looked slightly distressed. She didn't answer him right away.

The music on the soap opera had reached a crescendo. Byron regretted that he'd probably prevented Gladys from witnessing the climax du jour.

"Did you attend the town picnic on the 4th, Gladys? I was there, but I don't recall seeing you."

"I baked some Bundt cakes and brownies for the dessert tables, and ate my dinner there with the Freemantles. I left right after that. I don't like stayin' out after dark. It's too hard to see drivin' home. There's too many deer out movin' around—especially along the river."

"So you came straight on home?" he asked.

She nodded but didn't volunteer any details. The TV set was now blasting an ad for Tide laundry detergent.

Byron felt like Gladys was hedging about something. He began to feel like his instinct to come out and talk with her had been right. "You didn't go back by the cemetery, then?"

Gladys wearily pulled out a chrome kitchen chair and sat down. She pushed a second chair out for him.

"You'd best sit down, too. This is gonna take a bit."

Byron obeyed her and took a seat at the table. He waited for her to continue talking.

She took her time.

"After dinner at the river, I had to run back out there on account I left my good shears sittin' on top of one of them stones by the sycamore trees." She picked the pair in question up off the table and showed them to him. "John, at the florist shop, got these for me. They're made special for people with arthritis, and they're real easy to use. I didn't want 'em to get rained on."

"So did you see anyone else out there on that second visit?"

Byron could tell she was unsure about how to answer. "Yes. But he didn't see me."

"Who was it?"

"It was that Jenkins boy."

"David Jenkins?"

Gladys nodded. "He was over by his daddy's grave, so I didn't want to disturb him. I figured he was payin' his respects—even though that man never done anything to deserve that."

"Was that it? You just saw him visiting his father's grave?"

"Well. I went on about my business, walkin' on to get my shears. That's when I heard the racket."

"What kind of racket?"

"It was like hammerin' and such. I peeked back over toward where he was, and that man was on his feet goin' wild, smashin' that headstone with some kind of big rock or somethin'. He was actin' real crazy, too—cryin' and hollerin' just like Beau used to get sometimes. I could tell he was outta his head, Sheriff. It scared the tar outta me and I didn't wanna stay around to watch. So I just headed for my car. I come back home."

"You said he was using a rock or something to smash the headstone?"

"I don't really know what it was. He was swingin' it too fast."

That explained the broken statue of the angel Gabriel they'd found near the scene. It had been knocked off the top of a nearby monument. That must've been what David had used as a make-shift club. The angel's head had been snapped off, and one of its wings had been mixed in with the headstone rubble.

"Gladys? Do you remember what time you were out there?"

"It was right after dinner, so maybe seven or seven-thirty. It was just before dark, I know that. I heard the fireworks start up as soon as I got back here."

"So you think you saw David out there around seven or seven-thirty?"

Gladys thought about it. "I reckon it was closer to seven—maybe a little bit after that when he started actin' crazy. It took me about twenty minutes to drive home. There wadn't no traffic on account of everybody bein' at the river for the fireworks."

"And David was still at the cemetery when you left to head home?"

Gladys nodded. Byron was surprised when she reached out and laid a gnarled hand on his arm.

"Don't be arrestin' that boy for this, Sheriff. If you'd a known how mean that man was to him growin' up, you'd be surprised somebody hadn't done this to that grave sooner. If somebody has to pay for them damages, I'd like to try and cover it. That boy was always real good to my Beau."

Byron patted the top of Gladys's hand. "I don't want you to worry one bit about any of this, Gladys. Nobody is going to get arrested—for anything."

*At least, not David Jenkins, thank god . . .*

Avi was adding a second pack of Splenda to her coffee. Syd was amused. It was incredible how alike she and Maddie were.

She figured the sweet tooth must be a professional thing. She recalled Dorothy mentioning that Celine had one, too.

They'd met up with Avi at the inn so Maddie could drop off her new set of keys to the clinic. They were on their way to Junior's to pick up Syd's Volvo, so Maddie made the quick detour on their way out of town. When they arrived, Avi was sitting downstairs in the big front parlor, drinking coffee and scanning real estate listings in the local paper.

"Finding anything worthwhile?" Syd asked.

Avi closed the paper. "Alas, no. Not unless I want to share a two-bedroom mobile home with a single mother and three kids."

"Is that really all that's available?" Maddie was incredulous. "Maybe you need to widen your net."

"You think?" Avi agreed. "I was hoping I wouldn't have to go so far out of town. It kind of negates the reason for staying overnight here in the first place."

"How much room do you need to have?"

Syd's wheels were turning.

"Not much. Just one room, with a bath and a small kitchen—or access to one. Fortunately, I have a small footprint."

"All your books, notwithstanding," Maddie added. "We're going to need to get you another bookcase."

"Yeah." Avi faced her. "About that. I was wondering if we could turn that big hall closet into a library. Both you and Lizzy could store stuff in there, too."

"Which hall closet?" Maddie asked. "The one across from the kitchen?"

"Yeah. There appears to be nothing stored in there but cleaning supplies and a prehistoric wine fridge—which I've been meaning to ask you about. I realize things are unconventional here in the hinterland, but it does seem like rather an esoteric appliance for a medical practice."

Syd shot an incredulous look at Maddie. "Don't tell me you moved that thing from the barn to your clinic?"

"Hey . . . I had no choice. Once Henry told David it was working again, I knew I had to relocate it." It was obvious Syd wasn't buying it, so Maddie hauled out the big guns. "Come on, honey . . . it's got bottles in there I've been saving for the wedding."

"Oh, almost thou persuadest me, Agrippa. You haven't been saving *anything* for our wedding. I can barely get you to discuss it without breaking out in hives."

"That's not true, and you know it." Maddie sounded offended by Syd's assessment.

"Um," Avi interrupted them, "not to sound a trumpet before my good deeds or anything, but I *am* a rather brilliant shrink—and it appears the pair of you might benefit from a few hours of what we in the trade like to call 'billable time.'"

"Thanks, Avi." Syd frowned at Maddie. "We'll take that under advisement."

"Well, if you're offering anything like a family discount,"

Maddie suggested, "I'd love to get your assessment of Henry."

Avi looked surprised. "What about Henry?"

"Remember I asked you to keep an eye on him at dinner the other night?" Maddie prompted. "To see if you could detect any signs that he might be depressed or worried about anything?"

"Yes," Avi replied. "I remember."

"We're worried that he might be getting bullied at school," Syd added.

"Have you asked him about that?" Avi queried. Maddie and Syd exchanged glances. "I thought not."

"It's not like that," Maddie explained. "We simply don't want to introduce a possibility that might not have occurred to him."

"In case he isn't experiencing any of that," Syd added hastily.

"The two of you know that the road to hell is paved with good intentions, right?"

Maddie sighed. "So you're saying we should ask him outright?"

"If you're worried he's being bullied by someone, yes. You'll be able to tell a lot by how he responds. If he hedges or acts like he doesn't want to discuss it, you might have grounds for concern."

"And if he doesn't?" Syd asked. "Henry is uncommonly suggestible. I don't want to scare him."

"What does his father say?" When neither of them answered, Avi continued. "So you have this concern, but you haven't mentioned it to Henry's dad? Why not?"

"Okay . . . I'll say it." Syd replied. *"Uncle*. We didn't want to tell James we were worried about it until we knew something concrete. It didn't seem like a good idea to tell him we feared Henry might be getting bullied because he has two mommies."

"James does know his son is living with an out lesbian couple, right?"

Maddie nodded. "Of course, he does."

"Then I would imagine he considered this possibility when

he left Henry in your care. Would you agree?"

"I suppose so." Syd sighed. "To be honest, we didn't want to amplify any potential barriers to going through with the formal custody arrangement."

"The adoption, you mean?"

"Well, no." Maddie explained. "Originally, we did discuss adoption. But honestly, it seemed like a better idea for Henry—and for James—to share custody, with us as primary caregivers. Henry needs to know his daddy is going to remain engaged in his everyday life."

"That's a very good decision. I'm glad you opted for that solution. Especially since it seems Henry's father wants to stay involved with his son."

"James is a good man, and he loves Henry." Syd smiled. "We're all very fortunate about that."

"So, the reality is that Henry has two mommies, *and* a daddy. Right?"

"Right." Maddie agreed. She looked at Syd. "I don't know about you, but I feel like an idiot."

Syd took hold of her hand. "Together in all things."

Avi watched their exchange. "As much as I hate to shatter this moment of epiphany, I think Henry's dilemma is a lot simpler than you imagine."

Syd was all ears. "You do?"

"Oh, yeah. It's as simple as one, two, three." Avi took a moment to consider. "Or was it four, five and six?"

Maddie chewed the inside of her cheek. "Could you be a tad less vague? I think we've already demonstrated our level of obtuseness where our son is concerned."

Avi laughed. "I was counting up the biscuits he kept passing to Lizzy."

"Lizzy?" Maddie seemed perplexed. "What does Lizzy have to do with this?"

"Oh, dear god . . . *that's* all this is?" Syd threw back her head in amazement. "How on earth did I miss *that?*"

Maddie was looking back and forth between Syd and Avi. "Would one of you care to enlighten me? I think the subtitles dropped out during this part of the opera."

"You *did* complete a standard psych rotation, didn't you?" Avi asked. "This is pretty textbook stuff. Henry isn't being bullied: he's in love."

"In love?" It was clear Maddie realized she was missing something. "With Lizzy?"

"Unless I miss my guess. Which," Avi added, "I rarely do." She smiled at them. "If you ask me, the kid's got great taste, too."

Maddie was still trying to take it in. "Well, I'll be damned."

"She's right, Maddie. Every time Henry *sees* Lizzy, he morphs into some kind of Cheshire cat." Syd slowly shook her head. "I don't know how we missed this."

"With *Lizzy?*" Maddie repeated.

"Why is that so hard for you to comprehend?" Avi asked.

"It's not *that*," Maddie explained. "Of course I can understand why any guy—or child—with a functioning brain stem would find Lizzy attractive."

"Not just any *guy* . . ." Avi pointed out.

"Yeah." Maddie raised an index finger. "We'll get to *that* later. But how do we mend Henry's little heart if Lizzy moves to Colorado with Tom?"

"I don't think we'll have to cross that bridge, honey. Tom called me this morning. He said Lizzy broke up with him."

"She did?" Syd could tell Maddie was trying to conceal her excitement at the news. "I mean . . . I'm sorry for Tom—and for her. It can't have been an easy decision."

"No. But I think it was the right one for Lizzy. I love my brother, but he continues to demonstrate how *not* ready he is to make any kind of lasting commitment. To Lizzy, or to anyone else."

Maddie considered Syd's observation. "Your mother is gonna

go ballistic when she finds out."

"That's nothing compared to how my father will react." She looked at Avi. "Dad pretty much wants to canonize Lizzy."

"George really likes Lizzy," Maddie agreed with a smile. "He likes me a lot, too."

Syd rolled her eyes. "He's a man of simple tastes."

Avi laughed.

"We need to boogie if we're gonna make it to Junior's before he closes." Maddie got to her feet and withdrew a shiny set of keys from the pocket of her slacks. "Here you go." She handed them to Avi. "I guess this makes it official."

Avi took them from her. "I feel like there should be more ceremony here."

"Cake? Ice cream?" Maddie prompted. "Exotic dancers?"

"That could work as a start."

"How about you come to the house on Tuesday night for tacos?" Syd suggested. "We can invite Lizzy, too, and test your theory about Henry."

Maddie shot Syd a wary glance, but Syd ignored her.

"Okay." Avi tossed the keys into the air and caught them. "I'm not ashamed of being transparent enough to accept."

"So what do we owe you for the therapy session?" Maddie asked.

Avi took a moment to consider Maddie's question.

"What?" Maddie prompted her. "Do you prefer to be paid in small bills with non-sequential serial numbers?"

"How'd you guess?" Avi grinned. "I'll slip an invoice under your door."

# Chapter Seven

*Recorded Interview*
*Preliminary Inquest Investigation*
*Death of Mayor Gerald Watson*

"James Edward Lawrence, Corporal, U.S. Army Transport Corps. Now stationed at Fort Hood, Texas."

*I hope the signal doesn't drop out again. I only have twenty more minutes left on my lunch break.*

"Yes, sir. I reenlisted at the end of June, about ten days before the picnic on the 4th of July. I went to the picnic with my son, Henry. He was really excited to see the fireworks. He still lives in town with Dr. Stevenson and her partner, Miss Murphy. We share joint custody of him."

*I really don't understand why they've been so hell-bent on talking with me. I didn't even know the mayor. At least I could do it this way and not have to fly back to Virginia. That wouldn't have gone over well with the CO.*

"Yeah. I did see the shouting match between Mayor Watson and David Jenkins. It was right before the debate was supposed to start. The mayor showed up loaded for bear. He started it all. David pretty much stood there while the mayor went off on him. I never heard David say anything to him, in fact."

*That man looked like he wanted to crawl beneath one of the tables and hide. It was like he folded up on himself. I could see how scared he was—I'd seen that same look on the faces of some of the guys in Afghanistan.*

"The mayor was all ramped up about his daughter, and he was accusing David of behaving . . . inappropriately toward her. But none of us who were there standing in line to get dessert saw anything like that. David and the little girl, Dorothy, were joking and teasing each other—more like brother and sister, you know? All in fun. He was trying to get her to take one of each dessert, and she was complaining that she'd never be able to eat that much. It all seemed pretty innocent to me."

*When Watson grabbed that girl by the arm and jerked her away, I wanted to take his head off, myself. I don't think I was the only one who felt that way, either.*

"I was with my son, Henry and my friend, Rita. Rita Chriscoe. We were in line together when all this happened."

*Shit. Rita said if they talked to me, they'd probably ask about her . . .*

"After Watson took off with his daughter, I went up and helped Raymond Odell set the tables back up. Watson had pushed David into one of them and knocked it over. There were plates of cake and cookies and stuff all over the ground."

*Rita disappeared about that time, too. She wasn't still there with Henry when we finished cleaning up. He said she just left without saying anything to him.*

"No sir, I don't know where David went. All I know is he ran off and his partner followed him. That's Michael Robertson. They run the inn in town."

*I didn't see Rita again that night, either.*

"Henry and I stayed on and watched the fireworks. We left for Troutdale at about 8:30. I didn't hear anything about what had happened to the mayor until the next morning."

*Come on, man . . . let's wrap this up. Oh, shit. Here it comes.*

"No, sir. I don't know where Rita went after the whole dessert fiasco. I suppose she wandered off to get more smokes out of her car. She'd been trying to quit, but had fallen off the wagon, and had pretty much been smoking up a storm all day."

*That's not really a lie. I hope it's enough to call the damn dogs off her.*

"No, sir. I didn't see Rita or David again that night. Like I said, Henry and I watched the fireworks and left right after they were over."

*I wish like hell I could say Rita had stayed on with us.*

"Yes, sir. That's all I know about what happened. I hope it ends up being an accident, like they say. I think everybody associated with that man has already suffered enough."

Dorothy was trying really hard not to show how nervous she was. Dr. Heller had brought her to the doctor's office and said she'd stay there in the waiting room until Dorothy's appointment was over. That way, if it got too hard or too scary, Dorothy could leave.

But she didn't want to leave. She knew it meant a lot to Dr. Heller for her to be here, and she thought she could do it. She owed a lot to Dr. Heller. And when Dr. Heller had asked her to think about doing this, Dorothy felt like she needed to. Talking about her father was never easy—and it was going to be really hard, now. She knew Dr. Zakariya was going to ask her questions about him. Probably more questions than anyone had ever asked her about him.

Most people shied away from doing that.

She guessed that was because sometimes when people asked, they were just being polite and didn't really want to know the truth about what was happening to her at home. They just did it because they felt like they were supposed to. She could always see the looks of relief on their faces whenever she'd shrug and say she was fine.

But Dr. Heller had never done that. Neither had Dr. Stevenson or Miss Murphy. Or David. David always asked like he meant it, too. She was lucky to have so many people who really seemed to care about her, and weren't afraid to show it.

And there was Buddy, too. He had always been really nice to her. She knew he tried in his quiet ways to protect her. That's why she couldn't let her father hurt him that day at the river. She had to stop him in the only way she could.

*Now he was dead.*

And she was here to have to talk about it with this doctor. The doctor would try to tell her she wasn't responsible, but she knew she was. She hit him and he died. Nothing could ever change that.

But as much as she trusted Dr. Heller, she had still never told her very much about everything her father had done. It was too hard—and she worried that if people knew *everything*, they'd blame her for all of that, too.

That was the part that always scared her most . . . worrying that maybe she *had* done things to make him act the way he did.

When Dr. Zakariya came out to the waiting room to greet her, she looked really happy to see Dr. Heller. They shook hands and made small talk for a minute. Dr. Zakariya made a comment about how much Dr. Stevenson looked like her mother.

That was true. They were both *really* pretty women—tall, with the same dark hair and blue eyes. But Dr. Heller's hair was short and had streaks of gray in it. Dr. Zakariya asked if Dr. Heller wanted some coffee while she waited. Dr. Heller said that would be great, and the nurse, Mrs. Hawkes, jumped up to fetch it for her.

Then they walked down a hallway to Dr. Zakariya's new office.

Dorothy could tell that Dr. Zakariya—*Avi*, she asked Dorothy to call her—was trying to make her feel less nervous.

She apologized that her office was still kind of messy. There were books stacked in piles along two of the walls, and some framed diplomas leaning against the side of her desk. There was some artwork in there, too. One of the pictures was of a big group of lines and squares painted in all different colors. Dorothy liked that one. It reminded her of some of the pictures at Dr. Heller's.

Dr. Heller liked modern art and had explained to Dorothy that paintings like this one dealt with abstract depictions of light and color in ways that pulled the viewer into a shared sense of space.

Dorothy just knew that to her, the colors looked warm and alive, and seemed to work well painted next to each other. Dr. Heller said that was exactly right, and that what Dorothy was seeing was the artist's idea of harmony.

Avi noticed Dorothy staring at the big painting.

"Do you like that one?"

Dorothy nodded.

"Me, too. I don't really understand what it is, but I know I like how it makes me feel."

"How is that?" Dorothy hadn't meant to ask any questions, and she was a little embarrassed by her outburst.

Avi was looking at the picture now. "Safe, maybe? Like it's kind of a reminder that things in the world that seem really different can still exist in harmony?" She looked at Dorothy. "How about you? What do you see in it?"

"It looks happy to me. The colors are bright . . . like warm days in the summer before it gets too hot."

"I never thought about it that way, Dorothy. But you know? I think you're right."

Avi sat down on the sofa and waited for Dorothy to take a seat. She sat gingerly on the edge of the upholstered chair on the other side of a small coffee table.

"I grew up in Minnesota," Avi explained. "So our summers

lasted about twelve seconds. You get a lot more hot weather here in Virginia."

"That's really true this year. Buddy says the fall is going to be late."

"Who is Buddy?"

Dorothy had no idea why she was rambling so much.

"Buddy is a man who does a lot of different kinds of work for people. Yard work and gardening, mostly. He's at Dr. Heller's a lot. And he used to work at our house, too."

"The house you shared with your father, you mean?"

Dorothy nodded, but didn't share any more details.

"Have you spent any time back at your house since the 4th of July?"

"Just to get clothes and things. I can't stay there by myself now. And we don't know what's going to happen to the house now that . . ." She didn't finish her sentence.

"Now that your father has died?"

Dorothy stole a look at Avi, but the doctor's expression looked pretty normal. "Yes."

"Do you miss being there? At your own home?"

"I guess not really. I miss not having my mother's things. But I don't . . . I don't mind not staying there anymore."

"When did you lose your mother?"

"I was little when she died, so it's been a long time ago. My father didn't talk about her ever, so being able to go to the attic and look at her things was the only way I got to know anything about her."

"What was her name?"

"Eva. She liked to sew and bake. I have a lot of her books, too."

"I understand that you like to read, too. And bake."

Dorothy nodded.

"It sounds like maybe you're a lot like your mother, then."

"I hope so."

"Dr. Heller told me you're quite an exceptional piano player. Did your mother like music, too?"

"I don't know. I never knew much about music until I met Dr. Heller—and David. Buddy likes music a lot, too. But he talks about it in ways that are hard to understand. Everything with him is always tied up with math and numbers, so I don't always follow what he describes. Dr. Heller says he's a kind of musical ... *servant?*"

"Um, do you mean *savant?*"

"Yes. That's the word she used. I'm sorry I got it wrong."

"That's okay. I get words wrong all the time, too."

Dorothy was pretty sure that wasn't true. Avi had too many diplomas leaning against her desk not to know the meanings of most words. She was probably a lot like Dr. Heller and Dr. Stevenson.

Roma Jean called them *brainiacs* ...

"I get a lot of things wrong all the time," Dorothy said. "Even though I try really hard not to."

"I suppose that's something we can talk about, Dorothy. The things you think you get wrong."

"Is that why I'm here?"

"I hope you're here because you want to be. More importantly, I hope maybe you'll discover that sharing some of your feelings can help you make sense of them—kind of like looking at that Rothko painting over there. Maybe together, we can connect all those squares into something that feels better—like one of those summer days, before it gets too hot. Does that sound like something you'd be willing to try, Dorothy?"

*Was it?* She really didn't know.

But she'd come here today because she'd told Dr. Heller she would try. She knew it was going to be a lot like trying to make those key change transitions in the Beethoven sonata they'd been working on. Dr. Heller called it "articulation." But whatever it was called, Dorothy couldn't get it right—no matter how hard she tried. The notes were always changing. Her fingers were too clumsy. The sounds were too broken. Never smooth or connected like they were supposed to be—like they were when Dr. Heller played them first.

She wasn't very hopeful about any of these conversations—and she had no idea where they would go. But she was here because she said she'd do this. So she supposed she needed to at least try.

"Dorothy? It's also important that you know nothing you share with me in here will ever be discussed with anyone else. Not Dr. Heller. Not anyone."

She looked at Dr. Zakariya and tried to sound more confident than she felt.

"Okay. I guess I can try."

Sonny had been able to talk Bert and Buddy into eating dinner at Aunt Bea's, instead of making Salisbury steak at his house. He knew the hardest part would be getting Buddy to agree to skip working on projects that night, but when Sonny explained that Amazon hadn't delivered the carton of new rolls of car tape they'd ordered on time, he agreed—*after* rambling on for nearly ten minutes about broken ratios and how things weren't right. It wadn't like Sonny disagreed with Buddy about any of that. After all, a delivery date was a delivery date, and businesses should do right by their customers. But he supposed Amazon was so dern big it could pretty much do whatever it wanted to—golden ratios or no.

Sonny could tell Bert was relieved, too. They'd ended up having to spend another whole afternoon out at the cemetery weeding and running the zero turn, and only just finished up a little before six o'clock. They were both tired from working outside in the sun for so long. It was really hot today and there'd been nary a breeze up there.

They sat down with their plates of country steak and creamed potatoes and had just started to eat when Bert saw Rita Chriscoe come in. They hadn't seen her since the 4th, so Bert waved her over to say hello.

"How you been, Rita? Hot enough for you today?" Bert asked.

"I wouldn't make a dog stay outside in this heat, and that's for sure," Rita agreed. "How you boys been doing?"

"Fair to middlin'," Sonny said. "We just finished up out at the cemetery. Them weeds is out of control from all the rain. You eatin' in or gettin' takeout?"

"I thought I'd grab something quick and just eat here."

"Well, go on and get it and come back here. You can eat with us." Bert looked at Sonny to second his invitation.

"Yeah, Rita," Sonny chimed in. "I can slide right over. We got plenty of room in our booth."

They were sitting in their usual booth—the big one near the front window. It had the best view of the parking lot, and any action going on across the town square at the sheriff's department.

So far, it had been a slow night on both counts.

"Sure," Rita said. "Why not? Be right back."

Sonny watched her head for the front counter, where they dished up the food. He thought she looked tired, and wondered if maybe she'd just got back from one of them long hauls Cougar's was now into. She walked like her back hurt. He shifted on the vinyl bench seat. *He knew what that was like . . .*

"She looks tired, don't she?" Bert asked.

*It was always that way. People said they pretty much could finish each other's sentences.*

"Yeah. I think it's been hard on her since James Lawrence left to go back in the army."

Bert agreed. "Them two was gettin' to be pretty good friends, wasn't they?"

"Seems like it."

"Slow down inhalin' that supper, Buddy." Bert laid a hand on his son's arm. "Try to wait up on Miss Rita."

Buddy looked over at his father with those clear, round eyes of his. "It's Wednesday. Car tape was supposed to come. No car tape on Wednesday isn't right."

Bert sighed. "You wanna take this one, Sonny?"

"Maybe we can fix things another night, Buddy—after the shipment gets here?" Sonny did his best to sound upbeat. "I can make us some Salisbury steak then."

"Salisbury steak is on Wednesday. No car tape isn't right." Buddy continued eating his generous serving of stew beef.

Rita rejoined them and sat down next to Sonny. She had two pieces of fried chicken, some slaw and a biscuit.

"I don't normally come in here after six," she explained. "The food's been sittin' too long in that steam table, and the gravy gets too gooey for my taste."

"I don't mind it." Bert sopped up some of the gooey gravy with a piece of his biscuit. "It's still better'n what I could make at home."

"Heck. Sakrete mix tastes better'n what you could make." Sonny nudged Rita. "He can't cook for nothin'. It's a wonder he ain't poisoned Buddy."

Buddy looked across the table at Rita. "Late is not right. Waiting too long is not right. Being late hurts the little things."

Sonny could tell Rita didn't know how to respond to Buddy's rambling. "He run out of car tape," he explained. "The new stuff didn't get here today like it was supposed to. That's why we're eatin' in here tonight."

"Buddy's a stickler about things bein' on time," Bert added. "It upsets him when they aren't."

Buddy was still gazing at Rita. "Late things hurt Goldenrod."

"He means Dorothy," Sonny explained. "He calls her Goldenrod. He has nicknames for everything. Sometimes, they get all mixed up in his mind."

"He doesn't sound to me like he's mixed up," Rita muttered.

"She shall know the truth," Buddy quoted. "And the truth shall make her free."

"Buddy, stop pestering Miss Rita, so she can eat her supper."

Buddy shifted his gaze to his father. "The orange dog comes for her at night."

"You know what, fellas?" Rita pushed her plate away. "I wasn't as hungry as I thought. Either of you want this chicken? I'm tired and I think I'm gonna shove off."

"You don't have to run off, Rita." Bert apologized. "Buddy don't mean nothin'. He's just been all het up about poor Dorothy and how upset she's been about what happened to her daddy. He gets like this sometimes—and once he starts fixatin' on somethin', it's hard to get him off it."

"That's the truth," Sonny chimed in. "He's like a dog with a bone. He'll just keep worryin' it to death."

"Being late hurts the little things." Buddy chanted. "The truth shall make her free."

"No offense taken." Rita slid out of the booth and got to her feet. "You all take care." She touched Buddy on the arm before advancing toward the door. "Don't you worry about that dog, Buddy. I got a feeling it'll be movin' on real soon."

Sonny watched her leave.

*Yes. Miss Rita sure did look tired tonight . . .*

Maddie had a hard time concealing her excitement when Lizzy told her she'd decided to accept the partnership offer.

They were sitting in Maddie's office. Lizzy had asked for a few minutes to talk with her at the end of the day, after they'd each finished their final appointments.

"As happy as I am, it matters more to me that you're sure about this." Maddie wanted to assure Lizzy that she could take as much time as she needed "The last thing I want to do is push you into making a decision you may not be ready for."

"You haven't pushed me at all. And, yes. I'm very sure. It's the outcome I always wanted, but never thought possible."

"To tell the truth, it's what I always wanted, too. It just took some time to be sure the practice could sustain it. Once the Wilson Clinic closed and we inherited most of their patients, it was clear we had the revenue stream to comfortably add your position on a permanent basis."

"That I get," Lizzy replied. "But you didn't have to offer me a share of ownership in the practice."

"Of course I did. That part was a no-brainer."

"I appreciate it, just the same. It's one hell of an opportunity for me."

"Well, don't give me too much credit. I'd be an idiot not to do everything in my power to keep you here. You're the best NP I've had the privilege to work with. I didn't want to give you any escape route once I had a shot at ensnaring you."

"Too bad Tom never looked at me the same way."

Maddie detected the underlying sadness and resignation in her voice. "I wish I knew what to say to make that part easier."

"I know. Unfortunately, there isn't anything anyone can say at this point—including Tom."

"For what it's worth, I think he needs to have his head examined."

Lizzy laughed. "You're a lot more delicate than Syd."

"Oh, yeah? What did she say?"

"Well, she seemed to think examining his head wouldn't really be possible since it was shoved so far up his . . . wiz wang."

"She actually said *wiz wang*?"

"Well . . . not exactly."

Maddie rocked back in her chair. "I didn't think so. Syd

doesn't tend to mince words."

The phone on Maddie's desk buzzed. It was Peggy, telling her that Syd and Henry were in the waiting room. Maddie told Peggy to send them back.

"Speak of the devil," she told Lizzy. "Syd and Henry are here."

"Oh. Are you heading out now?"

"I hadn't planned on it. They must just be in town for some errand."

"Want me to give you some privacy?"

"No. Stay put." Maddie waved her back into her chair. "I'm sure they'd both love to see you."

Henry came barreling into Maddie's office with Syd following at a more modest pace.

"Maddie!" he cried. "You'll never guess what we got at the . . ." He skidded to a halt when he saw Lizzy. "Oh." His tone changed immediately. "Hi, Lizzy."

Maddie was surprised to see him blushing.

*Well I'll be damned*, she thought. *Avi was right.*

Lizzy got to her feet and crossed the room to greet him.

"Hello there, little man." She hugged Henry warmly. "What a treat to get to see you today. Hi, Syd."

"Hi, Lizzy. I apologize for bursting in on you like this. Peggy didn't tell me you two were in a meeting."

"Oh, we're through." Lizzy looked at Maddie. "Aren't we, boss?"

"I suppose so. Sport? You want to let go of Lizzy's leg so we can all sit down?"

"Don't bother with that." Lizzy tousled Henry's mop of hair. "I need to get going. I have a stack of charts to plow through before I can get out of here."

Maddie noticed that Syd was watching Henry closely, too. They exchanged meaningful glances.

"Are you coming for taco night, Lizzy?" Henry looked up at

her with a hopeful expression.

"Well . . ." Lizzy seemed uncertain how to respond.

"Please do," Syd urged her. "I was going to invite you, anyway. That's partly why we stopped by."

"In that case, I'd love to join you. Thank you. Is there anything I can bring?"

"You can bring Avi," Henry declared. "Syd's going to invite *her*, too."

It was Lizzy's turn to blush.

"So much for nuance." Syd apologized. "We already invited her the other day."

Maddie cleared her throat. "How about we just accept we're all in agreement about tacos, which, in and of themselves, are worthy of robust approbation?"

"Maddie," Syd asked, in a lilting voice, "do you ever get tired of lugging that briefcase around?"

"What briefcase?"

"The one between your *ears*."

Lizzy laughed. "I'd love to come eat tacos with all of you, regardless of any nuance."

"Knock, knock." Avi appeared outside Maddie's door. "I thought I heard friendly voices in here."

"Avi!" Henry finally dislodged himself from Lizzy to rush over and greet his new friend. "Lizzy is coming for taco night."

"*Seriously?*" Syd spread her hands in defeat. "Who needs the Internet with this kid around?"

Avi smiled.

"Tuesday night," Maddie clarified. "It's a thing."

"It's great to see you two." Avi beamed at Syd. "I'm so glad I resisted my better instincts not to butt in when I heard you two arrive. Rudeness tends to pay off sometimes."

Another thought occurred to Avi. "If you don't mind my asking, will the usual family party be in attendance on Tuesday night?"

"Probably," Syd replied. "The three of us, David and Michael, and probably Dorothy."

"Sometimes Dorothy comes home with me on the bus," Henry explained. "She likes taco night as much as I do."

"I don't blame her a bit for that, Henry." Avi faced Syd. "It appears I have a fly, in the shape of a conflict of interest, in the taco ointment. Since I've recently entered into a therapeutic relationship with one member of the dinner party, I'll, sadly—*very* sadly—have to decline your generous invitation."

"Oh." Enlightenment dawned for Maddie. "*Of course*. We hadn't considered that."

"It's my loss, believe me." Maddie saw Avi steal a glance at Lizzy, who in Maddie's view was looking pretty disappointed by the circumstances, too.

"Well, we'll be sure to reconnect for another occasion, soon," Syd promised. "In the meantime, I think I may have a solution to your housing dilemma."

"You do? Your timing is perfect. I've nearly decided my only remaining option is to rent a thirty-year-old Winnebago."

"Does that mean you've given up on the single-wide that came furnished with a divorcee and three kids?" Lizzy shook her head. "I thought that sounded like a sweet deal."

"Yeah?" Avi's tone was doubtful. "Maybe if you're into Sam Peckinpah movies."

Lizzy was undaunted. "It's an acquired taste, I'll admit."

"Well, I think I have a solution that can save you from the nomadic life." Syd warmed to the drama of her announcement. "The remedy came to me this afternoon from on high . . . literally."

"So, don't keep me in suspense," Avi said. "What is it?"

"It's the upstairs *apartment*—meaning, upstairs above the library."

"That's *right*." Maddie slapped a palm against her forehead. "Why didn't we think of that sooner?"

"Probably because it was too obvious. And it's perfect for

you, Avi. I actually lived there when I first came to Jericho. We only use it now for storage. It'll be easy enough to relocate the inventory that's up there." She shot a look at Maddie. "It's mostly copier supplies. I'm sure the county would love to have the revenue—*if* you want me to pursue the possibility for you."

Avi was in transports. "Are you kidding? It sounds perfect."

"Do you want to go see it, first?" Syd asked.

"I don't think I need to—especially not if you lived there."

"It's pretty Spartan," Maddie cautioned. "As I recall, it has a dorm-sized fridge and a Barbie stove."

"Gee, let me think about it." Avi raised and lowered her hands in imitation of a scale. "A spartan apartment above a library—*or* one room in a single-wide that comes furnished with three kids?"

"Don't forget the divorcee," Lizzy added.

"I'll contact the library board. Now," Syd took hold of Henry's hand, "we need to be on our way. We have to stop by Food City on the way home."

"We're out of cat food," Henry explained.

"So, we're all agreed?" Syd pointed at Lizzy. "Tacos. Tuesday. Be there." She waved at Maddie. "Aloha, baby cakes. Don't stay too late."

They left. Maddie could hear Henry chattering all the way down the hall.

"Tell me the honest truth about something." She faced Avi and Lizzy. "How worried do I need to be that Syd appears to be the last person on the planet who still watches *Hawaii Five-O?*"

Byron and Celine were relaxing on her patio with glasses of wine. Dorothy was inside, practicing the elusive Beethoven sonata. Celine was doing her best not to listen in too closely. She thought it had been significant that Dorothy had announced her intention to work on the piece after they'd finished dinner. That was a change. Normally, Dorothy would retreat to her room to read.

Byron asked Celine if she'd made their plane reservations for the New York trip.

"In fact, I did. I thought it made sense to take an early evening flight on Friday, instead of heading up Saturday morning. That will allow us a full day for sightseeing, since Dorothy has never been to the city before."

"That sounds like a great idea. Any thoughts about where all you'll go?"

"I have a few. Dorothy specifically asked if we could tour the Steinway factory."

Byron smiled and cocked an ear toward the music coming from inside the house. "That one's not hard to figure out."

"No. But it will be a challenge to figure out how to get us in there. They only do tours on Mondays."

"Do you know anyone who can pull some strings?" Byron amended his comment. "Wires?"

"Good one. I do have one contact I can try. Maybe we can get in if we don't ask for a full-blown tour, but just to see the suite where they present the finished pianos to buyers for demonstration. That's what I'm hoping for. The factory is all the way up in Queens, so it's a twenty-minute cab ride, minimum. I thought we might do that later in the day, before the concert."

"How long has it been since you've been back to the city?"

*How long had it been? Eight years? Ten? Many . . .*

"A long time. It'll be an experience for both of us."

"Gonna lay some demons to rest?"

Celine smiled. "Or maybe unearth a few new ones. It could go either way."

The music slowed. Then stopped. Then restarted before stopping again.

Dorothy was still struggling with articulation during the key transition.

Byron snapped his fingers. "You weren't going to listen, remember?"

Celine met his eyes. "I know. It's . . . a disease."

"No. I wouldn't go that far. It's more like a control thing."

"Control?" Celine was surprised by his comment. "What makes you say that?"

"Because it's the same way I get whenever Charlie talks about her father being back in town. I pretty much want to go get him and drag his useless ass to the county line."

"Well, unlike me, you've at least resisted temptation to interfere."

Byron didn't reply.

"Byron? You *have* stayed out of it, haven't you?"

He finished his wine. "Define 'stayed out of it' for me."

"Oh, no. Byron . . . what did you do?"

"What makes you think I did anything?"

"Don't kid a kidder. The same thing that makes you so certain I'm fighting an impulse to rush into the house and help Dorothy master that transition."

"Right. I get it." He stretched his long legs out and crossed his ankles. "Maybe I had a . . . *chat* with Manfred."

"A chat?"

"That's what I call it. A chat."

"So I suppose you just ran into him in the normal course of a day?"

He studied her with narrowed eyes. "You know, the county should hire you to conduct those inquest interviews. I predict they'd wrap the investigation up in record time."

"Don't obfuscate."

"Okay, so maybe I went and found him."

"And where was he when you had this chat?"

"Bone Gap. He and his common law wife were having some kind of solitary praise-fest in the church there."

"Praise-fest?"

Byron shrugged. "They were at the altar, speaking in tongues."

Celine was shocked by his admission. "And you interrupted that?"

"No, I did *not.* I sat down quietly at the rear of the church until they finished."

"I guess that's something . . ."

"Hey . . . you have to agree that Manfred's actions getting on that bookmobile and accosting Roma Jean and the kids couldn't go unacknowledged. I had every right to go and caution him. In fact, I had a responsibility to do so."

"I suppose that's true."

"And that man's piety is about as deep as the wine in this glass." He held up his empty wineglass. "Mark my words: Manfred Davis is an unredeemed charlatan, and he's up to no good."

"You may be right. But Charlie is an adult—as you've said yourself, many times. With a good head on her shoulders. Why not trust her to resolve this situation?"

"What makes you think I don't trust her?" Byron's tone was sharp. It was unlike him to react to anything so defensively. He seemed to think better of his comment almost immediately. "God. I'm sorry, Celine. I have a hard time staying impartial when it's something that has the potential to hurt her. She's already been through too much in her young life."

"Don't I know it?" When Dorothy's stuttering piano performance resumed, Celine inclined her head toward the sound. "Equal in all things, it appears."

Byron refilled their glasses from the bottle that sat in an ice bucket on the table between them. It was nice—a sparkling rosé they'd sampled and liked on a recent visit to a winery in North Carolina. "I'll drink to that."

Thunder rumbled in the distance. There had only been a modest chance of a storm this evening, but it appeared the odds were improving. Celine scanned the clouds gathering over Buck Mountain.

"So much for our hiatus from the rain."

"Buddy will be happy for the benefit to all his little plants. But I don't think this will amount to much. I predict it'll blow in and move on as fast as it came up."

"Maybe Manfred Davis will do the same thing?"

"Maybe." He clinked rims with her. "Here's to exorcising old demons, whenever they rear their nasty little heads."

"You'll get no argument from me on that one." She sipped her wine. It had a nice, dry palate that was lovely with its berry overtones. "You mentioned the inquest. Are the interviews nearly completed? It seems like they've been going on for weeks now."

"Nearly. I think they have only a few more to finish. One subject is proving to be ... *elusive*. And that's slowing the process down."

"Really?" Celine was intrigued. "Are you able to elaborate?"

"Not really. But the good news is that I think I stumbled across the reason for it—and it's completely un-sinister. The examiners don't appear to me to be finding anything suspicious or chargeable—beyond the fact that the man was pretty universally despised."

"That's good news."

"It really is. The truth is that we may never know what actually happened to Watson."

"I don't know how much that will help Dorothy. I fear she is still riddled with guilt about hitting her father with that piece of driftwood."

"She was only protecting Buddy."

"We both know that—but I don't think she believes it. It's not something I can exactly coerce her into talking about."

"Well, there is one thing related to Dorothy that we're going to have to figure out how to share with her."

"That sounds ominous."

"Yeah. It seems Watson had no immediate family—and left

no will. *Typical.* He also left behind a ton of debt—so much so, his estate will be assessed to pay it all back. There will be next to nothing left for Dorothy's care or education."

"That's demonstrably unfair for her, but hardly surprising, given who he was."

"Yeah. It gets worse. The county is going to seize his property and sell it at a public auction. And since the land is the only thing of real value—and they're persuaded nobody will ever want to live in his house—they're going to have the fire department burn it down."

Celine was aghast. "Burn it down?"

"Yeah."

"Byron . . ."

"I know. We have to tell her. And we have to allow her the chance to get anything she wants out of there."

"I had already determined that I'd like to manage Dorothy's living expenses—including college. No matter what way an ongoing custody arrangement unfolds. But this? How on earth do we tell her about this?"

"I honestly have no idea. I guess it's possible she'll be relieved."

There was another rumble of thunder—closer this time. Celine watched the swirling cluster of dark clouds advance toward them. She felt overwhelmed by her sad realization that Byron's suggestion about how Dorothy might respond to this news was more than a remote possibility: it was a certainty.

Byron seemed to have another thought. "How did her therapy session go?"

"I have no idea. She said very little about it, except to mention that Avi was nice and that she had artwork like mine."

"That kid doesn't miss much, does she?"

"That kid doesn't miss *anything*. She reminds me a lot of David at her age. I mean, in those rare instances you can see beneath Dorothy's cloak of . . . damage." She thought about her comparison. "Maybe damage isn't exactly the right word. David certainly had his share, too. But Dorothy seems more resigned to hers. Not in the sense that she chooses it—but more in the sense that she's so used to living with it, she's learned to accept it like a second skin she cannot shed."

"Damn . . ."

"I told you: still waters run deep."

"Celine?" Byron took hold of her hand. "That's the last thing you need to explain to me."

"So, we wanted to share this idea with you, James—so you could take the time you need to think about it."

Henry and James had finished their regular FaceTime chat a few minutes ago, but Maddie and Syd asked if he could stay on the line a few minutes longer so they could talk over something with him. He agreed right away, and Maddie feared he might think there was some problem. She wanted to set his mind at ease right away—as soon as Henry ran off to feed Before. In as few words as possible, she summarized their thinking that instead of adoption, they should consider a continuing joint custody arrangement.

James had been surprised, but didn't seem unhappy at the suggestion.

"Okay. But why would you want to do it this way?" he asked. "I know you wanted to be sure you'd be taking care of Henry permanently—that I wouldn't change my mind and want to take him back again."

"That's still true," Syd explained. "But you're Henry's father, and you're a good one, James. Henry needs to have you in his life in all the ways he's been used to—that you've both been used to. We don't want to interfere with that."

"I don't know that I did such a good job with him before I

reenlisted. You both know that. Henry wasn't getting what he needed from me, and I knew I'd never be able to do better by him."

"You did the best it was possible for you to do, James. Nobody could ever ask for more than that. Henry knew it—and we knew it, too." Maddie wanted to drive home the message that they were invested in James remaining involved in Henry's life—as a co-parent. "We believe adopting Henry, changing that fundamental understanding he has—*and* you have—would just end up confusing him. He needs to know his daddy is still . . . well. His daddy."

Syd was nodding energetically. "It's really that simple."

"I don't know what to say." James sounded overwhelmed by their suggestion. "I guess I don't get why you'd be willing to do this."

"Because, James." Maddie spoke softly to him. "We sincerely believe the four of us are a family. You matter to us as much as Henry does. And, as Henry would be the first to point out, families stay together."

He smiled. Maddie thought his eyes looked watery. That didn't surprise her—she was near tears herself.

"Take the time you need to think it over, okay?" Syd smiled back at him. "We're not going anyplace."

James nodded. "Thank you both for considering this. I really appreciate it."

"It seems like the right thing for all of us, James." Maddie knew they needed to let him go. He'd already stayed on the call longer than his lunch break allowed. "Let's make a date to talk again soon."

James agreed, and they signed off.

"I think that went very well." Syd seemed genuinely pleased. "Don't you?"

"I really do. I'm surprised he was so unprepared for the suggestion."

"That's our fault, I think. We were so adamant with him about our conditions when he first asked us to take Henry on permanently."

"I know," Maddie agreed. "But I think we were right to let him know the decision had to be binding. What if he'd reenlisted in the army and it didn't work out? We couldn't risk Henry getting bounced around again."

"James doesn't want that any more than we do."

"Agreed. We're both more confident about that now."

"These decisions are always so fraught with legalities. Your mother with Dorothy. Us with Henry. None of it is uncomplicated."

"It shouldn't be, Syd. Not when you're dealing with human beings. Especially when those human beings are children."

"I know. Still . . ." Syd didn't complete her thought.

"Still . . . what?" Maddie asked.

"I was just thinking about how much simpler it was with David and your father. When it became clear that David was better off staying here, his parents allowed it to happen. No drama and no legalese."

"I wouldn't exactly say there was no drama. Far from it, in fact."

"What kind of drama?" Syd was intrigued. "No one has ever said much about how those arrangements actually happened. I assumed it was a gradual transition."

"It was gradual, but it wasn't uncomplicated. Phoebe was a wreck about it—even though she realized David was a lot safer being out of their house."

"But she had to know how horribly her husband was treating their son?"

"Oh, she did, all right. But nobody called those things by name back then, Syd—especially not in a closed, rural community like this one. David's father was an unabashed cretin who couldn't accept the fact that he had a gay son. He wanted nothing more than for David to disappear—so he wouldn't be reminded of his implied failure as a parent. And as wonderful as she is now, back then, Phoebe had to walk a tightrope between her love for her son and her *own* struggles with his emerging sexuality. As parents, they had no context to understand what they understood to be David's 'choices.' And, sadly, they had little curiosity or support for the concept of broadening their perspectives. All Phoebe knew was that David would be safe and cared for here with my father. And she decided it was better to keep him here in town, where she could still be involved in his life, than to leave him to his own devices. His father, on the other hand, just wanted him gone—and he didn't care much where he went as long as he was out of his sight."

"That's unconscionable. There are too many people like him—and like Charlie's father."

"I wholly agree with you on that."

Syd's frustration reached a boiling point. "I don't understand how any parent could violate their sacred obligation to love and care for their children. It's the most basic covenant we make."

"Covenants are broken all the time, sweetheart."

"Well it's criminal, and they shouldn't be. Not ever."

"You know what?" Maddie put an arm around her. "Henry is blessed with a great dad, and an equally great mom."

Syd leaned into her. "*Two* great moms."

"Let's just pray that our self-styled parental three-way saves him from at least a few years of hurt and disappointment."

They heard two sets of footsteps pounding toward them on the porch outside the kitchen.

Henry and Pete were back from the pasture, and they'd soon be clamoring for food.

"From your mouth to god's ear, Sawbones." Syd kissed her on the ear before getting up from the table where they'd set the laptop. "Come on. Let's make some supper."

# Chapter Eight

*Recorded Interview*
*Preliminary Inquest Investigation*
*Death of Mayor Gerald Watson*

"That's correct. I run the Riverside Inn with my partner, David Jenkins. I've lived in Jericho for nearly eight years. My last name is Robertson, with a *t*. I came here from Charleston, where I went to culinary school. But I'm originally from Aiken, South Carolina."

*God. I just know they're going to ask me if I was with David after the fight with Watson . . .*

"Yes. I was catering a lot of the food that day with Nadine Odell. We had just set up the dessert tables when the mayor showed up."

*How much do they know already? Do they know I couldn't find him? Do they know I have no idea where he went?*

"That's right. Mr. Watson was angry and shouting at David for talking with his daughter. David wasn't doing anything but teasing Dorothy about which desserts to try. But Watson was furious and out of control. He said some horrible things to David and made some offensive accusations. There were a lot of people standing there who witnessed it all."

*What would it mean if I refused to answer their questions? Do I have a legal right not to? Would it just make things look worse for David?*

"David never did anything to provoke him. In fact, I was the one who told him to back off when he grabbed Dorothy and yanked her away from us. Nobody should ever treat a child like that—parent or not. It was obvious she was terrified."

*David was like I'd never seen him before . . . like he'd vacated. He was practically comatose. It was almost as if Watson had been trying to drag* him *away—instead of Dorothy.*

"David *never* touched him. Not once. And he never threatened him, either. Watson shoved him hard and he fell backward into one of the food tables. You can ask anyone who was there. Nobody provoked that man. All the while, his daughter was begging him to stop and to leave us alone. She didn't want him to hurt anyone."

*God. Don't ask me. Please don't ask me.*

"He did wander off for a bit. I think just to compose himself. It had all been pretty embarrassing. We were all focused on picking up the desserts that had been knocked all over the ground. It was a big mess, and everyone was trying to help."

*How am I going to handle this? I should've had an answer prepared . . .*

"David reappeared after just a bit. He helped to finish clearing away the food. We watched the fireworks. No. We didn't find out about Watson until later, when all the police and EMTs arrived. We didn't see Dorothy again that night, either."

*Maybe they'll let it drop? Maybe they won't ask me?*

"Well . . . no. I don't actually know where he went when he left to pull himself together. He told me he'd just gone for a walk. He was back in just a short amount of time, though. I'm not really sure how long it was. Maybe an hour? Not much longer than that, though, because Nadine and I were still cleaning up."

*Please, god. Let somebody else have seen him. Let somebody else have told them where he was.*

"Yes. If I remember anything else, I'll be sure to let you know."

Celine had been through the National Immigration Museum on Ellis Island many times. Her parents had taken her to tour the island facility at the mouth of the Hudson River for the first time on her tenth birthday, to teach her about their experience arriving in the United States in 1950, just four years before the immigration station closed its golden doors. It had been hard for her to comprehend that her parents had not always lived in their Manhattan neighborhood, but had first arrived in the city with little more than their musical instruments and their aspirations to pursue performance careers on some of the greatest stages in the world.

Those dreams had mostly been realized by the time Celine had been born. Wandering among the towering displays of photographs that depicted the gaunt faces of haggard-looking travelers, she found it hard to reconcile the life she lived in the luxury of their Upper East Side apartment with the battered suitcases and canvas bags these weary hopefuls clutched.

She remembered her father crouching beside her as she stared up at one image of row after row of immigrants, waiting to be processed. "Remember this, *Bärchen*. These are your humble beginnings. Always be grateful for the gifts you have been given."

She had always remembered his words. But years later, her beloved Papi had turned his face away when she entered his studio and told him she no longer wished to study the piano at Juilliard.

"*Du bist nicht meine Tochter*," he'd said. *You are not my daughter.*

Her father's quiet disappointment had been harder to bear than her mother's strident rejection of her plans to pursue a career in medicine. Things were much simpler for her mother. Celine was a *Weisz*. And a Weisz pursued only one path: a lifetime of fierce dedication and devotion to music.

But today wasn't about revisiting her past experiences: it was about giving Dorothy the chance to create her own. She'd been mostly silent on the boat ride over from the Battery. Celine could sense the girl's unabashed astonishment as they approached the Statue of Liberty. It had been palpable. And Celine understood it. Even having grown up in the city, she'd never fully understood the power of what the monument represented until she approached it for the first time from the water. The ubiquitous clicking of cell phone cameras and the incessant chattering of tourists in a dozen different tongues could not detract from the enormity of what she knew Dorothy was feeling.

Their stroll through the museum at Ellis Island appeared to be having the same effect.

"Your *parents* came to New York through here?" Dorothy asked in amazement. Other questions followed in quick succession. *What did they do? Where did they go? Did they know anyone else in the city? What kind of jobs did they get?* Celine answered them all with as much detail as she could supply. The truth was, she knew very little about how her parents managed once they passed through here. Her mother preferred to gloss over any of the hardships they had endured—choosing, instead, to impress her daughter with how far hard work, industry and endless *practice* had brought them.

"You must study, *Töchterchen*. That is how to make your way in this world. Nothing is given to you. You must earn it through hard work."

Dorothy asked if they could see the apartment building where Celine had lived. And the music school, too—the place she called "Juilliard." *Was their apartment near the school? Could Celine walk there from home? Could they go there today, too?*

Celine said yes to everything. Her attempt to finagle an

abbreviated tour of the Steinway factory in Queens had failed. The facility was closed to the public for repairs right now. Not even the regular Monday tours were happening. But the kind manager she spoke with took an interest in her plight, and made what turned out to be a very helpful suggestion: why not take Dorothy to tour the new Steinway Hall on 6th Avenue? He explained that all of their latest concert grand and salon models were on display there, and pointed out that the opulent 19,000-square-foot facility featured a seventy-four-seat recital hall. With luck, they might get a peek at a potential buyer, test-driving a few models before purchase.

Since Steinway Hall was only a fifteen-minute walk from their hotel in Midtown, Celine thought it should be the highlight of their day, and the last thing they did before grabbing an early supper and attending the concert. The walk to Carnegie Hall from the Warwick Hotel would take less than two minutes, so they had plenty of time for Dorothy to tarry and indulge her passion for the pianos.

The first thing that caught Dorothy's eye when they stepped inside the exquisite showroom was a breathtaking installation made of glass by artist Spencer Finch. Called *Newton's Theory of Color and Music*, Finch's brilliantly colored creation recreated the visual spectrum created by Isaac Newton, which assigned colors to each note on the chromatic scale. Finch used that scale to replicate the exact chromatic sequence found in a seminal work by J.S. Bach, represented by a series of alternating colors on long glass tubes, each internally illuminated by fluorescent light. The work was a stunning display of color and carefully controlled order.

Celine drew Dorothy's attention to the particular piece of music the installation represented: Bach's *Goldberg Variations*.

Dorothy was nearly overcome with excitement—a reaction Celine had never seen the girl express. She was captivated by how the expression of such raw emotion overspread her young face.

"This is the music Buddy loves so much—from that recording you played for him. He counted the number of bars. Over and over, he talked about how Bach put God inside the music."

"I remember," Celine told her. "Clearly, Buddy and this artist have something in common. You'll have to tell Buddy about this sculpture when we get home."

Dorothy was gazing up at the soaring tubes of color. "I can't believe it. This must be what Buddy sees when he listens to music—all these colors and patterns. It all makes sense now."

Celine had to agree. Buddy's synesthesia did give him the uncanny ability to "see" the colors in the music—unlike the rest of them, who could only listen to it. "Maybe we can find a photo or poster of this to take to Buddy. Do you think he would like that?"

"I know he would."

They spent the better part of two hours looking at all the various pianos on display. Dorothy was especially intrigued by Steinway's Spirio line of digital player pianos. The high-resolution instruments recreated live performances with perfect tonality and fidelity. Selections in the Spirio library comprised an extensive roster of performances by the world's leading artists—both contemporary and historic. And it was all controlled by a special app available for iPad. The pianos could also capture live performances and immediately play them back.

"Why would you ever need to learn how to play the music if you can buy one of these?"

Celine had to admit that Dorothy's question had some merit. "I suppose," she suggested, "that without the artists who can play the music, the Spirio library would be pretty limited."

"That's true." Dorothy agreed. "And you'd miss out on all the best parts, too."

"What are those?"

"Feeling the way the keys move under your fingers and how the notes flow out from inside you just exactly the way you play them—whether you get them right or wrong. How you feel the sounds, and how the music keeps echoing inside the room—even after you're finished. Like it's been set free and can do what it wants once it's been released." She looked up at Celine. "Does that sound weird?"

"No." Celine had been so overcome by Dorothy's simple explanation, she was finding it hard to articulate any coherent response. "It sounds exactly right to me."

During the walk back to their hotel, Celine took a slight detour along 57th Street so they could duck into the Brooklyn Diner to get a bite to eat before the concert. She thought the place had enough authentic New York ambience to be engaging to Dorothy, and it also featured an expansive menu that included many more accessible options. Dorothy seemed genuinely impressed by the number of selections. It became clear to Celine in short order that she longed to try one of nearly everything.

In the end, Dorothy opted for a bowl of the homemade chicken noodle soup that was served with a biscuit top, and Celine chose the pan-seared teriyaki salmon.

They agreed to split an Oreo milkshake.

Throughout their meal, Dorothy was uncharacteristically talkative. She seemed to be thriving on the sights, sounds and infectious energy of her first New York experience. More than once, she asked Celine if it had been hard for her to leave the city to move to California. Celine explained that she'd actually left New York to live in Virginia, when she'd married Maddie's father—but agreed that, yes, there had been parts of her life in New York she'd missed very much.

"What parts?" the now unabashed Dorothy wanted to know.

"Well," the depth of Dorothy's curiosity amused Celine, "ready access to so many first-rate musical performances, for one thing. And I missed the bookstores and some of the restaurants."

"I know you missed *this* place. It's terrific."

"I bet that biscuit isn't as good as yours, though."

"It's different." She could tell Dorothy didn't want to blow her own horn. "But it's still really good. And the noodles are amazing."

"I think that's because they're homemade. Homemade is nearly always better."

"I'd love to learn how to make noodles." Dorothy spooned one up. "I wonder if it's hard?"

"Tell you what . . . when we get home we'll give it a try."

"Can we?" Dorothy's eyes were alive with excitement.

"I don't see why not. I'm sure Byron would love them."

"I know he would. As long as we didn't put them in chicken soup."

"Don't worry about that. There are a lot of vegetarian dishes that use noodles. I have several cookbooks we can go through. I'm sure we'll find something."

Thinking about going home must've reminded Dorothy about their Steinway Hall visit.

"Thank you for buying that poster for Buddy. I know he'll love it."

"I'm just glad they had one for sale. I want Buddy to see the sculpture as much as you do. It will be a special reminder of all the conversations we had about Bach and *The Goldberg Variations*."

"And that man who grunted while he played them on the piano."

"You mean Glenn Gould. Yes. He had a very unique style."

"I wonder if Mitsuko Uchida will make noises when she plays tonight?"

Celine smiled. "I somehow don't think so. And we won't be close enough to the stage to hear her, if she does. Are you excited about the concert tonight?"

Dorothy nodded. "I've never been to a real one before."

"I think your trip to hear the Richmond Symphony counts as a real concert."

"Maybe. But that was all Christmas music. It wasn't like the music you and Buddy and I love."

Celine was touched by Dorothy's simple admission. "I'm glad you love it, too."

"I didn't know anything about it. Not until that day David brought me to your house and you showed me your piano. It was . . . weird."

"What about it was weird?"

"I don't know." Dorothy made a subtle shrug. "I guess it was like that thing that happens sometimes when you meet a new person—but they don't seem new. They seem like someone you've always known." She looked down at her lap. "That's probably a stupid thing to say about something that's not even alive."

"No. It isn't. I understand perfectly what you're describing. Buddy would, too."

Dorothy met her eyes. "I felt at home right then—like I was in a place I belonged."

Celine's heart melted. "I hope you still feel that way, Dorothy."

She gave Celine a shy nod.

Celine didn't suppress her smile.

"Do you want some more of this milkshake?" Dorothy pushed the icy, tall glass toward Celine. "I feel like I'm drinking the whole thing."

Celine knew Dorothy needed to move their conversation to less emotional ground.

"Sure." She took up her spoon. "I'll never turn down a frozen Oreo."

It had been Maddie's turn to work with Henry on his math problems. Syd was busy on a conference call with several of her bridesmaids.

Dear god . . . *bridesmaids*. One or two, Maddie could get her head around. *But twelve?*

The concept of twelve was becoming a problem as difficult for Maddie to solve as was finding an effective way to get Henry to understand how prime numbers worked.

*And why were kids expected to grasp abstract concepts like prime numbers in the damn third grade?*

In her view, they still should've been reading about Dick, Jane and Sally . . .

But she realized this enriched learning curriculum was part of Henry's "gifted and talented" classes at the local elementary school. More than once, she and Syd had discussed the merits of sending Henry to attend one of the private academies located in neighboring counties. But each time, they'd backed away from that prospect, believing that a solid public school education, combined with significant home involvement on their part, would serve him better in the long run. Socialization was important for Henry. So was having the opportunity to form close, lasting relationships with the children who were his neighbors. He'd have plenty of time later, once his interests evolved and narrowed, to decide what direction he wanted to take for focused or advanced study.

Frankly, she hoped he'd go to medical school—and one day take over her practice. But Syd said that was a pipe dream, and he'd be likelier to become an engineer—or a zookeeper.

According to her, it could go either way.

In the end, it didn't much matter what he chose to do, as long as he found happiness and came home for holidays.

She really wanted that holiday part to happen . . .

She'd helped Henry create a graph that listed all numbers from one to one hundred, in ten rows of ten. Now she was helping him identify which of the numbers were prime numbers: meaning they were numbers that were only divisible by one or themselves.

He seemed to get that concept, but it took him a while to

do the math on each number as he progressed through the rows. Eventually, Henry realized that *even* numbers were not prime numbers, and *odd* numbers were.

Of course, it then occurred to him to ask Maddie about fractions, and a brave new world of disappointed hopes opened before her.

It occurred to her that Buddy would've been a better person to teach Henry about these concepts. She decided to facilitate that idea by inviting Buddy to taco night on Tuesday.

For tonight, however, they'd accomplished enough, and it was time to get Henry ready for bed. They were nearing the end of his *Danny the Champion of the World* book, and things were getting very exciting in the Gypsy caravan where Danny lived with his mechanic father, who moonlighted poaching pheasants. Henry told Maddie that Roma Jean had a big stack of books on hold for him when they finished this one. Maddie didn't mind one bit. Reading to Henry before bed was one of her favorite parts of the day.

When she finally made it back downstairs, Syd was just finishing up her call. Maddie saw that she'd made copious notes in one of her array of color-themed notebooks—each one pertaining to a different aspect of wedding planning. She supposed this one was the "bridesmaid" handbook.

The whole thing was making her slightly depressed—and irritated.

As usual, Syd picked up on her mood.

"How'd the math lesson go?"

"Okay." Maddie was noncommittal.

"You don't sound very convinced."

"No." Maddie thumbed through Syd's notes. "It went fine. I think he made some progress."

Syd watched her reaction to the notes she'd made during the call.

"Is something bothering you?" she asked.

"What makes you ask that?" Maddie hadn't meant for her tone to be so sharp, and regretted the words as soon as they'd left her mouth. "I'm sorry, honey. I didn't mean to snap at you."

"Uh huh." Syd reached out a hand to take the notebook from her. "What's really eating at you? Or do I even need to ask?"

"Come on, Syd. Let's not do this tonight. Okay?"

"Oh, no you don't." Syd pulled out a chair. "Take a seat, Dr. Stevenson. We're doing this all right. And we're doing it right now."

Maddie knew better than to argue with her. She dropped onto the chair with all the elegance of a sack of potatoes.

Syd followed suit and sat down at the table opposite her. "So, do you want to tell me what's going on with you and why you're so despondent? I somehow think it has nothing to do with prime numbers."

She was right about that. *Mostly because twelve wasn't prime for anything . . .*

"It's just . . . do we really need *twelve* bridesmaids? When David told me about it, I thought he was joking. But," she gestured toward the notebook, "I guess he wasn't."

"I fail to understand why any of this is so upsetting to you."

"Don't you?"

"No. I genuinely do not. I would have hoped you'd be as excited and as invested in this event as I am. But every step of the way, you've dragged your feet and avoided taking part in any aspect of it. I'm beginning to think maybe you don't really want to marry me at all."

"Syd. That's ridiculous, and you know it."

"How am I supposed to know that, Maddie?" Syd's exasperation was clear. "Through osmosis? Certainly not because you've made any effort to be invested in any of the planning."

"To be fair, you and David haven't seemed very interested in *having* me be involved in the planning."

"That's not true. I can't even get you to work on the guest list."

"Oh. Right. Because I have to fill my share of . . . how many seats do I get? A hundred? A hundred and fifty? The scope of this thing is ludicrous, Syd. I don't even know that many people."

"Of course you do—you just don't care enough to think about it."

Maddie sat back and folded her arms. "So, you don't think *any* aspect of this is just the tiniest bit over the top? You honestly think the scale of what you're planning is appropriate for us, and for the town we live in?"

"Clearly, it doesn't much matter what I think, since you've already decided it isn't."

"Honey . . ." Maddie dropped her arms and tried to lower the temperature of their discussion. "All I want is to be married. *To you.* That's all I've ever wanted. I don't need two hundred guests, a couple dozen attendants, hyper-foraged crudités, *haute couture*, arbors choked with lilies, or a hundred freaking doves to show the world how much I love you, and how committed to our life together I am. *I just want you.* Plain and simple. Isn't it possible for us to dial some of this back . . . just a little bit? Maybe meet in the middle someplace?"

"You sound like we're negotiating a treaty, not planning our wedding."

"Now that you mention it . . ." Maddie attempted a joke, but Syd wasn't ready to see the humor in anything just yet.

"Fine." Syd abruptly pushed back her chair and collected her notebooks. "We can just call the whole damn thing off."

"Wait a minute . . ."

"No. *You* wait a minute, Maddie. I explained why this was all so important to me—and I thought you understood it. I even allowed myself to believe you respected it. Apparently, I was mistaken."

Maddie got up, too. "Syd. Come on. Calm down about this. You're not even acting like yourself. Whenever the topic of this wedding comes up you morph into . . . I don't know—some kind of Bridezilla."

*Okay. Not the smartest thing to say . . .*

Syd's green eyes blazed. "Like I said. You can relax, now. The wedding is *off*."

She left the kitchen and stormed up the back stairs to their bedroom.

Maddie watched her go in a daze, not really sure if Syd meant the Cecil B. DeMille wedding was off, or their *marriage* was off.

And right then, she was too damn chicken to follow her and find out.

Avi had finished installing shelving units in the former supply closet at the clinic. She told Lizzy that Maddie had agreed to her idea to convert the little-used space into a shared resource library. For her part, Lizzy didn't have many volumes in her own office to contribute, although it was true that she tended to keep most of her reference books at home.

The renovated space was looking pretty good. There was even room for a small table and chair along one wall, and Avi had appointed it with a desk lamp and hung a vibrant modern art print on the wall above it.

Lizzy'd stayed late to help Avi transfer boxes of books from her small office into the space.

"You know what?" Lizzy observed. "If this room had a window, I'd think about moving in here, myself."

"Yeah. It is kind of claustrophobic for long-term use. Although the hum of that wine fridge adds a certain homey charm."

"Why *is* that thing in here? I don't remember it being here before."

Avi took the box from Lizzy and set it down on the floor. "I gather it's some kind of family drama involving Maddie, David, and Maddie's drive to protect some vintage bottles of hooch."

"Oh. *That*. It's true. Maddie says David could find truffles in the Sahara."

"An unsung talent, to be sure. He sounds like a useful friend, to me."

"Have you met him yet?"

"I did about a hundred years ago, when I spent some time here with Maddie and her dad. I remember David being as vibrant as a live wire: full of spark and energy—with great fashion sense."

"That about sums him up. He and Maddie have been best friends forever."

"I can see why. She tends to have more . . . gravity."

Lizzy was pulling books from the box and examining their titles. "These appear to be about," she turned one over and scanned the copy on the back, "something incomprehensible."

"Lemme see." Avi leaned over her shoulder. "That's not incomprehensible. It's Anna Freud's definitive exposition of ambiguity in the child's superego."

"Of course it is." Lizzy handed the book to her. "Don't you ever read magazines?"

Avi shot her a withering look. "Magazines?"

"Sure. You know . . . *Red Book, Family Circle, Garden & Gun*."

"*Garden & Gun?* You have to be joking."

"Nope. You should check it out. Top-tier writers and photographers. It's a coffee table-worthy lexicon of Southern culture."

"Hence the gun part?"

"It's a somewhat regrettable, yet undeniable, building block of social discourse south of thirty-six degrees, thirty minutes—or what untutored Yankees call the Mason-Dixon line. Guns rank right up there with grits, Jesus, and The Whiskey Trail. You should check it out. I think there are copies in the waiting room."

"Seriously? I need to get out more."

"You seem to be doing all right."

"You think so?" Avi asked.

"I do. I've never seen anyone ease into life in this community as seamlessly as you have."

"I appreciate the compliment, but I'm not sure how 'seamless' it's been. I tend to overcompensate for my unconventional presentation. That probably comes across as a comfort level I don't actually feel."

Lizzy handed her more books. These seemed to be as obtuse in content as the Anna Freud volume.

"What do you find to be unconventional about your—*presentation*, as you call it?" She asked Avi the question out of genuine curiosity.

"You mean apart from my manifestations of boi-ish charm and preference for androgynous dress?"

"Well. Yes. I don't find those things to be remarkable at all."

"Nurse Mayes. Be careful or you'll quite turn my head."

Lizzy fought the sudden blush she felt advancing up her neck.

*Great. Just what she needed.*

Fair skin be damned. She remembered how her English lit professor at Vanderbilt defined instances of blushing in Victorian literature as "erections of the head." She'd never been able to look at Jane Eyre or Elizabeth Bennet in quite the same way after that.

"Don't do that." She chose to meet Avi's taunt head on.

"Don't do what?"

She wanted to blurt, *Tempt me to behave like a dog in heat.* But she refrained. She wasn't that courageous. And she was too confused about the escalating power of their obvious . . . *whatever in the hell it was.* Even if she'd *had* a name for it, she wasn't ready to use it. She didn't trust her perceptions right now—about *anything.* And she sure as hell didn't trust her instincts.

"Tease me," she said, instead. "I feel like I'm in uncharted waters with all of this, and I'm foundering."

Lizzy's direct admission led Avi to quickly abandon her former tone.

"I'm sorry." She extended a hand to reassure Lizzy, but seemed to think better of it. "My behavior has been . . . inappropriate, to say the least." When Lizzy didn't reply, Avi continued, "I honestly don't know what I'm doing."

"Don't you?" Lizzy hadn't intended to issue her response with the flirtatious abandon of tossing down a gauntlet. Yet every passing second, their *tête-à-tête* felt more like a confounding duel between willing adversaries who kept switching sides.

"Maybe I do." Avi's honest, self-effacing response didn't make things any easier. Neither did the look in her dark eyes.

*Beyond this point there be dragons*, Lizzy's tired mind reminded her. She knew what she needed to do. It was easy. She needed to concoct some flimsy excuse and leave—extract herself from a cascading impulse to rush headlong into clear and present danger. Space inside this closet had become too small—too close, and no longer able to constrain the leviathan that had reared up between them.

She closed her eyes in a last-ditch effort to save herself. "I need . . ."

When she didn't finish her statement, Avi gently prompted her. "What do you need?"

Lizzy did look at her, then, aware that Avi's image had begun to shift in and out of focus. She swayed and extended a hand toward Avi to steady herself, while she fought to clear her vision.

"I need," she repeated, as she fumbled forward.

*I'm doing this*, her mind and heart chanted in time with the blood pounding through her veins. *I'm doing this because I have to.*

The speed and strength of her advance nearly knocked them both to the floor. But Avi held on tight. She held on as Lizzy kissed her, finally surrendering the reins and allowing her wildest impulses to run free.

It was nearly 10 p.m. when Celine and Dorothy arrived back at their hotel room after the concert. Mitsuko Uchida had obliged and delighted the enthusiastic audience by playing two encores, both selections from her extensive Mozart repertoire.

Dorothy sat forward, perched on the edge of her seat throughout most of the performance. Celine didn't blame her one bit. Uchida's playing had been spectacular and alive with nuance. When the acclaimed pianist skillfully and fluidly navigated the transition from down-tempo E minor to double tempo A minor—a mirror of the same thing Dorothy had been struggling with—the girl gazed at Celine with a look of sheer amazement, and a flood of recognition. Celine understood all that Dorothy sought to communicate. Her experience of such restrained and nuanced articulation in live performance had communicated more meaning than a thousand lessons ever could.

*She understood it now.*

*That* was the unwritten part of mastering music theory. That was the part that couldn't be taught. It had to be felt. It had to well up from deep inside you. Its true meaning derived from the power and force of its nonverbal expression.

And that was at the heart of the connection they shared with each other, and with Buddy.

When the concert ended and they made their slow way out of the fabled venue, Dorothy didn't try to mask how overwhelmed she felt by the entirety of the experience: the magnificence of the great hall, the refinement of the stately paneled walls and gleaming wooden floorboards of the stage, the glow of the elaborate chandeliers, and the perfect acoustics that allowed even the faintest musical timbre to vibrate beneath their feet.

She peppered Celine with questions during the short walk back to their hotel. Celine did her best to field them all. Dorothy was excited to return home and revisit the Beethoven sonata with a fresh perspective. She seemed persuaded that she understood it now.

Celine didn't disagree with her one bit.

After they'd changed and gotten ready for bed, it occurred to Celine that it had been six hours since they'd eaten their early supper at the Brooklyn Diner.

"Are you hungry?" she asked Dorothy.

She could tell Dorothy wasn't sure how to answer. Celine knew she probably didn't want to make a fuss about anything.

"I'm asking because I'm feeling a bit peckish. Maybe a little bite of something would be nice?"

"Okay," Dorothy agreed. "Where would we go so late?"

Celine smiled. "Not far. We can order room service."

"Really? They'll bring food right to us here?"

"I think that can be arranged." Celine retrieved the menu from a credenza drawer. "Let's see what's available."

The selections offered after 10 p.m. were more limited, but still sufficient to meet their needs. They decided to share a charcuterie and cheese board and added two cups of tomato soup. The server promised the food should arrive within thirty minutes. While they waited, they stretched out on their beds and shared their most memorable details from the day.

Celine worried about keeping Dorothy awake so long, but the girl seemed unfazed by the lateness of the hour. Instead of finding the city oppressive with its noise, traffic and crush of people, Dorothy seemed to find it all exhilarating. Celine found this to be an astounding reaction from someone who'd never ventured more than a handful of miles from her home in Jericho.

They hadn't had time that day to visit Lincoln Center so Dorothy could see Juilliard—but Celine thought they could squeeze it in before heading to LaGuardia to catch their late-afternoon flight back to Charlotte.

Something told her there might be visits back to the city in their future.

"I want to get a souvenir for Henry." Dorothy gave it some thought, but apparently couldn't come up with a winning idea. "What do you think he would like?"

"Maybe an alarm clock that works?" Celine suggested.

Dorothy laughed. "Yeah. He'll never get that broken one back together."

"How about a New York Yankees cap? He's always wearing hats."

"That's perfect!" Dorothy's excitement was infectious. "He loves baseball. And it'll look a lot better than that ratty Quakers hat Maddie gave him."

"We should be able to pick one up at their team store in Times Square. It's only about a ten-minute walk from here. We can grab a cab from there and shoot up to Lincoln Center."

"Is that where Juilliard is?"

"Yes. It's part of the whole complex. We just need to be back here by one-thirty so we can meet our car to the airport."

"Will you like visiting there again?"

"To tell the truth, I haven't really thought about it. I haven't been back there in many years. I'm sure it's changed a lot. I don't know how much we'll actually get to see—but we can walk around the complex and you can see the opera and city ballet houses, too. Maybe one day, we can come back for a performance there. Would you like that?"

"I'd love that. Maybe Miss Murphy could come, too? She loves opera. She's always listening to it while she's cooking. Dr. Stevenson always complains and says it sounds like Rosebud howling."

"That sounds like her." Celine smiled. "But we'll definitely invite Syd to join us."

Dorothy was looking around their room. "I've never stayed

in a hotel before. Are they all this nice?"

"Not all of them, no. But I've always liked staying here because it's close to so many things."

"Papa said only bad women stayed at hotels. I think he meant my mother."

"When did he say that?"

Dorothy shrugged her narrow shoulders. "Some time after she left us. I don't remember it very well."

"That's right. You were very young when your mother passed away, weren't you?"

"Yeah. Only five. I remember her, though. She always smelled like lilacs, and she was a really good cook, like you. Only not as fancy."

"I know you miss her a lot. I'm sorry you didn't have more time with her."

"Me, too. Everything changed when she left. Papa got . . ." Dorothy hedged. "Angrier. I think he blamed me for making her leave."

Celine was treading carefully. It was unusual for Dorothy to be this self-revealing. She didn't want to ask too many questions or scare her back into her customary silence.

"I don't think you could've done anything to make her leave, Dorothy. Adults do things for all kinds of reasons. I'm sure it would make her sad if she knew you thought that."

"Maybe. I don't know." Dorothy was plucking at a loose thread on her bedspread. "He said she didn't want me anymore, so she ran away from us."

Celine bit her lip to keep from expressing the rage she felt welling up inside.

*How could any parent say that to a child?*

"I didn't know your mother, but from what you've told me about her, that doesn't sound like something she'd ever do. I'm sure she loved you very much. It would be difficult not to."

Dorothy raised her eyes to Celine's face. "I tried to learn

how to be good enough, so I wouldn't upset him. Sometimes, it worked, but not always."

Celine recalled the day Dorothy had allowed her to examine the welts on her back. The recollection made her half sick.

"Was that when he'd hurt you?"

Dorothy nodded.

Celine wanted to ask a follow-up question that had been haunting her, but was afraid it would push Dorothy back into hiding.

So she stayed silent.

After a minute or two, Dorothy continued her halting narrative.

"It was only when he'd been drinking that he'd do . . . other things." She stole a furtive glance at Celine. "I never told anybody about it."

"Dorothy?" Celine waited until Dorothy looked back at her. "Did your father rape you?"

Dorothy dropped her eyes. "Sometimes. He'd be in a rage and would always tell me it was my fault—that I made him do it. But I never wanted that . . ." Her eyes met Celine's. "I promise I never did."

"Oh, honey. I believe you." She hastily wiped at her eyes. "Hear me, Dorothy: I *believe* you."

"I'm sorry, Dr. Heller. I didn't mean to upset you. I shouldn't have said anything."

"*No.* No, Dorothy. You were absolutely right to tell me. I promise I'm not upset with you—and I'm not afraid to know about this. I'm just so sad and sorry he did this to you—all of it. Listen to me, please: this *never* should have happened to you—not ever. It wasn't right."

Dorothy tried to smile, but didn't quite succeed. "Now you sound like Buddy."

"Buddy understands a lot more than we do."

"I know. I always feel like he knows everything."

More than anything, Celine wanted to wrap her arms around the girl—to hold her close and promise that nothing like this would ever happen to her again. But Dorothy had clear boundaries—ones that probably had taken most of her short life to develop, and Celine needed to respect them.

"Would it be okay if I came over there and sat beside you—just for a little bit?"

Dorothy nodded permission. "But you don't have to worry about me. I'm really okay, I promise."

"I know you are." Celine got up and carefully closed the space between their beds so she could sit down beside her. "It's me who needs to be close to you right now. Is that okay?"

Dorothy didn't reply, but she seemed to understand the subtle shift in their dynamic.

Celine was careful not to touch the girl, but Dorothy immediately leaned into her.

They sat that way until a knock at their door advertised the arrival of their late supper.

"If we drink any more of that, we'll be awake all night."

Lizzy had refilled her own coffee cup, and was offering more to Avi.

"What difference does it make?" she said. "I'll be awake all night, regardless."

"Good point." Avi held out her mug. "Top me off."

After their unrestrained encounter in the makeshift closet library, they agreed that it was probably a good idea to sit down and see if calmer heads could prevail. For her part, Lizzy had been tempted to flee and not look back on how insupportable her behavior had been. But Avi, being Avi, had the wherewithal to insist they needed to sit down—right then—and talk through what had occurred.

*What* had *occurred?* Even now, after two cups of coffee, Lizzy had no framework to understand it. Her . . . *unbridled* assault on Avi wasn't like anything she'd ever done before. She didn't recognize herself. And she was mortified that, if it had been left up to her, she'd have kept right on going.

It had been Avi who'd come to her senses first. And that only happened after they'd stumbled back against one of the unsecured shelf units, and a book had toppled off and hit Avi square on the head.

They were sitting in Lizzy's office, and Avi continued to absently rub a hand over the spot.

"Are you sure you don't need some ice for that?" Lizzy asked.

"No." Avi dropped her hand. "It really doesn't hurt, I promise. I just keep thinking about the irony."

It had been the Anna Freud book that had fallen and struck her. Avi had carried it with them to Lizzy's office like some kind of talisman. It sat on the small table between their chairs.

"What the hell *was* that?" she asked.

"Which part?" Lizzy was pretty confused about every aspect of what had transpired between them.

"Yes. Exactly my point."

"I honestly don't know what came over me." Lizzy made the mistake of meeting Avi's eyes, and her determination folded like a cheap lawn chair. "That's a lie," she confessed. "I knew what I was doing. I'm mortified . . ."

"Why are you mortified for giving in to an honest impulse?"

"Precisely because it *was* an impulse. Aren't you the one who's supposed to be an authority on impulse control?"

"That depends."

"Oh, come on." Lizzy rejected Avi's hedge. "Depends on what?"

"In this case, it depends on how powerful my *own* impulses are. I'm still human."

Lizzy had no response to that admission.

"Believe me," Avi continued, "if the esteemed Dr. Freud hadn't smacked me upside the head, we wouldn't be sitting here right now, calmly discussing this like we're on the set of some talk show."

"It'd have to be Springer or Maury Povich."

"Are you *always* so dour?"

"Only when I act like a shameless floozy."

"Floozy?" Avi deliberated. "I wouldn't go that far."

"I see you noted no objection to the 'shameless' idea."

"Look. It happened. We *both* participated. I *am* guilty of egging you on. In fact, I have to take the hit for behaving inappropriately toward you almost since we met. So there's plenty of culpability to spread around here—more than enough to weave two hair shirts."

"Ordinarily, I wouldn't be this . . . flummoxed. But I'm barely out of my relationship with Tom. And even if that weren't the case, you'd still be a . . ." Lizzy didn't complete her sentence.

"A woman?" Avi suggested.

"I'm sorry." Lizzy raised a hand to rub her forehead. "I'm not handling this very well. It isn't about *that* . . . not really. I mean, I've never spared a single thought about *any* of this before. It's always been perfectly natural to me. It's just never been *about* me." She dropped her hand. "Until now."

"Sometimes attractions between people just happen—like a straightforward hormonal or chemical response. They don't always have to imply anything greater than that."

"Is that what you think this is?"

"For me, you mean?"

Lizzy nodded.

Avi drummed her fingers against the side of her mug.

Lizzy answered her own question. "I didn't think so."

"But that doesn't mean it has to signify anything greater for *you*, Lizzy. This isn't some kind of 'you break it, you bought it' retail rule. You get to take the time you need to decide where this belongs in your own self-understanding. And my job is to give you the space to do that without interference."

"It must suck to have to be so reasonable all the time."

"You have *no* idea." Avi looked like she meant it.

"All right." Lizzy took a slow, deep breath. "Thank you for this, Avi." She set her coffee mug down. "I may as well head for home so I can get started on yet another sleepless night."

"I'll be right on your heels in *that* relay race."

Lizzy got up and collected her bag and keys. "Will you lock up?"

"Sure. I'm gonna hang here a bit longer." She snagged the book from the table beside her chair. "Dr. Freud and I have some unfinished business."

"See you tomorrow?"

Avi smiled. "Count on it."

Lizzy paused just outside the door. "There *is* one part of this whole process that really does suck."

"What's that?"

Lizzy sighed. "You're a great kisser."

She left before Avi had a chance to reply.

Syd had no idea where Maddie went after their argument. She'd been shocked when she heard the Jeep start up and slowly leave the property. Watching the glow of her taillights disappear behind the pond filled her with fear and regret.

How had she allowed things to get so out of hand? It wasn't what they did. They'd never had an argument like that before. And Syd had never stormed out of a room that way, either—not even when she'd discovered the truth about her ex-husband's latest infidelity.

*She was ashamed of her behavior.*

And she continued to be heartsick and disappointed by

Maddie's stubborn resistance to even *try* to engage with any aspect of the wedding planning. She thought they'd reached an understanding about all of this the last time they'd locked horns about the scope of the wedding. Maddie had really seemed to accept how important staging the perfect event was to her—how much Syd wanted it to atone for her first mistake, marrying Jeff.

But tonight, Maddie had retreated to her earlier posture of casting aspersions on all of it. She hadn't minced words, either.

*Bridezilla*, she'd called Syd.

That was the thing that stung her so badly and had pushed her over the edge.

*But she still wished she hadn't stormed out like that.* How many times had she lectured Henry about never walking away in anger?

*Too many times to count.*

And where had Maddie gone at this hour? It wasn't like her just to leave like that. Maddie never walked away from a fight. Syd had fully expected she would follow her upstairs so they could talk it through.

Maddie *always* wanted to talk things through. It was a hallmark of their relationship.

*Until tonight.*

She picked up her cell phone for the twentieth time and thought about texting her: *Where are you? When are you coming home?*

But she didn't.

Whatever had driven Maddie to leave was something Syd knew she needed space to figure out. Even though not knowing where she'd gone—and if she'd be coming back—was eating her alive. She couldn't imagine her life without Maddie. Not now. It would be impossible. The two of them were meant to be together. How was it her father characterized them?

*Like Ferrante & Teicher.*

Her father was such a nerd.

They actually were a lot more like . . . Wallace & Gromit.

She smiled. *Sans the penguin . . .*

At least she could still find *something* to smile about. That had to mean they'd be able to work this out and find some kind of common ground. Didn't it?

But first, Maddie needed to come home.

She checked the clock over their bedroom fireplace for the zillionth time. Maddie had been gone for nearly two hours now. Syd was beginning to panic. What if she didn't come back tonight? What would she tell Henry in the morning? And how would she ever live with herself for driving her away?

She finally decided to head back downstairs and make some hot tea. She didn't really want it, but at least it would give her something to do. She'd just finished filling the kettle with water and putting it on to boil when she heard the sound of a car outside.

*Thank god, thank god . . .*

She didn't know whether to go outside to meet her, or to wait for her to come into the house.

She didn't have long to deliberate. She heard Maddie on the porch outside, and the kitchen door opened. Maddie looked surprised when she saw Syd standing beside the stove.

"I was afraid you'd already gone to bed," she said awkwardly. "I'm sorry I was gone for so long."

"It's okay," Syd lied. "I'm just happy you're back."

Maddie took a cautious step toward her and Syd quit pretending and rushed into her arms.

"I'm sorry, I'm so sorry," she muttered into Maddie's chest.

Maddie held her tight and kissed the top of her head. "I'm sorry, too. I acted like an ass."

"We both did." Syd raised her head and Maddie kissed her. "I never should've stormed off like that. It was wrong and I regret it."

"I regret that I drove you to it." Maddie kissed her again. "Let's not fight anymore, okay? I don't like it."

"I don't like it either."

"Syd, it matters to me that you know how much I want to marry you. And I swear to you that I'll never say another word about any arrangements you want to make. I promise."

"I know you do. I've never doubted that for an instant. I was just angry and disappointed and I overreacted. I promise we can scale it all back . . . it's your wedding as much as mine. I know we can find some common ground."

"I'd really like that. And I pledge to take things more seriously, too. I even started working on a mental list of invitees, so I can fill out my pitiful half of the guest list."

"Did you really?"

Maddie nodded. "Pete and Rosebud count, right?"

Syd socked her on the arm. "Asshole."

"True. But I'm your asshole."

Syd moved in for another kiss. "You certainly are."

The teakettle started whistling and Syd grudgingly extracted herself from their embrace so she could take it off the heat. "Do you want some tea?"

"Why not? Maybe it will help me sleep."

"There are other remedies for that."

"Tease. Don't make promises you don't intend to keep."

"Who says I don't intend to keep it?" Syd fixed their cups of tea. "We can drink this upstairs."

"Hold that thought." Maddie held up an index finger. "I got you something, but I left it on the porch."

Syd was intrigued. She waited while Maddie went back out to the porch to fetch her present. When Maddie returned, she was carrying the biggest bunch of white Peruvian lilies Syd had ever seen. There had to be three dozen of them.

"Where on earth did you get those at this hour?" Syd took the bouquet from her. "They're gorgeous."

The flowers were exquisite. Most of the buds on the long stalks weren't open yet, but they all smelled wonderfully like spring.

"Let me put it this way," Maddie explained. "If ever you're tempted to doubt the depth of my love for you, or my commitment to this wedding, I want you to remember this night—and the five Walmart stores in four counties I had to scour to find all of these."

Syd hugged the bouquet to her chest. "Dear god, I love you."

"You'd better," Maddie warned. "I used *your* Visa card to pay for these."

# Chapter Nine

*Recorded Interview*
*Preliminary Inquest Investigation*
*Death of Mayor Gerald Watson*

"My name is Nadine Odell. Raymond is my husband. He didn't do *anything* to provoke that man. Watson was there with his goons, trying to make trouble about some shrubs we had growing beside the entrance to our café. It was the kind of ridiculous mess that man created all the time. He wasn't happy unless he was stirring up trouble for somebody else. He was demanding that we cut the shrubs down, and Raymond was arguing with him. That's when Watson called me an offensive name and Raymond, doing what any decent husband would do, slugged him. This all happened a long time ago. It's ancient history. You can ask Sheriff Martin about it. Watson even dropped the damn charges."

*I can't believe they're bringing that mess up. Why do they even know about it? We didn't have any worse trouble with that pitiful man than any other business owner in town.*

"I do work with Michael Robertson from time to time, over at his inn. In turn, he helps me out at the café on busy nights. I've been doing that for more than a year now. That's how we ended up collaborating on a lot of the food for the annual town picnic at the river."

*I wonder if they found out about that blue Rust-Oleum? I never should've let myself get so mad at that man. It wasn't Christian. David was the only one who knew I spray-painted those nasty words on Watson's damn car. And I know they haven't talked with him yet . . .*

"I was there when the mayor pushed David Jenkins into that table full of desserts. Half the town saw it. It was ridiculous. David wasn't doing anything wrong—and he for sure wasn't hurting the mayor's little girl. Those two were friends. Watson was off his rocker."

*I think maybe Michael is right: they seem too interested in David. Dear lord, I hope that boy has enough sense to have a good alibi to explain where he went.*

"No, sir. I don't know where he went. After Watson dragged his daughter off, David and Michael left the vendor area. I didn't see either of them again for a while after that. I don't know how long it was, either, because I was too busy trying to clean up the mess that sad excuse for a mayor made."

*You ask me, the whole town is gonna be cleaning up that man's mess for years to come . . .*

David Jenkins didn't seem surprised when Byron showed up at his office on Monday morning. In fact, Byron thought David met him with something like resignation. He waved Byron inside and got up himself to close the office door.

After David reclaimed his seat behind the desk, Byron sat down to face him.

"So, what brings you here today?" David asked. "Or do I have to guess?"

"It's nothing ominous. But I have some information that I hope will be welcome to you."

"And what is that? Are you finally going to do something

about that damn outhouse display those knuckleheads who run the thrift store think adds old world charm to Main Street?"

"No. It's not that kind of welcome news."

"Too bad. Well . . . hope springs eternal, as the saying goes."

"I'll get to the point." Byron decided to cut to the chase and save David the trouble of working so hard to cover his anxiety. "Bert and Sonny were working out at the cemetery the other day, and they discovered that someone had vandalized some graves."

David turned white. "Why tell me this?"

"Because one of the graves was your father's."

David exhaled slowly. "Couldn't happen to a nicer guy."

"That's what I heard. But it turns out that Gladys Pitzer was there that day. She'd stopped by after the picnic to pick up some shears she'd left behind after decorating the graves for Independence Day."

"Oh, shit . . ."

"She saw you there, attacking the headstone with a bronze statue. She didn't want to embarrass you by letting you know she'd seen it, so she got out of there as quickly as she could."

"I'm . . . *humiliated*." He sounded like he meant it. "I don't know what to say."

"I've given that some thought, David. And I think this discovery means you don't have to fear sitting for your inquest interview."

"What do you mean? You can't tell me I'm not their chief suspect in Watson's murder."

"For starters," Byron began, "we don't know that Watson *was* murdered—and we won't know until the autopsy is completed. And beyond that, the timing of your visit to the cemetery means you couldn't have been present at the river when Watson died."

David was visibly shaken by Byron's announcement. Byron watched him fight to retain his composure.

"David? We may ultimately learn that there was some kind of misadventure leading up to Watson's death. But this makes it clear that you could not have been involved in whatever happened that day."

"Sweet Jesus . . ." David choked back a sob. "I've been so terrified. I figured everyone in town assumed it was me—and I had no way to prove I wasn't there. Even Michael . . ." He didn't continue.

"What led you to do what you did that day at the cemetery is something private, for you to work through. Well, except for the damage to the Hawkes memorial. I'm afraid you'll have to pay to repair that statue."

David held up a hand. "It's done. I'm so ashamed . . ."

Byron got to his feet. "Like I said, your reasons are personal and I don't need to understand what led you there or why you did what you did. Just do me one favor?"

"What is it?"

"Call the medical examiner's office and make a date to sit for your damn interview. I don't want you to get cited for being stupid."

"Could they actually do that?"

"Let's not find out. Okay?"

David nodded. "Thanks, Byron. I mean it."

"Don't thank me—thank Gladys."

David was no longer trying to hold back his tears, so Byron left him in peace.

He hoped for the sanity of everyone in town that Watson's damn autopsy report would show up soon.

Dorothy's sharing of details from her trip to New York City took up most of her second meeting with Dr. Zakariya. Dr. Zakariya seemed really interested in her reactions to the visits they made to Ellis Island, the Steinway showroom, the concert at Carnegie Hall, and walking around Juilliard. She asked Dorothy to try and describe her reactions to the sights, sounds and smells of the city.

That was especially true when Dorothy talked about Ellis Island and the music sculpture.

"What about those two places affected you the most?" Dr. Zakariya wanted to know.

Dorothy tried to explain how the glass sculpture was tied into the important part music played in her life, and in her friendship with Buddy—and how seeing it had been like a concrete representation of everything Buddy tried to explain about Bach and *The Goldberg Variations*.

"It was kind of freaky," she said. "Almost like it was waiting there for me to find it."

"It's great when things happen that way," Dr. Zakariya agreed. "Too often, they never do."

"We got a poster of it for Buddy. He hasn't seen it yet, but Dr. Heller says we can give it to him on Tuesday night."

"Ah." Dr. Zakariya smiled. "The infamous taco night?"

Dorothy had been surprised by her question. "You know about taco night?"

"I do. Henry invited me to come, too. But I declined."

"Why? Do you have other plans or something?"

"No, Dorothy." Dr. Zakariya smiled. She was really pretty, and her smile made her look especially nice and friendly. "Remember I told you that everything between us would stay private?"

Dorothy nodded.

"Well, part of that means I need to be careful not to intrude on your life apart from these conversations. It's a boundary we both need to protect. If we do things socially, especially around other people, we might blur the lines that protect the confidentiality agreement we made."

Dorothy admitted that she hadn't thought about anything like that.

"Does that mean Dr. Heller can't talk with you about . . . anything, either?"

"Not about anything that concerns what you and I talk about, no."

"What about things I tell her that you don't know about?"

"Not those either. It's up to you to decide what you want me to know."

Dorothy took some time to consider that information. She had thought that maybe Dr. Heller would tell Dr. Zakariya about what they had discussed in their hotel room after the concert. She expected Dr. Zakariya to bring it up and ask her about it. She'd pretty much worried about that all night . . .

Now she knew that wouldn't happen.

What did that mean for her? Should she keep it secret, the way she had always done?

Well. *Until she told Dr. Heller.*

But Dr. Heller *asked* her about it . . . nobody had ever done that before. And Dorothy didn't want to lie to Dr. Heller. Not about anything.

Dr. Heller had said they needed each other—and sometimes, Dorothy knew it was *her* job to be the stronger one in their relationship. Like when Dr. Heller had that nightmare and Dorothy went in to wake her up. She wasn't used to adults being vulnerable—and not being ashamed to show it.

It was a lot to try and sort through. Dr. Zakariya was being silent—not asking her any questions while she tried to figure it all out.

Dr. Heller hadn't brought anything up again after Dorothy told her the truth about what her father had done. She acted like she always did. But Dorothy knew she wasn't pretending their conversation had never happened, the way most people did when they found out about things they'd rather not know about. Dorothy had had a lot of experience with that . . . especially all the times at school when she'd been unable to hide her bruises.

She knew her teachers saw them. She knew the bus driver saw them. But nobody ever asked her about it. Not until Dr. Heller did that day at her piano lesson.

Dorothy had known that day that she could trust Dr. Heller.

She looked at Dr. Zakariya. *Could she trust her, too?*

"What are you thinking about, Dorothy?" Dr. Zakariya asked. "You seem to be struggling with something."

"It's . . . I told Dr. Heller some things after the concert. I wondered if she'd tell you about it, but I guess she didn't."

"No. She did not. But you can, if you feel safe doing so. You know I won't pressure you one way or the other."

*Did she feel safe?*

"She asked me about my father . . . if he ever did things to me . . . besides hitting me, when he got mad." She hesitated. "I told her he did."

Dr. Zakariya did not look away from her. Her expression didn't change, either. Both of those things made her feel a little better.

"Did you tell Dr. Heller what kinds of things he did?"

Dorothy dropped her eyes to the floor before she nodded.

"It took a lot of courage for you to do that, Dorothy." Dr. Zakariya's voice was gentle. "Would you like to tell me, too?"

Dorothy had come here because Dr. Heller had asked her to. But now, she knew it was up to her to decide if she wanted to tell the truth . . . about everything. She looked up at Dr. Zakariya.

"I think so . . ."

"I'm not saying they think David had anything to do with Watson's death."

Nadine was making a dozen small skillets of sweet potato cornbread. It was a favorite recipe of hers—one she'd found years ago in a cookbook written by a North Carolina chef. A lot of people came to the café just to order small pans of it as appetizers. The cookbook said it was best when served with a lot of honey ginger butter.

She had Michael mixing that up for her. It was his turn to help her out today.

"What *are* you saying, then?" he asked her.

"I'm just agreeing with you that they seem a little too interested in where he went after Watson pushed him into that table of food."

"When the hell are they going to finish that damn autopsy?"

"Why?" Nadine asked. "Do you think it'll make things any clearer?"

"I don't see how it could make things any worse. Do you?"

Nadine didn't tell him that she thought it could make things a *whole* lot worse—especially if it showed that somebody *had* killed the worthless man.

"Quit whisking that butter so hard," she warned him. "You're gonna turn it into a sauce."

"No, I won't." Michael set the bowl aside. "I just wish I could get him to be straight with me, Nadine."

"Ain't that above your pay grade, boy? I don't think the Lord Himself could make that boy straight."

"Very funny." Michael rolled his eyes. "You know what I meant."

Nadine started ferrying her little skillets to the big oven.

"You just need to give it time. No matter how long it takes."

"Are you quoting Diana Ross?"

Nadine yanked the ubiquitous hand towel out of her apron and threw it at him. "Don't you blaspheme in my kitchen."

"How is it offensive to God to take Motown lyrics in vain?"

Nadine grumbled something unintelligible.

Michael sighed. "I know you're right. It's just so hard to make sense out of his behavior."

"He's just scared. Anybody with two eyes can see that."

"Yes—but scared about *what?*"

"Probably about whatever in tarnation he was doing that he doesn't want you—or anybody else—to know about."

"I guess that's possible."

"It's more than possible," a voice said from the entrance to Nadine's kitchen. "It's pretty damn insightful—which in my mind, shows some greatness of intellect, Nadine. Color me impressed by your powers of perception."

It was David. Neither of them had any idea how long he'd been standing there.

"Where'd you come from?" Nadine demanded to know. "It ain't nice to sneak up on people that way."

"If you must know," David explained, "I just had a very illuminating visit from the sheriff." He looked at Michael. "I wanted to come right over here to tell you about it . . . and to apologize for acting like such a jerk."

Nadine knew that was her cue to exit.

"Watch that timer for me, so those things don't burn," she ordered Michael, as she headed toward the door to the dining room. "I don't want to have to make that mess over."

"You don't have to leave, Nadine," David apologized. "I don't mind if you hear what I have to say."

"Well maybe *I* mind—and I'd rather not be involved in your private business." She waved a hand at them dismissively before exiting the kitchen. "Get on with it and be quick about it. I'll be up front."

Once she'd left the kitchen, she said a silent prayer that David had brought good news.

Lord knew, they all could use some.

Once they were alone, David crossed to where Michael stood, and took hold of one of his hands.

"I'm truly sorry for acting like such an asshole. I was just ashamed of what I did that day, and I was too embarrassed to tell you about it. I hope you can forgive me."

"Of course I can forgive you." Michael had no idea what David's meeting with the sheriff had done to bring about this change in his demeanor, but he wasn't going to look a gift horse in the mouth. "What did you not want me to know?"

"That part is a lot more complicated." He leaned against the prep table where Michael had been working. "You know how I ran off after Watson took Dorothy away. What you don't know—and what I refused to tell you—was where I went." He met Michael's eyes. "The truth is, I went to the cemetery."

"The cemetery? Why in the world did you go there?"

"You're gonna have to just go with me on this. Like I said, it's complicated."

"Okay."

"When Watson grabbed Dorothy the way he did, something inside me snapped. It's hard to describe. But it was like watching a home movie of my own childhood—and the way my own father behaved toward me. I looked into that girl's eyes and I knew . . . I just *knew* what he was doing to her. *I could see it*—just like I could see it all the times it happened to me. Every bit of it came flooding back like it had just happened yesterday. And I knew I couldn't hide from it anymore."

Michael squeezed his hand, but wasn't sure what to say.

But David wasn't finished. "Watson was brutalizing his daughter . . . we all suspected that. At least, I did. But in that one moment, I understood the extent of his brutality. I knew that he was abusing her sexually, too. *It was obvious to me.*" He searched Michael's eyes. "It was obvious because my father did the same thing to me—and I never told anyone about it, either. I hid it—just like Dorothy was hiding it. I hid it because that's what we thought we were supposed to do."

"David . . ." Michael stepped forward to embrace him, but

David held him back.

"No. Let me finish, okay?"

"All right." It was an effort, but he stepped back.

"Seeing him drag her off the way he did . . . the truth of it all cut me like . . ." He cast about the kitchen. "Like one of those knives. I *had* to run. I had to get out of there because I knew I wouldn't be able to hold it together. So I ran. I got in my car and I took off. I don't even know how I ended up at the cemetery. When I got to my father's grave, I just stood there staring at it . . . knowing he was dead, but not gone. *He'd never be gone.* Not as long as I kept hiding the truth about who he really was. About everything he'd done to me when I was a child—just like Dorothy. So I fought back . . . *finally*. I hit him with anything I could get my hands on—and I kept on hitting him until there was nothing left of that damn monument but broken pieces of granite. I screamed at him for all the ways he'd hurt me, and for all the years I kept silent about it. For all the times I blamed myself, *because that's what they do to us*. They make us buy in to their conspiracy of silence—and everyone around them colludes with them, too, because the truth is too horrible to face. And I kept right on screaming because Watson was doing the same thing to Dorothy."

Michael was overcome with rage and sadness by David's revelation. He knew he was totally out of his depth and struggled to know how to respond. But right then, he owed it to David to listen. To hear what he was finally willing to confess.

"I didn't know until this morning, when Byron came to see me, that Gladys Pitzer had been at the cemetery when I was there. She saw me and witnessed the whole thing. Byron got involved when they found out the grave had been vandalized. He knew Gladys had been there doing flowers, so he went to ask her if she'd seen anything." He smiled sadly at Michael. "She had."

"I'm so sorry," Michael said. "I'm so sad and sorry this ever happened to you."

"I know you are." David kissed his big hand. "And I'm sorry I never told you about this before now—and that I acted like such a jerk when you tried to get me to tell you where I'd gone."

"Tell me what I can do? Tell me what *we* can do together to make this better. I don't want you to be afraid any more. Not of him. Not of anything."

David hugged him. "Believe me, my furry prince. You do it in a thousand ways, every single day."

"I hope so. I want to."

David gave him a final, warm squeeze and stepped back. "Do you want to hear the only good news to come out of this nightmare scenario?"

"Yeah." Michael used Nadine's hand towel to wipe his eyes.

"Byron told me that dear, unsuspecting Gladys Pitzer gave me a gift—the one thing I desperately needed."

"What was that?"

"An alibi."

Michael's jaw dropped.

*Yes, Virginia,* he thought, *there is a Santa Claus* . . .

Byron had arranged to take Dorothy to the house she'd lived in with her father, so she could identify the personal belongings she wanted to retrieve before the house was destroyed. Celine was gratified when Dorothy asked if she would ride along with them.

When they'd told Dorothy the decision the county had made to burn the house down before selling the land at auction, Dorothy had shown little reaction. Celine didn't know what to expect and wondered if Dorothy would be sad to lose all connection to the place she'd once lived with her mother. But if Dorothy had any of those feelings, she didn't express them. Her only question was whether she could keep some of her mother's things—the two boxes of books and personal effects her father had kept stashed in the attic. Byron had been quick to assure Dorothy that she could retrieve anything she wanted from the house, and he would help her remove it.

Celine had been happy to see that Bryon had brought Django along when he came by to pick them up. Dorothy asked immediately if Django could go, too, and Byron said, "Of course."

Celine had never been to the house where Dorothy grew up. She knew it was located in a rocky, mostly undeveloped part of the county the locals called Babylon Hill, and that it overlooked part of the New River. As they drew closer, she became more than a little bit anxious about seeing it—especially knowing all she now understood about the magnitude of the horrors the girl had experienced living there with her father.

In her view, the place couldn't go up in flames soon enough.

But this was part of Dorothy's journey—not hers. Her job was to provide whatever comfort and support Dorothy would ask for—or allow.

When they drove up the long, rutted lane that led to the property from the county road, Celine could see the remnants of a small vegetable garden, and a clearing that contained a burn can surrounded by neatly stacked piles of tree branches and other yard waste. When Byron drew up in front of the house and shut the car off, Celine was surprised by how small the place was. It really wasn't much more than a story and a half. Its most distinctive features were its large front porch, and how much in need of a paint job its clapboard siding was. There were no curtains at any of the windows, but she supposed they wouldn't be necessary out here, where there were no other houses within a mile. She noticed that the area beneath the big porch was raked clean.

She figured Dorothy was responsible for that. Or perhaps, Buddy. Dorothy had shared with her that Buddy sometimes did outside work for her father.

Byron turned in his seat to ask Dorothy if she wanted him to accompany her inside.

"No," she said. "I only want a couple of things. I know where they are, and it won't take me very long."

She got out of the car and Django hopped out with her.

The house was locked, but Dorothy knew where to look for the spare key, hidden beneath an old bucket filled with now-dead geraniums. That struck Celine as sad. She recalled a greeting card Maddie had once sent her many years ago. "To believe in life," it read, "is to believe there will always be someone to water the geraniums."

Not here. Not anymore.

Dorothy unlocked the door and stepped inside. Django trotted right along behind her.

*Django certainly wasn't an orange dog . . .*

"You know you have to let her do this, right?"

She looked at Byron. "I know. But I don't much care for it."

"How about we go and wait for her on the porch?"

Celine agreed and they approached the house. It was quiet out here. She couldn't hear any traffic noise from the county road—or any sounds from the river. There were no birds singing, either—even though she saw what looked like a homemade feeder hanging from a rope tied to a roof truss above the porch. She didn't see any evidence of floodlights outside—not on the house and not on any posts or poles. She could only imagine how dark it must've been out here at night. Dark enough to conceal the damage Watson had systematically visited upon his own child.

Dark enough for Dorothy to study the stars, as she'd often shared with Henry—stars that lit up the night sky above the appalling landscape below.

*Yes. This place couldn't be gone soon enough.*

Django came clattering out onto the porch. Dorothy followed behind him, carrying a cardboard box. Byron met her and took the box from her.

"Do you need help carrying anything else out?" he asked.

"There's only one more. It's heavier, but I can carry it."

She ducked back inside—with Django at her heels.

Celine watched Byron follow her with his eyes.

"You know you have to let her do this, right?" she quoted.

He made a face at her. "I hear you." He looked down at the contents of the box. "I wonder what this stuff is?"

"I'm guessing those are the attic boxes she talked about—the things that were her mother's."

Dorothy was back a minute later, carrying a larger box full of books. She handed it to Byron.

"That's everything. That's all I want."

"Are you sure?" he asked. "We can stay for as long as you need."

"I'm sure," she replied. "I only want the things that belonged to my mother." She looked back at the house. "Nothing else in there means anything to me."

Celine could tell Byron wanted to press her to be sure, but she stopped him.

"Do you want me to lock the door for you?"

"It's okay." Dorothy gave her a slight smile. "I can do it."

Byron loaded the two boxes into the trunk of his car while Dorothy locked the house and returned the key to its place beneath the bucket of dead plants. Celine waited for her to descend the wooden steps and walked with her to the car. Dorothy did not look back at the house.

"Are you okay?" Celine asked.

Dorothy kept her eyes focused ahead of them, on Byron's car.

"I will be," she said.

—~— —~— —~—

Maddie and Syd stood on the porch and watched David leave. He'd stopped by unexpectedly on what he called, "the second leg of his apology tour."

"Think Hugh Grant without the hookers," he added.

But the tale he'd shared with them about Gladys, and his unplanned flight to the cemetery after the 4th of July altercation with Watson, was very welcome news. Especially to Maddie, who'd begun to worry that David was emerging as a potential lead suspect if Watson's autopsy showed any indications of misadventure.

Now they could all relax. David was now willing to account for his whereabouts during that critical hour—and he had a witness who saw him there.

But the mystery of what had happened to Gerald Watson would continue to churn and disrupt the lives and serenity of nearly everyone in Jericho until they knew, with certainty, what events had contributed to his death at the river.

David shared other revelations with them, too—gruesome and disturbing details about the extent of the abuse he'd suffered at the hands of his father. Maddie had been sickened by his admission of all he'd endured. She felt indicted by her own obliviousness and failure to recognize what had been happening to him.

"How could I not have known about that?" she asked him. "Why did I not see it?"

David tried his best to reassure her. "Because I hid it from you—and from Mama." He gave a bitter laugh. "It figures that keeping this a secret was the only thing my father and I ever agreed on."

Syd gave up on decorum and got up to wrap her arms around David from behind. "I'm so sorry this happened to you."

David leaned into her. "Thanks, Blondie. I'm sorry, too. That bastard stole years of my life from me."

Maddie had never been prouder of her best friend—or more impressed by the courage it took for him to own the truth about his past.

Even though she was overwhelmed by the callous way his innocence had been stripped away by the one person he should've been able to trust the most.

*How could this happen? How could a parent ever damage a child in this way?*

She thought about David—and Dorothy. Charlie, too. *All of them.* And how many others like them did they cross paths with every day? The silent victims . . . the ones with no voices to cry for help.

She reached across the table to take hold of David's hand.

"It's okay, Cinderella," he said softly. "You were always there for me. You took care of me in all the ways I didn't know I needed."

"I hope I always will," she pledged.

David left shortly after that, saying he had one more stop to make before it got too late.

Syd leaned into her as they watched his car drop out of sight.

"Dear god. When is this all going to stop?"

"Watson, you mean?"

"Not just him," Syd explained. "Everything that created him. Everything that created a thousand more just like him. Everything that feeds this ugliness and allows it to flourish. It just needs to stop."

"I know. It's like trying to find your way through the fog of nuclear winter—even though the sun keeps shining. What we thought we understood has been turned upside down. We can't tell up from down anymore because we're all spinning around inside Yeats's apocalyptic gyre, and the center isn't holding."

"God. How do we keep Henry safe?"

"We have to keep telling him the truth—about everything. No matter how difficult it is. We have to show him the same kind of courage David has just shown us. And we have to promise that we'll never turn our faces away if things get too hard, and it would be easier or more expedient just to ignore them. The only way to push back the darkness is to stand in the light."

Syd tightened her arms around Maddie. "I knew you'd know the answer."

"I don't know about that. Sometimes, I don't think I understand anything anymore. But I do know *one* thing: if you and I can manage to stay as constant and steady as we are, we'll probably do okay."

"I think so, too."

Maddie kissed her hair. "I'm too agitated to head back inside. Do you want to walk down to the pond?"

"Sure. We can see how Henry's fish are doing."

"Since the water usually looks like it's boiling, I'd say they're multiplying like locusts."

"It might be time to fish a few out," Syd agreed.

They left the porch and started their slow descent toward the pond.

"Good luck breaking that news to Henry," Maddie told her. "He's not going to be happy about seeing any of his little buddies end up on somebody's dinner plate. He's probably given them all names."

"Me? Why do I have to do it?"

"Because the need for it derives from fish with overactive libidos. Ergo, *your* territory."

"Someday you'll have to explain this division of labor to me."

"It's simple: I handle anything requiring sober reflection or poetry, you handle all things related to making whoopee."

"Making *whoopee?*"

"Why not? It sounds better than ichthyologic orgies."

"You're certifiable . . ."

"Like I said," Maddie squeezed her hand, "constant and steady."

—⁓— —⁓— —⁓—

Roma Jean decided to stop by Charlie's house on her way home. She knew she couldn't stay very late, but she'd been worried about how Charlie was dealing with the sudden reappearance of her father, and she just wanted to check on her.

She'd felt bad about having to tell Charlie about her run-in with him on the bookmobile after he and the two Bone Gap women had shown up. But she knew she had to. Manfred Davis had seemed so different during that encounter. Emboldened, maybe. She'd been a little afraid of him and his undisguised anger about the nature of her relationship with Charlie.

That Mrs. Black didn't help, either.

Charlie said Mrs. Black had been partly responsible for the awful way the girl, Jimmie's, parents had shipped her off to live with some crazy snake-handlers in Kentucky. And all because Jimmie and Charlie had discovered they liked each other.

*Okay. Maybe they more than liked each other...* But that didn't justify what had been done to Jimmie, or what Manfred did to Charlie. Nothing could ever make that kind of reaction all right.

Buddy had covered the back window of her Caprice with heavy plastic and secured it with car tape, just until she could get it back out to Junior's to get it fixed. *Again.* The plastic was so thick, Roma Jean couldn't see through it to back up, so she had to park on the street, instead of pulling into Charlie's driveway. Not many people out here ever parked along this road because it was kind of narrow, but Roma Jean felt better about it when she saw a beat-up white van pulled off on the shoulder, just past Charlie's house.

This time, she decided not to wait outside. She got out her key to unlock the door, but was surprised when it just pushed open. That was strange. It wasn't like Charlie to leave her door unlocked.

*Oh, well. Maybe she was running late this morning and forgot?* Roma Jean forgot stuff like that all the time. Four times out of five, she'd get all the way to the library only to realize she'd left the bookmobile keys at home on the kitchen counter beside the door.

Roma Jean went inside to sit down and wait for Charlie to get home. She hoped it wouldn't be too long. Her mother was making two kinds of pasta salad for the market tonight, and she needed Roma Jean to help her weigh it up and put it into plastic containers.

"I might've known *you'd* show up here."

The voice scared her half to death. She knew she jumped about a foot into the air. When she dared to take a tentative look into Charlie's living room, Manfred Davis was sitting there, holding a pile of papers.

"I come here tonight to see my girl, and pray for her delivery from the evil influence of you and your kind." He threw down the paperwork he'd been holding. It looked like mail . . . bills and store fliers. *He's been going through Charlie's mail,* she thought.

"Does Charlie know you're here?" She tried to stop herself from shaking.

"I'm not bound to tell you anything, Jezebel." He got up and advanced toward her.

Roma Jean instinctively backed toward the kitchen.

"I don't know what you want, but you have no reason to accuse me. I just stopped by to see her."

"Is that so? Does Charlene give out keys to anybody who wants to just *stop by?*"

"I know she told you to leave us alone. You need to listen to her, Mr. Davis."

"Don't you dare tell me what I need to do where my own blood is concerned. You're nothin' but a two-bit whore, and what you're leadin' my girl into will make her burn in hell for all eternity."

He stepped closer. Roma Jean could see the rage simmering

behind his eyes. There was no one who could help her now. She knew that. Her only hope was to hold him off long enough to make her escape. She backed up again, and pulled out a metal kitchen chair to place between them.

"Coming here like this isn't going to help you reach her, Mr. Davis. It'll just push her further away."

"Maybe I don't care so much about *what* she thinks," he sneered. "Not when the two of you are carryin' on like a couple of filthy Sodomite dogs. There's only one kind of teachin' your kind can understand—and it ain't got nothin' to do with prayer."

He reached for the chair, but Roma Jean shoved it at him with all her might. It got tangled up with his legs and she heard him cursing as she ran out the door.

She ran as fast as she could, but he overtook her. She cried out when he grabbed her by the hair from behind and brought her to her knees.

"Let go of me!" she screamed. The pain was excruciating as he half dragged her toward the house.

"You'd best be tellin' them perverted demons to let go of you, girl." He yanked her to her feet.

Roma Jean kicked him in the shin and tried to run again, but he tripped her.

"Get up, you whore." He grabbed her by the arm. "We got business to take care of inside."

"Manfred!" A woman's voice shrieked. "Stop it! *You're hurting her.*"

Roma Jean was dimly aware that a woman was approaching from behind the white van.

"You stay outta this, Glenadine," Manfred warned the woman off. "Me'n this harlot got some things to take care of. You get back in the van and leave me to the Lord's work."

"That ain't the Lord's work." Glenadine approached him. Roma Jean saw she was holding a cell phone. "You're actin' crazy. You need to let this gal go."

"Goddamn it, woman." Manfred approached Glenadine and gave her a shove. "You get back in the fucking van, like I told you."

"Don't you curse at me." Glenadine grabbed his arm and tried to pry him away from Roma Jean. "You got to stop this craziness, right now."

"Get *off* me, woman!" Manfred backhanded Glenadine across the face. The blow sent her staggering and she crumpled to the pavement.

Roma Jean broke free from him and ran to help Glenadine. The woman had blood oozing from a cut on her lip. She was shaking so hard, Roma Jean could barely hang on to her.

"You stay away from me, Manfred Davis," Glenadine sobbed. "I don't never wanna see you near me or my babies again."

He scoffed and started toward them, but the sound of a siren stopped him dead in his tracks.

"What'd you do?" he hissed at Glenadine. She didn't answer him. "What'd you fucking *do*, woman?" He spat his question at her again. "Answer me when I ask you a damn question."

"I did what any decent, God-fearin' person would do when a mad dog was loose. I called the sheriff."

He gave her a murderous look.

"Give me the fucking keys."

Glenadine ignored his order. "You'd best be on your way, Manfred. Them sirens is gettin' closer."

Roma Jean saw him struggle with whether he most wanted to kill them—or to run for his life.

In the end, he chose self-preservation. He didn't get very far. Two sheriff's cars roared in from opposite directions and cut off his escape route. She saw Bryon get out of one. Charlie's father tried to run, but Byron was able to grab him and slam him against the side of his car before putting him in handcuffs.

"Are you okay, young lady?"

It was the woman, Glenadine.

Roma Jean looked down at her. Her bloody lip had already swollen to nearly twice its normal size.

"I am now." Roma Jean told her. She pulled a tissue out of her pocket and used it to gently sop up some of the blood. "Thank you, Miss Glenadine, for saving my life."

"He had no call to do what he did to you. Violence like that ain't never what the Lord wants. It's not His way. I'm real sorry about comin' up here with him. It was wrong. He ain't the man I thought he was."

"Don't you worry about me, okay? Let's get you inside and get some ice on that lip."

Roma Jean helped the small woman stand up. She knew they'd both be sporting bruises from head to toe tomorrow. She was sure about one thing: once Byron got finished with Manfred Davis, he wouldn't be dispensing his rogue form of divine justice on anyone for a *long* time to come.

They slowly made their way to Charlie's small porch.

That was when they heard the blare of another siren, and a third cruiser screeched to a halt out front.

Roma Jean recognized this one.

Charlie had arrived.

It was starting to get dark when David arrived in Fries. It always amazed him how most of these small towns seemed to roll up and go into hiding once the daylight faded. Even the smattering of storefront businesses that struggled to keep going pretty much closed down at five o'clock. Only a few people continued to live in the cookie-cutter mill houses that lined the narrow streets, hugging the hillside above the river. They all disappeared at night, too—heading inside to watch game shows or Fox News while they ate supper off metal trays in front of their TVs.

Growing up, he remembered how the old cotton mill in

town had been a hive of activity, and its big parking lot was always filled with cars. He and Maddie would sometimes come over here after school with Beau and a couple of other kids whose fathers worked at the mill. They'd all get Cokes at the market on Main Street, and dare each other to hike out across the old Bedford Dam that harnessed river water to power the looms in the mill.

Now the place was little more than a ghost town.

But Gladys still lived here—alone in the same house she and her husband bought from the mill back in the early '70s.

David could see the lights burning in Gladys's front room, although her curtains were closed tight.

*He hoped she wouldn't greet him at the door with her squirrel gun . . .*

He parked in front of her house and walked to her side door to knock. Nobody in the county ever used their front doors—not unless they were selling something or were there to witness for Christ.

After he knocked, Gladys's porch light blazed to life. He saw her peek at him from behind a gauzy curtain before she unlocked the door and stood blinking down at him with confusion.

"Hi, Gladys. I know it's late, but I was hoping I could talk with you for a minute. I promise not to keep you very long." She continued to eye him with a wary expression, so he hastily added, "I just wanted to thank you for helping me out with the whole cemetery thing."

She unlocked her screen door and stepped back so he could enter her small kitchen.

"I didn't tell him much," she said, once he was inside. "Bert and Sonny saw that damage, and he come out here askin' about that headstone and wantin' to know if I saw anything. He know'd I was out there doin' flowers for the 4th."

"It's okay, Gladys. You did right telling him the truth."

"Well, I don't know about that. I hope you ain't in no trouble . . . I told him it was your right to do what you needed to out there—you wasn't hurtin' nobody."

"I'm not in any trouble," David assured her. "Except for maybe what I did to that angel statue. But I'll make that right. It's not a problem at all."

"I was only out there after the picnic because I left my good shears out there—them ones John got me that have the big handles. I didn't wanna lose those. They're just about the only ones I can use with my arthritis."

"It's lucky for me you were there, Gladys. The fact that you saw me saved me from a whole heap of trouble." Gladys looked unsure about David's meaning. "Everybody knows I had a fight with the mayor right before he got . . . before he *died*. After he pushed me into that food table, I kind of freaked out and took off. Nobody knew where I went, and I couldn't prove that I wasn't there when Watson died. You seeing me at the cemetery—even though I was outta my head—really saved me. I came here to thank you."

Gladys seemed embarrassed. "I didn't do much."

"That's not true. Byron told me you even offered to pay for the damage I caused. I can't tell you how much that meant to me, Gladys. And I want you to know how sorry I am that I scared you that day. I wish I hadn't done that. It wasn't right."

"Don't you worry none about that. Your daddy did you wrong, and you had every right to be mad at him. He had no call to treat you the way he did. He wadn't a good man. I always knew that."

"No, ma'am," David agreed. "No, ma'am, he wasn't."

"Have you had supper yet? Are you hungry?"

David knew Gladys wanted to move on. "I did eat before I came out here. But thank you." He gestured toward the bags of decorations on her kitchen table. "Byron said you were working on the Veterans Day decorations. How far along are you?"

"Not very far. I can only tie a few of them bows at a time. My hands is too bad."

"What are you watching on TV tonight?"

Gladys turned her head toward the living room, where there were sounds of cheering and clapping.

"*Wheel of Fortune* is on right now. But it's almost over."

"What's on next?"

"*Dancing with the Stars.*"

"I love that show!" David exclaimed. "How about I watch it with you and maybe tie some of these bows while we're sitting there? We can critique all the outfits."

Gladys only took a moment before accepting his offer. She collected the bags of ribbon and florist wire, and handed them to him.

"Do you want some ice tea?"

David said he'd love some, and carried the two bags into her living room.

# Chapter Ten

*Recorded Interview*
*Preliminary Inquest Investigation*
*Death of Mayor Gerald Watson*

"My full name is David Arthur Jenkins. I'm the acting mayor of Jericho, and I run the Riverside Inn with my partner, Michael Robertson. No, sir. I don't have any siblings. My father is deceased and my mother now lives in Gulfport, Florida. She'd been a teacher here in Jericho until she retired, about two years ago."

*I feel like such an idiot for putting this off so long. I'm lucky they didn't arrest me for being stupid.*

"That's right. Mr. Watson and I were supposed to have a debate that day at the picnic. It was scheduled to end right before the fireworks. That's when he showed up by the dessert tables and went after me for talking to his daughter. He was acting like a total lunatic, too."

*Are they going to want me to tell them what he accused me of? How he accused all of us of polluting the community with our perverted lifestyles? Do they need that much detail?*

"He said I was an evil influence on his daughter and he wanted me to stay away from her. Then he launched into a tirade where he pretty much lashed out at everyone in town he disapproved of—me in particular. He said he'd refuse to debate me because it would sully the dignity of the office. That's when he shoved me into the dessert table and everything got knocked over. It was during that pandemonium that he grabbed Dorothy by the arm and dragged her off."

*We all just stood there and let him do it, too. We all stood by and watched while he took that little girl off to . . . to do god knows what. If there's any guilt to be had, it belongs to all of us for not protecting her—especially after we all saw what he was, and how terrified she was when he hauled her away. I won't ever forget that look in her eyes. It was like standing in front of a mirror.*

"No. I did *not* follow him, and I don't know anyone else who did, either. I got up and left so I could calm down and try to get my head together. Yes, sir, I did leave the park. I went to the cemetery to see my father's grave. I guess I was gone about an hour or so. I got back in time to help Michael and Nadine finish clearing the food away. That was right before the fireworks started. No. We didn't stay. Michael and I were still too upset about what had happened with Watson and the debate. We packed up our things and went home."

*I wonder if they know about the cemetery and the damage I did to those graves? Maybe I should tell them I already said I'd pay to repair that bronze angel statue . . .*

"We found out about what happened at the river after we got home. Nadine Odell called to tell us. We didn't go back out there—Michael said we'd just be in the way. The only thing we worried about was what would happen to Dorothy—who'd take care of her that night. We were going to offer to keep her with us at the inn, but Nadine said she was going to go home with Dr. Heller. She's Dr. Stevenson's mother. She had been giving Dorothy piano lessons and they'd become friends. Michael and I knew that Dr. Heller's was a safe place for Dorothy to be. We were glad that worked out. The whole thing was horrible, and we all knew the real nightmare was just beginning."

*I don't know why they didn't ask me about Gladys... I wonder if Byron already told them? Why else would they be taking me at my word for where I went when I ran off?*

"I honestly don't know what I'll do at this point. Eventually, there'll be a formal election to replace Watson as mayor. I only agreed to do this on a temporary basis because none of the council members wanted the job. To tell the truth, I think I'll be a lot happier sticking to what I know, and helping my partner run our business. Watson cast a long shadow in this community, and it's going to take years to be rid of the stench he left behind."

*And for people like Dorothy, it'll take a lifetime.*

Maddie arrived at her clinic on Tuesday morning to be greeted by two pieces of breaking news.

The first revealed itself when Peggy told her with a raised eyebrow that Lizzy and Avi had both called in to say they were running late. Maddie wasn't too sure what suspect variables Peggy had added together to arrive at her implied suggestion that the two of them were off together someplace, "playing hooky"—but she knew she'd be a lot better off not asking. Satisfied that neither of them would need to have any appointments covered or canceled, she told Peggy it was fine, and retreated to the safety of her office.

She stopped by the kitchen to get a cup of coffee, and ducked across the hall to take a peek at the new clinic library.

Avi had made a lot of progress. The space actually looked pretty good. She'd even put some kind of woven cloth on top of Maddie's wine fridge, and had placed two pretty nice pieces of hand-thrown pottery on top of it. They looked like a couple of the Jugtown vases from the waiting room.

Syd was still griping at Maddie to bring the damn fridge back home. She had told her she would, just as soon as she could figure out a good place to hide it from David. The problem was, she was running out of hiding places. Maybe she should ask Michael if she could stash the bottles in their own damn wine fridge at the inn?

*That'd be the last place he'd ever look . . .*

She got the second piece of breaking news when she sat down at her desk and booted up her computer.

The district medical examiner in Roanoke had completed Gerald Watson's autopsy, and had sent copies of the report to her and to Byron Martin.

*Here we go,* she thought as she waited for the attachment to download.

The first thing she did after opening the file was scroll to the section detailing the conclusions reached about Watson's cause of death.

**Primary Cause of Death**

a. Laryngospasm

b. Asphyxiation

**Other Significant conditions contributing to death, but not resulting in it/underlying causes**

Chronic alcoholism, enlarged liver, smoking, blunt force trauma.

*Manner of Death:* Accident

**Primary Cause of Death:**

a. Acute Intoxication

b. Ataxia

c. Acute respiratory distress syndrome

Maddie closed her eyes and felt the surge of relief she'd hoped for, but had believed unlikely.

Then she read the full autopsy report.

Watson's blood alcohol level at the time the autopsy had been performed was .23, which meant that at his actual time of death, he'd been well beyond the legal limit for intoxication. He also had dangerously high cholesterol levels and signs of liver damage consistent with late-stage cirrhosis. There was evidence that he'd suffered two head traumas prior to death, showing signs of cerebral contusion limited to soft tissues and bone. Watson's brain showed no signs of epidural or subdural hemorrhage, although minor swelling was noted. There was also evidence of an indirect orbital floor fracture of the right eye.

The ME went on to cite the presence of small stones and vegetation clenched in the subject's hands and beneath some of his fingernails, further suggesting that Watson had been conscious before entering the shallow water.

In summary, Watson was an advanced alcoholic—based on examinations of his esophagus, heart, and fatty liver—who was legally drunk at the time of death. The head injuries he sustained weren't severe enough to kill him, but his alcoholism led to obstructive laryngospasm and consequent respiratory arrest, resulting in the onset of sudden death.

*Watson's death had officially been ruled an accident.*

Maddie sat back and removed her reading glasses. This was a surreal outcome. Although she'd known about the phenomenon of laryngospasm, she'd never encountered a single case of it in all her years of practice. She wondered if her mother had? She'd be sure to ask her about it, once they could discuss all of this in greater detail.

The good news was that Watson had not been murdered—*by anyone*. Maybe now, the town could begin to heal.

Her phone buzzed. Peggy told her Sheriff Martin was on the line. No doubt, Byron had just read the report, too.

"Did you read it?" he asked as soon as Maddie answered.

"Yes. I just finished."

"So, tell me if I'm reading this thing right."

"If by that, you mean the report says they found no evidence that Watson was murdered, you'd be correct."

Byron blew out a breath. "Jesus H. Christ."

"Yeah. Looks like we all dodged a huge bullet on this one."

"No kidding. I can't even imagine what this will mean to Dorothy—not to mention half the other people in this town."

"I know," Maddie agreed. "I guess we'll have to pray it's enough evidence to free Dorothy from believing she killed her father."

"Yeah. Do you think it's all right for me to tell Celine?"

Maddie thought about it. "It probably is. But you might want to give it twenty-four hours, just to allow time for due process. I'd guess this will allow the inquest team to wrap up their interviews pretty quickly and the word will get out soon enough."

"Okay. Fair enough. By the way, what the hell is *laryngo-spasm?*"

"It's a spasm of the larynx that cuts off an individual's air supply. Under these circumstances, we'd probably call it 'dry drowning.' There was no water found in Watson's lungs, meaning he didn't die from being face down in the water. The laryngospasm he suffered could've occurred at *any* time—it just unhappily occurred that day."

"Is that a common thing?" he asked.

"No. It's extremely rare, in fact."

"*Damn* . . ." He absorbed what Maddie had explained. "Kind of hard not to see the hand of providence in this one. We're sure gonna have a lot to celebrate once everybody finds out about this."

"Ain't that the truth? Hey," she got an idea, "I know you and Mom are dropping Dorothy off later for tacos—why don't you just stay and join us? It'll be intimate . . . just our usual cast of thousands."

"I don't see why not. Let me ask Celine."

"Fantastic. I've got a couple bottles of great wine I've been hiding here at the office. I'll bring them home tonight. Even if nobody else knows the reason, you and I can celebrate."

"Maddie? Why in hell are you hiding wine at your office?"

"It's a long story, Byron. I'll tell you tonight."

Celine had been in her studio, thinking through some new musical selections that might be right for Dorothy. Already, the girl's musical vocabulary had expanded beyond rudimentary methods to school her in keyboard patterns of scales, arpeggios, and chords. A mastery of that basic keyboard vocabulary was rightly considered essential to play and interpret repertoire—and Celine believed that Dorothy had now advanced beyond that intermediate point, and was ready to tackle a more standard piano repertoire—like the sonata she'd been wrestling with.

She believed that etudes, in particular, would be especially appealing to Dorothy, since they were generally built upon repeating patterns that, once established, expanded to introduce quick changes and shifts—all designed to increase the performer's flexibility and coordination.

She'd finally decided on two etudes written by Viennese composer Carl Czerny—who had always been one of her mother's stalwarts. Czerny, as her mother had declared, provided an essential introduction to the work of Beethoven, who Celine knew was rapidly becoming one of Dorothy's favorites.

*"Du musst gehen, bevor du rennst, Tochter." You must walk, before you can run.*

Celine had only been ten years old when her mother sat her down to teach her the first Czerny etude of many.

*She wondered if she still could play it from memory?*

She was halfway through *Op. 261, No. 13* when she realized

Dorothy had arrived home from school. The girl stood just inside the doorway to the studio, listening—but being careful not to intrude.

"Hi there." Celine stopped playing. "I didn't hear you come in."

"I'm sorry. I didn't mean to interrupt you. I just thought what you were playing sounded really beautiful."

"It is," Celine agreed with her. "In fact, I was just thinking about this as a good piece for you to learn."

"Me? Do you think I could?"

"I absolutely think you could. Would you like to work on it with me?"

Dorothy nodded enthusiastically. "I don't have any homework tonight. Our math teacher was out today so we had a study hall. I finished everything there."

"Well, that's especially fortuitous since tonight is taco night."

"I know. I thought we could practice before you take me over there. Henry wanted me to ride home with him on the bus, but I told him I wanted to practice before dinner."

"And what did Henry say about that?"

"He looked at me like I was crazy, but he got over it when I told him we were bringing him a present from New York."

They both started when Celine's doorbell rang—which was remarkable because nobody ever rang the doorbell out here.

"I wonder who that could be?" Celine pushed back the bench and got up to answer the door.

"Maybe Amazon?" Dorothy suggested.

"Could be. But they usually just leave things on the porch."

Celine opened the door and was surprised to see Rita Chriscoe standing there.

"Rita," Celine greeted her. "This is a surprise. Would you like to come inside?"

"No ma'am." Rita looked uncertain. "I'm here to talk with Dorothy for just a bit . . . if that's okay with you?"

"Um," Celine looked over her shoulder at Dorothy, who was now standing beside the piano looking at sheet music, "sure. She just got home from school. Let me go and get her."

Dorothy seemed surprised and somewhat confused when Celine told her Rita Chriscoe was there to see her. But she dutifully followed Celine to the foyer.

"Hey, Miss Rita," Dorothy greeted her. "Dr. Heller said you're here to see me."

"I am, if that's okay with you?" Celine was intrigued by the way Rita was looking at Dorothy. Her expression was almost shy.

"Sure," Dorothy said. "It's . . . fine. Do you wanna come inside and sit down?"

"If it's all the same to you," Rita glanced at Celine, "I'd rather, maybe, sit outside someplace? I promise not to stay too long."

Now Dorothy looked at Celine, plainly inviting input.

"Why don't you two go sit on the patio? I'll just finish working on the etude. Would you like something cold to drink, Rita?"

"No, ma'am. Thank you. I won't be here too long."

"Come on, Miss Rita." Dorothy urged her inside. "We can go out through the kitchen. It's closer."

Rita meekly followed her and the two of them left the house.

*I wonder what in the world this is about?* Celine knew that Rita had once been close friends—and possibly more, if the rumors were to be believed—with Dorothy's mother, Eva. Maybe she'd heard about the impending destruction of the house, and was here to commiserate with Dorothy? Maybe she wanted to ask for some special keepsake?

Or maybe she'd *brought* some special keepsake she wanted Dorothy to have?

Either way, it was strange. She hoped it didn't portend anything more serious. Dorothy already had enough parental baggage on her plate.

—~— —~— —~—

All the way over here, and for most of the night before, Rita had practiced what she wanted to say to Dorothy . . . to Eva's little girl. But now that she was here, she had a hard time getting the words to come out. She'd even called James Lawrence to tell him about what she'd decided to do. She didn't know how he'd react, but she figured he knew a lot more about kids than she did, and she wanted his advice about the best way to approach the girl.

James had listened to her story without saying much of anything. Rita figured that was because she had pretty much just confessed to being a murderer, and he was probably trying to figure out how fast he could get off the phone. But when she finished talking, she realized he hadn't been thinking that at all.

"Well, Rita," he said. "That's about the saddest thing I've ever heard. I'm sorry all of that happened to you. I remember when you told me how you'd once had a shot at happiness. But I had no idea you'd been talking about Dorothy's mother."

*That was it? That was the first thing he thought about?*

"Did you hear what I said?" she reminded him. "I said I was there with him at the river, and I saw him go into the water. He begged me for help, but I walked away and left him there to die."

"I heard you," James said. "But that doesn't mean you killed him."

"Well, it ain't like the man *chose* to die with a chestful of muddy water. He was screamin' at me, but I didn't help him—" Her voice choked. "*I didn't* . . . And instead of doin' right and turnin' myself in, I ran away like a dog. I ran away and I let Eva's little girl go right on believin' she killed her papa."

She heard James sigh. "Rita, I can't make that part right for you. Nobody can. But if you think telling Dorothy the truth about what happened that day will help her not to blame herself, then I agree that's the right thing for you to do."

James didn't offer any other advice. But he did tell her that if she wanted to come to Killeen, he knew a place she could stay until she could figure things out.

James Lawrence was a good man.

Now she was here to try and make things right with Eva's girl.

It was harder than she thought it would be—and she'd already decided it was gonna be plenty hard.

"I hope me showin' up here today didn't scare you," she began.

"No," the girl said. "Not really."

"I come out here because I have some things I need to tell you about . . . about that day at the river."

She saw the way the girl's face changed. Her skin seemed to get tighter-looking. But she didn't say anything.

"The truth is," Rita continued. "I was there, hidin' in the bushes, when you'n Buddy were down there with your daddy. I followed you down there from the food tables after he drug you off. I knew he was up to no good, and I wanted to stop him from hurtin' you . . . anymore. I hid when Bert's boy showed up. I saw everything that happened."

Dorothy began to look more agitated. "You saw me hit him with the piece of wood?"

"I saw you stop him from hurtin' Buddy . . . we both know he would'a kept right at him. He was so outta his head. You did right to save your friend."

Dorothy dropped her eyes. "I killed him."

"*No!*" Rita hadn't meant to bark the word at her. Dorothy recoiled and Rita reached out a hand to try and claw the word back. "No," she said more gently. "You didn't kill him, Dorothy. *I was there*. I saw him after you'n Buddy escaped. I talked to him. He was alive and tryin' to get up. He was alive and still madder'n a hornet—and just as hateful, too. We had words . . ."

"He was *alive?*" Dorothy said the words so quietly, Rita

wasn't sure she'd heard them right.

"He was alive," Rita repeated. "Hear me, Dorothy: you didn't kill your daddy." *I did,* she thought. But there was no reason to dump that on Eva's little girl. What she'd done was her own hell to endure.

Rita had one more thing to apologize to Dorothy for. "Your mama and I were . . . well. We were friends. *Special* friends. And she made me promise that I'd always look after you, even if she couldn't. She wanted to make sure you'd be safe and protected from . . . from anything bad. That day at the river, I knew I'd failed my Eva. I didn't keep my promise to take care of you, and I'm sorry about that." She forced herself to look Dorothy in the eyes—eyes just like Eva's. "I'm sorry I didn't protect you from him. He was a bad man and he didn't deserve your mama—and he wadn't never worthy to be your papa. But you need not carry this burden about what happened to him that day around no more. It don't belong to you. So you put it down now, and let it rest." She slowly got up from her chair. "I'm gonna go on. There's one more person I need to see. You take care now, little girl." She gestured toward the house. "It looks to me like you found a safe place to be at last."

She turned away and began the slow walk back to her car.

"Miss Rita!"

She stopped dead in her tracks. *The girl had followed her*. She tried to blink away her tears, before she turned around.

Dorothy closed the distance between them, and threw her arms around her without saying a word. Rita stood there rigid as a statue, before awkwardly wrapping her arms around the girl's small frame, and hugging her back.

Then, as quickly as it started, the hug was over. Dorothy released her and took off running toward the house.

—~~— —~~— —~~—

Roma Jean ended up spending the night at Charlie's after all. Charlie had been so upset and concerned about her after she learned the details of what all had happened with Manfred, she'd insisted that Roma Jean stay so she could keep an eye on her.

The truth was that Roma Jean didn't really want to leave Charlie that night, either. Even if that meant her mama would have to weigh up all that pasta salad by herself. Roma Jean made the phone call to her mama short and sweet, and kept details to a minimum. There'd be plenty of time later on to face all the doubt and disappointment she knew her parents would express once she got back home. But for right then, she explained that Charlie had just experienced a traumatic family event, and needed to have her best friends around her. That meant Roma Jean was going to stay—and that was final.

She'd been surprised when her mama appeared to back down as quickly as she did. At least, she got quiet—which was about as close to backing down as her mama ever got. Probably that was because Roma Jean almost never used "that tone" with her. It occurred to her that maybe she should exercise her burgeoning adult privilege more often—especially if it meant her parents would be less vocal expressing their judgments about what was and wasn't acceptable behavior. She'd already been thinking that once she graduated from Radford and began pursuing her online library science degree at East Carolina, she'd approach Charlie about the possibility of moving in with her.

She thought that decision would be simple. Charlie was always looking ahead to the day they could be together—really together—full time.

Roma Jean was excited about that prospect, too. Charlie's house was nice enough, but it was missing some homey touches she knew she could provide. Like better curtains in the front room—ones that didn't look like refugees from the '80s. And maybe a new set of bath towels . . . ones with a higher thread count that might actually sop up water, instead of just spreading it around.

It took a couple of hours before all the police reports and tending to Glenadine got sorted out. Byron told Roma Jean she'd have to come down to the station at some point, but said he had enough to hold Manfred overnight, so she could just come down in the morning. That was fine with her. Her head hurt from where Manfred had grabbed her by the hair, and her knees and elbows were all scraped up from the pavement.

Charlie had hovered over her like a nursemaid, cleaning up her scratches with hydrogen peroxide and triple antibiotic ointment, and giving her Tylenol for her headache. She wanted Roma Jean to go and lie down on the bed, but Roma Jean refused. She wanted to stay awake and be near Charlie. So Charlie wrapped her up in a fleece blanket like a sushi roll, and they sat close together on the sofa.

The worst part was how Charlie kept apologizing for what Manfred had done.

"It's not your fault," she told Charlie for the umpteenth time. "You didn't know he was going to be here—and you didn't know I was going to be here, either."

"I should've made him leave. I knew he was lying about why he came back. He'll never change."

"Well, we all know that now. And Byron says he'll be going away for a long time. Glenadine is pressing charges, too. She doesn't want him threatening her anymore, either."

"I won't ever forgive him for hurting you." Charlie gently kissed the top of her head. "I would've killed him if I'd gotten here first."

"Then it's good you didn't. And he didn't hurt me as bad as he hurt you." Roma Jean looked up at Charlie's worried face. "You have to stop this, Charlie. We both need to get over it and move on. I don't want that man or the memory of this to keep growing until it becomes this big thing between us. He's gone. We both need to let him be gone."

Roma Jean could tell it took an effort, but Charlie smiled at her. "I'll try. I promise."

"Good." Roma Jean snuggled back into her shoulder. "This place is barely big enough for two people, as it is. If *he* crowds us out, we'll have to move."

"*We'll* have to move?" Charlie asked.

"Well, yeah. I mean, after college, when I move in here."

"Roma Jean?" Charlie drew back to look at her.

"You want me to, don't you?"

It didn't seem to take any effort for Charlie to smile now.

"Hell yes, I want you to. I didn't think you'd ever do it."

"Well, that's dumb. You think I'd be scared off by Grandma Azalea's crazy reminders that loose women end up meeting bad ends . . . like getting capped by car thieves in video games?"

"I don't think she meant *that* kind of bad end . . ."

"Why not? It's a lot more relevant to her current beliefs. And it sure beats having your entrails lapped up by a pack of wild dogs—like that woman in the Old Testament she's always running on about."

"Honey . . ."

"I don't know why Rock Star doesn't just set one of their stupid car heist games back in Bible times. They'd have a lot more fresh material to draw on."

"Sweetie . . ."

"If you read all those religious stories, you know there probably had to be about a thousand harlots running wild in every *one* of those ancient towns. All I can say is that the Israelites had to be up to *something* besides the Lord's work to keep all those women in business."

"Baby, please . . . you have to stop."

Roma Jean blinked up at her. *Oh man. I went off on one of*

*those jags again . . .*

"I'm sorry, Charlie. I guess I got carried away on one of my silly rants."

Charlie raised her hands and gently took hold of her face. Roma Jean felt a thrill race through her body at Charlie's sweetly intimate touch.

It was always like that between them.

Charlie's hands felt warm and strong, and her kiss was making Roma Jean forget all about Old Testament stories.

Roma Jean sank back against the cushions and pulled Charlie along with her.

"Are you sure about this?" Charlie's voice was husky. "I don't want to hurt you."

Roma Jean pulled her head down for another long kiss.

"Now who's being silly?"

Byron was wrapping a final few things up before leaving the office to head for Celine's. He was frustrated that he couldn't share any details about Watson's autopsy results with her—or with Dorothy—tonight, but he knew Maddie was right. They needed to wait until they were sure the final report had been entered into public record.

It was impossible to guess how much relief this news would bring to a community that had been so badly shaken by what had happened on the 4th of July. He hoped the town residents would breathe more easily, quit eyeing each other as suspects, and begin to find ways to reclaim the innocence the place had lost. For all its fall from grace, Jericho was still an extraordinary place full of good and well-intentioned people. Maybe in time, the pace of life here would settle back into its normal rhythms.

For his part, he'd welcome having the worst job of his day be disarming Gladys Pitzer's car alarm.

He finished his paperwork and had one last bit of business to take care of. Roma Jean Freemantle and Glenadine Langtree had each filed assault—and, in Roma Jean's case, unlawful restraint—charges that were sufficient to keep Manfred Davis in custody until he could appear before the magistrate—which would happen tomorrow, or possibly as late as Friday. In addition, Charlie had filed unlawful entry and trespass charges—and Byron had rounded those out with citations for resisting arrest and evading capture.

With luck, Manfred Davis would be looking at some hard time. And Byron wanted to walk the paperwork over to the courthouse himself.

He'd just finished putting all the requisite forms into a folder when someone knocked on his office door.

"Come on in," he called out.

The door pushed open, and he saw Rita Chriscoe standing there. She stared at him uncertainly before stepping inside.

"I need to talk with you, Sheriff."

"Sure, Rita. Come on in and take a seat."

Rita closed the door behind her before sitting down in a chair, across from his desk.

Byron didn't like her coloring. She looked unusually pale to him—paler than she normally looked with her head of bright red hair.

"Are you okay, Rita? Do you need a glass of water or anything?"

Rita shook her head. "No. I just got some things to tell you about me and the mayor, and what all happened that day at the river."

"What do you mean, Rita? Didn't you already make your statement during your inquest interview?"

"I made a statement, but I didn't tell everything. There's more you need to know."

"All right." Byron pulled a yellow notepad from a stack on

his desk and picked up a pencil. "Do you mind if I take a few notes?"

"No, sir. That'll be fine. It won't take too long." When Byron nodded, she continued. "What I didn't tell nobody was that I was down there that day, by the water, where Watson drug his little girl. I saw what happened."

Byron put down his pencil and folded his hands. "You saw Watson down there with Dorothy?"

"Yes, sir. I followed them after he pushed David Jenkins into that table. I knew what that man was capable of and I wadn't gonna let him hurt that little girl no more. I hid in the bushes when I heard that whistle blowin', cause I didn't know for sure who was comin'. After that, things happened real fast."

"It's okay, Rita." Byron spoke in the gentlest voice he could muster. "Take your time."

"Bert Townsend's boy, Buddy, showed up blowin' some kind of whistle—and he was yammerin' all kinds of crazy stuff, tryin' to get Watson to let Dorothy go. But Watson attacked him—kicked him so hard in the shin, I thought he'd busted Buddy's leg. That boy was writhin' on the ground cryin' and Dorothy was tryin' to get her daddy to stop and not to hurt him anymore. But Watson kept right at him. That's when Dorothy picked up a piece of driftwood and hit him square across the back of the head. He went down, and Dorothy got Buddy up so they could get away from there. Watson kept tryin' to stand up, but couldn't manage it. So they had time to get up the bank and go for help. That's when I come out from behind the bushes."

"You're saying that Watson was conscious when Dorothy and Buddy left?"

Rita nodded. "He was sittin' on the ground holdin' his head when he saw me. Then he really went crazy. I don't have to tell you how much that man and I despised each other—you pretty much got to see it firsthand that day at Freemantle's Market. What you maybe don't know is that Watson hated me because of what happened between me and Eva."

"You mean his wife?"

"Me and Eva didn't mean to fall in love . . . neither of us planned on anything like that when we joined the same bowling league. It just happened." She dropped her eyes. "Like those things sometimes do. But Eva was plannin' to leave Watson—and take her little girl with her. We were gonna find a way to be together—someplace away from here, so he couldn't get to her." She met Byron's eyes. "He used to get liquored-up and beat her somethin' awful. She said she knew it was only a matter of time before he started goin' after Dorothy, too. She wanted to get away from him—whether I was in the picture or not. But by then, I *was* in the picture . . . and I wanted to make a life with her—and her little girl. When Watson found out about us he went crazy. He beat Eva 'til she couldn't stand and threw her outta their house. She was only stayin' at the motel until we could figure somethin' else out. We knew we had to move fast, so we could get Dorothy away from him." Her voice faltered.

Byron got up and got her a bottle of water. "Here, Rita. Drink some of this."

She took it from him, but didn't open it.

"We planned to get Dorothy the next day at school—before she went home on the bus. But that night . . . the night before we were gonna get her and take her with us, he found out where she was stayin'. I know because two people saw his car in the parking lot there. The next morning, they found Eva in her room, dead. They said it was a drug overdose . . . but Eva never took pills for anything. Not even a headache. *He killed her.* And he knew I knew he killed her. That's why he hated me. And that's why I hated him."

Byron was having a hard time keeping his composure. He didn't have reason to doubt a single word of Rita's story.

But she wasn't finished yet . . .

"Like I said, when he saw me comin' toward him that day at

the river, he went nuts. Started callin' me all kinds of names. Told me to stay away from him and his daughter. I told him I knew what he did to Eva— and just saw what he did to Dorothy—and to Buddy. I told him I was gonna go get the law. He managed to stand up and tried to take a step toward me, but he was still too shaky. He slipped and fell down hard, and hit his head on some of the rocks. I could see he was bleedin', and I started over to help him—but he cursed me even worse . . . called me a cunt and a whore. He tried to drag himself away from me—and he told me I could go to fucking hell." She looked at Byron. "So I left him there. *I left him there to die*."

"Rita . . ." Byron began.

"I know." She held up a hand to stop him. "I know what I done. I let that man die—and I hurt Eva's little girl. I knew she thought she killed him, but I didn't come forward and tell what I knew. Eva made me promise to look after her . . . and I let her down. I can't never forgive myself for that, Sheriff." She wiped at her eyes. "I went out there to Dr. Heller's today so I could tell Dorothy she didn't kill her daddy. I went there before I come here to turn myself in. I had to try to make that part right, if I could. I never should'a let that little girl think she killed that worthless excuse for a man. He was a monster and he deserved what he got. But I know that don't excuse me for lettin' him die, and for lettin' that little girl suffer. I know I did wrong."

"Rita," Byron said softly. "Rita, I need you to listen to me. We got Watson's autopsy report today. His death was ruled an accident. He died because of a health condition he had that didn't have anything to do with drowning. He had no water in his lungs, Rita. He didn't drown. He didn't die from hitting his head. He had a spasm in his throat, and he suffocated. It could've happened to him anyplace, Rita. *Nobody killed him*. Not Dorothy. Not you. Not anybody."

"What do you mean, nobody killed him? I left him there to die. I didn't help him."

"I don't know what to say about that part, Rita. It's going to be something you'll have to find a way to make peace with. But there's no duty to rescue in Virginia. State law doesn't require you to help him—or anybody. Deciding to walk away might be hard for you to live with, but it wasn't a crime."

Rita looked shell-shocked by Byron's explanation. He could tell she still didn't believe him.

"I'm not under arrest?"

"No, ma'am. You are not. And I want to thank you, Rita, for coming here to tell me the truth about what happened that day. I especially want to thank you for going and trying to help Dorothy. That took a lot of courage, and you should feel good about it."

"There ain't much to feel good about in any of this, Sheriff."

"I think I understand that. But try to be kinder to yourself, Rita. Today, you kept your promise to Eva. And I think you've helped her daughter in a way no one else could have."

Rita did cry, then. But even that, she did without much of a fuss. Byron passed her a box of tissues.

"Do you want to sit here for a while, Rita? You're welcome to stay as long as you need."

"No. Thanks, Sheriff. I'll head on home, now." She stood up.

"Do you want me to give you a lift? I can have somebody drop your car off later."

She blew her nose and stuffed the tissue into her front pocket. "No offense, but I'd rather not take a trip in a police car today."

"No offense taken." Byron smiled at her, and stood up to shake her hand. "You take care of yourself, Rita. You did right by everyone today."

She nodded without speaking and left his office.

Byron dropped down into his chair. *What the serious fuck?*

He picked up the phone to call Maddie.

—w— —w— —w—

Dorothy told Celine about Rita's confession as soon as she got back inside the house.

Celine was dumbfounded by the revelation, and she could tell that Dorothy had been stunned by Rita's account, too. It surprised her that Dorothy seemed willing, if not anxious, to discuss the details of what Rita had shared. Celine made them a pot of tea, and they sat together at the kitchen table while Dorothy did her best to process everything Rita had shared with her.

"She told me she was good friends with my mama. I didn't know that. She said she came to see me today because Mama made her promise to look after me. She kept apologizing to me for not keeping her word."

*God bless you, Rita Chriscoe . . .*

"Do you think she's right?" Dorothy asked her.

"Right about what, sweetie?"

"Do you think Papa didn't die in the water because I hit him?"

Celine chose her words carefully. "It sounds to me like it was very difficult for Rita to come here today, and to apologize to you for keeping silent about what she saw after you and Buddy left to get help. Do you agree, Dorothy?"

Dorothy nodded. "I do. She was very upset about it all."

"Then it wouldn't make very much sense for her to come out here and not tell you the truth, would it?"

"I guess not."

"How do you feel right now?"

"Better, I guess. I'm still sorry I hit him so hard." She looked at Celine. "Mostly I feel bad for Miss Rita. If she was Mama's friend, I want her to know she really did help me."

Celine dared to reach across the table and pat Dorothy's

hand. It was a new kind of intimacy for them, but one Dorothy seemed to take comfort in. "How about we think of ways to check in on her now and then—just to be sure she's doing okay?"

"I'd like that. I don't want her to feel guilty about me." Dorothy finished her tea. "She said something else to me before she left."

"What was that?"

"She looked at our house and said it seemed like I'd found a safe place to live."

Celine smiled at her. She didn't miss Dorothy's choice of words: *our house*. She was fairly certain it hadn't been an accident. Dorothy didn't have many of those.

"Do you think that's true?" she asked her.

"Yes." It was simply stated, but Celine knew it spoke volumes.

"What would you think about staying on here with me, permanently—after everything is settled?"

"Do you think I could?" Her tone seemed neutral, like she was afraid to give too much away.

"I feel pretty sure we can work it out—as long as it's something we both want."

Dorothy dropped her eyes to the table. "Do you want it?"

"Yes, I do, Dorothy. I want it very much."

Dorothy raised her eyes and met Celine's gaze. Then she smiled.

"I want it, too."

"Okay." Celine knew it would be undignified and would probably scare the girl half to death, so she fought her impulse to jump up and race around the house like a quokka. "It sounds like we have a plan."

Dorothy quietly collected their teacups and carried them to the sink.

"Should we have my lesson now?" she asked.

Normally, Celine would've said yes without thinking. In fact, it would've been more customary for *her* to be the one to suggest they head for the studio, so she could help Dorothy master a new piece of music. Yet, something about that felt . . . *tone deaf* to her. She didn't want to use music as a knee-jerk method to avoid living in the moment—like her own mother had always done. Like she'd tried to do—unsuccessfully—with Maddie. Dorothy needed time to decide if she wanted to choose this path—and only after she'd had the chance to experience the rest of what life could offer her, now that she'd been shown a way out of her dark world of fear and isolation. What she needed, more than perfecting a Czerny etude, was learning how to have a childhood . . . *right now, while she still had a chance.*

"I have a better idea," Celine told her.

Dorothy seemed surprised. "What's that?"

"After you left for school this morning, I drove over to the Haynes Greenhouse and bought some plants."

"New plants for the garden?" Dorothy asked.

"No. New plants for *us.* Geraniums. I know it's late in the season, but if we pot them and keep them on the west side of the house, we should be able to have blooms until the first frost. Then we can winter them inside and keep them safe for next year."

"I love geraniums. They're my favorite."

"I thought you might. I love them, too."

"Buddy said the frost will be late this year."

"I remember," Celine told her. "We're lucky we can count on Buddy to let us know when it's time to bring them in from the cold."

"He will, too." Dorothy smiled at Celine. "I'm ready. Let's go."

"This is the last one we had in the chest freezer." Maddie handed Syd a two-pound package of ground beef. "Do you think it'll be enough with what you already have?"

"It'll have to be." Syd had already browned the onions, and was ready to add the extra meat to the taco mixture. "I wish I'd known we were getting ready for fleet week."

"Hey . . . *I* didn't invite any more people than *you* did." Maddie snagged a tortilla chip from a big basket. "Besides, you're always going on about how much you love having tons of people around and big piles of coats on the bed."

"That's *Thanksgiving*. This is a Tuesday."

"Tweedledee and Tweedledum. Taco night is just as sacred, in my view. Besides, we can serve cafeteria-style, and everybody can find a place to perch." Maddie snuck another chip.

"Stay out of those. Where's Henry?"

"He's out feeding the menagerie."

"Did you finish grating cheese?"

"Do you not see the four Band-Aids on my good hand?"

"Which hand is your good hand? You'll have to remind me."

"Play your cards right, and I will later on."

Syd looked at her warily. "Why are you in such a good mood?"

"Aren't I always?"

"Let me think . . . *no*."

Maddie laughed and leaned against the counter. "Do you think David will be surprised when he sees the wine I brought home for dinner?" Maddie had chosen four bottles of a 2013 Elizabeth Spencer Napa Valley Cabernet. She'd been saving them for a while now, and they'd reached their perfect window for drinking.

"I'd say that's probably a safe assumption. Why are we celebrating?"

"No particular reason." Maddie hated not telling Syd the news about Watson, but knew she'd be able to soon enough. "I just thought we deserved it."

"What time are the boys arriving?"

"Should be any minute now. David said he was picking Michael up at the inn. Michael had some kind of to-do there today, so David hoped he wouldn't get held up."

Syd was doing a credible job getting the two-pound block of frozen ground beef to cooperate. Once it had nicely browned, she added it—along with the other beef and onion mixture—to a Dutch oven. It was the only vessel they had that was large enough to accommodate so much taco mix.

"I feel like we're feeding the five thousand."

"With one exception," Maddie observed. "Knowing this crowd, there won't be twelve basketfuls left over."

They heard a commotion outside and Maddie walked to the door to see what was going on.

"It's just Byron and Mom with Dorothy. Oh," she added. "Buddy, too."

"Buddy?" Syd was surprised. "Really?"

"Yeah. I forgot to tell you I invited him. He's going to help Henry with prime numbers."

"Inspired idea. Did I tell you he stopped by the library yesterday?"

"No. How come?"

"He must've been in town for some reason. I gather he saw Roma Jean's car and noticed the broken back window. Roma Jean and I were up front, setting up tables for the book sale. Buddy never said a word to us, but walked straight to the drawer where I keep that roll of car tape, and took it outside. He came back inside a few minutes later, returned the tape to the drawer, and left."

"Buddy likes order."

"Hard to blame him for that. We could all use a bit more of it right now."

"Knock, knock." Celine entered the kitchen from the porch. She was carrying a large white bag, and deposited it on a bench beside the door. "Thanks for the invitation. I feel guilty not contributing anything."

"You two are welcome *any* time." Syd told her. "It's a treat for us that we got you to agree to stay and join us. Where's Byron?"

"Henry corralled everyone for a trip to the pond. I declined and said I wanted to get off my feet."

"Are your feet bothering you?" Maddie asked with concern.

"No." Celine smiled at her. "I heard a rumor about some good wine, and thought I might luck out and get a jump on the crowd."

"Is that a hint?" Maddie asked.

"If it isn't, I must not be doing it right."

"I'll pour." Maddie selected three glasses and poured them each a hefty serving.

"Why thank you," Syd took her glass. "Are you afraid we'll run out?"

"You mean before we eat? *Who cares?*" Maddie sipped her wine and made happy noises. "Oh, this is *soooooo* good." She eyed the bag Celine had brought in. "What's in the bag, Mom?"

"Presents," Celine explained. "For Henry and Buddy. Things Dorothy picked out for them in New York."

"That's so sweet. How was the trip?" Syd asked. "We haven't seen you since you got back."

"You know, I think it was wonderful. The concert was excellent and Dorothy seemed to be in her element. As much as she enjoyed hearing Uchida, I think the real highlight of the trip for her was Steinway Hall."

"Hard to blame her for that. I remember my first trip there, after they closed the old showroom on West 57th." Maddie slowly shook her head. "I grumbled the entire time about what a travesty the new place was certain to be—but, wow. It's spectacular. I remember being completely blown away."

"Do you remember the Spencer Finch installation?" Celine asked.

"Is that the glass sculpture that's based on the chromatic

scale?" Syd was excited. "I've always wanted to see that."

"Yes, it is," Celine explained. "And Dorothy was completely captivated by it. One of the presents in the bag is a poster of it for Buddy."

"Ooohhh. He'll love that. It replicates *The Goldberg Variations*, doesn't it?"

Celine nodded. "It's breathtaking."

Maddie looked back and forth between the two women. "Do you two need a moment?"

Syd tossed a cherry tomato at her. "Put your troglodyte hands to work and dice some tomatoes for the salsa."

"I'll do it." Celine approached the counter and butted Maddie out of the way. "I don't want you to cut yourself."

"Seriously, Mom? You're not the only person in the room with an MD after her name."

"No," Celine agreed. "But neither am I the only MD in the room wearing *four* Band-Aids on her right hand."

"That's not my fault . . . I blame that vat of cheese that's now causing the table to sag."

"Wimp." Syd craned her neck to look out the window toward the driveway. "It looks like Lizzy is here."

"Good. I can't wait to ask her about why she and Avi both played hooky this morning."

"Hooky?" Celine sounded intrigued. "What's *that* about?"

Maddie shrugged. "You'll have to ask Dear Abby, here. Syd is the one with her finger on the pulse of burgeoning relationship intrigue."

"You know how I hate to gossip . . ." Syd wielded her wooden spoon. "But I think there's a little something-something brewing there."

"Didn't your brother just . . ." Celine began.

"Exit, stage left?" Syd suggested. "Yes. And if you ask me, it's good riddance for Lizzy."

"Yeah . . . well. 'For what do we live but to make sport for our neighbors?'" Maddie quoted. "Lemme pour Lizzy a glass. I'm sure she could use it."

Lizzy joined them inside and was surprised to see Celine.

"Oh, Dr. Heller," she said. "I didn't know you'd be here."

"Hello, Lizzy," Celine greeted her. "And, please—call me Celine. Dr. Heller sounds too much like I could be the mother of a forty-year-old spinster."

"*Forty?*" Maddie was incredulous. "Forty? Jeez, Mom. And you criticize *my* math skills. Besides . . . I won't be a spinster for long."

"That's true," Syd agreed. "You'll begin serving your life sentence in approximately one hundred and twenty days . . . just in time for your fortieth birthday."

It was Maddie's turn to toss a cherry tomato at Syd, who caught it handily and popped it into her mouth in one fluid motion.

"*How butch!*" A voice bellowed from the doorway. "I always suspected you were a closet softball player. Lemme guess . . . *shortstop?*"

David had arrived.

Michael followed along behind him, wrangling a large tray of . . . something.

"What's that?" Maddie asked him.

"Cupcakes." Michael deposited the tray on the kitchen table. "About three dozen of them."

"I'd be the last person to look a gift horse in the mouth," Syd noted, "but where'd you get three dozen cupcakes?"

"He *made* them." David was making rounds, kissing all the women—except Maddie, who glowered at him. "He catered some kind of *Quinceañera* soirée this afternoon."

"Isn't that a mixed metaphor?" Maddie asked.

"I'm *ignoring* you. As I was saying," David continued, "the girls in attendance ended up being pretty typical fifteen-year-old Skeletors—so they ate like chickadees." He fluttered his fingers at Michael. "I *tried* to tell you they'd rather have artichoke toast."

Michael rolled his eyes. "I thought the kids would enjoy them."

"Sure," David agreed. "*The kids*. Henry . . . Maddie. They should each be able to dispatch a clear dozen."

Lizzy was admiring the intricate designs on the cupcakes. "These decorations are incredible. I've never seen this much icing on a cupcake."

"It's all in the Number 48 star tip and the pastry bag," David explained. "Michael uses the same one to apply styling gel to his hair."

"It's how I maintain great loft." Michael selected one of the cupcakes, and whispered to Lizzy. "Wanna split one?"

"Oh, *no* you don't," Syd warned from the stove. "I've got my weight in taco meat simmering up here. Nobody eats *nothin'* until we make some headway on all this damn food."

"Sheesh." David made a beeline for the wine. "Who knew we were dining in Hell's Kitchen?"

Maddie cut him off at the pass. "May I help you with something?"

"Is this an academic question?" he asked her. "If not, could you make yourself about nine inches shorter, cultivate a sense of humor, and kindly shift about three feet to the left?"

"Don't make me stop this car, you two," Celine cautioned them using her sternest, professorial tone.

"*Now* you've done it," David whined. "You've upset Stanford Hopkins."

Lizzy was confused. "Who is Stanford Hopkins?"

"It's a long story," Maddie and Celine answered in unison.

"It's her editorial *nom de plume*—an homage to her advanced degrees." David poured two glasses of wine and carried one over to Lizzy. "Come with me, you captivating, redheaded minx of a Florence Nightingale. I'll spirit you away from these cretins and regale you with highlights of my award-winning tenure as a literary icon, and the esteemed Dr. Heller's role as my translator."

"Literary?" Michael appealed to Celine. "Is that what we're calling it now?"

"No." Celine resumed dicing tomatoes. "It's still garden-variety, gay German porn."

"I *beg* your pardon . . ." David steered Lizzy out of the kitchen. "It's *edge* fiction."

Maddie motioned him along toward the doorway. "Cast not your swine before pearls."

Michael watched them leave before facing the rest of the group. "He's baaaaaack."

They all laughed.

'Give the man a glass of wine," Syd told Maddie. "At this rate, he'll need a box to go."

"Box?" Michael asked.

Syd nodded. "After we polish off these bottles, Franzia is all we have left. I fear David already drank everything else."

Michael was aghast. "Is he *still* doing that?"

"You're kidding me, right?" Maddie handed Michael his glass. "I've resorted to hiding the good stuff at work."

Celine laughed. "No wonder Byron told me to ask you about why you had a wine fridge in your clinic."

"Wait'll you see how good it looks, Mom. Avi covered it with some kind of snazzy tapestry thing and a couple of those nice pieces of Jugtown pottery you picked up during your last trip to Seagrove."

"To use David-speak, Avi is the hot-looking boi, right? That's b-o-i," Michael clarified for Celine. "How's that arrangement working out so far?"

"Great. I think she'll build up a client base in no time."

"Why isn't she here tonight? She could've hitched a ride with us."

"Well, that's complicated." Maddie glanced at her mother. "Avi's been talking some with Dorothy, so socializing with her outside the clinical setting would be a breach of protocol."

"Maddie?" Syd interrupted. "I think I see Charlie's cruiser pulling in. I forgot to tell you I left my cell phone at the library. Roma Jean said she and Charlie would drop it off on their way to dinner."

Maddie headed for the porch. "Want me to invite them to stay and eat?"

Syd smiled at her. "Why the hell not?"

Henry was torn between pestering Charlie with endless questions about her police car, and clinging to Lizzy like a dryer sheet. It really was adorable. They were lucky Lizzy was such a good sport about it. More than once, she'd caught Syd's eye and winked at her.

*Too bad my clueless brother didn't have the sense or taste our son has . . .*

"No, Henry," Charlie was explaining. "The car isn't equipped with booster rockets—but it can go pretty fast. You have to be careful, though." She glanced at Roma Jean. "You never know when you might encounter a wayward flock of canned peaches."

"It is that time of year," Byron agreed.

Buddy was still poring over every minute detail of the glass sculpture depicted in the poster Dorothy and Celine had brought him from New York. He'd recognized the chromatic scale represented by the dozens of glass tubes in the photo immediately.

"Bach is in the music," he said. "The canons are God."

Dorothy seemed overjoyed by Buddy's reaction to the poster. Syd saw her share a satisfied smile with Celine.

For his part, Henry was thrilled with his New York Yankees cap. He asked Maddie if he could wear it inside the house, since it was a special occasion. Maddie said he could, but only until they sat down to eat supper.

Michael and David were arguing with Byron about which one of them had the best pesto recipe.

Byron was insisting that his version, with blanched almonds and cilantro, was the gold standard.

"You have to use *fresh* cilantro stems, to make that," David was insisting. "And it's not in season right now. Ergo, you cannot make decent pesto in late August. That dried stuff is for shi—"

Michael kicked him to stop his use of the expletive.

"Ow!" David complained. "Why'd you kick me?"

"Kids?" Michael warned.

"Oh, pish posh. Maddie's heard curse words before." David was rubbing his shin. "That's gonna leave a *mark*. Now I won't be able to wear capris for a week."

Byron laughed.

"You're right," Michael said to him. "I could've spared us all a lot sooner."

Syd smiled. Michael was right: *David was back*. How wonderful it was to see him being . . . *David* again.

Celine and Maddie were sitting at the kitchen table, deep in conversation about something. Probably Dorothy, she guessed. She wondered if Maddie had decided to ask her mother about Dorothy's music education? Celine looked at ease . . . more relaxed and at peace than Syd had seen her look lately.

Hell. They *all* seemed more relaxed. Something had changed—but she wasn't sure what.

Maddie was laughing at something her mother had said.

*God, the woman was so damn gorgeous.* Even now, after all their years together, a simple glance from Maddie could still dissolve her into a hapless pile of goo.

She couldn't wait until they were married . . .

An idea occurred to her. And once she started thinking about it, she couldn't stop.

The oven timer dinged.

It was time to take the taco shells out.

*And it was past time to take care of some other business, too . . .*

"Maddie?" she called out to her. "I need you for a minute."

Maddie excused herself from Celine and joined Syd by the oven.

"What's up?"

"I want to get married," Syd told her.

"I know, honey. I do, too." Maddie looked around at the bowls of food. "Is it time to get this show on the road?"

"Not exactly. It's time to get *our* show on the road."

Maddie was confused. "I'm not sure I'm following you."

"Meaning, I want us to get married. Here. Tonight. *Right now.*" She waved a hand to encompass all of their assembled family and friends. "While everyone is here."

"What? Are you . . . is this . . . I mean . . ." Maddie looked as dazed as she sounded. "You want to do this *now?* For real?"

"*Yes.* For real. I've never been more certain of anything in my life. I feel like I've been wandering around in some kind of insane fog. *It's crazy.* Everything I've ever wanted is already here. You. Henry. Our friends." She took Maddie's face between her hands. "*This is right.* This—all of this—is who we are." She kissed her. "Come on, hot stuff. Time to put your money where your mouth is . . . let's *do* this."

She could tell Maddie was blindsided by her sudden change of heart, but that didn't stop her from kissing her back soundly before grinning like a Kewpie doll, and proceeding to whistle at their company.

"Heads up, everybody!" she called out. "It seems like the chef, here, would like to tend to one not-so-small order of business before we eat." She smiled down at Syd. "You wanna give them the news, blondie?"

Syd leaned into her. "We've decided to get married. *Right now*—with all of you as witnesses."

"What?" David shot to his feet first. "Without *telling* us

first? I didn't even press this shirt."

"Seriously?" Michael asked with incredulity. "*This* is the first thing that occurs to you? Unless I miss my guess, Versace, this means *you'll* be the one officiating."

"Officiating?" David brightened up immediately. "That's *right.* I'm the effing mayor of this one-horse hamlet. *And* since I already filed your licenses last week, there are no impediments. So it's a great idea to do this now, before I resign."

"*Resign?*" Maddie was shocked by his statement. "You're quitting?"

"You're kidding, right?" David waved a hand. "Of *course,* I am. This town is only one Ferdinand away from a Bolshevik revolution. No way I want to be all up in any of *that.* I mean . . . olive drab pants and bad facial hair? *I don't think so . . .*"

Maddie beamed down at Syd. "I knew he'd get there . . ."

Celine was suddenly in front of them. "My girls." She hugged them both. "I couldn't be happier."

"Come on, come on." Byron was corralling everyone. "Let's all crowd together in here. Two by two. Hustle it up. Come on Henry, Dorothy. Henry? Take your hat off, okay buddy? No . . . not *you*, Buddy. You're fine." He faced Syd. "Where do you two want to stand?"

Maddie gazed at her mother with wonder. "Who turned him into Marie Kondo?"

"I can't talk about it." Celine squeezed her daughter's hand. "Do you have Oma's ring?"

"Yep. It's upstairs in my bureau." She kissed Syd on the temple. "Lemme go and get it."

"Bring yours, too," Syd called after her.

"Mine?" Maddie was confused. "*I* have one?"

"Of course you do, nimrod. It's at the back of your sock drawer."

"My *sock* drawer?"

"Uh huh. I knew it would be the last place you'd ever look."

"I could've told you that, Kemosabe," David scoffed. "I mean, the whole world knows you only ever wear the *same* five pairs." He bent to whisper to Lizzy, who was fiddling with her cell phone. "She's just like Einstein: all black, no patterns."

"Yeah." Maddie headed for the stairs. "*What-ever.* Back in a flash."

"You're really sure about this, Syd?" Celine asked her. "No dress? No big spring wedding?"

"I'm absolutely sure. Not an iota of hesitation. Well . . ." she deliberated. "Maybe just one. I wish my mom and dad could be here."

"We're here, honey!" a voice boomed out.

Syd was shocked. It was her father's voice. She looked past Celine to see Lizzy holding up her iPhone. There were her parents, smiling away on the tiny screen, looking like they'd just won the lottery.

"I FaceTimed George," Lizzy explained. "I thought you wouldn't mind."

"We're so happy, honey." Syd's mother gushed. "As much as I hate not being there with you two, I'm thrilled I don't have to wear the shoes."

Syd looked at Celine for support. "This is my struggle."

Maddie came back down the stairs carrying the two ring boxes.

"Did you look at yours?" Syd asked.

Maddie nodded, shyly. "It's perfect. It's *exactly* like Oma's. How'd you pull that off?"

"I have my ways." She winked at Celine.

"Yes, you do." Maddie clapped her hands. "So, are you ready?"

"After I get one more thing."

Syd crossed to the wide windowsill near the back door and retrieved the vase of ghost lilies. "Roma Jean?" she called out. "I need you for a minute."

Roma Jean joined her in the kitchen. "Nice going, Miss

Murphy. I just knew you'd ditch the *Say Yes to the Dress* jazz in the end."

Syd laughed. "Do you think you could not call me Miss Murphy right now?" Syd pulled a white lily out of the vase and handed it to her. "Especially since you're my maid of honor?"

"No way!" Roma Jean glanced over at Charlie, then back at Syd. "Me? For real?"

"For real. I was going to ask you anyway—but now you don't have to buy the dress."

"Take the offer, RJ," David called out. "I *saw* the dress . . . believe me, you'd *never* wear it again."

"I'd love to . . . *Syd.*" Roma Jean blushed. "I've never been a maid of honor before. What do I do?"

"It's simple," Syd explained. "You have one job: you hold Maddie's ring, and hand it to me when it's time."

"That reminds me . . ." Maddie cast about. "Where's my best man?"

"I'm here, Maddie." Henry pushed forward. He'd put his new Yankees cap back on. "See, Syd? I'm wearing a *hat.*"

Syd smiled at him. "You look very handsome in it, too."

"Okay, Sport. Here's Syd's ring. You hold on to it tight until I ask you for it. Okay?"

He nodded and took the ring. "I won't drop it."

They all moved into the family room. Syd carried the rest of the lilies, and she and Maddie took their places in front of David, with Roma Jean and Henry at their sides.

Pete had somehow decided to accompany Henry, and the big dog sat looking dignified and proper beside him, at full attention. Of course, that meant Rosebud assumed *she* should be in attendance, too—so she made her presence known by constantly rubbing against the side of Maddie's leg.

Maddie tried to chase her off, but David stopped her.

"Will you kindly leave that tuxedo cat alone? She's the *only* one here who showed up appropriately attired." He cleared his throat. "Okay. I had to look this service up, so forgive me for having to improvise."

The entire group gave him their full attention as he wielded his cell phone with a flourish.

"Dearly beloved," he began, "we are gathered here today to celebrate one of life's greatest moments, the joining of two hearts—and to give recognition to the worth and beauty of love. By so doing, we add our solemn testament to the covenant, which shall today be undertaken by these two women.

"Should there be anyone who has cause as to why this couple should not be united in marriage . . . *yadda, yadda, yadda* . . . we're totally skipping this part . . ."

He faced Syd. "Okay. Who gives this woman to be wed?"

David waited for George to shout, "Her mother and I."

David faced Maddie. "And who gives this woman to be wed?"

"I do." Celine smiled at her daughter. "Proudly."

"We have all come together on this, the most sacred of taco nights, to witness the joining of these two lives. For them, the extraordinary has happened. They met each other, fell in love, settled some hefty fines for past-due books, and are now finalizing their journey with a commitment made before us all."

The rest of the ceremony was a seamless, happy blur for Syd. She remembered them each making their vows and exchanging rings—then David concluded the short ceremony with his customary dramatic flair, and it was done.

*They were married.*

Maddie was happier than Syd had ever seen her before.

*Everyone* was happier than she'd ever seen them before.

Syd was filled with joy—and a surprising amount of . . . *calm.* She knew that was because this, *finally*, had been right. *Exactly right.*

She tugged on Maddie's hand. "So, whattaya think?"

"I think we done good." Maddie kissed her warmly.

"Too bad we don't have any champagne to serve with all those cupcakes."

"*Au contraire.*" It was David. "I happen to know where there are *two,* highly-coveted bottles of Duval-Leroy."

"*Where?*" Maddie demanded. "In your other suit?"

"Nice try. Check the fridge," David told Syd. "It's in the crisper drawer, behind the rotting leeks and Napa cabbage."

Syd shrugged and went to check the fridge. Sure enough, she discovered the two bottles of premier cru champagne. She lifted one out with amazement.

"How the hell did *those* get in there?" Maddie was flabbergasted. "I thought you drank them up months ago."

"Duh . . . I've been saving them for something special. That's why I hid them in the crisper drawer." He batted his eyes at Maddie. "I knew it would be the last place you'd ever look . . . I mean, after your sock drawer."

Syd returned the bottle to its resting place. "Now that we have the cake and champagne toast part of the ceremony covered, how about we eat some tacos and get this party started?"

"Hear, hear!" It was Syd's father, still broadcasting live from Lizzy's iPhone. "Mom and I will try to get down there within the next couple of weeks, honey. We'll celebrate with you two then."

"I love you both so much." Syd blew her parents a kiss. "It means the world to me that you were here—even remotely."

"Bye, honey. Bye, Maddie." Syd's mother waved. "See you soon, Henry."

"Bye, Gramma!" Henry tugged on Syd's arm. "Can I have a cupcake first?"

"*No.* And you still have to do your homework after supper, so don't ask about that, either."

Henry's face fell.

"Don't worry, Sport." Maddie put an arm around him. "Buddy

will help you with your prime numbers chart."

"A new covenant has been born." Buddy had managed to be first in the food line, and was busy piling cheese on his taco. "The golden ratio is restored."

Maddie looked at Syd. "Do you think he means the cheese?"

"No." It was Dorothy. "He means the wedding. Buddy likes it when things happen the way they should."

Buddy looked up at them from his plate. "A new covenant is right. The transitions are complete."

"He's right about that." Syd smiled. "About the *only* thing we're missing is tying it all off with some car tape . . ."

"Ask, and ye shall receive." David opened a drawer in the big pine sideboard and withdrew a roll of the ubiquitous tape. He slapped it down on the table next to the trays of hopelessly overwrought *Quinceañera* cupcakes.

"Hell," he declared, "hath retreated to its box. However," he nudged Maddie, "you're *still* on the hook for the deposit on those doves . . ."

Maddie was too happy to care. She looked around their crowded kitchen. All of their friends were huddled close together, laughing and grabbing plates from a tall stack Syd had placed at the end of the counter.

After all, it was Tuesday night—and everybody was ready for tacos.

# Chapter Eleven

## *Prime*

On Friday, Dorothy asked the bus driver to let her off at the old bookmobile stop, near the river. It was a familiar place to her, this bend in the road that overlooked a shallower swath of water. All the rain they'd had recently had swollen the river to higher levels than were common through here, but she knew she'd still be able to cross it, if she proceeded carefully and took her time jumping from rock to rock. She hitched her backpack up higher on her shoulders and carried her shoes in her left hand to prevent them from getting wet. Dr. Heller had just bought them for her, and she didn't want to ruin them. They were the first shoes she'd ever had that fit her feet and didn't leave blisters on her soles.

The smoke was already pretty thick through here, and the slight breeze blowing in from the north made it swirl above the water in crazy patterns. The air smelled like soot and wet wood—the same way smoke from their burn can would smell when they loaded it with dried brush, and burned it with the trash.

It took longer than usual to make her way across the river. Muddy, swirling water surged over her feet in some places, but she managed not to slip. Once she'd made it safely across to the other side, it was a short climb up the bank and into the clearing that led to the house.

Or to what was left of the house.

It was still burning. There were two fire trucks and several men wearing hats and bright yellow coveralls, watching over it. They stood back at a distance, near her overgrown vegetable garden. The men held rakes and long poles with hooks on their ends. Dorothy stayed back out of their sight. She was sure they wouldn't want her there.

She hadn't known what to expect when she made her decision to come here and watch the house die. Part of her thought it might make her sad, even though she knew she never wanted to live here again. That's why she hadn't told Dr. Heller that she was coming. It was something she needed to do by herself.

Most of the porch roof was gone, but bright orange flames still flashed and lapped at the sides of the empty attic window, where she'd retreat to watch the stars and try to identify the constellations pictured in her mother's book.

No one would be here to see the stars anymore. But Dorothy knew that didn't matter. They'd still be there every night—high above the treetops, shining down on what once had been, and soon would be gone. The stars would always be there—long after any reminders of the life she'd lived here had ceased to exist, and all that remained was a ravaged landscape dotted with poppies.

She understood that now. Everything that happened *happened.* Then it stopped happening, and all of it became part of the past. Sometimes the past got so big and so full it overwhelmed her. But it was still *past* . . . and the important part was to remember that it was over, and she could choose not to let it hurt her anymore.

She watched the fire burn. Each part of the house it took fell to the earth and became part of the past. *Her past.* She thought about the fire, and the water she'd crossed to witness it. Fire and water were like opposite ends of the same thing. One consumed, the other nourished. But from her hiding place at the edge of the woods, they existed together. One consigned the bad things that had happened here to the past, and the other carried them away.

Still . . . she knew with certainty that some part of the fire would stay alive inside her—like a pilot light, burning forever.

She didn't hear Buddy's scooter approach until he stopped near where she stood.

There would've been no way for him to know she was coming here today, but she wasn't really surprised to see him. *Buddy just knew things.*

He watched the fire with her in silence. After the roof fell, he told it her it was time to leave.

"Goldenrod is right. The ratios are restored." He looked at the diminishing flames. "The orange dog has gone away."

Dorothy smiled at him. He handed her his homemade helmet.

"The Quiet Lady waits. It's time for Goldenrod to go home."

Dorothy climbed on the back of his scooter and rode out with him—past the stand of ragged trees that hid the rutted lane, and out of the smoke into the sunlight.

# About the Author

Ann McMan is the author of eleven novels and two collections of short stories. She is a two-time Lambda Literary Award winner, a nine-time winner of Golden Crown Literary Society Awards, a three-time IPPY medalist, and a recipient of the Alice B. Medal for her body of work. She resides in Winston-Salem, NC with her wife, Salem West, two precocious dogs, and an exhaustive supply of vacuum cleaner bags.

# Acknowledgments

If Daniel Defoe hadn't already coopted the title, this book would have been called *A Journal of the Plague Year.* Few of us would be able to deny the impact the Covid-19 pandemic has had on nearly every aspect of daily life in the past year. For my part, the pandemic, coupled with free-floating election year angst, rendered me all but speechless . . . a feat most people who know me well would claim to be impossible. The fact that you're holding this book right now ranks, in my experience, as one of the great wonders of the world—right up there with the Hanging Gardens of Babylon.

*I'm not kidding.*

Thanks for this are entirely due to a small group of incredible people. Susie Bright, my straight-shooting producer at Audible, was gracious enough to move my submission deadline—*twice*. I will always be grateful to her for her supreme indulgence and unwavering trust. My dear friend, Christine (Bruno) Williams, was the one who encouraged me to write this story when I was persuaded I could not. "Why not channel everything you feel and fear right now into the book?" She suggested. "Let that be your voice. Let us all see how you find your way out." So I did. And special thanks are due to the pair of Evenflo Position and Lock™ baby gates that Salem West cruelly employed to barricade me into our dining room until I finished writing this novel. It was a slog—and my dearest hope is that the finished product doesn't manage to read like one.

To the many followers of the entire Jericho series: your words of encouragement mean the world to me. I hope I didn't disappoint you.

As always, I derived constant inspiration from the longsuffering Cherie Moran, who selflessly walked away from fame and fortune as the film industry's leading animal colorist. Cherie, in the ninth month of her pregnancy, had nearly completed the application of Grecian Formula to *all* of the spots appearing on the cast of *101 Dalmatians* in the recent Disney Studios reboot of the classic tail [sic]—when her water broke, and she embarked on an epic labor that lasted longer than the first season of *Bridgerton*. Cherie selflessly walked away from her meteoric rise in the world of Technicolor Makeup Magic to bring writer Sandra Moran into the world. Cherie? I speak for us all when I say we shall *always* be in your debt.

My Bywater Books family has sustained me through thick and thin. I am, as always, grateful for the steady hands of Marianne K. Martin and Salem West, who give us all a publishing home to be proud of Kelly Smith, Fay Jacobs and Stefani Deoul are as essential to me personally as they are to the success of our company. (And, Fay? We won't talk about that time Bonnie cut Salem's hair with a Flowbee.) My editor, Nancy Squires, was the best partner I could've had in the quest to make this a better book. Elizabeth Andersen constantly kept me on the straight-and-narrow—and I'm *finally* off em dash probation. I'd also like to thank our superlative family of authors (including Michael Nava and our extended family at Amble Press) for inspiring me to work harder every day. You're all the best there is, and I'm grateful to call you friends. I also plan to continue stealing liberally from every one of you.

Finally, my eternal love and thanks are due to Buddha, Dave and Ella—my family. Without you, I'd be lost (even though I wouldn't get far, because I'd still be unable to figure out how to open those damn baby gates).

–Ann McMan

Winston-Salem, NC

At Bywater, we love good books by and about women, just like you do. And we're committed to bringing the best of contemporary lesbian literature to an expanding community of readers. Our editorial team is dedicated to finding and developing outstanding writers who create books you won't want to put down.

For more information about Bywater Books, our authors, and our titles, please visit our website.

**www.bywaterbooks.com**